WARMASTER 3:
GAMBOLING COIL

MELISSA MCSHANE

CHAPTER ONE

Aderyn stood outside the door to the Starling Inn, shivering in the pre-dawn air. "I'm sad we won't be coming with you to Finion's Gate," she told her grandfather.

"So am I," Marrius said. The old man didn't look like the chilly morning affected him, though he wasn't dressed any more warmly than she was. "It's been good getting to know you and your friends. Quite a lucky coincidence, eh?"

"It was." Aderyn hugged him. "Thank you. For everything. The **<Wayfinder>** has already been indispensable."

"Someday I hope you'll use it to bring your siblings home." Marrius patted her shoulder.

Aderyn hesitated. There was something she'd been thinking of for a while now, something that maybe wasn't any of her business, but now that it came to saying goodbye, she couldn't bear not telling him. "My parents always told us kids that family was for keeps," she said. "That we'd be brothers and sisters for life. But now I wonder— that was after you fought, and maybe they meant family in the bigger sense."

"I'm not sure—" Marrius began.

"Please, don't say it's different, or that I don't understand," Aderyn said. "You said things I know you regret, and I'm sure Mother feels the same. I think you should take a chance on returning. It's never too late to apologize until you're dead."

Marrius burst out laughing. "Is that your father's saying, or your mother's?"

"Neither. It's the personal wisdom of your granddaughter. Please. You'll be back in Guerdon Deep in a couple of months, and from there it's only a week's travel to Far Haven. I would love to return someday and find you and Mother have reconciled." Aderyn kissed his cheek. "You've got two months to think about it. Plenty of time to make a decision."

"I'll consider it," Marrius said with one of those smiles that said he'd already made his decision. "It's too bad there isn't anyone in Elkenforest who can cast *world door*."

"There are three spellslingers in the city who are high enough level to have access to the spell. A Tidecaller, a Windwarden, and a Bonemender. The Tidecaller doesn't know it, the Windwarden knows it but not how to reach Obsidian, and the Bonemender wanted more money than we have." Aderyn scowled. "Maybe that won't matter for you. Or—but you won't want to abandon all your things. *World door* is just for people and what they can carry."

"It's a sad truth that I'm attached to my possessions," Marrius said, pretending despondency. "Don't worry, Aderyn. After meeting you, I feel the loss of my family connections more powerfully. And who knows? Maybe I'll reach Far Haven and one of your siblings will have returned."

"That would be wonderful."

They hugged once more, and then Marrius waved goodbye and set off down the street in the direction of the gate where the caravan and his wagon waited. Aderyn waited until he was out of sight, then returned inside.

On her way upstairs to her room, she met Isold coming the other way. "I thought you would be at the caravan, saying goodbye to your ladies," she said with a grin.

"We made our farewells last night," Isold said, his grin matching hers. "I don't exactly regret the quest that makes our paths diverge, but I will miss them."

"I still don't understand how you can manage six relationships at once."

"Well, it's more by way of being a single relationship with six people, though the distinction is a fine one." Isold's smile deepened. "I assume you're satisfied with the one you have with just one person, yes?"

Aderyn blushed. "Well, of course."

"Don't be embarrassed. I watched Owen tie himself into knots trying to figure out how to court you, and I'm happy things worked out."

"You knew, and you didn't say anything?"

"I thought it would embarrass him if he knew his secret attraction wasn't so much a secret. And I don't like interfering in other people's romances. It's too easy for that to be misconstrued." Isold continued down the stairs. "I'm for breakfast, and then I understand we need to discuss our options."

"We'll be down soon."

She let herself into her suite and heard Owen moving around in the bedroom. "I'm back," she called out.

Owen appeared in the doorway, fully dressed and with his hair combed. "You saw Marrius off?"

"I told him he should go to Far Haven. I think he might do it."

"That would be great. Hey, come here."

Aderyn joined him, and he drew her into his embrace for a wonderful kiss. Three days had passed since Owen had told her he loved her, three wonderful days and three glorious nights, and she still tingled all over when they kissed. Owen slipped his arm around her waist to pull her closer. "You hungry?"

"I can't remember." She kissed him in return.

Owen chuckled and let her go. "Let's eat. We need to talk, all of us, about what to do next."

Weston and Livia had joined Isold in the private parlor where paying guests ate. Livia's eyes were closed nearly to slits, and she cradled her mug of coffee in both hands like it was all that was keeping her upright. "I swear I'm awake," she said.

"I'm glad, because I want to discuss our plans," Owen said.

"What more is there to discuss?" Isold asked. "Our inquiries about level sixteen spellslingers were for nothing, unless we've suddenly discovered twenty-five hundred gold in the sofa cushions."

"I still can't believe that Bonemender wanted so much," Aderyn groused.

"It's an expensive spell," Isold said. "In terms of a spellslinger's reserves if nothing else. Only one person can be transported with each casting, and my understanding is that that particular Bonemender would only have been able to transport four of us before becoming incapacitated."

"I know. It still irritates me. We're back to looking at a couple of months' journey across the continent, longer because we'll have to avoid the dangerous places. Even the thought that we'll gain enough experience that we'll be high enough level to risk Obsidian by the time we get there isn't reassuring."

"Well, here's the thing," Weston said. "When we were running around town, searching for information on the Repository, one of the rumors I heard was about a way to get from one place to another quickly, without *world door* or a million *transport* hops."

"You didn't take that rumor seriously before," Owen said.

"That's because I thought it was ridiculous and a joke someone wanted to play on me." Weston wiped his mouth with his napkin and pushed his empty plate away with finality. "But Livia and I were at a tavern last night with a Herald who told stories, and the Herald repeated the rumor in more detailed and less flowery terms. Enough detail that we're convinced it's true."

Aderyn found her appetite had vanished, replaced by anticipation. She made herself eat a few more bites before pushing her own plate away. "I remember what you said about the rumor, that it was a dungeon that moves around while you're inside so you exit in a completely different place. That could be exciting."

"Or it could deposit us even farther from Obsidian than we are now," Owen said. "I'm not thrilled about the possibilities."

"I'm sure there's more to it than that, or Weston wouldn't bring it up."

"There is," Livia said. She drained her mug and set it down with a *tock*. "Defeating this dungeon, in addition to experience and treasure, gives adventurers the chance to travel anywhere in the world they choose. Anywhere."

Owen whistled. "Okay, I'm listening."

"It's still not a lot of information." Weston looked uncharacteristically serious. "The Herald said its name is Gamboling Coil, which doesn't tell me anything, and that it's an intermediate dungeon, standard type. Which still means we could expect any number of things."

"'Gamboling' means traveling in a carefree, whimsical way," Isold said, "and a coil is, among other things, a puzzle or difficulty. To me that suggests that despite being a standard type, the dungeon probably offers puzzle challenges as well as—or maybe instead of—traditional monsters to fight."

"So, where is it?" Aderyn asked. "If it's too far away, we might as well walk to Obsidian after all."

Weston removed a folded piece of paper from inside his jerkin. "According to the Herald and her companions, Gamboling Coil follows a strange pattern. It moves every few days, but it's a different number of days each time. And they couldn't predict where it chose to move."

"So, not helpful," Owen said.

"Just wait." Weston spread the paper out on the table. It was covered with numbers and tiny, neat handwriting. "They'd enlisted the help of a Windwarden with *scry* to figure out the pattern. When an adventuring team defeats the dungeon and uses it to travel, Gamboling Coil stays in the spot they move to for five days. Then, if no one else has come along in that time, it moves and stays in the new place another five days. Then ten in the next place, fifteen in the next, twenty-five, then forty. Then it starts over with five days."

Owen's lips moved in silent calculation. "Hey. I know that pattern. That's a multiple of the Fibonacci sequence."

"Is that a spell?" Weston asked.

"It's math. It's like the only math thing I remember. Each number is the sum of the previous two, so it goes 1, 1, 2, 3, 5, 8, and so forth. Except the dungeon has multiplied each number in the sequence by five." Owen pursed his lips. "I'm not sure how that helps, unless the location the dungeon moves to is also determined by a Fibonacci spiral. It's the squares of the—" He took in their uncomprehending faces. "You know what? Never mind. It's complicated. And even if I'm right about where it goes, that it travels in a spiral, unless we know how far the jumps are, we couldn't use the numbers to find it."

"Finding it shouldn't be hard," Weston said, "if this team was telling the truth. They failed to defeat the dungeon, so it hasn't moved since its last jump, and according to the Windwarden they consulted, it had been at the location they found it for thirteen days. That location is about three days southwest of Elkenforest. They left Gamboling Coil six days ago."

"Nineteen days," Owen said. "That gives us time to find it before it moves again."

"The <**Wayfinder**> can lead us right to it," Aderyn said. "I hate to jinx us by saying it's easy, but... it sounds easy."

"Let's get resupplied and head out tomorrow morning," Owen said. "It might be there for all forty days, but if it's going to move after twenty-five days, we don't have a lot of time."

"And let's hope that Herald hasn't spread the story to any other adventurers," Isold said.

CHAPTER TWO

The companions left Elkenforest an hour after sunrise the following day. Even Livia was alert, and Aderyn thought she must feel the same eagerness Aderyn did to not complain even once about the brightness of the sun. None of them spoke more than was necessary, which added to Aderyn's cheer. She loved that her friends were all close enough that nobody needed to fill the silences with chatter.

It was going to be a hot day, as hot as it ever got in summer this far north, but Aderyn hadn't left her cold-weather gear behind. Obsidian was supposed to be wet and cool half the year and wet and cold the rest of it, and she felt it showed a positive attitude to plan ahead for that. She strode across the untilled fields south of Elkenforest as they headed southwest. Several miles ahead, an arm of the forest extended across their path. They would reach it just as the sun was at its hottest.

"If those adventurers were right, it will take us three days to reach Gamboling Coil," Owen said as they walked. "In the vicinity, at least. The earliest the dungeon will move is five days from today, so we've got time, but once we're close, we'll need the <**Wayfinder**> to guide us more directly. I wish we knew more about the dungeon so we can be prepared."

"I hesitate to depend on rumor," Isold said, "but from what I've heard, the dungeon may be a standard type, but its reactions to adventurers are random."

"Is it aware, like Winter's Peril was?" Aderyn asked.

"That wasn't one of the rumors, no, but I've started to believe many more dungeons are sentient than is commonly assumed. It's the sort of thing adventuring teams would keep secret, because knowing to expect a self-aware dungeon would give any team a huge advantage." Isold shrugged.

"The Herald said its beauty concealed danger," Livia said. "And that the environment itself was a threat. She wasn't more specific than that."

"That's good to know." Owen stepped around a hole half-hidden by scrub grass. Then he stopped. "That hole is too regular. Everyone stay alert."

Aderyn scanned the ground around her. There were several holes within sight, scattered yards apart, each nearly perfectly circular. On a whim, she Assessed the holes and got nothing. "I don't—"

Something popped out of a hole a short distance away. It was a small, furry creature with black and white markings around its eyes that made it look like it was wearing a mask. Small paws hung limply in front of its compact brown body. It made a chittering sound and dove back into the hole.

"Did everyone see that?" Owen said. "Anyone know what it was?"

"I didn't look that way in time," Isold said.

"It moved too fast," Aderyn said.

"I don't see an end to this patch of ground where the holes are," Weston said. "Let's run."

Running was difficult across the rough terrain, and Aderyn's gaze fixed on the ground so she was only barely aware of more of the creatures popping up to watch them pass. She didn't dare Assess them on the run and risk tripping or stepping in a hole. Probably they were low-level monsters who wouldn't attack adventurers of their level, and running was stupid. But that wasn't a chance smart adventurers took.

Then Weston said, "They're coming for us! Form a defensive circle!"

Aderyn stumbled to a halt and turned so the others were at her back. Dozens, maybe hundreds, of the creatures poured across the fields. There were enough of them they made a solid wave of furry bodies. Aderyn took a defensive stance and Assessed them.

Name: Gopheroon

Type: Magical beast/swarm

Power Level (solitary): 1

Power Level (swarm): 6

Vulnerable to: area-damage attacks

Gopheroons are pack animals who kill by overwhelming their prey. Scattering the pack prevents them attacking, as an individual gopheroon will not risk death by attacking alone.

"Livia, we need area damage!" Aderyn shouted. "If we scatter the pack, they'll flee!"

Livia shouted something incoherent and stomped her right foot. An enormous crack of thunder split the air, and the ground undulated outward from the point of impact, racing to meet the oncoming wave of gopheroons. They met in a titanic crash that sent small furry bodies flying through the air. Despite her tension, Aderyn felt like laughing at the sight. But *thunderstomp* hadn't dispersed all of them, and there was nothing funny about their teeth and claws.

Livia changed her stance and waved one arm from left to right like sweeping the top of a table, calling out a few nonsense words. Instantly, the ground sagged, and half the pack of gopheroons disappeared into a morass of mud. The monsters at the edge of the [**Earth to Mud**] effect scrambled to free themselves. The rest of the pack, divided now to either side of the mud puddle, slowed their approach, and then every gopheroon fled in a different direction, disappearing down holes and sometimes clawing each other as they scurried over one another to get to safety. In seconds, all that was left was a giant puddle of gloopy brown muck.

**Congratulations! You have defeated [Gopheroon Pack].
You have earned [1200 XP]**

Aderyn breathed deeply to calm herself. "I don't know if that was a good omen on this trip, or a bad one."

"I don't believe in omens," Livia said. "They just make you look for excuses not to take responsibility for your life. But did you see how fast those little monsters broke and ran? If I believed in omens, I'd call that a good one."

"I think of it as a nice warm-up," Owen said. "Let's hope everything we face is as easily defeated."

"Or we should hope this is the easiest challenge, and we're going to face far more difficult monsters and earn enough experience for three levels," Weston said.

"When you put it like that, I don't know which to hope for," Aderyn said.

"Whichever you hope for, do it as we walk, because gopheroons are not intelligent enough to learn from the past," Isold said, "and they might come after us again in a few minutes."

"Isold, when you tell the story of this combat," Owen said, "leave out the part where we ran away from a bunch of level one rodents."

"I'll make it sound more noble," Isold promised.

ADERYN LET THE THOUGHT OF GAMBOLING COIL FILL HER as she willed the <**Wayfinder**> to point the way there. "It's pointing southwest. The dungeon hasn't moved yet."

"We've still got two days before it moves next. Assuming it moves at exactly midnight on the twenty-sixth day, which I realize isn't a given. If we miss it, we'll know because the <**Wayfinder**> will suddenly point elsewhere." Owen rose and offered her a hand up. "Let's keep going."

"I sort of wish—I mean, not really, because I'm grateful for what it does, but it would be nice if it indicated how close my heart's desire is more specifically than just how the glow gets deeper," Aderyn said. She cupped the <**Wayfinder**> in both hands and set off after Owen.

Even knowing the dungeon's pattern didn't reassure her, because suppose the Herald and her team had lied to send them after an impossibility? Adventurers didn't generally help each other gain advantages over dungeons, if only out of jealousy over someone succeeding better than they had. The fact that this team had been so cooperative made Aderyn suspicious. But the <**Wayfinder**> continued to point in the right direction, so she was willing to go on taking a chance.

It had been an uneventful three days out from Elkenforest, with only one other fight, and they'd killed the three blight boars who'd attacked easily. That was twenty-seven hundred experience they'd each gained as they traveled. Aderyn hadn't been keeping strict count, since leveling happened at the system's whim, but she felt they were drawing close to level ten.

Her unspoken feeling was that level ten was the lowest level at which anyone dared to go to the city of Obsidian. The city wasn't precisely lawless, but sometimes its law was "whatever I can get away with." Her parents wouldn't say more about the place than that it was perfect for the kind of adventurer who liked gaining experience by defeating or killing people more than monsters. Aderyn felt a squirming, guilty excitement when she contemplated going there.

The way southwest took them from plains to forests, plains to forests, in a regular pattern. Currently, they strode through a stand of fir trees, not bothering to be stealthy. As Weston pointed out, making noise would scare off anything smaller than they were that would waste resources if they had to fight it, and anything higher level would discover them no matter how stealthy they were. So they walked, and stayed alert.

Knowing they were coming up on the deadline made them all walk ever faster until Owen pointed out they wouldn't be able to enter Gamboling Coil immediately if they did reach it that night. "We need to be at our peak, which means a full night's rest," he said. After that, they resumed their normal pace. Aderyn didn't stare at the pointer constantly and risk tripping over her feet or loose stones or roots; she glanced at it occasionally, making sure they stayed on the right path. No one spoke now.

Sunset approached without a sight of the dungeon. When Owen said, "We need to make camp. We'll go on in the morning," Aderyn's hands and shoulders sagged from weariness. Her eyes felt bleary, and even though she hadn't stared continuously at the warm red light, it felt burned into the backs of her eyeballs.

Someone took the <**Wayfinder**> from her hand and slipped it into the <**Purse of Great Capacity**>. "Sit over here," Owen said, steering her to a spot at the base of a tree. Aderyn sat, and discovered the ground was soft with moss and only a little lumpy. "You look dead on your feet. Give us time to build the fire, and then you can help cook dinner."

"I haven't done anything all day but walk, same as you."

"Walk, and use the <**Wayfinder**>, and you've done that for at least six consecutive hours. You've never used it that long before. I think it might take something out of the user, based on how exhausted you look." Owen kissed her and squeezed her shoulder. "Just rest for a bit."

Now that she was sitting, Aderyn realized she was unusually tired. Not just her aching shoulders, which made sense given how she'd held the <**Wayfinder**> in an unnatural position all that time.

Her feet and legs and lower back ached in a way they hadn't since her very first days on the road. She closed her eyes and listened to the sounds of camp being made: the whoosh of the *breeze* that Livia swept the forest floor clear with, the knock of firewood as someone collected some of the many loose branches in the area, the snap of a <**Matchlighter**>—probably Owen's, he loved using the magic item —and then the crackling sound of flames, accompanied by the pitchy smell of fir wood.

The tiredness passed quickly, and she joined her friends in boiling dried meat for soup. With that and the last of their bread, now very stale, she ate until she was contentedly full. "I've heard it's possible to bake bread over a campfire," she said.

"It is, but it requires skills I lack," Isold said. "And none of us are such gourmands as to demand fine dining in the wilderness."

"*I* would like fine dining in the wilderness, but I'm too impatient to be a good cook," Weston said.

"I'm satisfied with—what is it?" Owen asked Weston, whose head had jerked up like a hunting hound's.

"Something's coming," Weston said, rising to his feet. "From the east."

"Spread out," Owen said.

Aderyn followed him to a position opposite Weston that left Livia with a clear shot at whoever this was. She couldn't hear the creature—and then she did, the shuffling sound of several feet passing through the leafy undergrowth, not trying to be silent. Soon, she caught glimpses of figures. People, not monsters. She didn't relax. Out in the wilds, the distinction between human and monster was sometimes blurred.

CHAPTER THREE

When they came more fully into view, but were still a good ten yards away, Aderyn Assessed the trio, opting for the faster Level Assess over a Full Assess.

Name: Joran

Class: Deadeye

Level: 7

NAME: MICAI

Class: Spider

Level: 7

NAME: FIANA

Class: Tidecaller

Level: 7

"Level seven, all of them," she murmured to Owen, who stood just far enough away that they could separate for **[Outflank]** if necessary.

Owen nodded. He stepped forward. "Hey," he said. "Do you need something?"

"We saw your fire and thought we should introduce ourselves," the man in the lead, Joran, said. He was stocky, but moved with lithe grace, each step touching the ground only lightly. He carried his bow unstrung over one shoulder, but Aderyn saw the brace of throwing knives within easy reach of his hand, remembered Deadeyes had the skill Precise Shot, and didn't let down her guard.

"We didn't want you discovering us and thinking we were trying to conceal ourselves," the woman, Fiana, said. She was slim and beautiful, with fair hair and pale blue eyes, though her skin was almost too pale to look human. On a whim, Aderyn used Skill Assess on her. She knew nothing about a Tidecaller's capabilities, and that might be dangerous.

Name: Fiana

Class: Tidecaller

<u>Class Skills:</u> **Knowledge: Magic (7), Perceive Magic (6), Elemental Blast (geyser, ice spray) (8), Create Water (6), Mage Armor (ice slabs) (6), Eroding Ice (3)**

The second man, Micai, just nodded in greeting. Aderyn had never seen anyone who looked more like a Spider than Micai. Despite his having armor proficiency, he wore ordinary if close-fitting clothes in shades of dark gray and green, and he moved with such smooth confidence he made his teammate Joran look like a stumbling buffoon.

"That was smart," Owen said. "We'd rather not make enemies if we can help it."

"I'm Joran," Joran said. "This is Micai and Fiana."

Owen introduced himself and the rest of the team. "Are you hunting," he asked Joran, "or on your way somewhere?"

"Just hunting," Joran said, so casually it was like he'd preceded his words with *The following is a big fat lie.* "You?"

"Same," Owen said, telling Aderyn he'd realized the lie as well.

"This is a good mid-level area for monsters. Have you had much luck? I'm not sure we would have wanted to hunt this area when we were level seven. You're bold."

Owen had sounded genuinely admiring, but Joran's shoulders stiffened as if he'd felt insulted. But he only said, "We're doing well. Should reach level eight in only a few more encounters."

"We're nearly level ten ourselves," Weston volunteered casually.

"Well, good luck to you, then," Joran said. "We're over that way, but I'm sure neither of us is in the business of kill-stealing, if there's an attack tonight."

"Of course not," Owen said. "Thanks for coming over. You didn't have to be so courteous, and we appreciate it."

Joran relaxed slightly. "Thanks." He nodded, and the three of them turned and walked away.

When the sound of their footsteps had faded, Aderyn began, "I think—"

Weston raised a hand for silence. He had the intent look he got when he was listening hard. Finally, he said, "All right. They stopped for a bit in what I'm sure was within that Spider's range of hearing, but they're gone now."

"I was going to say, I think they were hoping for a lower-level team they could defeat," Aderyn said. "Though why they thought a lower than level seven team would be out here alone, I don't know."

"They were definitely poised to attack," Weston said. "That unstrung bow was a ruse."

"There are only three of them, and they're two levels lower," Owen said. "Nothing changes except we have a specific threat to keep watch against tonight. Aderyn, did they have any skills we might need to worry about?"

"They were low enough level I didn't think finding out their skills mattered. I hope that wasn't a mistake." Aderyn cast back in memory for what she'd Assessed. "But I think—Livia, do Tidecallers get both water and ice spells?"

"They do," Livia said. "But when it comes to class skills, every time they get a new one, they have to choose whether to take the water or the ice version. So you'll get Tidecallers who specialize, or Tidecallers who do both but aren't as good with either."

"I think Fiana is the latter. She had two different Elemental Blasts." Aderyn considered further. "There wasn't anything that struck me as particularly dangerous to us."

"Then let's settle in for the night," Owen said.

They'd fallen into a standard watch rotation, Isold, Livia, Owen, Aderyn, and finally Weston, who would have risen that early anyway. Aderyn and Owen spread their bedrolls near one another as Livia banked the fire. Then everything was silent except for the noises of a billion insects and one hunting owl calling out to the night, *hoo hoo*.

"We're so close," Aderyn whispered to Owen. She fumbled around in the dark until she found his hand and clasped it. "This time tomorrow we might be in Obsidian, did you realize?"

"That's more optimistic than I'm comfortable with," Owen said. "As we talked to those retired high-level adventurers in Elkenforest, I asked some of them their advice on, well, everything, but especially what to expect from dungeons. And they had stories of dungeons that take days or even weeks to defeat. We've only faced two so far, and they were small. We have no idea how big Gamboling Coil is."

That hadn't occurred to Aderyn, and it dashed cold water on her imagination. "I guess that's possible."

"Sorry, I didn't mean to ruin your hopes."

"No, I'm glad you said something, because it would be worse to go in thinking it would take a matter of hours and then be in there for several days." She squeezed his hand lightly. "I can be excited instead about the prospect of reaching level ten. That's got to happen soon."

"I'm looking forward to that, too. Though I'm still glad new levels bring surprises. I would hate to miss out on what's happening in the moment because I'm so focused on a skill that will open up several levels from now." Owen put his other hand over their joined ones. "Sleep well, Aderyn. I love you."

"I love you, too." The words thrilled through her as if more of them were touching than just their hands. She lay on her back, staring up at the black fir branches, until she fell asleep.

A shout woke her from a dream of sailing down a black river in a boat made of a giant silver spoon. Owen roared, "We're under attack!"

Aderyn scrambled out of her bedroll and snatched up her sword, lying near to hand. The night was as black as the river in her dream— and then the clearing was full of light as Livia shouted a few nonsense words and cast *daylight*. The sudden transition from night to day disoriented Aderyn, but not enough that she couldn't see three hulking forms, low to the ground, that froze as if the light had disoriented them too.

In that moment of their bewilderment, she Assessed them:

Name: Hulking Horror

Type: Abomination

Power Level: 6

Immune to: elemental damage earth, elemental damage air

Resistant to: weapon damage

Vulnerable to: elemental damage fire, elemental damage ice, *daylight***, sunlight**

Special attack: engulf

The hulking horror absorbs everything it passes over, leaving a trail that is a clear indicator of its presence. While it appears small, it can expand to engulf a creature three times its apparent size. Its digestive juices are caustic but not fully acidic, and a creature engulfed by a hulking horror may take days to die. Of course, this also means there's time to rescue that person, so don't lose hope!

Aderyn didn't have time to puzzle over that last sentence. Blue lines rolled across the hulking horrors' dark, menacing bodies, crossing and intersecting until they cohered into red-tinged blue spots of light at what looked to Aderyn completely random places on their bodies. She called out what she'd Assessed, her skill [**Amplify Voice**] making her words echo through the trees. "We have to hit them hard for damage to count, but go for the... oh, damn, they don't have a regular anatomy for you to aim for!"

"I see it through the <**Twinsword**>," Owen said. "Weston, strike where I do!"

"Livia—" Aderyn began.

"I know. No earth attacks. *Thunderstomp* wouldn't knock them over anyway, as low as they are to the ground," Livia replied. She chanted, and a pit opened up under the farthest hulking horror, dropping it ten feet. "But I can do crowd control. Go, Aderyn!"

Aderyn circled around to where she was on Owen's far side, but immediately discovered the hulking horror could perceive its environment in every direction and [**Outflank**] was useless. Her new sword, the one they'd bought in Elkenforest with some of the treasure from Winter's Peril, was magical, unlike her previous sword, but her skill wasn't good enough to be much of a threat against the constantly moving monster.

"Aderyn!" Isold shouted.

She stepped back, startled at hearing her name. Isold faced the second hulking horror, his whole body rigid with concentration as he stared it down with [**Fascinate**]. "I've got its attention, but I don't know for how long," he ground out between gritted teeth. "If you can hit it, do it now."

The blue vulnerable spots were still visible, one at where its forehead would have been if it had a head, two low and on opposite sides from the first. Aderyn paced toward it, conscious of how the third hulking horror was steadily making its way up the side of Livia's pit. She reached a position near a vulnerable spot and thrust.

The hulking horror let out a terrible moan and twisted away from Isold in an effort to reach her. She thrust again, missed the spot, then struck with her third blow. The monster stiffened again, and then sagged.

Two identical system messages flashed, one only seconds before the other.

**Congratulations! You have defeated [Hulking Horror].
You have earned [1150 XP]**

Livia shouted again, and another pit overlapping the first appeared, dropping the hulking horror from where it had nearly climbed to the top. The friends all gathered at the new pit's edge, watching the monster begin its inexorable climb.

"I can't do that all night, and I bet now it's got our scent it won't be enough for us to get beyond its sight and hope it forgets about us." Livia looked thoughtful. "I suspect if I drowned it in mud it would crawl out eventually."

"The *daylight* spell weakened them," Aderyn said.

"If we beat on it hard enough, we'll eventually kill it," Weston suggested. "If its vulnerable spot was visible, I could throw daggers at it until I ran out."

"Owen, did you say you saw what I did? The vulnerable spots?" Aderyn asked.

"I did. Sort of blue lights with a red aura, right?" Owen stepped back as the hulking horror neared the lip of the pit. "This sword was an incredible find. All right, Weston, watch where I strike—that worked before."

Aderyn moved to the side. "If you draw it out, I can hit where it's weak on the other side. **[Outflank]** won't work, but Weston's right —we'll get it eventually."

With three of them against the lone monster, it didn't take as long as Aderyn guessed it would have without the effects of *daylight*. When it finally stopped moving, and the monster defeat message had disappeared, she said, "That was unexpected."

"And suspicious," Weston said. "We get ambushed by not one, but three of these creatures, and they just happen to be immune to elemental earth damage? Right in the middle of the night when we're least likely to be alert?" He sounded grim, his usual good humor gone.

"You think it was on purpose?" Aderyn said. "That other team?"

"I think he's right," Owen said. "This seems far too deliberate. And look at this." He walked around to one side of the dead monster and pointed with his sword. "That looks frostbitten. Like a spell-slinger with ice magic goaded it."

They stared in silence. "Well, that fills me with a desire to find their camp and sink it in mud," Livia finally said.

"Tempting," Owen said, "but what we're going to do is move our camp as quietly as possible, and head out for the dungeon at first light. They know they can't face us in a fair fight, and now *we* know they're a dishonorable enemy. We could defeat them easily if we forced the issue, but it would be a waste of our resources just before we enter a dangerous dungeon."

"I agree," Isold said. "If they are after Gamboling Coil as well, we need to move quickly."

"What makes you say that?" Livia asked.

"It's a stretch, I know, but the monsters in this area are a little too powerful for a team of level seven, and Gamboling Coil is the only other thing that might be a draw. And it *is* the appropriate level challenge for them." Isold looked thoughtful. "True, I can't explain how they knew to look here, but otherwise, I'm confident of my guess."

"Then let's definitely get moving," Owen said.

They walked for about half an hour before settling in again, not really making camp so much as finding places to spread their bedrolls. Aderyn stayed awake, since it was now her turn for watch. She was on edge, jumping at the littlest sound, wishing she'd paid better attention to where they'd gone so she would know where to anticipate an attack from the other team. Those bastards and their nasty trick. Half of Aderyn's jitteriness came from her desire to find the three and beat them senseless.

When her watch was over, she shook Weston awake and tried to sleep, but succeeded only in napping, all her nerves still on edge. She woke not quite rested, but not exhausted, and figured that was the best she could expect after a night like that.

This time, they all walked rapidly, with Owen keeping close to Aderyn so she wouldn't walk into a tree as she focused on the <**Wayfinder**>. No one spoke. Urgency drove Aderyn hard enough that she kept going when the others all stopped, and only looked up when they all said her name.

They were near the edge of the forest where it opened on another broad plain, but rather than ending abruptly, here the forest grew in such a way that it nearly encircled part of that plain, like a clearing half a mile wide. At the far side of the clearing stood a tiny house. "House" wasn't the right word, Aderyn decided; it was more of a shack, only big enough for one room that wouldn't be larger than a tall man could lie down in. Its thatch roof reminded her of home in Far Haven, but that was the only resemblance to the houses she recalled.

"That's not it," Livia said. "It's too small."

Aderyn consulted the <**Wayfinder**>. "This is pointing right at it."

The shack quivered like a tremor had struck it and it was deciding whether to fall over. Then it rose into the air. Aderyn gasped. Two giant, muscular green frog legs sprouted from beneath it. They flexed, and the shack leaped fifteen feet in the air and came to rest some forty feet from its initial position. It settled into place, and once more it was an ordinary shack.

Congratulations! You have completed the quest [Find Gamboling Coil].

CHAPTER FOUR

They stared at the shack in silence. Aderyn took the opportunity to Assess it.

Name: Gamboling Coil

Type: Standard dungeon, intermediate, victory condition variant C

Power level: 8

Inhabitants: various

Traps: various

Reward: coin and/or random item drop plus instantaneous world transportation

Getting through the door is the first challenge.

She repeated this to the others. Weston said, "Great. How are we supposed to get into that thing?"

"We'll approach it and see what happens," Owen said. "Let's go. If that other team managed to locate our trail, they'll be following us now."

The clearing looked no different from the rest of the plains—tall grasses, yellow at the tips and green at the roots, with occasional leafy shrubs growing lone and proud above the sea of waving grass. Sometimes they came across places where the grasses were crushed and matted as if a couple of giant feet had trampled them. Aderyn's gaze flicked to the dungeon the first time they found one of these spots. Just at that moment, Gamboling Coil gathered itself on its powerful frog legs and leaped, landing closer to her and her friends.

"I think we might have to chase it," she said.

"It stays still for a few minutes before it leaps," Isold said.

They were within a dozen yards of the dungeon when it quivered and leaped again, sailing over their heads and settling fifty feet away. "That's it," Owen said. "Time to run."

They sprinted for the little shack. Its door hung invitingly ajar, swaying as if the latch was broken. It didn't take long for them to cover the distance, but when Isold, in the lead, had only a few yards left to go, the dungeon gathered itself and leaped again. This time, it landed behind them and to the right. Aderyn veered to avoid running into Owen, who'd stopped beside Isold.

"That's not good," Owen said. "Aderyn might be right that we're in for a chase. That sure looked like it knew what we wanted and avoided us."

"Let's try once more," Isold suggested. "We don't know for sure that this isn't part of its pattern. It might not have a pattern."

They ran, pushing themselves faster. This time Isold nearly had a hand on the door when the dungeon leaped, and he had to duck to avoid being knocked over by the frog legs. The dungeon landed thirty feet away with its back to them. Aderyn imagined she could hear it laughing.

"That's it," Livia said. "I'm not a runner."

"We have to catch it somehow," Weston said.

"Or we can try *transport*, teleport ourselves to the door," Livia said.

"Oh." Weston sounded embarrassed.

They walked, keeping a good distance between themselves and the shack, until they could see the door. "Gather round," Livia said, directing them to stand facing one another with their arms around each other's shoulders in a circle, with Livia facing the door. She chanted a few nonsense syllables, and in the next breath, they were at the door, pressed against the frame. "No," Livia said, "we were supposed—"

The shack lurched, shoving them all off balance, and they tumbled to the ground as it leaped again. Aderyn looked up from where she lay sprawled across Weston's back. The shack jerked and jiggled exactly the way someone laughing uproariously would. "I hate that thing," she said.

"We should have arrived inside the door," Livia said, sounding annoyed. "There's some kind of *transport* block on the dungeon."

"Well, we're just going to exhaust ourselves running after it," Owen said. "Any other ideas?"

"I have one more thing I can try," Livia said. She pushed herself to her feet and dusted herself off. "It can't run away if it can't jump."

She strode toward the shack, stopping when she was still several yards away. Taking a wrestler's stance, she clenched both fists at shoulder height and spoke several words that almost made sense.

The ground beneath the shack dipped so it was sitting in a small round depression. Immediately it rose on its powerful frog legs, or tried to. Fat ropy tentacles the color of mud entangled those legs, gripping them and pulling the thing back to earth. The dungeon strained against the tentacles, but they crept higher, sliding around and over the shack until only the door was still visible. The shack quivered once more and then was still.

"Hah," Livia said with pleasure, and lowered her hands. "*Immobilize.* That was deeply satisfying."

"I thought you'd use **[Earth to Mud]**, keep it stuck that way," Aderyn said.

"I considered it, but we'd have gotten stuck, too, crossing the mud field to get in," Livia said. "Though I would have done it if *immobilize* hadn't worked. I didn't know if that spell would hold something as big as the shack."

"How long does it last?" Owen asked.

"I'm not sure. We'd better run." Livia made a pained face. "I hate running."

Weston took her hand. "It's good for you."

"So is reading, and no one ever demands successful adventurers do that."

"Less talk, more running," Owen said, and took off across the plain. The others followed, with Weston pulling Livia along behind so she could keep up.

The shack didn't so much as quiver when they came to a stop in front of it. Owen pushed the door open on pure blackness. The doorway might have been painted on, it was so perfectly black and without depth. "Hold hands. I don't want to get separated," Owen suggested.

They joined hands, and Owen stepped forward. It looked to Aderyn, immediately behind him, as if he was walking into a vertical pool of ink with how his body disappeared so completely. She swallowed nervously, and then it was her turn. She closed her eyes and stepped through.

Against her closed eyelids, a system message appeared:

**Congratulations! You have achieved [Enter Gamboling Coil].
You have earned [1000 XP].**

The doorway was cold, not bone-chillingly freezing, but the cold of a water trough on a spring morning. Aderyn shivered and kept going. Almost immediately, the cold sensation passed, and muggy warmth like a warm, wet cloth pressed against her skin. She opened her eyes and gasped.

The round room she stood in was more than thirty feet in diameter, with several doors or open doorways leading off it, but she made note of those automatically, the adventurer in her looking for means of escape. What the rest of her saw was color everywhere. Great swirls of paint in vibrant, deep colors, reds and violets and greens and garish yellows, covered the walls and the ceiling and even the floor. Aderyn kept walking, barely aware that Isold had emerged behind her. The swirls had an almost hypnotic effect—not a literal one, because she could look away easily as she examined the room, but one that figuratively compelled her to stare in amazement.

"Look at it," she said in awe. "It's *hideous*."

"It's a '70s nightmare," Owen agreed. "I mean, it reminds me of a time in my world's history. But even then nobody thought of throwing clashing paints around in these quantities." He dropped Aderyn's hand and walked forward to touch the wall. "It's plaster."

Behind her, Weston said, "I didn't think I'd ever say this, but this dungeon has no taste."

Greetings!

The system message that appeared in front of them was echoed by a voice that boomed through the chamber. Aderyn felt instantly embarrassed about having criticized the dungeon. She'd never heard one speak before, and it made her feel like she'd been gossiping within earshot of her target.

You must be VERY clever to have found your way in! I'm always happy to welcome clever adventurers. Don't go anywhere! You'll want to know the rules first.

This message wasn't accompanied by a voice, but Aderyn could imagine the speaker—male, enthusiastic, with a dramatically intense voice that swooped up and down like a slide flute.

Another system message appeared, along with a voice repeating the words:

Assessing now. Please wait.

This voice was different, female and smooth and calming, the sort of voice you'd want to hear on your sickbed because even bad news would be easier to deal with coming from her. Lights flashed throughout the room, colored circles that made the companions look spattered with color like the walls.

Assessment complete. Prepare for instructions. Failure to obey will nullify the dungeon experience and may result in adventurer death. Have a nice day.

So, her voice wasn't so reassuring, after all. Aderyn turned in a slow circle, trying to see where the voice had come from, but the lights were still flashing and she saw nothing out of the ordinary. Well, nothing weirder than what they'd already seen.

The lights stopped flashing, and another system message appeared.

Oh, don't listen to her, she's such a downer. Let's begin. Your goal is to gain a threshold amount of experience to defeat me. That's such a negative term, don't you think? Defeat? I won't make this easy on you, so I suppose defeat is the best word.

Aderyn again scanned the room. After Winter's Peril, where the dungeon had spoken to them directly, she wasn't surprised at the possibility, but this dungeon's words were so... so *chatty* that despite the lack of sound, she couldn't help looking for someone who might be the person behind the system messages.

I see that your average party level is [9] and you have experienced this dungeon [0] times. Your goal is therefore [18,000 XP]. You can gain this experience any way you like. I offer many challenges of varying degrees of difficulty.

"Does that mean we could, um, experience the dungeon more than once?" Owen asked. He, too, had his head tilted back and was turning in a slow circle.

Of course! I love repeat visitors. It's so friendly, don't you think? But you're getting ahead of yourself. You haven't defeated me even once yet.

"Right. Sorry." Owen lowered his head. His eyes met Aderyn's. Aderyn shrugged. "Are there more rules?"

Oh, yes. How silly of me. Each room, once cleared, resets itself after an interval. I won't say how long, because that would be boring. Uncertainty is, after all, the spice of life! This means you can defeat a challenge more than once, but take care—if you manage to win against something very dangerous, you may have to face that challenge again. And, of course, if you decide I'm too difficult, the door behind you will let you leave.

"We're not trapped here?"

Of course not! I'm not like other dungeons, selfishly insisting on forcing adventurers to complete the whole challenge. I have confidence in my ability to provide a challenging yet rewarding experience. Doesn't that sound like fun?

"Right. Fun," Weston said sourly.

Don't be grouchy, young Moonlighter. You chose to come here, after all. It's not like I came into your house and dragged you out of it. And you want the ultimate reward, right?

"Which is?" Weston asked.

You know, treasure, experience—and of course the chance to travel anywhere in the world. That's why you came, isn't it?

"Then we should get started," Owen said. "Thank you for the explanations."

Thank me?

The booming voice spoke as the words appeared. It sounded bewildered.

"Well... sure. You were really helpful."

No one's ever thanked me before. It's usually "let's go, no need to listen to rules, argh argh my leg."

"Um." Owen hesitated. "Why 'argh argh my leg'?"

That's about the point where some threat they weren't expecting tears off a limb. It's what happens when people don't listen to perfectly reasonable instructions.

There was no voice this time, but wounded pride resounded through the message anyway.

Owen cleared his throat. "Well. Yes, we wouldn't want that."

I'd like to give you hints, but that's against the rules. You understand.

"Of course." Owen gestured to the others to gather close. "Thanks again, and... I guess we'll get started?"

Enjoy your adventure!

The system message vanished.

CHAPTER FIVE

Aderyn turned to Owen. "That seems straightforward enough. Defeat enough of what's in these rooms, gain a total of 18,000 experience, and on to Obsidian. I don't want to get ahead of myself, because it could be very hard, but at least it's not complicated."

"There are five exits aside from the front door. Let's take a look before choosing," Owen suggested.

They spread out through the room. Aderyn chose the door immediately to the left of the entrance. The swirling pattern continued across it, though the swirls were slightly faded so the door didn't disappear against the walls. It had an elaborate brass knob shaped like a chrysanthemum at its center rather than to the side. Aderyn couldn't tell which way it opened. She pressed her ear to the door and heard nothing beyond.

She turned to see what the others had found. Livia and Weston stood at the empty doorways opposite the entrance. From her position, Aderyn could just barely see that they led to corridors, one painted bright green, the other an eye-watering fuchsia. Owen stood next to a door directly opposite Aderyn's, and Isold was looking at the third door, just to the left of Owen's. Aderyn couldn't make out any details that differentiated those doors from hers.

Owen gestured, and they all met in the middle of the round chamber. "Any preferences?" he asked. "I couldn't hear anything behind my door."

"Neither could I," Isold said. "My guess is that Gamboling Coil doesn't want to give anyone an advantage in the form of knowing what's in a particular room before entering."

"Those corridors aren't well lit, and even I couldn't see past ten or fifteen feet," Weston said. "We decided not to illuminate them with *orb of light* in case that alerted something."

Aderyn held up her compass. "This still works. It might not show actual north, but what matters is that it's consistent inside the dungeon. So those two archways are north, the two doors on that side are east, and the one I looked at is to the west. But that doesn't help us decide."

"Then we're back to guessing," Owen said. "Weren't there any differences between doors?"

"Mine has a handle like a chrysanthemum," Aderyn volunteered.

"That's different. The handle of mine is shaped like a rose," Isold said.

"And mine looks like a pinecone," Owen said. "Isold's door, then. I hate chrysanthemums. They're so showy."

They gathered in a loose group in front of the rose door, and Weston examined it for traps. "Based on that conversation with the dungeon, either Gamboling Coil will have no traps because it thinks they're juvenile, or it will have many traps in its desire to 'challenge' us," he said. "This door's clean." He turned the rose knob, which was also in the center of the door, and pushed the door open.

The wild paint scheme didn't continue in the next room, which instead was covered in soothing blue and green swirls. Many thick, waist-high walls made a maze that filled the enormous room. The friends stepped forward, scanning the room for movement.

"I don't see any other doors," Aderyn said.

"There's an arched opening over there, to the east," Weston said, pointing. "Who knows where it leads. It might just loop around back to this room."

"Let's make that our goal," Owen said. "We should at least figure out how to get out of this place. Maybe the maze is the challenge, except the walls are short enough to see over, so if it is the challenge, it's not much of one."

Weston led the way through the narrow, twisting path. Owen was right; it wasn't much of a challenge. Aderyn cast her gaze around the room, looking for another exit. Movement caught her eye, and she grabbed Owen's arm. "There's something there."

"What is it?"

"I'm not sure. It moved fast, like a cat."

They all stopped to look in the direction Aderyn pointed. Then Livia shouted, "There!" and blasted a hail of stones at the far wall. Something howled, and suddenly a creature appeared in front of them. It had the narrow muzzle and lean flanks of a hunting dog, but it raked razor-sharp claws across Aderyn's chest, scoring the front of her leather jerkin. Faster than thought, Owen drew his sword and skewered the creature. His sword passed through its body, which began to fade.

"What are those things?" he shouted. "Ghosts?"

"Fade dogs," Isold exclaimed. "Look, there's another!"

The fade dog he pointed at loped across the tops of the walls like a cat, bounding over gaps and running straight for the team. Aderyn drew her sword and Assessed it.

Name: Fade Dog
Type: Magical beast
Power level: 7
Immune to: none
Resistant to: none
Vulnerable to: none

Fade dogs, despite the name, are felines with the appearance of hunting dogs. They are capable of casting *skip* at will, magically jumping a short distance from one space to another without passing through the area between. When a fade dog *skips*, it leaves behind a perfect image of itself that gradually fades away. This peculiar ability affects the damage done by its claw attacks, which require multiple healings as the injury extends into the past and future. If monster power level were based on how annoying a creature is to fight, you'd stand no chance against them.

Blue lines of light slid over the contours of the fade dog's body, cohering at spots in a row from the base of its throat to the lower curve of its abdomen.

"It *skips*," Aderyn shouted. "Try to hit its underside, and if you strike and feel no resistance, don't waste time—that's just an image!"

Aderyn saw more than a dozen fade dogs, but only three of them were moving. She climbed to the top of a maze wall and flailed at one of the images. That didn't make it dissipate faster. She gave up on that and, leaping like the fade dogs, ran across the walls after Owen, who was chasing one of the runners. Abruptly, it turned on him, and Owen struck it a glancing blow down one narrow flank. The bleeding fade dog froze and the image began to fade. Aderyn hopped over to stand next to Owen. "This is worse than chasing the shack," she said.

"We need to be smarter about this," Owen said. He surveyed the room, and Aderyn did the same. Isold was advancing on one that kept *skipping* away from his attempts to use [**Fascinate**] on it. Weston and Livia stood in a slightly wider space, with Livia taking that same wrestler's stance she'd used to *immobilize* Gamboling Coil but not apparently having any effect, and Weston waiting, poised to leap as soon as she caught one of the fade dogs.

Owen ran to where Weston and Livia were, and Aderyn followed him. "*Immobilize* doesn't work," Livia said. Her words were clipped and sounded tense. "And they're faster than my *elemental blast*."

Aderyn's eye fell on the wounded fade dog, whose right side was bloody all down its rear leg. It *skipped*, leaving behind an image, but its injury made it easy for Aderyn to keep track of the real dog. She watched it do this several times until she became aware that Owen was addressing her. "They always *skip* the same way," she said.

"I said—what was that?" Owen asked.

"Look at the maze. Look at the floor tiles. It's a grid. And they always *skip* the same way—five squares to their right and two squares forward, with a pause like they're catching their breath. Watch the bleeding one."

They all watched. Weston let out a heartfelt curse. "I should have seen it."

"Maybe it needed a Warmaster's vision," Owen said, gripping Aderyn's shoulder briefly. "I know what to do. Aderyn, go after the bleeding one, but don't attack it."

"I understand."

Aderyn climbed back onto the wall and made her way slowly toward the wounded fade dog. It pretended not to notice her, but it was tensed, ready to *skip* when she lunged for it. She got to within ten feet and waited, not looking away from the monster. Soon, she heard Owen say, "I'm ready," in an ordinary, conversational tone of voice.

She ran forward, shouting and waving her sword in a way that would be completely useless if this was a real attack, and reached the fade dog just as its image froze. A yowl of pain split the air. Turning, she saw Owen crouched on the wall, his arm extended in a perfect lunge, his <**Twinsword**> thrust deep into the fade dog's belly. The monster curled in on itself, batting at the sword as if it could pull it out with its paws. Its movements became feeble, and finally it sagged in death.

Congratulations! You have defeated [Fade Dog].

You have earned [2000 XP]

Owen withdrew his sword and cleaned the blade on the fade dog's short, thick fur. "There. Everyone partner up."

The second fade dog managed to claw Weston's arm, but after that one strike it fell to Livia's *elemental blast* of head-sized stones, timed to arrive in the fade dog's destination exactly as it appeared there. Isold was waiting for the third, and **[Fascinated]** it so Aderyn and Weston had all the time in the world to position themselves for killing blows.

When the final monster defeat notice faded, another system notice appeared.

That was really well done! I'm so impressed. You have earned [6000 XP] toward your goal, which means you only need [12000 XP] more to defeat me! Go you!

"I can't tell if it's mocking us or not," Weston said, extending his arm to Isold for him to use the **<Wand of Minor Healing>**. It took three attempts before the bleeding stopped. "Not even I am that relentlessly positive. About anything. Including Livia."

Of course I'm not mocking you! You must be a very insecure person to assume genuine encouragement is some kind of trick. I am always pleased when adventurers succeed. It's so much better than the alternative.

"What's the alternative?" Aderyn couldn't help asking.

Having to mulch the bodies.

Silence fell. Owen cleared his throat. "Let's move on, shall we? There are two other doors and that arched opening. I'm guessing that one door near where we entered leads back the way we came. I want to try the archway rather than the door. If our fight made enough noise to draw attention, anything beyond that archway would have come to investigate, so I'm guessing there's no danger right there."

"Unless the monsters have to stay in their rooms," Aderyn pointed out. "Or they roam the corridors."

"Can we just stick with my guess? If I'm wrong, feel free to criticize."

"If you're wrong, none of us will be in a position to criticize," Livia said.

They walked across the tops of the walls, leaping the gaps, directly to the archway, which opened on a corridor painted such a bright yellow it seemed to radiate light. It made an immediate left turn, then turned right after a dozen paces and came to an end in another dozen. They all stopped in front of a pair of doors, spaced about five feet apart.

"Those might go to the same place," Owen said, "or they might be two different rooms."

"They both lead north," Aderyn said, consulting her compass.

"Either way, we have to pick one," Livia said. "Take the one on the right."

"Why that one?"

"No reason. This place is getting to me. I'm starting to feel frivolous and carefree. It's unsettling." Livia shuddered dramatically. "Next thing you know I'll be dancing through a field of bluebells reciting poetry."

"Let us proceed before that dire event happens," Isold said with a smile.

Weston checked the door. "Still no traps. Don't let me get complacent." He opened the door and peeked inside before throwing the door open entirely. "There's nothing here—or, more likely, nothing visible."

"You don't think we'll have to fight invisible creatures, do you?" Aderyn said. "I hated fighting boggarts, and they weren't even fully invisible."

"Let's not anticipate trouble," Owen said. "Spread out and look around."

The walls of this round room were painted in a rainbow gradient that never ended, running through the gamut of colors until violet turned to rose and merged with red. Unlike the maze room, whose floor had been perfectly square stone tiles, the new room had a floor of packed earth covered with a thin, loose layer of grit that crunched beneath Aderyn's boots. She walked cautiously forward, examining the ground for tripwires or pressure plates. Finding traps wasn't one of her skills, but it shouldn't be hard to detect anything big.

"I don't like this," Weston said. His voice echoed in the emptiness.

"Maybe it's been cleared and hasn't reset yet," Livia suggested.

"That's what I don't like. We're the only adventurers here, or so I thought. If this room is empty of threats, that means someone else beat us to it." Weston's grim tone unnerved Aderyn. He was only ever serious when true danger threatened.

She tilted her head back to look at the ceiling, which was a shallow dome painted, unusually, solid white rather than in gaudy colors. Hidden lights shone on its surface, brightening the room. "It's got to be—"

She took a step, and the ground moved beneath her feet as a hidden switch depressed with a click. "—a trap," she concluded, and the floor fell out from beneath her.

CHAPTER SIX

Aderyn screamed and clawed at the floor, trying to halt her slide down an incline toward the newly-revealed pit. The others were shouting, words that were unintelligible over the *whopwhopwhop* sound coming from below. Aderyn stretched out her arms and legs so she was spreadeagled. Maybe if she was a wider shape, there would be more of her to stop her descent. It worked— sort of. Her slide became erratic and slowed, but she didn't stop.

"Grab her!" Owen shouted. "Doesn't anyone have a damn *rope?*"

"It's Aderyn who's got the rope!" Weston called out.

Then she heard Livia's voice, and suddenly she was mired in goopy, thick mud. Her progress halted. Breathing heavily, she lifted her head and said, "What's below me?"

"Don't worry about that," Owen said. "Just hold on. We'll make a human chain."

She felt her body slip with a slight jerk as the mud seeped down the slope. "Better make it fast."

Owen lay on his stomach and inched over the edge of the slope. Behind him, Isold crouched, holding Owen's ankles and scooting himself forward as Owen moved. Aderyn reached for Owen's hand. The *whopwhopwhop* sound grew louder. "Sorry," Weston said.

"Keep trying," Owen replied through gritted teeth. "We've almost got her."

Aderyn slid a little farther. Her feet dangled over open air now, and globs of mud fell into the pit, splattering against something that made the *whopwhopwhop* become higher pitched. "What am I about to fall into?" she screamed.

"I said don't worry about it," Owen said. "Give me your hand."

Their fingertips brushed, and then Aderyn slid out of his reach. She could feel emptiness beneath her knees, and a cool wind blew across her legs. "Owen!"

"Lower me faster!" Owen shouted. "Aderyn, grab onto something!"

"There isn't anything!" She slipped again, rapidly descending a few inches. The edge of the slope dug into her thighs. She thought about looking below, but decided that might throw her enough off balance that she'd fall faster. Whatever was down there, she didn't need to know.

Owen's hand came into view again. "Aderyn!"

She reached for him. Their hands clasped. Then her muddy palm slid through his fingers as she dropped farther. Now her entire lower half dangled free, and gravity was pulling her down faster. The edge cut into her stomach as sharply as if the sloping ground was a plate rather than a cliff. She raised her knees, squeezing the edge of the slope with her legs like clenching that plate between her belly and her thighs. It stopped her fall, but tension in her legs told her she wouldn't be able to maintain that position long.

She looked up at Owen, whose face was intent on her. He didn't seem to be moving closer. She stretched out her arm, but now their fingers weren't even close to touching.

"I said lower me, Isold!" Owen shouted.

"I can't go any farther without sending us both to join her," Isold grunted.

The whirring *whopwhopwhop* sound grew louder and faster. Owen's eyes widened in fear. Seeing his terror sent a spike of fear through Aderyn as well. "Owen," she whispered. "Owen, I'm sorry."

Painful cramps shot through her thighs, and involuntarily she relaxed her grip. Immediately, her slide resumed, slowly but inexorably. She screamed—

—and the whirring sound slowed and came to a stop.

Unable to hold her position any longer, Aderyn fell. To her surprise, it was a fall of only a few feet. She tried to stand, collapsed as her tortured legs wouldn't support her, and then Owen was there, lifting her up and holding her tightly despite the fact that she was covered in mud.

"That was close," he whispered. "Oh, Aderyn. I thought I'd lost you."

Aderyn held him and waited for her breathing to calm down. "It was a bottomless pit, wasn't it," she said. "I was afraid to look."

"Worse," Owen said.

She turned in his arms to look behind her and let out a gasp. Dozens of circular blades, all with wickedly gleaming edges, filled the ten-foot-wide pit. Some were within touching distance of where she had fallen. "Spinning blades," she said faintly.

"They were more spread out when they were rotating," Owen said. "If you'd fallen, they would have sliced you into a thousand pieces. I swear when we reach civilization I'm buying myself a hundred feet of the best rope available."

A thunk echoed through the room, and Weston appeared at the edge of the pit. "It's disabled permanently now," he said, "though maybe not—"

You have received [1500 XP] for disabling the [Spinning Slicing Filleting Blades of Doom Trap], putting you at [10,500

XP] still needed to defeat me. Amazing work! That could have been messy!

"What the *hell*—" Owen shouted, his arms closing tightly around Aderyn.

"Don't shout at the dungeon, sweetheart," Aderyn said. "It's not our friend, remember? No matter how encouraging it is. Yelling only risks it turning on us and making things harder."

"But only fifteen hundred experience?" Owen released Aderyn and regarded them both. "Fine. Let's get up there, and Livia can rinse us off. Good thing this place is warm."

Aderyn still felt cold after Livia's *drench* washed away most of the mud, mainly because *drench* produced ice water. She changed into her spare shift and shirt and wrung muddy water out of the ruined one. Beside her, Owen did the same. "All right," he said, his voice shaking with cold, "so it's not as comfortable as I suggested."

"I'm alive. That's as comfortable as I need to be." Aderyn quickly stripped out of her trousers, squeezed water out of them, and gingerly put them back on. "We'll dry soon enough."

"Hurry," Weston said. The others were standing with their backs to them to give them what little privacy they could. "I said it was permanently disabled, but that's only until the dungeon gets around to resetting the trap."

"Did you all check the other doors?" Owen asked.

"One of them is an archway that leads to a hall," Livia said. "That hall turns back the way we came. That second door we saw outside a minute ago does lead to this room. The other three doors, we don't know, but two of them head north and the other goes east."

"Let's keep moving north, just to stay consistent," Owen said. "Check the door on the left."

That door led to a corridor with walls painted a deep turquoise. It extended out of the range of the room's light. "Hmm," Owen said. "How about the other one? Based on the halls we've seen so far, that hall will probably twist and turn so we'll end up not knowing where we are in relation to the rooms we've passed."

After establishing that this door wasn't locked or trapped either, Weston turned the door handle and pushed open the door on a room hotter and wetter than the rest of the dungeon. "It's a jungle," he whispered.

"Why are you whispering?" Livia asked.

"Because I can't see more than a few feet ahead of me thanks to these plants, and anything might be in there."

"Very smart," Aderyn said. "I don't suppose this is actually outside? It would be unlikely, but still."

Weston sniffed. Then he took a single step inside and turned his head first one way, then the other. "It's indoors. There's no air movement, and I saw the ceiling, so unless the sky is suddenly only thirty feet above us and painted a nice bright green, we're still inside Gamboling Coil."

The others all followed Weston, and Isold shut the door quietly behind them. Aderyn marveled at the greenery, all the trees that looked nothing like any trees she was familiar with, the broad-leaved bushes, the yellow and green striped grass. The air smelled rich with loam, the kind of earth that would grow anything that stood still long enough to take root, and it was dim with mist that diffused the light and made everything feel comfortably close. It was hard to stay afraid, even in such an alien environment, when the air felt like a warm blanket that shut out the cold of winter. Unseen birds sang in the trees, unfamiliar songs like raucous coughs or high, thin whistling or murmurs that sounded almost like speech.

"I don't hear anything moving around," Weston said.

"I'm guessing whatever is in here is a monster rather than a trap," Owen said. "Something sneaky, something with camouflage. We need to stay together. Getting separated could be fatal."

Aderyn consulted the compass. "Should we continue north, or stay with the walls?"

"The monster or monsters here will almost certainly see us before we see them. If we're going to defeat them, we'll have to wait for them to attack." Owen searched the nearby bushes as if despite his words he could find the creature. "So we might as well blunder around in the open."

"I'll take point," Weston said. "Isold, stay close to the middle. Anything that jumps us will be moving too fast for **[Fascinate]** or **[Suggestion]**."

They shuffled around until they were in a loose group centered on Isold. Aderyn marveled as she always did that a man Weston's size didn't make any noise as he moved through the undergrowth. She pushed aside ferns as tall as she was and scanned the jungle that lay beyond them. The heat and dampness warmed her without drying her off, and her trousers stuck to her legs unpleasantly. Nothing moved beyond the five of them except the bushes and plants they passed through.

The birdsongs moved with them, following them, and Aderyn searched the canopy but still saw nothing. Fear that the monsters here were flying ones struck, reminding her of past encounters. She listened closely for any change in the music that might mean something was diving at them, and became increasingly disconcerted.

"I think some of those birds speak words," she said. "Or sing them."

"I don't hear words," Owen said. "Are they talking to us?"

"I don't think so," Weston said. "It sounds like 'worms, worms, worms, we eat worms.'"

"And it's cheerful," Aderyn added. "Like worms are the best thing ever."

"So long as they don't consider us worms, we're fine," Owen said.

Aderyn moved another branch with leaves the size of her palm and jerked back. Two yellow eyes stared at her from the darkness beneath the trees. They blinked, and then they were gone. Something big rustled the bushes with its passing.

They all stopped and stared into the undergrowth. "It's gone," Weston said.

"For now," Livia replied.

Owen drew his sword. "We've got its attention. Keep moving. It knows it has the upper hand with its concealment."

Aderyn drew her sword as well. She hadn't liked the way those eyes had looked at her, like they could Assess her down to her core. Her whole body felt stretched to the breaking point, every nerve on edge, every inch of her skin tingling with anticipation. The birds' songs maddened her now, the repetitive tunes and the constant *worms, worms, worms* filling her ears so she couldn't hear anything else.

To her right, the bushes rustled as a big, dark shape ran past. It was gone too quickly for **[Improved Assess 2]**, but Aderyn tried it anyway and got nothing. Again, they all stopped, drawing closer together as if by instinct. Aderyn's pulse throbbed in her ears, drowning out the birds. Nothing happened. The bushes were still again.

With a snarl, something leaped from the bushes behind them, knocking Weston over and forcing the others back. Black fur over rippling muscles blended with the dark greens of the plants, and a red mane hung lank over a long muzzle with teeth like daggers. Its jaws closed over Livia's arm, and she screamed.

Aderyn stepped back, her mind a white blank of terror, and seized reflexively on the one thing she could do.

Name: Sanguisuge
Type: Abomination
Power level: 10
Immune to: Mind-affecting spells and skills
Resistant to: Bludgeoning damage
Vulnerable to: none

Special attack: Blood drain

The sanguisuge attacks from the shadows, separating its prey from the group to devour it in solitude. Its bite allows it to drink the blood of its victim, reducing the victim's maximum health pool. The sanguisuge regenerates its own health when it feeds in this way. Extremely dangerous.

"Get her away from it!" Aderyn shouted, just as the sanguisuge gathered itself and leaped over their heads into the bushes, taking Livia with it.

CHAPTER SEVEN

They ran, following the sound of thrashing plants that Aderyn was terrifyingly aware was probably made by Livia's body. She couldn't see her friend or the sanguisuge, but she heard Livia chanting and then a muffled thump like the biggest fist in the world slamming into flesh. "It doesn't take as much damage from bludgeoning weapons," she gasped. "That was *thunder punch*. She can't disable it."

"What else?" Owen said.

"It drinks blood and heals that way. Isold's mind control skills won't work on it. We have to get Livia and get out of here." [**Keep Pace**] dragged her along beside Owen, and she'd never been more grateful for it. Getting separated from the others might make her the sanguisuge's next victim.

The bushes stopped moving. Aderyn and the others stumbled to a halt. "Where is it? Where is she?" Weston exclaimed.

"Livia, scream if you can!" Owen shouted.

A shrill, penetrating scream shattered the air. Weston immediately dashed away, and Aderyn ran after him. She couldn't tell where the sound had come from, but Weston had no such problem.

Again, bushes rustled, and they heard the scream again. This time, it was weak, frightening Aderyn with possibilities. Weston changed direction. Aderyn's legs ached from the exertion coming so soon after she'd strained herself in the spinning blades trap, but she kept running.

They burst through a bank of ferns into a more open space. The sanguisuge crouched over Livia, its jaws still locked on her upper arm, its throat pulsing like it was swallowing. Livia lay unconscious and far too pale beneath it. Weston shouted a challenge and threw himself at the monster, which didn't stop draining Livia. His wild swings and thrusts glanced off the sanguisuge's black fur.

"Come on!" Owen shouted to Aderyn. Aderyn Assessed the monster again. The blue lines of light slid and intersected without ever coalescing into the blue spots that indicated weaknesses. Still, she had to do *something*.

She ran at the monster's head. Every creature that had a face was protective of it. Instead of slashing, she smashed the sword's pommel across the bridge of the sanguisuge's nose. As she'd hoped, the monster roared, a terrible, bloodcurdling sound, and let go of Livia. Aderyn noticed briefly that no blood flowed from the terrible deep wounds on Livia's arm, but that was all she had time for before the sanguisuge turned on her.

Then Owen was beside her, his **<Twinsword>** at the ready. "Weston, grab Livia," he said. "We have to get out of here. Back the way we came. Aderyn, we're covering the retreat."

Aderyn nodded.

The sanguisuge snarled and lunged for Aderyn. She brought her sword up and thrust at its face, making it step back. Owen slashed in the direction of its throat and backed up a few careful steps. "Isold—"

"I will keep you from falling," Isold said from behind them.

Step by step, Owen and Aderyn backed away, barely keeping the sanguisuge at bay. After a few steps, it snarled again and backed up before leaping into the bushes. Aderyn lowered her sword. "It's going to try to get behind us."

"Run," Owen said, and the three of them bolted for the exit.

The sanguisuge kept pace with them. It ran silently, without the snarls and growls that had chilled her to her core, the only sign of its passage the rustling of the bushes. The simple sound terrified Aderyn as nothing else ever had, filling her with a primal fear of things that came for you in the darkness.

The open door that appeared in front of them relieved Aderyn's heart. She'd lost track of direction and hoped this wasn't some other door, open to new horrors. Relief gave her new energy, and she sprinted ahead of Isold and Owen and through the doorway, nearly tripping over Weston and Livia, sprawled on the floor. Then the others were through, and Isold slammed the door shut and leaned against it, gasping for air.

You failed to defeat the [Sanguisuge]. It's all right, this doesn't make you failures! Well, it sort of does, but it's nothing personal.

Owen's lips thinned as he held back what Aderyn was sure would be a spectacular outburst. She clasped his hand. "I'm having trouble remembering the dungeon isn't actually antagonistic to us."

"I could do without the motivational messages," Owen replied.

Weston held the unconscious Livia in his lap. "She's not dead," he said. "But she won't wake up. It drank her blood."

Aderyn focused on the team roster, as Owen called it, that showed the names and statuses of the teammates, always faintly visible until she brought it to her attention. Livia's health bar was almost gone, and what remained pulsed a deep, heart's-blood red.

Isold crouched on the floor beside the two and withdrew the **<Healing Stone>** from his belt pouch. "I don't know how well this will work. It's more powerful than the wand, but—"

"Just do it!" Weston commanded.

Isold pressed the <Healing Stone> to Livia's wounded arm. A deep green light welled up from beneath her skin, healing the punctures. Her health bar quivered and grew by half an inch, but the red pulsing remained. Isold had the inward-turned expression that said he was watching this as well. He removed the stone and sat back.

"Do it again," Weston said. "She's still injured."

"I'll try again, but I'm not sure the stone knows that blood loss is an injury, given that we all make our own blood, all the time," Isold said. "If the <Healing Stone> sees that Livia is already naturally replenishing her blood, it might not think—though of course it doesn't have a mind to think with, but you take my meaning... at any rate, it's possible it won't regenerate her lost blood." Isold pressed the stone to Livia's arm again, and they all watched the team display. Aderyn willed the little bar to rise, but it simply quivered.

Livia stirred. "Did we kill it?" she murmured in a faint voice.

"Don't worry about that, dearest, just lie still," Weston said. "What are we supposed to do now?"

"We go back to the entrance, and hope that's a safe location to wait Livia's recovery out," Owen said.

Weston rose and picked Livia up, cradling her gently in his arms. "And if—"

"She'll recover," Aderyn said. "It will just take time." She wished she was as confident as she sounded. At the moment, everything felt like failure.

The pit trap hadn't reset when they poked their heads through that doorway. They circled the room's perimeter anyway, just in case. The maze, too, was empty of fade dogs, and the team returned to the entrance without encountering anything dangerous.

The entrance was too garish and garishly lit to be truly comfortable, but Aderyn sat with her back against the wall and let Owen lie with his head in her lap. She ran her fingers idly through his hair and made herself think of nothing. It didn't work. Memories of the sanguisuge intruded, frightening her once more. When she managed to stop thinking about that, her gaze fell on Livia, reclining against Weston with her eyes closed. They'd nearly lost two people in the space of half an hour. The dungeon's bright colors and cheerful messages felt like taunts now.

"We could leave," she said. "The door's right there."

"There's no guarantee a cross-country journey will be any less dangerous," Owen said. He, too, had his eyes closed, but his voice was strong. "We need to be more cautious, that's all."

"We were as cautious as we knew how to be back there," Weston said sharply.

"Then what do you suggest, Weston? Take on a six-week trip with who knows how many challenges that might also kill one or all of us?" Owen's voice matched his for sharpness.

"Please don't argue," Livia said faintly. "Adventuring is dangerous. We all knew that when we accepted the Call. We have to keep going. If we leave and come back when we're higher level, the challenge here will likely be even greater. And there's no thundering way I'll give this stupid frivolous place the satisfaction of driving me away."

"I agree," Aderyn said. "We beat two of the challenges this place threw at us. I don't want to give up just because we couldn't beat the third. The dungeon is power level eight—its other challenges can't possibly *all* be as terrible as the sanguisuge."

"The what? Is that its name?" Owen exclaimed, sitting up. "That sounds terrifying even if you don't know what it is."

"Yes. I guess 'blood-sucking lion' isn't punchy enough." Aderyn hugged Owen and rested her cheek briefly on his shoulder. "We'll rest until Livia is better, and then we'll go the other way."

As she said this, she checked the team roster. Livia's health still hovered at about a third its normal length, and it still pulsed red, but it was higher than it had been even a few minutes earlier.

"We might as well eat something, then," Owen said.

They ate dried meat and nuts washed down with stale water and tried to get comfortable in the hideous entrance chamber. Isold curled up and napped. Aderyn took a turn resting her head on Owen's lap and was almost able to sleep. She drifted in and out, barely falling asleep before her awareness of her surroundings penetrated her sleepy brain and jerked her awake. Finally, she sat up and raked her fingers through her hair before retying her ponytail. Surprisingly, she did feel rested.

Owen had his head tilted back and his eyes closed, but he said, "Did you sleep at all?"

"Sort of." She leaned against his shoulder. "I feel better, though. Less tense."

"Good." He fell silent again.

Aderyn checked the team roster. Livia's health indicator had risen to above half its normal length, and it was blue again. "Isold," Aderyn said, "I think you should try healing Livia once more."

Isold sat up and rummaged around for the **<Healing Stone>**, but then set it aside and drew out the **<Wand of Minor Healing>**. "We are running low on charges with the stone, and if you are, as I believe, suggesting we see if healing will have an effect, better to try with a more bountiful resource."

He scooted to sit next to Livia and activated the wand. As usual, its tip glowed green and bubbled over with a frothy green liquid that rolled over Livia's arm. Livia said, "There's no wound, so maybe it won't work."

Aderyn was keeping an eye on the roster. "No, it worked!" she exclaimed. "Just not by much."

Livia's eyes focused on the middle distance as she, too, examined the team roster. "Three-quarters full," she said. "That's good enough for me."

"What if we encounter something dangerous, and that missing one-fourth is the difference between life and death?" Weston demanded.

"It's not going to come to that. And I will be careful." Livia kissed him. "You're the optimist, dearest. Tell me I'm wrong, and you wouldn't do the same."

Weston sighed. "I'd be the first through the door. All right, where do we go next?"

"It should be the chrysanthemum door," Aderyn said. "That's the only one that goes for sure in the opposite direction to where we've been."

"Reasonable," Owen said. "And if it turns out to double back, we'll try another."

Weston was already examining the door. "No traps." He turned the knob and opened the door to reveal a corridor painted a vibrant orange.

Owen made a face. "I don't like chrysanthemums *or* the color orange. I'm choosing not to see this as a terrible omen."

Aderyn, who liked how cheerful chrysanthemums were, decided not to comment.

CHAPTER EIGHT

The corridor extended some twenty feet before turning left, then right, then right again, turning back on itself. No doors appeared, not even the secret ones Weston checked for. Finally, the corridor straightened out and ended at a door painted turquoise blue with a knob shaped like a beagle's head. Weston looked at it for several seconds. "This place is weird," he finally said, and examined the door as he'd done every time before. "Still clear, but after the pit trap and the sanguisuge, I'm even less inclined to take chances."

Owen gestured him aside when he pronounced the door safe. "Don't enter right away. Let's look first."

Aderyn looked, and wished she hadn't. The room was painted in the same vibrant swirls as the entrance chamber, but these swirls moved, slowly rotating in any of a dozen directions. It gave Aderyn the impression that the room itself was tumbling in slow motion along its horizontal axis. She swallowed against unexpected nausea.

Livia pushed past them into the room. "This is assault," she declared, standing with her hands on her hips in an aggressive manner. "I say we bypass this room and go somewhere less directly antagonistic."

Aderyn followed Owen into the room. "I don't see any monsters." The room, like the pit trap room, appeared completely empty, but the floor was of smooth gray marble tiles one foot square instead of packed earth. Three doors and two arched doorways exited the room, some to the north, others to east and west.

"Everyone stay close to the wall for a bit," Weston said. He tipped his head back and surveyed the ceiling. "What do you think those circles are?"

Aderyn looked up. The ceiling wasn't tall, no more than ten feet, and at its center was a row of black glass circles, ten foot-wide circles in a neat line. "I hope they don't spray acid, or blast fire, or anything like that."

Weston shrugged. He walked slowly to the center of the room, testing each tile before putting his weight on it. When he was close to the center, several marble tiles lit up, glowing with a warm yellow light. "Look at that. Twenty-five lit tiles, five on a side."

"How can marble glow?" Aderyn said. "It's stone."

"Translucent stone, if it's thin enough," Livia said. "Though it would have to be a very bright light."

"I've seen things like that in my world, electrical lights," Owen said. "Weston, be careful."

"I always am." Weston put a foot on the nearest lighted tile, the one at the corner. Immediately, the tile and its two nearest neighbors turned dark. Weston stepped again, to the next lighted tile. It went out, as did the one adjacent to it, and two others turned on again. "This is fun," he said, and raised a foot to step again.

"Stop," Livia said. She'd circled the room and was now staring down at one of the tiles. "It's a test."

"A test of what?" Isold asked.

"Of whether we're smart enough and patient enough to read the rules instead of jumping in at random. No offense meant, dearest."

Weston jumped over the series of lit and unlit tiles and joined her. "There are rules?"

"On this tile. Wait, I'll make them clearer." She spoke a few words, and a gout of mud dropped onto the tile and splattered. Livia ignored Weston's complaint and gestured. A strong wind pushed the mud away from the tile, leaving behind traces in grooves that hadn't been visible before.

Aderyn crouched to see better. "It *is* rules."

"So, what do they say?" Owen asked.

Livia crouched beside Aderyn and read aloud. "It says, 'Extinguish the lights.' And below that are two more lines, in script, not printing. The first says 'Light breeds darkness and the reverse.' The second says, 'Step here to begin,' and there's a curly arrow to this other tile. It's a puzzle."

"I get it," Weston said. "Stepping on a lit tile turns it dark *and* darkens the adjacent tiles. Stepping on a dark tile does the reverse. I don't know why we need the other tile, since we already lit the thing up, but—"

"I think we should make sure there aren't any other instructions," Livia said.

"But I understand how it works," Weston said.

"It's too simple a puzzle if that's all it takes," Livia insisted. "Let's all spread out. These instructions were by a door, so maybe there are others."

"Spread out," Owen said.

Aderyn crossed to the nearest archway. All the tiles seemed smooth and blank. She dropped to her knees and felt along the surfaces of the tiles. "There's more!" she exclaimed. Peering close, she read, "'Trust to the patterns you see.'"

"There wasn't a pattern before. Maybe that refers to once the puzzle is activated." Owen was on hands and knees like Aderyn, feeling around at the door opposite her. "Here's another one: 'The race goes not to the swift, but to the efficient.' I have no idea what that means."

"I think it means the puzzle isn't on a timer," Aderyn said. "That's a relief. I'm still not sure I understand how the lights work in practice."

"The one beside the door we entered by says 'Sometimes moving forward means taking a step back,'" Weston said.

"And this door here has the message 'Three times success equals victory,' which I take to mean we have to solve the puzzle three times," Isold added.

"The last one says 'Ten steps is your limit,'" Livia said. "So, we have to extinguish the lights, we have to do it three times, if we can do it in only a few moves it's better—maybe we earn more experience?— and if we take more than ten moves, it's over. Or maybe it means it won't let us take more than ten moves per puzzle." She stood and stretched. "There's no time limit. I say we take it slowly and figure out the solution before doing it."

"Then let's activate the puzzle," Owen said.

Isold, who was closest, stepped on the indicated tile. This time, the black glass circles lit, one at a time, and then turned dark the same way until the entire row of circles was unlit. The square of twenty-five tiles flashed on and off three times, then most of them remained dark. Ten squares continued to glow with warm radiance.

Weston walked around the puzzle, followed by Livia. "There's your pattern," he said. "Two small crosses of five lights each, with a dark tile at the center between them."

"That one's obvious," Livia said. "Somebody jump on the tile at the center of the cross."

Owen took a long step that put him on the indicated tile. All five lights surrounding it went out. The first of the glass circles lit up. "I see how it goes," Owen said. He stepped to the center of the second cross. All those lights went out, leaving the square of tiles dark. Another glass circle glowed.

"Isn't that it?" Aderyn said.

Owen shrugged. "Those lights from above are really warm, though. I hate to think how hot the puzzle square will get when they're all lit." He hopped over the tiles to stand beside her. Immediately, the tiles flashed on and off again three times, and the two bright circles went dark.

"That was an easy one," Livia said. "This one is harder." There were only five tiles lit up this time, spaced apparently at random.

Weston regarded it closely. He stepped on the corner tile. "No, that one's dark already!" Aderyn exclaimed. Above, one of the lights turned on.

"That's the trick," Weston said. "I'm taking a step back." Now the pattern looked like a small half circle, two darkened tiles on the edge of the square surrounded by four lit ones. He stepped on one of the dark tiles, and the pattern changed to show a single lit tile with one more bright one on each side. One more step, and all four remaining tiles went dark. Weston stepped back and again the square flashed three times.

"I don't know how you're doing this. I can't see which squares will light at all," Aderyn complained.

"Well, this isn't really tactics, so a Warmaster's vision wouldn't engage," Weston said. "It's a matter of following the rules, and I can't believe I just said that."

"One more," Livia said.

"From where I stand," Isold said, "it looks like two dark columns between three light columns, with the center horizontal row blacked out."

Weston and Livia circled the puzzle in silence. Aderyn's nerves twanged. She hated that this thing made no sense to her, not because she felt she should always know everything, but because she felt so unable to aid her friends. "Is it the one in the middle?"

"I don't think so," Weston said. He placed a tentative foot on a dark tile. It and its neighbor lit up, and the two above and below it darkened. Weston gazed at the puzzle, remaining so still he might have feared accidentally making a move that would count against him. Finally, he touched the tile again, reversing his move.

"That's two chances gone," Owen said. "Sorry. You know that."

"I do, in fact, realize," Weston said with a grin. "So it's not the middle... in fact, it's not any of the dark tiles."

"Corners," Livia exclaimed. "It's the corners. But you might not have enough moves left."

"I guess we'll see," Weston said.

He stepped lightly onto a lit corner tile and then, with breath-taking grace, leaped from that tile to the next corner and the next until all four corners were dark. Six glass circles were lit, and they radiated heat Aderyn could feel even from where she stood to the side. Weston must be broiling.

Eight lit tiles remained in what to Aderyn looked like an hour-glass: three tiles in a row, then one below them, then a dark tile, then one, then three. Weston, sweat beading his hairline, didn't even pause. Quickly he stepped from the center tile in the first row of three to its counterpart on the other side of the square and then stepped away like he was walking off a stage. The entire square was dark.

The moment Weston's foot left the final tile, both the tiles and the glass circles flashed more rapidly than before until Aderyn had to cover her eyes to keep from becoming dizzy.

Congratulations! You've successfully solved the [Light and Dark Puzzle]! What's more, you only made two mistakes. Reading the rules is important, don't you think? Your reward is [4000 XP], putting your total at [11,500 XP]. You only need another [6500 XP] to defeat me! Keep on trying, and remember—you only truly fail when you give up!

"There were four exclamation points in that message," Owen said sourly. "True sign of a deranged mind."

"Shhh, it might hear you," Aderyn said.

I did hear you, and I'm deeply hurt that you don't appreciate my motivational messages. I really do want you to succeed, you know. Would you prefer "Strangers are friends you haven't met yet"? It's not relevant, but it's very catchy. Or there's always—oh, this one is better— "Impossible is just an opinion." That's good, isn't it?

Owen opened his mouth to reply. Aderyn overrode him with an elbow to his ribs and the words, "Those are very motivational. Thank you."

I *do* like you people! Much better than the last group that passed through here. They shot the lights out before leaving without even attempting the puzzle.

Aderyn froze. "When was this?"

Oh, time means nothing to a dungeon. It could have been two weeks ago, or it could have been tomorrow. It's irrelevant, really, when you consider that in the long run, we're all dead. Well, *you* are. I'll be here long after your children's children's children have given up on adventuring. Now, good luck! And try not to get blood on the paint. It's so hard to get out without ruining something.

There was a pause, and then the booming voice said as if reading aloud the system message,

Oh, I almost forgot—

Welcome to Level Ten

Over her friends' exclamations, Aderyn said, "Wait—shouldn't we be worried about other adventurers being here? Suppose it was those three who sicced the hulking horrors on us?"

"It can't have been them," Livia said. "How would they have gotten here before us? And if they did, they couldn't have defeated the dungeon, because Gamboling Coil was still where the pattern predicted."

"It's not likely," Aderyn admitted. "It's just that one of them is a Deadeye, and when the dungeon said that about them shooting out the lights... I'm imagining things, I know."

"It's not impossible, though," Owen said. "And if they did enter, they might still be around. We'll have to stay alert. More alert, that is."

"And Livia was wrong about one thing," Weston said, putting his arm around Livia's shoulders. "Apparently sometimes things *do* demand adventurers read."

"There are worse things to be wrong about," Livia said.

CHAPTER NINE

"Let's take a few minutes to examine our new skills, and give Livia a chance to select spells," Owen said.

Aderyn had already called up Advancement.

Name: Aderyn

Class: Warmaster

Level: 10

<u>Skills</u>: **Bluff (6), Climb (2), Conversation (6), Intimidate (4), Sense Truth (10), Survival (3), Swim (1), Knowledge: Monsters (9), Knowledge: Demons (1)**

<u>Class Skills:</u> **Improved Assess 2 (16), Awareness (10), Knowledge: Geography (7), Spot (9), Discern Weakness (14), Dodge (9), Improvised Distraction (7), Outflank (10), Draw Fire (3), Keep Pace (10), Amplify Voice (8), See It Coming (6), Basic Weapon Proficiency (Swords) (4), Read Body Language (1), Basic Map Access (1)**

"Aderyn, do you have something called [**Read Body Language**]?" Owen asked.

"Is that another paired skill? How useful! And I have access to the system's maps, too." Aderyn recalled her parents' stories and whispered, "Map."

A blue outline map that matched the one her parents had given her grew to fill her field of vision. It wasn't as detailed as that one, but it showed all the cities she'd visited as small, labeled dots. Nothing was marked where she knew the cities of Branlight, Finion's Gate, and Obsidian lay. Apparently the system map only tracked what you actually visited. "Map close," she said, and the map vanished.

"I've decided on *hungry pit* and *banish demon* for my two new fifth-level spells," Livia said. "*Hungry pit* is just like *create pit*, except it closes over and swallows anything that falls into it, and *banish demon* is just what it sounds like. It's the sort of spell that becomes more effective as I gain levels, so I wanted to take it as soon as I could."

"I'm in favor," Weston said, grimacing. "I never want to count on surviving a demon encounter because the demon was too bored to devour me."

"I have an intriguing new skill called simply **[Shout]**," Isold said. "It is an attack that does not affect my friends, fortunately, but aside from that I'm not sure of the effect. Something to experiment with."

"And my **[Detect Traps]** skill has grown to include magical traps," Weston said. "I'm satisfied."

"Then I think we should continue on," Owen said. "Based on my earlier logic about corridors being safer places than rooms, I want us to take that archway to the west. When I was reading that tile, I saw that the arch leads to a yellow corridor. It's also the only exit that continues away from the entrance chamber."

"Reasonable," Isold said. "By all means, lead on."

Owen had understated the nature of the corridor. It wasn't just yellow, it was a painfully bright yellow, worse than the other yellow corridor, as if the paint glowed with light the way the tiles had done. As if that wasn't enough, the walls were covered in writing, thick black letters that said things like:

YOUR PASSION IS WAITING FOR YOUR COURAGE TO CATCH UP

and

DON'T BE AFRAID TO GIVE UP THE GOOD TO GO FOR THE GREAT

and, in what struck Aderyn as hopelessly circular,

DON'T LIMIT YOUR CHALLENGES, CHALLENGE YOUR LIMITS

"It's trying to cheer us on," she whispered to Owen.

"I'm not looking," Owen replied. "I'm afraid its enthusiasm might be contagious, and then you'll find me standing on a corner hawking *Chicken Soup for the Adventurer's Soul.*"

Aderyn was better now at recognizing when Owen's references to his own world were too complicated for an explanation and didn't ask. "This corridor seems to be going on for a long time. You don't suppose it's actually endless, do you?" The hall had immediately turned south, then doubled back on itself, and they'd already been walking for more than a minute without seeing a door or the corridor's other end.

"I doubt it. The point of these weird halls and all the doors is to keep us confused, have you noticed? So we think the dungeon is bigger than it is. It keeps us off balance."

"I don't like that we've been headed north for a while now. We wanted to go west."

"We wanted to go away from the entrance. I think the dungeon is actually a big circle, based on what we've seen so far."

You're really very clever! Yes, my rooms run in a circle, though they will be rearranged when you come back next time. It keeps things exciting.

"I thought you weren't allowed to give hints," Owen said.

That's not a hint, because it doesn't give you an advantage against any of my challenges. It's just my little way of acknowledging that I like you.

"Um... thank you?"

You're welcome. Enjoy your stay!

Owen muttered something under his breath. Aderyn said, "What was that?"

"Nothing I'd like to repeat." He slowed his steps. "Up ahead, the light changes. I think we've found an exit to this corridor, everyone."

They rounded a corner to find an archway through which silver moonlight reflected off low-hanging silver mist. Weston moved forward and stood with one hand on the side of the arch. "Another forest," he whispered. "Temperate this time. It's foggy, but I can make out oak trees. And it's chilly, like an autumn morning. I don't see or hear movement."

The others joined him, clustering around the entrance. "We'll stick with the walls this time," Owen said. "It was a mistake walking in the open before."

Weston nodded and pushed between two tall bushes with round leaves that emitted a warm, spicy scent when he moved them. Aderyn followed him and immediately found the wall. It was painted dark green and from beyond the bushes had given the impression that the forest went on forever.

They walked, stepping quietly, until they came to a corner. It wasn't a right angle, but was much wider, as if the room was a pentagon or some other shape with more than four corners. Weston paused to sniff the air. "I smell something. I don't know what it is. Something cold and damp."

"Keep moving," Owen said. "I want to know where the exit is before we go hunting whatever lives here."

After several minutes, Weston said, "There's a door. But it leads back south. It might go to the puzzle room." He examined it closely, then opened it, revealing a room with a marble-tiled floor. "And yes, it does."

Aderyn watched the trees and bushes as they continued to walk. Silver tendrils of fog threaded through the leaves, filling the room with an unearthly glow. The place was perfectly silent except for the sound of their footsteps and their bodies rustling the bushes, without even the chirrup of insects or the calls of the night birds to break the calm. Aderyn had to remind herself that something dangerous had to be here and that quiet and peaceful places, in this dungeon, were a trap.

Another two corners brought them to a short passageway, no more than five feet long, at the end of which was another door. Beyond it, a similar passage opened on a warmly-lit room that looked much larger than this one. "Leave it for now," Owen said. "We're almost directly opposite the hall we came from, if my sense of direction hasn't deserted me."

"We could move on, avoid this challenge," Livia said. "We're at a disadvantage here."

"Or we could see what it is, and flee if we have to," Aderyn said. "We only need another sixty-five hundred experience, and what if we get as much from this challenge as we did from the puzzle room?"

Livia muttered something under her breath. "I said I'm stupid," she repeated when they pressed her. "*Clairvoyance* should see through this mess. I can't believe it didn't occur to me."

"Because you've only ever used it on solid objects before," Weston said. "Try it now."

Livia recited a handful of nonsense words and then fell silent, slowly scanning the forest surrounding them. She stiffened and then took a couple of steps forward, apparently peering at the trunk of a large oak tree. "They're dogs," she said. "The same color as the mist

—no, actually I think they might be made of mist, at least partly. It's coming out of their eyes."

"Immaterial, then?" Owen asked.

"I can't tell for sure, but it seems likely. Or possibly they phase in and out of solidity." Livia stepped back, blinking rapidly to clear her vision. "They're off that way toward the center, about twenty yards. Seven of them."

"Then we can surround them," Weston said.

"That might not be the best option," Aderyn said. "If they're even partly immaterial, our weapons won't affect them."

"I can cast earth spells in here. The ground is dirt and stone." Livia looked like she was reviewing her spell list. "But they're all physical attacks, too. *Thunderstomp* will disorient them, but that won't be enough."

Owen nodded. "Let's move closer and see what **[Improved Assess 2]** says, at least."

With Livia in the lead, guiding them, they moved away from the wall and into the forest. The noise they made increased as they passed through the heavy undergrowth. Though it wasn't so much undergrowth, Aderyn observed, as it was thick bushes as tall as Weston, some of them bearing flowers that made them look better suited to a garden than the wilderness. Nothing the dungeon did surprised her anymore. That wasn't true. There were plenty of surprises left. Maybe it was more accurate to say the dungeon's design choices were always going to be erratic, and that was no surprise.

Livia stopped and waved a hand at the others to bring them to a halt. She stood behind one of the bushes, this one covered not only with thick leaves, but tiny furled blossoms, and gingerly moved a branch so light shone through a gap in the leaves. Without being told, Aderyn joined her and peered through the gap.

A break in the tree cover above let moonlight spill over the soft grass in the small clearing beyond the bush. Seven silver-gray hounds sat or sprawled beneath the light. One of them lifted its head, tilting it to face the unseen moon, and its throat muscles shifted like it was drinking something. They were so beautiful Aderyn at first forgot to Assess them, until Livia whispered, "Well?" and brought Aderyn out of her fugue.

Name: Misthound
Type: Magical beast
Power level: 2
Resistant to: weapon damage
Misthounds are mostly insubstantial, drawing their nature from fog and moonlight. They are wary of intruders and quick to attack anything that threatens the pack. They subsist on moonlight and starlight and you're going to feel really, really bad about killing anything that lovely, aren't you?

Aderyn swallowed. Then she drew Livia with her quietly back to where the others waited. "It's true, they don't take full weapon damage," she said. "Maybe we can just leave them undisturbed. They're only power level two, so they can't be worth much experience."

"What happens if we move on to the next room and have to retreat the way we did with the sanguisuge?" Owen said. "Power level two monsters can still do damage, and if we're fleeing, we might not be in a position to defend ourselves."

"That's true," Aderyn admitted. "And **[Improved Assess 2]** does say they're quick to attack if they think their pack is threatened. We wouldn't be able to run through this place without being challenged."

"I have an idea," Isold said. "I mentioned I have a new skill called **[Shout]**. If it is an attack with sound as I suspect, it likely affects any monster, immaterial or not. Though possibly the monster has to be able to hear."

"They're all grouped together, in case that matters," Livia said.

"It's worth trying," Owen said. "Go for it."

Isold crept up to the bush and then, terrifyingly, stepped into the open. Aderyn wasn't in a position to see the misthounds, but she heard a few yelps and then an awful growl. Isold drew in breath the way he did when he was preparing to sing. Instead of music, what emerged from his mouth was the single word *"Flee."*

The word built and echoed and surged in volume until it became a shout that shook the bushes. Immediately, the unseen hounds whined and yipped, and Aderyn heard a lot of scrambling of canine paws digging into the earth as they tried to get away from the sound.

**Congratulations! You have defeated [Misthound Pack].
You have earned [350 XP]**

Isold gestured, and the friends all gathered where he stood. The clearing showed evidence of what Aderyn had heard, the ground clawed up, leaves scattered where the not-quite-immaterial dogs had shoved through the bushes. "That hurt," Isold said, massaging his throat. "I'm glad I tested it in a relatively safe location. I think using this skill too often and too rapidly might impede my ability to use other skills, or to sing at all."

"Maybe it will get easier over time," Weston said.

"I wish I hadn't been right about how little experience they were worth," Aderyn griped. "Especially since that was a clever solution."

You're so right! That *was* clever. I'll consider altering the experience reward in future.

"What, not right now?" Owen asked.

If I chose to change the experience given for a challenge based on intangibles, I'd be no better than a variable dungeon. They're all so snooty about how good they are at assessing adventurers' actions and rewarding them appropriately. I believe adventurers prefer consistency.

"But you—" Aderyn began, then reconsidered her outburst. "I mean, aren't your random colors and the rearranging of the rooms and how varied the challenges are sort of variable already?"

Yes, but they're *consistently* variable. I always do what I say. That's why people come back. Well, that, and they get a free ride anywhere in the world. That's tempting, isn't it?

Aderyn gave up. "I get it. That's very generous of you."

I know! You're so polite. It's why I like you all so very much. You have earned [11,850 XP] toward defeating me, which means you only need [6150 XP] more. Keep going!

"That's never going to stop being unsettling," Owen said. "Where's the door?"

CHAPTER TEN

They huddled around the open door, peering into the room beyond. Orange light like the last rays of sunset filled it, enough to see by, but if it got any dimmer, they would have trouble. Again, the room appeared to be outdoors, but unlike the two forested rooms, this one had flat, open ground covered with fine new grass. From where Aderyn stood, she could see the trunks of widely-spaced trees, not very broad and covered with thick, bulging bark ridged enough it almost made handholds. They were tall enough their branches were well out of sight.

"No movement, and no sound," Weston said. "Let's take a closer look."

Owen nodded. The friends entered the room and spread out to make themselves a less inviting target in case anything in there had some variant on *mudball* or *stone sphere*. Aderyn gazed up in wonder. No branches sprouted from the trees; no leafy foliage blocked the reddish light of the unseen sun. Instead, the tree trunks forked and bent at right angles to create a vast network of tree limbs, each limb growing narrower until it was as flexible and narrow as a vine. From there, the vines rose toward the ceiling, which was at least fifty feet high, intertwining to make nets that swayed under their own weight.

"That's impressive," Owen said.

"There's no undergrowth to provide cover," Aderyn pointed out. "And I don't see anything on the ground. Do you suppose we have to get up there?"

"It shouldn't be hard," Owen said. "The trunks run straight for twenty feet before splitting, true, but look at how rough the bark is." He walked to the nearest tree and put a foot on a rounded extrusion, hitching himself up and reaching for more large bumps.

"That's not going to work for me," Livia said. "I don't climb."

"We'll help you," Weston said.

"Can we at least find out if it's necessary before we become arboreal?" Livia looked unusually pale. Aderyn remembered how terrified she'd been in the Repository, when they'd had to levitate to reach their destination and Livia had been separated from her connection to the earth.

"Fair," Owen said. "Let's find out what's in here."

The grass beneath Aderyn's feet was springy, like the ground wanted to give her a boost. She walked lightly to stop the bouncing that threw her off balance and alternated between watching the network of branches above and scanning the floor at ground level.

She saw movement straight ahead just as Weston said, "There's something there. Something big."

In the distance, a charcoal-gray shape sat up and then remained very still, poised as if it was watching them. It was too far away to be visible as anything but a bulging mass, but Aderyn strained to make out details anyway.

"It's coming this way," Weston said. "Um. It's moving fast. And it's *big*."

Livia stepped out in front of their group. "Let's give it a little warning," she said. She called out a few sharp words and stomped. A crack like thunder split the air, and the ground furrowed, driving in a straight line that made the earth rumble as it shot toward the oncoming monster. The moving earth hit the creature and made it stagger. As it regained its balance, Aderyn Assessed it.

Name: Clobbering Ape
Type: Magical beast
Power level: 7
Attacks: slam, special
Immune to: none
Resistant to: bludgeoning damage, *sleep*, poison
Vulnerable to: *levitation*, *fly*
Special attack: *thunder punch*

The clobbering ape is a magical relative of the common gorilla. It draws its strength from the earth. Its name derives from its ability to strike as with the spell *thunder punch*. Clobbering apes are weakened when they lose contact with the earth, but don't think that makes them a pushover.

The blue lines slid and intersected over the enormous muscular body. Everywhere the ape touched the earth, a red aura glowed, indicating invulnerability. Blue spots of light glowed at its arm joints and at the base of its spine.

"It's like an Earthbreaker," Aderyn exclaimed. "Draws strength from the earth, like Livia. Don't let it hit you—it has *thunder punch*. And if we can get it off the ground—"

The clobbering ape had built up speed and was now pounding toward them. It roared, a terrible sound that shook the trees. Aderyn guessed it was over seven feet tall, and it looked like it weighed more than all of them combined. "*If* we can get it off the ground," she managed weakly.

"Spread out," Livia said. "I've got this. Figure out how to tie it so we can hoist it into the air, but until then—" She cracked the knuckles of each hand, grinning evilly. "It's not the only one with *thunder punch*."

Aderyn scrambled to one side and grabbed for a handhold,

hauling herself up just as the clobbering ape barreled down on the much smaller Livia. Frozen in fear for her friend, Aderyn watched helplessly. Livia faced the ape in the square, solid stance so familiar to Aderyn. She cocked a fist back and waited. The ape raised both arms to hammer Livia into the ground.

Livia let fly her right hook. It slammed into the clobbering ape's face with a thunderous crack. The ape flew backward fifteen feet, tearing up the grass as it skidded away, finally impacting against a tree that cracked with the blow. The clobbering ape's tiny eyes looked bewildered, and it shook its head as if dazed.

"Go, *go!*" Livia shouted, waving at Aderyn. Aderyn felt as stunned as the ape. Livia chanted again, and the ground around the ape's fallen body churned wetly into mud, dragging it down. Then Aderyn scrambled up the tree, hoping nothing else would appear to challenge Livia while they were all too far away to help.

Climbing the tree wasn't hard, once she figured out the rhythm. The rubbery bark had millions of tiny gripping extrusions like fingers that clung to Aderyn's hands and feet and improved how well she held onto the wood. In only a few seconds, she reached the point where the tree trunks forked and bent into narrow paths. The others were already there, and Weston was trying to climb into the network of vines with no success.

"I'm too heavy," he said. "The vines themselves are tough, but they don't support a heavy weight. It needs to be Aderyn or Isold."

"What are we doing?" Isold said.

"We need to free some of those vines so we can lasso the ape," Owen said.

"So we can what?"

"It means catch it in a noose and haul it off the ground," Owen explained. He was scanning the ground, not the sky, and suddenly he said, "Crap. There's two of them. Livia!"

"I'll warn her, and help back her up," Weston said. "I'm no use here." He grabbed hold of the nearest tree and began a rapid descent.

The second charcoal-gray form of the clobbering ape was approaching from the other side. Shuddering, Aderyn made herself turn her back. Figuring out how to use these vines was the only thing she could do to help Livia now.

She ran up a narrow branch that sloped toward the ceiling. Normally she would have been terrified of walking on something only a few inches wide, thirty feet off the ground, but the wood continued to grip her boots firmly, and she felt as if she was running on solid ground. She had to slow as the branch continued to narrow until it was more like a pole than a ledge, but by that time she was within reach of the net of vines and could hold that to keep her balance.

She tugged on the vines, which gave slightly but didn't pull loose. They were rough to the touch and had a ridged surface that looked like it would take some effort to cut through. There were only a few vines, she realized, but they twisted and entwined with one another so completely they made a much thicker net. Gingerly, she hauled herself up, wedging her boot into a gap and reaching above her head for more handholds.

"Aderyn!" Owen shouted. "Cut one free!"

Aderyn used her belt knife to make a first tentative cut. To her surprise, the knife sliced through the vine easily, despite the hard, ridged appearance of its surface. She tugged the vine free, sliding it from its entanglement. It came loose, and she dropped it in annoyance. "Too short," she told Owen. "We need to identify—oh, I'm so stupid." She wound her hands more firmly into the network and Assessed the vine. Maybe it was just an ordinary plant, but if she didn't try, she'd never know.

Name: Climbing Creeper
Type: Plant

That was all—but no, it wasn't, because **[Discern Weakness]** showed the net as a glowing series of yellow points of various sizes. Aderyn identified the largest point she could reach and slashed it with her belt knife. It took much longer to work this vine segment free, and she looped it over and around her shoulder and waist to keep it from tangling itself. Finally, she wrestled it off her body and tossed the loose mass to Owen. "Try that!"

Owen looped it around his own body and ran, leaping from branch to branch, in the direction Livia and Weston had made their stand. The clobbering apes hesitated outside Livia's reach. One of them was covered in mud but didn't appear hampered by it. As Aderyn watched, that ape roared a challenge that rocked her teammates back a few steps. One vine might not be enough.

She climbed into the net again and searched for the yellow dot that identified the best place to cut. Beside her and a little above, Isold said, "Let me help. Pass me the free end."

Aderyn swiftly sliced the vine free and yanked on handfuls of it until it was long enough to pass to Isold. They worked in silence, hauling the vine rapidly through the net until it was loose. This one was even longer than the first.

"Down," Aderyn said. "We need to anchor this somewhere."

Awkwardly sharing the burden, they clambered out of the net and down to where the branches were broader. Owen had tied one end of his vine securely to a branch and now crouched, holding the other end, above where Livia and Weston fought. The free end was tied into a noose Owen was trying to loop over the nearest ape.

"This isn't working," he said, his hunched shoulders proclaiming his frustration as clearly as a complaint. Aderyn's passing thought that shoulders couldn't speak vanished as he added, "I know how to tie a running knot, but it's almost impossible to get the thing into the noose. It's going to have to be a point-blank approach."

Aderyn surveyed the branches nearby. "We have to get it off the ground, and none of us can cast *levitate*. So we need to tie a vine around it and use leverage to pull it up."

She ran with her half of the vine down the branch to where a few other, narrower branches hung over it. With a grunt, she heaved the mass of her vine over one of the upper branches and pulled so it hung down on either side. "That's half the problem solved. Assuming we're strong enough to lift the ape. Those things look heavy."

Owen picked up the longer end and looped it over his shoulders. "Watch for my signal," he said, and shimmied down the tree.

Aderyn watched as he waited for Livia to cast *thunderstomp*, knocking the clobbering apes off balance, before he ran to join her and Weston. Livia *thunder punched* the second ape while Weston and Owen huddled in conversation. Then Weston dodged the first clobbering ape and ran for the trees while Owen crouched, the noose he'd made in both hands. Aderyn's heart pounded so hard it shook her like *thunderstomp*. Weston swore a steady litany of profanity as he neared them.

Everyone moved at once. Livia snatched her **<Wand of Sleep>** from her belt and flicked it at the ape Weston had dodged, sending a shower of gray dust over it. Aderyn was about to shout a reminder that clobbering apes were resistant to *sleep* spells when the creature stopped, staggered, and waved a hand in front of its face before taking its next ponderous step—right into the center of the noose Owen had placed before it.

The noose tightened. The ape stopped again and looked down to see what it was snagged on. Then Weston stood beside Aderyn and Isold, reaching for the trailing end of the vine. "Pull!"

The loose vine slid, caught, was tugged free, and then took the full weight of the clobbering ape. Aderyn pulled with all her strength. At first, nothing happened, and she had visions of the vine snapping and sending them all tumbling to the ground thirty feet below. Weston's arms bulged, and his face and Isold's were both bright red with exertion. Then the vine moved, just an inch or two. Weston rearranged his grip and pulled again. With a smooth gliding motion, the vine slid over the branch. Aderyn risked a glance at the ground. The clobbering ape dangled by one foot, flailing helplessly at the vine. The bright blue light at the base of its spine now was a perfect target, and as Aderyn watched, Owen stepped up and thrust at the spot with his <**Twinsword**>.

Congratulations! You have defeated [Clobbering Ape].
You have earned [2500 XP]

They all let go of the rope, gasping for breath. "I don't think I can manage that twice," Weston said. "We'll need a different strategy."

Aderyn hurried to climb down, but stopped before stepping off the branch. "I think Livia has it in hand."

Owen faced off against the second ape, keeping it at bay while Livia took a familiar stance, legs slightly spread, knees bent, fists closed at chest level. She shouted a few words, and the clobbering ape lifted off the ground and slammed into the nearest tree. With another shouted invocation, dozens of *iron spikes* flew out of nowhere to impale the creature. Its head jerked, and then it sagged in death.

Congratulations! You have defeated [Clobbering Ape].
You have earned [2500 XP]

Aderyn hurried to descend. "That was amazing, Livia."

"It's always satisfying to have it out with something that can punch back," Livia said. "But I'm nearing the edge of my resources."

That was a stupendous battle! Most Earthbreakers give up when they see their best attacks aren't fully effective. You're wise to see that some effect is better than nothing. I'll need to see if I can turn that into a catchy inspirational motto. Unfortunately, it's not quite enough to defeat me! You've now earned a total of [16,850 XP], leaving you short of the victory

condition by only [1150 XP]. Don't give up now! You're so close!

"So close," Owen said. "Just one more encounter, maybe."

"But if Livia is almost at her limit, maybe we need to rest first," Aderyn said.

"Or we could push through and rest in Obsidian," Owen said. He shook his head. "Sorry. It needs to be Livia's call. She's the one who knows what she can do."

"Actually," a new voice said from behind Aderyn, "it's *our* call. Throw your weapons down, and nobody has to die."

Aderyn turned to see Joran approaching, followed by his teammates. The Deadeye had an arrow drawn and pointed right at them.

Owen stepped forward. "Don't be stupid. You're three levels lower—you can't defeat us. If anyone's going to die in this confrontation, it's you."

"You sure about that?" Joran sneered, and shot Owen in the chest.

Chapter Eleven

Aderyn screamed and grabbed Owen, who took an involuntary step back before sinking to the ground. His eyes were wide, and one hand pressed against the spot where the arrow had gone in, high on his chest. Then she ducked away from the ghostly form of Joran's next arrow, aimed at her head. "I did warn you," Joran said, nocking an arrow for another shot.

"You're right," Isold said, his voice throbbing with harmonics. "You did. What a clever attack."

All three of the enemy adventurers focused on Isold. The point of Joran's arrow dipped and sagged. "We..." the Spider, Micai, murmured. "Don't listen, he's trying—"

His words cut off as Weston's thrown dagger took him in the throat. Suddenly everyone was in motion, Joran backing away to give himself a better shot, Livia running at the Tidecaller, Fiana, as both of them shouted spells whose nonsense words tangled in the air, Isold crouching next to Owen with the <**Healing Stone**> clutched in one hand. "Pull it out when I say," Isold told Aderyn. "On three... two... one... *now!*"

Aderyn pulled the arrow free, sending blood pumping everywhere. She cried out and tried to stop the bleeding with her hands, but Isold pushed them away and held the stone against the terrible wound. Green light shone from beneath Owen's chest.

Congratulations! You have defeated [Micai the Spider]. You have earned [1500 XP]

Owen's lips moved. "Not yet," Aderyn said through her tears. "Almost healed. Just wait." She guessed Micai was dead, and part of her felt it should matter more that her team had killed a human, but with Owen's blood covering her hands, she couldn't bring herself to care.

She didn't even look around when the next system message appeared:

Congratulations! You have defeated [Fiana the Tidecaller]. You have earned [1500 XP]

"I feel fine now," Owen said, gently pushing Aderyn's hands to the side and sitting up. "That damn Deadeye. I'm going to take him apart."

Joran had disappeared, but Weston and Livia were staring up into the trees, watching something. "He went up. Looking for a vantage point," Weston said irritably.

"Let's see how good his vantage point is when he's got three feet of steel through his belly," Owen growled. He sheathed his sword and scurried up the nearest tree.

An arrow whizzed past Aderyn's shoulder seconds after she dove behind a tree. The next moment, the earth heaved and bulged as Livia's **[Excavate]** skill dug out a fortification and piled the excavated dirt high into a packed earth shield. Aderyn joined the others behind it. "I should help him," she said as Livia summoned water to wash Owen's blood off her hands and arms.

"Some things, a man has to do for himself," Weston said.

Aderyn stepped aside from the earthen bulwark anyway and nearly got an arrow through her skull. She ducked back under cover and listened. All was silent. Then she heard grunting noises like two men exerting themselves in close physical combat, and a scream, and a thud.

Congratulations! You have defeated [Joran the Deadeye]. You have earned [1500 XP]

Aderyn peeked out from behind the bulwark and saw Owen descending at a leisurely rate. She ran to meet him and threw her arms around his shoulders, not caring that he was still covered in blood. "That terrified me. If we hadn't had the **<Healing Stone>**, you might—"

"Let's not worry about what might have happened, okay?" Owen's kiss felt a little desperate, and his arm around her waist said he wasn't nearly so confident as he sounded. Again, Aderyn found it odd that she was attributing meaning to his movements... oh, yes. **[Read Body Language]**. She wasn't sure that was useful, but you never knew.

"I wish they hadn't attacked us," Owen went on. "It's like—I mean, I don't want to say they deserved killing, or that they made us do it, but they sort of did. And now—" His jaw clenched, and he fell silent.

"There's nothing that says we have to let someone kill us just so we'll be innocent of taking human life," Livia said.

"No. Of course not." Owen drew Aderyn closer and let out a breath that warmed her forehead.

"It still matters," Isold said. "Even though it was the right thing to do."

"I guess killing those adventurers doesn't count as a Gamboling Coil challenge," Weston said. "Too bad, because that was quite a workout." His voice shook enough to keep his words from sounding like a joke.

Of course it counts! I was just waiting for you to finish. We wouldn't want your success to be anticlimactic, right?

"We won?" Owen said.

Bright lights flashed, and unseen trumpets played a fanfare. The booming voice echoed the system message that played across their vision:

CONGRATULATIONS! You have defeated [Gamboling Coil] and gained [10,000 XP]! What an accomplishment! You should all feel very good about yourselves. Follow the path to the dungeon center, please, and again—way to go!

Across the room, a white spot on the wall grew rapidly until it was the size of a clobbering ape. It flashed brightly three times, and then it became a well-lit tunnel extending around a curve out of sight.

The friends exchanged glances. "I guess this is it," Owen said, and they all strode toward the tunnel.

The sound of music grew as they approached, twittering birdsong, but harmonizing in thirds as no birds ever did. Aderyn slowed to listen. "It's an actual song," she said in fascination. "Can you all hear that?"

"Singing our praises," Owen said. "It's embarrassing."

"I wouldn't have thought to rhyme 'good' with 'blood,'" Isold said. "Or with 'worm food,' for that matter."

"Let's walk faster," Livia suggested. "I don't want to know what happens in the second verse."

Though the tunnel's roof was low, it was painted white and brightly lit, and Aderyn didn't feel the least bit claustrophobic. She walked beside Owen as the tunnel snaked back and forth. The ground was soft and springy again, but not to the extent the clobbering apes' den had been, and the sense of gently bouncing back and forth soothed Aderyn's still-taut nerves. When they reached the end of the tunnel, she was calm again.

After everything she'd seen, she had expected the dungeon's center to be painted in bright colors, possibly colors that moved. But the central chamber, the dungeon's heart, was a dome painted a warm white like fresh cream, with white rugs covering the floor and a number of chairs, also white, drawn up in a rough circle surrounding a featureless white block at the chamber's center. The chairs were all that was strange about the room, and not just because there were no two alike. Aderyn sensed Gamboling Coil's eccentric personality in that choice, because there were traditional chairs like someone might have in their kitchen, and cushioned chairs someone might pull out for a guest, and then there were objects someone could sit on because they had legs and horizontal surfaces, but they didn't resemble any chairs Aderyn had ever seen.

Please have a seat. A few details remain.

The friends sat near one another. Aderyn noticed they all took chairs that were recognizably chairs. She eyed the white block curiously. It was a cube four feet on a side with rounded corners and had a shiny finish like it had been repeatedly lacquered.

Another system message appeared.

I'm glad you succeeded! I really do like you all very much. That's why I'm so happy to offer you this reward. I know you'll appreciate it.

Between one blink and the next, the white block's top vanished, revealing a hollow interior lined with purple velvet. Owen rose from his white kitchen chair and approached the block. His shoulders stiffened with annoyance. "What... is this?" he asked, reaching into the box and removing something golden and round the size of his palm with a couple of wide silver ribbons dangling from it.

It's your badge for having defeated me! The lettering isn't real diamonds, of course, because that would be ridiculous. But you can display this with pride everywhere you go!

Owen's jaw clenched. "Is this the *only* treasure—"

"Thank you for your generosity," Isold said swiftly. He stood and whisked the badge out of Owen's hand and showed it to the others. Sparkling letters on a golden circle read I DEFEATED GAMBOLING COIL! "This is a **<Periapt of Buoyant Support>**, isn't it? It fills the wearer with self-confidence in both combat and non-combat situations, improving their ability to strike true, increasing the damage done by their attacks, and providing them with a measure of protection from attacks that strike at their morale. It is an extremely valuable gift."

There's one for each of you. I have discretion in choosing which rewards to give successful adventurers, and while often I only hand out coin, you've been so valiant and so friendly I thought you deserved more. Go on, take them!

Aderyn accepted hers from Isold and examined it more closely. The golden circle was gold-washed steel, she discovered, and while the sparkling letters were just cleverly incised faceted concavities, the red stones fixing the silver ribbons to the periapt looked like real rubies. A large pin affixed to the back of the circle let her attach the periapt to her shirt near her shoulder. When she did, a feeling of confidence washed over her, lifting her spirits. The idea of tackling the city of Obsidian, full of predatory high-level adventurers, no longer daunted her. It didn't even matter that they knew almost nothing about their quest—she and her friends could accomplish anything!

The others were all smiling and nodding like they'd realized an amazing truth. Owen's jaw relaxed and he looked as if he'd never questioned the wisdom of the dungeon. "Thank you," he said to the air. "We're all very grateful."

Oh, it's my pleasure. Now, where would you like to go?

"Right now?" Owen's surprise matched Aderyn's. Achieving their goal had been so difficult it felt anticlimactic to simply leap to their destination, or whatever the dungeon did.

Of course. Aren't you in a hurry? Most adventurers are.

"Well, um, I guess." Owen resumed his seat. "How do we tell you where we need to go?"

I know everywhere I've ever been, and I've been everywhere in the world. Simply name your destination, or if you want to go somewhere between cities, indicate your preference on the map.

A spotlight shone on the wall, illuminating a giant map Aderyn knew hadn't been there before. She wandered over to it. It was more detailed either than her father's map or the system map, though she hoped by the time she reached level twenty, her system map would be that detailed. Tiny cities of different sizes covered the map, filling spaces she'd believed empty. She focused briefly on Guerdon Deep and was amazed to see the tiny city outline expand so details like the city gate and the places where the city melded with the mountain were visible. She blinked, and the picture shrank.

"We want to go to Obsidian," Owen said.

Oh, that's a terribly dangerous place. Are you sure? I wouldn't want anything bad to happen to you, and even at party average level [10] you'd be at a disadvantage.

"Yes, we're sure," Owen replied.
"Thank you for being concerned, though," Aderyn added.

Very well. I can't take you all the way in to Obsidian. There are rules about the distance I'm allowed to approach a population center. But I will open about five miles from the city gate. I hope that's sufficiently close.

"That's perfect, thanks," Owen said. "Should we hold onto something?"

Hold onto something? Oh, no. We're already there. Oh, of course, you saw the frog legs! That's just to make getting in a challenge. My actual mode of transportation is instantaneous.

Instantaneous world travel! It was one of the things Aderyn had dreamed of, when she thought about the days before the level cap or imagined a time when such wonders might come again. "You are amazing," she exclaimed.

Why, thank you! It's nice to be appreciated. Now, I'll open the passage—don't worry, it bypasses the rooms—and you're free to leave. I wish you the best of luck.

Another tunnel appeared, this one showing watery, dim daylight at its far end. The smell of rain on grass wafted toward them on a chilly breeze. Owen rose, prompting the rest of them to follow. "Thanks again," he said. "We may come back someday."

I hope so! Oh, one more thing. May I ask what quest takes you to Obsidian at such a low level?

Aderyn caught Owen's eye. She shrugged, and saw in his eyes that her shrug had conveyed the complex message *There's no harm in telling it, and maybe it will have advice.* Owen said, "I'm the Fated One, and we're searching for the quests that will lead me to my destiny.

The Fated One?

The booming voice echoed the system message, loudly enough that Aderyn winced. The next message was silent, but the words appeared with such force Aderyn almost imagined she could hear them.

You can't possibly be the Fated One. You're not nearly smug, haughty, condescending, high-and-mighty, or egotistical enough. I have seen and will see hundreds of Fated Ones in the course of my existence. It's simply not possible.

"But that suggests, does it not, that Owen *is* the Fated One, simply because he is nothing like the hundreds of would-be heroes," Isold said. "And we are pursuing the actual quests revealed by Tarani, centuries ago—how many of those so-called Fated Ones even knew her name, let alone that she discovered the way to accomplish the Fated One's destiny?"

There was a pause.

I've never known a Fated One who believed their destiny was

anything more than being famous and, forgive my coarseness, getting laid. You say you have a quest to accomplish?

"We do," Owen said. "Tarani left evidence in Obsidian about three of the four quests in the quest chain that leads to breaking the level cap."

How extraordinary.

Gamboling Coil added nothing to this statement, but Aderyn felt a tension in the air that said it wasn't done communicating. Finally, another system message appeared.

Awarding treasure for the completion of this dungeon is entirely my prerogative. I've already given you something wonderful, and really, I ought to leave it at that. But if you truly are the Fated One, you'll want as much help as possible. So, take this, with my good wishes.

Aderyn looked around for what Gamboling Coil referred to, but Owen was already bending to reach into the velvet-lined compartment. He held up a ring, and a narrow beam of light came out of nowhere to spotlight it, making Owen look like he'd taken a dramatic pose on purpose. Aderyn joined him, and together they looked at the ring.

It was a ring of hematite, black except where the light struck it and turned it silver. Tiny abstract figures of running cats circled the band, coming up against a row of three colored stones, sapphire, emerald, and ruby. When Owen slid it onto the middle finger of his left hand, it hung there briefly, far too big, before shrinking to fit him perfectly.

That is the <Ring of the Cat>. Some call it the Ring of Second

Chances. Three times, when you are in great danger, the ring will activate to save you.

"You mean like a cat's nine lives? Is that why it's called <**Ring of the Cat**>?"

You mean a cat's *three* lives.

"No, I—"

Aderyn grabbed his elbow to get his attention and shook her head, raising her eyebrows to convey the message *Don't get into a discussion about world comparisons, please.* Owen nodded. He ran a finger over the three stones, which still sparkled even though the light no longer shone on them. "Thank you. This could save my life."

That's the idea. Good luck, Fated One—good luck to you all! And do return someday. This has been such fun!

Dungeons had a strange idea about what constituted fun, Aderyn thought. But—no. Dungeons weren't supposed to be aware enough to have a concept of fun or terror or anything else. But Winter's Peril had been self-aware, and Gamboling Coil was too, and they couldn't be the only ones, could they? On the other hand, no one ever mentioned self-aware dungeons. So was that ignorance, or was this another aspect of being the Fated One—and if so, was it luck, coincidence, or Owen's presence rousing some personality otherwise buried deep?

CHAPTER TWELVE

One by one, they left the central chamber behind. The tunnel floor was spongy as before, but now the tunnel air also felt damp. Aderyn didn't know why until she emerged from the dungeon to find a great forest spread out before her, shrouded in a heavy mist that beaded on her clothes and hair. They stood at the top of a hill, looking out over a valley covered with pine trees, through which a heavily-used road ran. In the distance, a city lay at the top of a cliff, and beyond the cliff, the horizon was a sullen gray Aderyn realized was in motion. She recalled her map. The ocean. She'd thought the ocean was blue.

She turned to say this to Owen and saw the tunnel had disappeared. In its place, the shack squatted, giving every evidence of an alertly-interested dog. Impulsively, Aderyn waved, and the shack bounced once or twice before settling again.

"That reset its pattern," Owen said. "It will be here for five days, and then it will start its journey in a new spiral."

"How do you know?" Aderyn asked.

"It was what the Herald said, about how it starts again where the dungeon is steered." He put an arm around her shoulders and hugged her close. "But it doesn't matter to us. We're here!"

Aderyn made a face at being so close to Owen's filthy, bloody, torn shirt. "We should maybe clean ourselves up a bit—though you only had the two shirts, so I don't know how clean we can get them."

"Take it off and I'll wash and mend it," Livia suggested. "The other one's damp, but not as stained as this."

Owen changed his shirt while Livia performed her small magics. "And we've traveled so far west it's like we got those hours spent in the dungeon back," he said. "Now, I know we keep hearing that Obsidian is a lawless and dangerous place, but does anyone know anything more specific than that?"

Aderyn startled. "Assess. I keep forgetting to see if **[Improved Assess 2]** tells me anything about cities!"

"Go for it," Owen suggested.

Aderyn focused on the distant city and saw no messages. "I may be too far away."

"Let's start walking, then," Weston said.

They were within two miles of the city, according to Weston, whose sense of distance was unusually accurate, when Aderyn Assessed it and finally got a response.

Name: Obsidian
Status: Fortified City
Government: Factional hegemony
Civilization level: 13
Resources: Spiritsmith x1, Spellcrafter x2, Tidecaller x7, Windwarden x5, Flamecrafter x3, Earthbreaker x2, Bonemender x4; Crafters level 11; Hospitality level 5; Food supply level 10

Obsidian is ruled by the leaders of its seven major factions, all of whom work to keep the others from gaining control. All non-classed citizens of Obsidian are under the protection of, and pay tribute to, one of these factions. Visitors to Obsidian

are encouraged to temporarily join a faction so as to gain protection. However, joining the wrong faction may have serious repercussions. You have been warned.

"That's discouraging," she said when she finished repeating all this to her friends.

"We won't be there long," Owen said. "We'll keep our heads down and be in and out before any of that can matter to us."

"Unless we walk into the wrong part of town on the wrong day and get gutted," Livia said.

"I've got a magic ring to take care of that," Owen said, perfectly straight-faced. "The rest of you will be out of luck."

"You'd better hope that's not true," Aderyn said, matching his tone. "I've got all the money."

They paused to put on warmer clothes, then set out for the city again. Aderyn had never been so grateful for her warm coat, which was also water-resistant. The air wasn't all that chilly, but between the drizzling rain and the gray overcast and the looming pines, she felt cold enough that the coat was essential.

The pine trees grew close enough to the road to make her wary of a possible ambush. Probably that was unlikely this close to a big city, but there was no sense being careless. She noticed her friends paying close attention to their surroundings as well and made sure her sword was ready to hand.

The trees thinned out when they were half a mile from Obsidian, leaving the city and its high wall fully open to observation. Aderyn Assessed the city once more as they trudged up the slope, in case proximity gave her more information, but the same text appeared as before. She closed the Codex, though she wanted to read the information again, but experience had taught her that walking and reading the Codex were incompatible activities for everyone except Livia, and even she had trouble keeping a straight line while doing so.

Aderyn had imagined Obsidian to be hard and glassy like its name, but the walls, while black, were granite rather than volcanic glass, and their stones were worn around the edges like they had been there for centuries. She judged the walls to be no more than thirty feet high, and their tops were crumbling in places. Aside from this, though, the stones looked sturdy, and anyone assaulting the city would be in for a long, hard slog.

The nearer they got to the city, the more uncertain Aderyn felt. Her earlier excitement about visiting had faded, replaced by her awareness that they were a very low level for this city, they knew almost nothing about it, and they weren't even sure where to go to find the quests they needed. "Tarani's memorial" might not be enough to go on.

The city gates, bound in blackened iron, were black as well, black with paint that looked as if someone had slathered it on over the oak slabs. The sight of the gates cleared Aderyn's head. How ridiculous, wasting all that paint just to intimidate visitors! The guards in the towers overlooking the gates wore black as well. They would have looked just as ridiculous if not for their deadly-looking crossbows.

She slowed as they drew near, waiting for Owen to take the lead. Isold put a hand on Owen's shoulder. "Maybe I should do the talking, in case we need to be extra convincing."

"I don't want to take the chance that they'll be angry over having **[Fascinate]** or **[Suggestion]** used on them," Owen said. "Plenty of time for those when we're inside."

He strode forward, raising a hand to salute the guards. "We're adventurers, asking permission to enter Obsidian," he said in a loud, confident voice.

"Level ten adventurers," a female guard said, not disdainfully but with obvious suspicion. "Do you know what you're asking could get you killed?"

"Thanks for your concern," Owen said, as sincerely as if she'd expressed true worry over their fates. "We know Obsidian's reputation, and we're willing to take our chances."

"I'd turn you away for your own safety if I didn't know you're in just as much danger traveling cross-country to get back to the sanctuary cities. How are you so low level after a six-week journey?" She sounded curious now.

"We defeated Gamboling Coil, and it brought us here." Owen, with some embarrassment Aderyn thought was visible only to [**Read Body Language**], pointed to the <**Periapt of Buoyant Support**> pinned to his shoulder.

The guard leaned forward. She wore a pair of spectacles with gold rims that gleamed dully under the overcast and made her eyes look enormous even from that distance. She said, "Wait there."

Several seconds later, the small door set into the left-hand gate swung open, and the guard appeared. She wasn't completely clad in black; she wore a striped armband in several colors that weren't in the right order to be a rainbow, and the knit cap she wore was dyed violet. She strode up to Owen and fingered the badge he wore. "And you wear this? On purpose?" She chuckled. "I guess you must be tougher than you look. Well, whatever. Ten gold each entry fee."

Aderyn paid, and the guard removed her spectacles and jerked a thumb at the gate. "Welcome to Obsidian. Come inside for the orientation lecture."

Orientation. That might be related to the factions [**Improved Assess 2**] had mentioned. Aderyn followed Owen, some of her old eagerness returning. This encounter had bolstered her spirits. Obsidian couldn't be all bad if the people running it were this reasonable.

The little door led, not to the city, but to a short, low-ceilinged stone tunnel through the wall, lit by one lantern that flickered low and cast eerie shadows across the floor. The guard didn't stop, so Aderyn restrained her curiosity and didn't pause to look at the construction. Beside her, Livia let out a little sigh of contentment at being comfortably surrounded by her element.

The guard led them through a matching small door at the far end of the passage that opened on an inner courtyard. She waited for them all to emerge before shutting and locking it. She pocketed the key and said, "Do you want the cheap lecture, or the useful one?"

"Um," Owen said. "How expensive is the useful one?"

"Fifty gold."

Owen glanced at Aderyn. Aderyn mentally contemplated the dwindling size of their team's money reserve and nodded. Fifty gold could save their lives. She dug out a handful of coin and counted out fifty gold. The woman dropped the money into a bulging belt pouch. "Good choice. You're not what I expected of adventurers your level. Most of them can barely afford a night's stay at a rat-infested hovel after the trip here."

"We've defeated Winter's Peril as well as Gamboling Coil," Owen said. He managed to make the accomplishments sound like no big deal, and not at all like he was bragging.

The guard's eyes widened. "No kidding," she said. "Well, I'm impressed. Maybe you *won't* die in your first half-hour here. My advice to you, free of charge: keep your heads down, and pick a good faction. There are those in Obsidian who hunt low-levels like you."

"And what faction should that be? Actually, what factions are there?"

The guard indicated they should follow her with a jerk of her head. "You've paid for the expensive version, so let's get out of the rain while I deliver it. This place rains enough to wash the thoughts right out of your head."

CHAPTER THIRTEEN

From inside the wall, the gate looked more normal, unpainted and worn from centuries of Obsidian's bad weather. The back sides of the towers each had wooden doors, also not painted, through which guards passed in both directions. Their guide indicated they should enter the left-hand tower. Aderyn hung back so she could Assess the woman.

Name: Araceli
Class: Pathseer
Level: 16

Surprisingly, the tower was a single room whose whitewashed walls were dingy and in need of a fresh coat. Benches lined two of the walls, and a wooden table covered with enough dings and scratches Aderyn didn't know how it was still standing leaned against a third wall. A wooden coffer with no lock, big enough that if it was full of coin it would be immovable, sat atop the table.

Another doorway led to the stairs going up to the tower top, and as Aderyn and her friends entered, another guard, this one wearing a purple hat but without a colorful armband, strolled out of that inner chamber and brushed past their helper. She ignored him. Aderyn was developing an impression of the woman independent of Assess, and it wasn't a positive one. This guard struck her as someone who enjoyed exercising her power over newcomers a little too much. Aderyn wasn't thrilled about having put themselves at her mercy, even in this small way. With luck, this orientation lecture would be worth what they paid for it, and they'd never have to deal with the guard again.

"Have a seat." The woman removed her knit cap and shook out her short blond hair. "I'm Lieutenant Araceli. The rank doesn't mean what you think it does, but don't worry about that. Now, listen close, because if I have to repeat myself, it's going to cost you another fifty gold plus ten for pissing me off, all right?"

"We understand," Owen said.

Lieutenant Araceli stood with her legs slightly apart and her hands clasped behind her back. "Obsidian started as a place free from the constraints of law other cities demand," she said, her tone becoming the sing-song of someone reciting a memorized speech. "The adventurers who founded the city meant it to be a place to rest up between quests and monster hunting, both of which are plentiful all along the west coast. They didn't want to be burdened by restrictions and laws and bossy authorities."

Her voice lost the sing-song tone. "Which meant they got everything you always get from anarchy: filthy streets, no public amenities, and a need for constantly watching your back because there are no guards to do it for you. No non-classed people were willing to come here to provide things like taverns and brothels and shops because they were potential victims unless they put themselves under the protection of someone powerful, and what happens if that person gets killed?" She sounded more like herself now.

"The point is, Obsidian would have failed as a community if some of the more powerful adventurers, some of them the ones who'd founded the city, others newcomers who were fleeing other troubles, got together and hacked out an arrangement. Those seven were the founders of the new order." She tapped her armband, and Aderyn counted. There were seven stripes, yes, though three of them were white, black, and gray rather than colored.

"Each of the seven set themselves up as leaders of a faction," Araceli continued. "They originally called themselves tribes, but the bigger they got, the more ridiculous that sounded. Whatever. Each faction's leader chose a name they hoped would strike fear into the hearts of others. Grim, Vicious—that sort of thing—though nobody today calls them anything but Blue or Black, so that was useless posturing. And each faction staked a claim to part of the city and pledged to protect those within it, with the understanding that the leaders of the factions were immune to assassination by the others." Araceli grinned. "Assassination by their own, that's another story."

"How—sorry, I won't interrupt," Owen said.

"Very wise. There were other decisions, unofficial rules. After two of the faction leaders got into a minor war over a murder— somebody from one faction was killed by someone from another, and the fight was over how the murderer didn't know whose protection the victim was under—the factions started wearing colors." Again, she tapped her armband. "Gray, black, and white are the factions created by the founders of Obsidian. The other colors belong to the ones who were newcomers to the city at the time of the Dividing."

Aderyn took a closer look. In addition to the three neutral colors, there were red, green, orange, and blue.

"Not that it matters now, but you paid for the full lecture, so you get the irrelevant details too. Who knows, they might be useful." Araceli waved her cap at them. "Violet represents the only neutral power in Obsidian, and it's not much of a power, more a coordinating entity. The seven factions each contribute to fund the gate guards and the visiting adventurer admittance lecture, including selling faction affiliations."

She glanced briefly at Isold, who looked like he had a dozen questions pent up inside, and continued. "Adventurers who come to Obsidian, unless they're very high level, confident in their ability to defeat all challengers, or stupid beyond all reason, pay for a temporary faction affiliation. This gives you access to the amenities within your district and lets you pass most places in other districts. It depends on how powerful your patron is, right? Nobody wants to start a fight that could get the faction leaders involved."

"Unless starting a fight is the point," Isold said.

"I did say no interruptions, right?" Araceli glared at Isold. "But, as it happens, you're right. The colored armbands can make you a target just as easily as protect you. Visiting adventurers don't generally have to worry about this, because anyone interested in starting a war or making a point won't strike at some random armband wearer, they'll go after someone whose death will really hurt the faction. You're more likely just to be harassed. Stay in your district, and you'll be fine."

Araceli said this with the air of someone wrapping up a speech, so Aderyn asked, "Um. Can you tell us anything about the power dynamics between the factions? Who's at odds, and who's more powerful? If we're going to choose a temporary faction, we should know enough to choose wisely."

Araceli's eyes narrowed. "You're a Warmaster. What did you do to rank so high, bribe your teammates to carry you?"

Owen stiffened, and his hand closed into a fist. Aderyn held up a hand to warn him to stay silent. "Something like that. Is my question one we've paid for an answer for, or will it cost extra?"

Araceli's gaze flicked from Owen back to Aderyn, and she smiled, a mocking expression. "It's a wise question, and sure, you've paid enough. There's no actual ranking, not neatly from most to least powerful, because that changes frequently, but Black faction has been at the top for the last five, maybe six years. I'd avoid Orange and Green, because they're in a war and you don't want to get sucked into that at your level."

"Where can we pay for these temporary affiliations?" Owen asked. His hand was still clenched, but he didn't sound hostile.

"Right here." Araceli opened the large box, revealing that it was full of colored strips of cloth all tangled together. "Not Orange or Green, and you probably can't afford Black. Any other preferences?"

Aderyn hid her annoyance that Araceli hadn't given them more information and said, "How much are the others?"

"Red is fifteen gold, Blue is twenty, Gray is thirty-five, and White is fifty. Per person." Araceli idly stirred the mess with one hand.

Aderyn couldn't remember offhand what their finances looked like. One hundred gold to get into the city and for the orientation lecture had hit them hard, and they needed to be able to afford housing and food. She wished she could pour out the contents of the **<Purse of Great Capacity>**, but that would reveal not only how much coin they had, it would give away the magic item's secret. "Blue, then," she said, choosing the most expensive one she was sure they could afford.

"That's one hundred gold," Araceli said. "Payable now." She began sorting through the fabric strips with purpose, pulling out ones dyed a bright blue.

Aderyn dug around in her purse until she had ten large gold coins, hoping Araceli was too busy with her own task to notice how deeply Aderyn's hand could fit into the purse. She handed them to Araceli in exchange for five blue armbands, which she passed around to her friends. As they all helped one another tie them on, Araceli said, "One more thing. Obsidian uses a different currency than the cities of the safe zone. You'll need to change money if you want to pay for things here, other than entering the city, of course."

"Any advice on getting a good deal on exchange?" Owen asked.

Araceli snorted. "Other than the obvious, which is to go to a moneychanger in your own district? Don't expect a good rate of exchange even there. Some moneychangers see visiting adventurers as targets."

"That's helpful, thanks."

Aderyn was always impressed at how well Owen responded to sarcasm with a genuine reply, like the sarcasm had been genuine advice as well. She wanted to give a snide answer. She finished tying the armband around his upper left arm and extended her arm for him to do the same.

"One more thing," Isold said. "We are looking—"

"Oh, right," Owen overrode him. "Any advice on a good inn in the Blue district?"

"If you've got the money, the Blue Tern," Araceli said. "If you don't, the Golden Goose is clean enough for fastidious types, but it doesn't serve food." She was looking at Isold curiously, who was himself watching Owen in dismay.

"Great. Thanks. How do we find the Blue district?"

"Out the main street, keep turning left until the lampposts are marked with blue paint." Araceli closed the coffer. "Welcome to Obsidian. Hope you don't die."

Owen was already most of the way out the door.

When they were on the street and some distance from the guard tower, Isold said, "Why did you interrupt me?"

"Because you were about to ask where to find Tarani's memorial, and I did not want Araceli knowing what we're after," Owen said. "She's smart enough to guess all sorts of facts from that knowledge, such as that one of us is the Fated One, and suspicious enough to make assumptions about why the Fated One wants something from the memorial."

"But she's not a member of a faction. What difference does it make what she knows?" Livia said.

"If those violet-capped guards aren't on the take, I'll eat her hat," Weston said. "I'd bet anything you like that they sell information about visiting adventurers to anyone who has enough coin. And, speaking of coin, just how broke are we?"

At that moment, a carillon pealed, followed by the sound of a deep-voiced bell ringing the hour, twelve strokes. Aderyn waited to answer the question until the noise stopped. She cast her gaze about, searching for the clock tower, but didn't see anything nearby. "I won't know for sure until we get some privacy, but our team funds aren't looking good." She scowled. "Two hundred gold just to get into the city. It's a good thing we defeated Winter's Peril, because we would have been stranded outside Obsidian otherwise."

"We'll need to find out how much each of those inns charges," Owen said. "It might not be much of a savings if we pay more than the difference eating elsewhere." He made the first left turn off the main road. "I feel like I've got a target painted on my back. Or my arm."

The rain fell more heavily now, and Aderyn put up the hood of her coat and tried not to think about how wet the fabric was getting. She followed Owen without observing much of the city, other than to note the buildings were wooden rather than stone and were no more than two stories tall. In the dreary overcast, they all looked gray and depressed, with only a few lights burning behind windows despite how dim the sunlight was.

If the condition of the streets represented the effects of law and order, or whatever it was the factions delivered, Aderyn could barely imagine how filthy and garbage-strewn Obsidian had been in its early days. Her hometown of Far Haven prided itself on its cleanliness, and all the big cities she'd seen were, if not perfectly clean, at least mostly free of refuse. Here, broken crates and discarded burlap sacks piled against the foundations of every other building, and water flowing through the gutters carried with it things Aderyn didn't want to look at too closely. She suspected the place would stink any time the rain stopped.

Very few people shared the street with them, and none of them looked like adventurers—or at any rate, nobody they passed was conspicuously armed or armored, or wore large knapsacks, or strode like conquerors of the world. Only about two-thirds of the passersby wore armbands, which Aderyn found curious, but she had no way of discovering what it meant.

She had her head ducked against the rain, so it surprised her when Owen slowed and said, "That's a blue lamppost. I think we've found the right district."

The lamppost wasn't entirely blue; it had a wide blue band painted around its post just below the lantern, its color not quite matching their armbands. Aderyn paused to look around. The other lampposts lining the street bore the same markings, some of them more faded than others. "We're not really safe here, though, are we?" she said.

"Remember what Araceli said about the faction leaders not being immune to assassination by their own?" Weston said. "I'm guessing that applies all the way down. Specifically, other adventurers who chose this faction probably won't get in trouble for attacking or killing us, since there won't be any political repercussions. We need to be on our guard constantly."

"We need to change currency," Aderyn said. "How are we supposed to know where to do that? I don't even know what to look for."

"I believe that's it," Isold said. "That stack of coins." He pointed at a largish building that looked more solid and less rundown than its neighbors. Several signs adorned its front, but the one showing a hand holding a stack of yellow coins was the largest and the most freshly painted. "My **[Map Access]** skill has advanced to the point that I not only see the map of the city, but points of interest appear on it as I discover them."

Aderyn took a few steps toward it and was stopped by Isold's hand on her shoulder. "I think we'll need charm for this," he said. "Though not the magical kind. We don't know what the repercussions of using Herald's skills on someone are, particularly someone of our own faction and for the purpose of gaining monetary advantage. Let me have some of our money."

It made sense. Aderyn pulled out a handful of mixed coin and counted it. "That's about half of what we have left. I hope it will be enough."

"I suppose we'll see." Isold poured the money into his belt pouch. "I suggest the rest of you find somewhere sheltered to wait. Having all of us hovering over the moneychanger can't help our cause." Whistling, he strode across the street and entered the building.

The moneychanger's building had narrow eaves that provided only a little protection from the rain, but Aderyn and the others huddled into that protection anyway. Aderyn stood next to Owen and tried not to shiver. The rain soaked through the coat's padding, dampening her shoulders. "I already don't like this place," she said.

"Rain is great if you can sit inside watching it," Weston said.

"I can see why so many Tidecallers make this place their home," Livia muttered. "Plenty of raw material."

"I heard it never snows here, just gets rainier during winter," Aderyn said. "I'm not sure how much of a benefit that is."

"I'd rather have rain than snow," Owen said, eyeing the clouds. "You're all southerners. You've probably never seen a real snowstorm. People get trapped in their houses, some people die from the cold... rain is much better."

The door opened, and Isold emerged. "Here, take this, and let's go before that young woman comes to her senses," he said, handing Aderyn a fat purse.

"I thought you weren't going to use [Charm] on anyone," Owen said.

"I didn't. Not magical [Charm], at any rate. But she had the look of someone who believed I promised more than I did, and we should leave immediately." Isold set off walking at a rapid pace. "Though I did get a better than fair exchange rate, I think."

"Slow down," Aderyn complained. "Where are we going?"

"Anywhere, apparently." Owen sped up, and Aderyn felt herself accelerated by [Keep Pace]. "Though I wish I'd thought to ask for directions to those inns. Look, there's a sign with a tankard on it. Let's see if the barman is friendly."

CHAPTER FOURTEEN

N o one looked up when they entered the tavern, though the room was full of people seated at long communal tables. All of them were paying close attention to their meals. The tavern was muggy and warm by comparison to the chilly outdoors, and it smelled of stale beer and hot fried food. Aderyn's stomach rumbled quietly enough she didn't think anyone else heard. She stayed close to Owen as he crossed the tap room to the scarred oak slab that served as a bar.

A tall, lanky woman filling wooden tankards from a tapped barrel glanced over her shoulder at them. "One minute," she said. She served a couple of men wearing blue armbands who gazed at them with mild interest and then, wiping her hands on a towel tucked into her belt, sauntered over to Owen. "What can I get you folks?"

"Food, beer, and information," Owen said. "In that order, please."

The woman smiled. "A man after my own heart. Have a seat anywhere. Today's meal is deep-fried chicken and mutton-and-bean soup, with bread baked fresh this morning."

Aderyn's stomach rumbled again, this time loud enough the

woman noticed. Her smile broadened. "Always nice to be appreciated. Go on, sit if you can find a table. You're new in town, are you?"

"We are," Owen said.

"Welcome to Blue faction, then." She nodded and disappeared
through a door behind the bar.

Weston had already claimed one end of a trestle table. A few
other patrons scooted down to make room, though Aderyn couldn't
tell if it was politeness or the intimidating bulk of the giant Moonlighter that did it. It seemed **[Read Body Language]** only worked
on Owen. Since it was a paired skill, that made sense, but it was
unfortunate anyway.

Aderyn dodged someone who'd just entered, managing not to
wrinkle her nose at the smell of wet dog coming off the wolfskin the
man wore as a cape, and took a seat by Owen. She didn't feel like
talking about their business surrounded by strangers, and she guessed
the others felt the same. After a couple of minutes, a young man in
an apron who carried a platter at shoulder height approached them
and carefully set out plates. Each plate had two pieces of fried
chicken, a large bowl of steaming soup, and two thick slabs of brown
bread. The young man distributed spoons and left without a word.

Aderyn fell to eating. The chicken was drier than she liked, the
mutton soup a little too salty, but after seeing the condition of the
streets, Aderyn had expected much worse from the cuisine. And the
bread was astonishingly good, dense and rich and just sweet enough
to counter the saltiness of the soup.

The lanky woman approached their table with a double fistful of
wooden mugs sloshing over with beer. "That'll be five silver each for
the meal and another two for the drinks," she said as she set the
tankards down.

Aderyn reached into her purse and extracted a single large silver
coin. The number impressed on it was 50. She handed it over, hoping
she was right about the total cost. "And the extra is for information."

"Sure." The woman again wiped her hands on her towel. "What can I tell you for fifteen silver?"

"We're looking for a place to stay. Someone recommended either the Blue Tern or the Golden Goose," Owen said.

"The Blue Tern is a good choice," the woman said. "The Golden Goose isn't bad, but it got torn up two nights ago by a couple of feuding adventuring teams and I've heard it's temporarily closed its doors."

"That's good to know. So, can you give us directions?"

"To the Blue Tern? Sure. Stay on this street a quarter mile, turn right at the tailor's sign—needle and spool of thread—and then the Blue Tern is at the end of that street. It's a dead end, so no risk of missing it. You'll see the blue bird above the door. Anything else?"

"You're being awfully helpful for only fifteen silver," Owen said.

The woman laughed. "I like to get my money's worth out of new adventurers before you get yourselves killed. And on that subject, you want more to drink?"

"Not now, but we'll be back." Owen tilted his head as if he'd just had a thought. "Oh, there was one thing. You've heard of the adventurer Tarani, right?"

"Sure." The woman didn't sound as if she thought this question was suspicious.

"I was wondering, what faction was she? Or was that before the factions?"

"You must be new not to know that," the woman said, but not disdainfully. "Tarani was Grim faction. That's the Grays, in case you're even newer than I think."

"Yeah, we don't know all the names that go with the colors. Thanks again." Owen drank from his mug. "Good beer."

"Thanks. I brew it myself." The woman nodded in farewell. "Hope you don't die."

"I wonder if that's some kind of tradition," Aderyn said when the woman was gone. "Telling adventurers 'hope you don't die.' It's what Araceli said, too."

"Since it's what I hope for us too, it feels like good wishes," Weston said. He drained his mug and added, "That was a good way to find out what we need to know. If Tarani was Grim faction, Tarani's house, her memorial, is in the Gray district."

"And if I'd known, we could have paid for the Gray armbands and had free passage there," Aderyn groused.

"We might not have been able to afford it even if we'd known, so don't worry about it," Owen said. "Let's finish here and see how expensive the Blue Tern is, and hope it's not so much that we have to hunt for an alternative."

They huddled briefly outside the tavern, under the shelter of its narrow porch, listening to the rain pound the slate tiles of the roof with a dull rattling sound. "We could wait for the rain to stop," Livia suggested.

"I'm not sure it ever does," Owen said.

"Let's hurry, then," Weston said.

This time, Aderyn was closer to the rear of their group, though she told herself it wasn't reluctance to go on getting wet, it was... she couldn't think of a good reason for her to linger. Behind her, the tavern door opened and banged shut again, and automatically she glanced back. A group of three men stood under the porch roof the way their team had. None of them wore colored armbands, but they were clearly adventurers, because they were all armed with swords or long knives. One of them was the man she'd bumped into inside who wore a wolfskin as a cape.

Just then, the man in the wolf cape caught Aderyn's eye, and for a brief moment they watched each other. Then the man looked away, but Aderyn felt chilled by that moment's contact. She turned away and walked faster, but she put her hood back so she could better listen for anyone following them. For about two seconds, she heard nothing, and then she perceived the sound of footsteps.

Turning around to let the men know they'd been detected would be stupid, so instead she said in a low voice, "We're being followed. Don't look back."

"Who is it?" Owen asked quietly.

"Three men who were in the tavern with us. I didn't get a chance to Assess them. But they're definitely after us and I'm sure they're higher level."

"Keep walking, then," Owen said. "Weston, keep an eye out for a good spot for a confrontation."

"You can't want to start a fight?" Livia said. "They might be a much higher level, and no one here will intervene."

"I won't start a fight unless there's no other choice," Owen said, "but if we do, better it be somewhere we control the situation than letting them ambush us later. And if we lead them to the Blue Tern, that's exactly what will happen."

They were approaching a sign of carved rather than painted wood, larger than the others on the street. It depicted a spool of thread and a needle the length of Aderyn's arm. Another street joined theirs at that point, making a sharp left turn around a blind corner. "There," Owen said. "Get out of sight and be ready for an attack."

The footsteps were closer and more rapid now. Aderyn hurried around the corner and took up a position to Owen's right and a little behind. She, Owen, and Weston drew their swords and surrounded Livia, giving her a clear shot at anyone coming around the corner. Isold stood just behind her. Then they waited. No one appeared. Aderyn listened hard, but heard no footsteps. She and Weston exchanged glances, and Weston shrugged.

With a shout, the three men surged into view, swords held high. Livia called out a handful of curt nonsense words, and *elemental blast* battered the men with a rain of fist-sized stones. Their shouts turned to cries of pain. Aderyn was already Assessing them.

Name: Carsus

Class: Lone Wolf

Level: 13

<u>Skill Alert:</u> Flying Kick (6), Sunder (1)

NAME: KALON

Class: Swordsworn

Level: 13

<u>Skill Alert:</u> Parry (10), Dodge (10)

NAME: POLDOR

Class: Moonlighter

Level: 13

<u>Skill Alert:</u> **Improved Bluff (10), Dirty Fighting (7), To the Heart (10)**

The pulsing red text of Skill Alert startled her, but she didn't waste time exclaiming over this new development. "Moonlighter, Lone Wolf, and Swordsworn," she shouted, pointing to each in turn as the men recovered from the *elemental blast* attack. "The Lone Wolf will try to surprise you with a **[Flying Kick]** that can break your weapon, so close with him quickly. The Swordsworn is really good with combat maneuvers, and the Moonlighter is a dirty fighter who's experienced with **[To the Heart]**, so *don't* let him get close!"

"Aderyn, with me," Owen said. "Weston, see if you can take that Moonlighter, and Isold—"

The enemy adventurers had recovered from being battered by stones and were approaching more slowly. "This doesn't have to be a fight," the Lone Wolf said. He wasn't the one in the wolfskin cape, that was the Swordsworn, but he had a sneer as arrogant as belonging to any poser who thought animal skins made them look tough. "Give us your money, and you can walk away."

"Sure," Owen said. "Like you don't want the experience from killing us."

As he spoke, Livia chanted a few more nonsense words, and the earth beneath their opponents' feet churned into mud. All three halted and strained against the **[Earth to Mud]** effect. The Lone Wolf snarled. "I'll kill you extra painfully for that," he said, and wrenched one foot free. Beside him, the Swordsworn still struggled, but the Moonlighter freed himself and advanced on Weston.

"Go, go!" Owen shouted, and attacked the Lone Wolf, slamming into him with **[Charge]** and keeping him off balance so Aderyn could slip past, dodging the Swordsworn's awkward blow. Having seen the man's skill with combat maneuvers, she knew better than to think the attack was his best; he was distracted by being mired in mud, and the fact that he still had enough attention to swing at her said he was a dangerous opponent.

The Lone Wolf had drawn a second weapon, a long-bladed knife, and ignored Aderyn in favor of deflecting Owen's sword. He was still trying to get free, and after another second, he pulled his other foot out of the mud. Aderyn thrust at his lower back and scored a hit along his side. The Lone Wolf swore and turned to block her next attack, leaving himself open to Owen's next blow, a long slice along his left arm. Aderyn jumped back to avoid being skewered. She heard Weston cursing, and the sound of steel on steel, and then someone screamed her name and suddenly the Swordsworn was in her face and had used his own second blade to flick her sword out of her hands.

She backed away. The Swordsworn followed. Owen was shouting her name, but he was too busy fighting the Lone Wolf to help her. The Swordsworn's eyes gleamed as he raised his sword for the kill. Aderyn knew, looking into those eyes, that he would make it as painful as possible.

Someone stepped between them. Isold, completely unarmed, held up one hand palm out. The Swordsworn stopped, though he still held his sword high. In a quiet, almost conversational tone, Isold said, "Drop your weapons."

Both swords hit the ground with muffled thuds. The Swordsworn stared at Isold, his expression peaceful. "That's right," Isold said. "Keep looking at me. Aderyn, you might want to finish him now."

Aderyn retrieved her sword and then hesitated.

"Aderyn," Isold said more urgently. "He'll kill us both."

She'd killed creatures [Fascinated] by Isold before, but never a human. The Swordsworn trembled. In the next moment, he shook his head as if clearing it. His peaceful expression vanished. Swiftly, he snatched a dagger from his belt and lunged at Isold. Aderyn shoved Isold out of the way and thrust with her sword, piercing the Swordsworn's chest. Sharp pain flared along the outside of her left arm, but the Swordsworn collapsed.

Congratulations! You have defeated [Kalon the Swordsworn]. You have earned [6000 XP]

Breathing heavily, Aderyn hurried back to [Outflank] the Lone Wolf, but as she did, the man folded up over Owen's blade impaling his stomach, and the system message appeared.

Congratulations! You have defeated [Carsus the Lone Wolf]. You have earned [6000 XP]

A short distance away, the third attacker flung down his weapon, or tried to; ropy tentacles entangled him, holding him in place. "I surrender," he said, sounding completely unafraid. "Don't kill me. I'll leave you alone, I swear, just don't kill me." As if in emphasis, the bell in the still-unseen clock tower tolled five o'clock.

**Congratulations! You have defeated [Poldor the Moonlighter].
You have earned [6000 XP]**

"I guess that solves the problem of whether or not we kill you," Owen said. "Take their valuables, but leave that disgusting cloak behind. It stinks of wet dog."

"Aderyn, your arm needs healing," Isold said.

Aderyn held still for him to use the <**Wand of Minor Healing**>. She couldn't bring herself to look him in the eye. She'd nearly let him be killed by that Swordsworn because she was too squeamish to kill someone who meant to kill them. Guilt and embarrassment surged within her. Isold said nothing, but she was sure he blamed her for her reluctance.

Poldor the Moonlighter watched, still *immobilized*, and made no protest when Weston and Owen rifled through the fallen bodies' purses. Livia gathered up the abandoned weapons with *telekinesis* and asked, "Do we leave this guy his sword?"

Owen regarded Poldor closely. "If we're not going to kill him outright, we shouldn't do it indirectly by depriving him of his means of defense. Leave it." He surveyed the captive Moonlighter, who still didn't look afraid. "I guess that should teach you something about assuming lower-level adventurers are a pushover."

"It's true we thought you were easy pickings," Poldor said. "But we went after you because you're the Fated One."

Chapter Fifteen

Owen recoiled. "What?"

"You heard me," Poldor said. "You spared my life, so I figure you've earned that much. It's you, huh? The blond one. Right?"

"*You* haven't earned anything," Weston said. "Somebody told you wrong. None of us is the Fated One." He sounded so dismissive of the idea Aderyn would have been convinced if she hadn't known the truth.

Poldor tilted his head, all he could move, to look up at Weston. "Nice try. But you were noticed when you walked through the gate. The magic item that does it is one hundred percent accurate."

"Why do you want the Fated One dead?" Owen asked.

"We just wanted the money for seeing it done." Poldor twitched against his bonds and fell still again. "We don't care what our employer's motives are."

"And your employer is...?"

"No idea. He used a go-between to communicate and to deliver our payment. We never cared enough to trail the fellow back to his boss."

"You don't seem to know much of anything," Weston said. "Maybe we ought to kill you, after all. You'll probably go running back to this go-between to report your failure and let him know we're aware of him."

"Not likely," Poldor scoffed. "I may not know my employer, but he sure as thunder knows who I am. I wouldn't last a day if I reported I failed. He'll assume I talked—"

"Which you did," Livia said.

"Sure, but he'd assume that even if I'd told you nothing. No, I'm leaving Obsidian. So there's no reason not to tell you what I know."

"Unless you're trying to mislead us out of malice because we killed your friends," Weston said.

Poldor twitched again, and Aderyn realized it was an attempted shrug. "Believe that if you want. It's our employer I want to get back at. His information was that you were typical mid-level adventurers, but you—" He nodded at Owen— "you're a better swordsman than a level ten Swordsworn ought to be by far, and Carsus is—was— good, but he didn't stand a chance against you. That tells me we really were meant to be disposable, and that pisses me off."

"Fine," Owen said. "Who's the contact at the gate? Who identified us? Araceli?"

"She's got <**Spectacles of Truesight**>," Poldor said. "Those can be attuned to identify any characteristic, including whether someone is the Fated One. Guess she's in the pay of our employer, too, but most of the purple-caps are working for some faction or another."

Weston grunted as if acknowledging he'd been right.

"Are you satisfied that I'm being straight with you?" Poldor asked. "You want to let me go now?"

Livia gestured. Instead of loosening, the *immobilize* tentacles constricted. Poldor gasped, and his face reddened. "No," he wheezed. "I swear I won't betray you. Don't..."

Once more, Livia gestured, and this time, the tentacles relaxed and then crumbled into loose earth that pattered to the ground all around Poldor. The man drew in a deep breath. Finally, he looked afraid.

"That was a warning," Livia said. "If you do betray us, I'll make sure no one ever sees you again. So think about whether you want to be buried alive before you talk."

Poldor nodded. He backed away a few steps, then fled.

"That was dark, Livia," Owen said.

"What does that mean? Dark?" Livia glanced at the sky.

"No, it means—well, dark. Leaning on impulses to do scary things, I guess."

"Of course it was. He clearly needed more of an impetus to get out of town without turning on us." Livia dusted off her hands. "And we can't do anything about that lieutenant."

"She's level sixteen and has a bunch of friends to back her up," Aderyn said. "Besides, what's done is done. She already told her boss about us, and nothing we do to her can take that back."

"Which means all we know is that someone in Obsidian is tracking and killing Fated Ones," Owen said. "Not knowing the face of our enemy puts us at a serious disadvantage." He prodded the dead body of Carsus the Lone Wolf with his toe. "Let's get out of here and leave someone else to deal with the mess. We need to find the Blue Tern and hope it's a sanctuary of sorts, as much as we can expect in this city."

They backtracked to the sign of the needle and thread and turned right onto a dead-end street. Aderyn found herself walking faster and hunching her shoulders as if to defend against an unexpected blow. The knowledge that some stranger wanted Owen dead frightened her. Obsidian already had all these rules about the factions, and districts, and who knew what else, and adding the need to watch for assassins made everything so much worse.

The street wasn't very long, and soon the sign of a blue seabird became visible over the door of the two-story building at the end of the street. Now all of them walked faster, though the rain had diminished and wasn't much more than a persistent drizzle. Owen flung the door open, and they all rushed in, then had to stop because the room beyond was unlit and they stumbled over each other in their haste.

Aderyn blinked rapidly, but that did nothing to make her eyes adjust faster. "It's not empty, is it?"

"I smell cabbage cooking," Weston said. "Someone's here."

A door opened, shedding welcome light on the small room. Now Aderyn saw two more doors and a sign with letters she couldn't make out despite the new illumination. The woman who stood in the doorway was short and thin, and her voice, when she spoke, sounded elderly. "You don't need to come bursting in like this, you know. Don't care how wet it is outside, there's such a thing as manners."

"We're sorry," Owen said. "We're adventurers looking to rent a couple of rooms. Are you the innkeeper?"

"The Blue Tern isn't an inn, it's a hostel," the woman said. "I take paying guests who don't cause trouble. You lot look like trouble to me." She glared at the swords Livia still held close to her side with *telekinesis*.

"We assure you we bring no trouble with us," Isold said, stepping to the front of the group. "We traveled here from Elkenforest, and we simply wish for shelter. Your hostel was recommended highly. May we ask how much you charge for rooms?"

The woman eyed him. "Smooth talker. You're a Herald?"

"I am."

"Don't go trying your magic ways on me, or I'll kick you out faster than you can say 'don't kick me out.'"

Aderyn quickly Assessed the woman.

Name: Phedera

Traits: suspicious, tenacious, loyal, honorable

The woman crossed her arms over her chest and glared at all of them. "I charge ten silver per person per night. Boys in one room, girls in another—I don't hold with immoral behavior. Meals are part of the charge, and they're served at seven a.m., noon, and six p.m. on the hour. You miss mealtime, you're out of luck. If you're involved in a feud with some other faction, don't go bringing it here or I'll kick you out. Understood?"

"Yes, ma'am, we understand," Isold said. "We would like two rooms on those terms."

The woman, Phedera, sniffed haughtily. "Sure. Follow me."

The room she'd come from turned out to be a dining room with a long trestle table and a couple dozen backless stools lined up along it. The smell of cabbage was stronger here, but the door Phedera opened led to a stairwell rather than a kitchen. The rickety stairs creaked underfoot, but the walls were grimy enough Aderyn trod on the center of each step to avoid touching them, even though that was noisier.

Upstairs, a dimly-lit hallway extended away from the stairs, with ten doors opening off it. Phedera led the way to the third door on the right and opened it. "This one and the next one. Should be enough space. Payment for three nights in advance." She held out a gnarled hand.

Aderyn concealed a sigh over their dwindling resources and withdrew one gold coin and another fifty-silver piece. The hostel keeper made the coins disappear into her apron. "Seven, noon, and six," she reminded them. "Don't be late." She marched back to the stairs and descended in a loud chorus of creaks.

Aderyn peeked into the room. It had a window, so it wasn't completely dark the way the entry had been, but the watery sunlight wasn't enough to illuminate the room fully. Livia conjured an *orb of light* and tossed it to float at the center of the ceiling. "It's not as bad as I feared," she said. Three narrow beds filled most of the space, each with a small clothespress at its foot. Colorful rugs beside each bed cheered the place considerably, as did the red curtains drawn back to each side of the window.

Aderyn tipped the water jug and saw it was empty. "This will be fine," she said.

She heard noises that indicated the men were exploring their room next door, and exchanged glances with Livia. "Immoral behavior, huh?" Livia grumbled. "It's probably just as well. These beds aren't made to hold more than one person."

"You don't suppose she'd rent out that third bed, do you? I hate the idea of sharing with a stranger."

"It's not like we were planning to leave anything here unattended." Livia dropped her knapsack on the bed and stretched. "How much did we take off those men?"

"Owen and Weston still have their purses. Let's find out."

They ended up gathered in the women's room, where Owen and Weston poured out the contents of the looted belt pouches onto the spare bed. Owen whistled. "That's a lot. Guess their employer pays well."

Weston stirred the pile with his forefinger. "There's enough odd coin here that I feel safe guessing they were paid in ten-gold coins, since there's a total of exactly twenty such coins totaling two hundred Obsidian gold."

Aderyn dug into the **<Purse of Great Capacity>** and sorted the regular coin from the Obsidian currency. "So, they were each paid one hundred Obsidian gold, and then there's, let's see, another thirty-three Obsidian gold, fifty-eight silver, and twenty copper from the would-be assassins. We have thirty-two Obsidian gold, sixty-seven silver, and fifteen copper, plus what amounts to forty gold in mixed coin of our own currency. More than two hundred and sixty Obsidian gold in total, which is more comfortable."

"Let's make sure everyone has a handful of Obsidian coin in case we're separated," Owen suggested. Aderyn doled out money to each person and poured the rest back into the purse.

"And we can sell those weapons. Three swords and a knife—they aren't the highest quality, but they should be worth something," Weston added.

"If we were anywhere else, I'd say we have time to take care of that before six, but we don't know this city. And I want to show up for dinner, if only to show Phedera we're decent, clean-living folks who never cause trouble." Owen grinned. "Let's call it an early night. It's been a long day, and I'm exhausted."

His saying that brought all the day's events back to Aderyn, and all her muscles suddenly ached. "I'm not sure I'll make it through dinner without falling asleep in the boiled cabbage."

Weston made a face. "Boiled cabbage. Slimy and smelly. My least favorite food."

"It's good for you, you health-obsessed ox," Livia teased.

"They boil the health benefits right out of it. It's good for nothing except maybe..." Weston tilted his head, pretending to search for a conclusion to that statement. "I give up. It's good for nothing."

"There will have to be more than just boiled cabbage on offer," Isold said, "if only because other vegetables are even cheaper."

"If there's even a shred of meat served with this meal," Weston said, "I will eat the boiled cabbage happily."

There wasn't.

Chapter Sixteen

Weston emerged from the weapons shop, scowling ferociously. He dropped a small clinking bag into Aderyn's hand. "Imagine a shopkeeper not willing to haggle," he grumbled. "That's thirty-five Obsidian gold for the lot. I know those weapons are worth twice that."

"It's money we didn't have to work for," Aderyn pointed out.

"Of course we did. You got knifed for it, in case you've forgotten." Weston tapped Aderyn's upper left arm, where a faint stain on her coat was all that remained of the wound the Swordsworn had inflicted. Livia had mended the tear earlier that morning, but scrubbing hadn't been able to totally eliminate the bloodstain.

Aderyn deliberately didn't look at Isold. "I guess that's like work. At any rate, we got something out of those thugs. Do we care about finding out who hired them? Or should we pursue our main quest?"

"Finding who hired them is too much of a distraction," Owen said. "We'll have to stay on our guard, but we were doing that anyway. Let's stick to discovering Tarani's memorial. Do we know where Gray district is?"

"I made inquiries. It's on Obsidian's north side," Isold said. "My informant suggested we take the long way around, through Red district, as the direct route passes through Orange, which as Araceli said is in the middle of a war with Green."

"I thought the other districts wouldn't attack us because they wouldn't want to start a fight they might not be able to win," Livia said.

"According to the woman I spoke to, both Orange and Green factions are using the war as an excuse to attack adventurers of other factions who pass through." Isold's lips tightened. "On the basis that no other faction wants to get mixed up in the conflict, and adventurers are temporary members only and therefore expendable."

"Which is no more than we suspected," Owen said. "All right. Do you know the route, Isold?"

"I have a map, drawn for me by that helpful woman." Isold withdrew a rolled sheet of paper from inside his coat and held it open for the others to see as they clustered around.

"That's really well drawn," Weston said. "Almost a professional's work. Certainly an artist's."

"She is, in fact, an artist. In exchange for this information, she asked me to sit for her." Isold's smile replaced his grim expression. "I look forward to it."

"This wouldn't be a *naked* sitting, would it?" Owen asked.

"She is a professional, Owen. Of course she asked me to pose nude." Isold's smile broadened. "I anticipate it will be mutually satisfying."

"We haven't even been in this city for twenty-four hours," Owen said. "Fine. But on your own time, right? Let's get moving."

The rain had stopped overnight, and the cloud cover that morning was sparse, with the sun peeping through the clouds as it rose. Obsidian in sunlight still looked gloomy, though, its wooden shops and houses more obviously weather-beaten and the unpaved streets tacky from the previous day's rain. Mud caked Aderyn's boots before she'd gone twenty paces, making her feel as if Livia's **[Earth to Mud]** skill had gone horribly wrong.

She let Isold and his map lead the way west and kept a careful eye on their surroundings. Maybe Owen could focus on their quest despite having essentially a price on his head, but she couldn't stop seeing that feral, hungry expression on the Lone Wolf's face. It was small comfort they'd killed him. Once their unknown enemy found out his hired thugs had failed, he might send others, higher-level adventurers, and if that went on, eventually he'd find someone capable of killing her and her friends.

The streets were thronged that morning as they had not been the night before, with pedestrians and riders and a couple of carriages, and carts selling food lined the streets. The smell of hot sausages made Aderyn salivate. Breakfast had been gruel with a dollop of honey, filling but bland, and sausages would be so invigorating. She made herself focus not on the carts and vendors, but on their customers, in case someone pretending to buy a cone of pine nuts actually intended murder.

But no one leaped at them, screaming, and by the time they left the food carts behind, Aderyn had stopped focusing on the people and could pay attention to the buildings. They were three stories tall rather than two and their paint was fresher, though it was more pastel in shade than she thought it had originally been. Still, the shades of blue and green soothed her.

She'd made note of the lampposts and their painted bands and had been aware when they crossed into Red territory and once more turned north. Idly, she considered the painted buildings. Why not red, or washed-out red? Maybe it meant something that the owners didn't feel compelled to extend their allegiances all the way to house color. Then again, they were in Red district, so there would be no point in red paint, because everyone already knew you were part of Red faction if you lived here. But she imagined a city painted to match its districts, and how colorful that would look if you were a bird flying overhead. It was a ridiculous notion, but it amused her.

The crowds again thickened as they drew closer to what Aderyn suspected was the center of Red district. No more tall houses with shared walls; mansions on properties separate from each other occupied all the available space. It wasn't a lot of space. Aderyn guessed the gaps between houses weren't more than ten feet. But by comparison to the rest of Obsidian, those mansions might as well have occupied acres of property.

These streets were paved, too, with worn-down cobbles that made the gutters look shallow. That meant the gutters had been installed after the streets were originally built. Aderyn kicked some of her mud overshoes off against the curb and felt less burdened. Immediately ahead, Owen was watching the crowds with his head held alertly high. It relieved her mind that he was taking the potential danger seriously even though he didn't want to do anything about it.

And the truth was, she couldn't argue with his logic. If they could get into the memorial, retrieve Tarani's records, and leave Obsidian, it wouldn't matter if someone in the city wanted all Fated Ones dead. They just had to watch out for attacks, not track down and stop the one promoting those attacks.

She saw her first gray-banded lamppost just as Isold said, "We're here. The memorial is half a mile north."

"Don't say anything cheerful," Livia warned Weston. "I don't believe in coincidence, but I do believe in jinxing yourself, so none of this 'It's been so easy' or 'Piece of cake.'"

"I wasn't going to say anything," Weston protested. "Except maybe 'almost there.' Does that count as cheerful?"

"I doubt it can jinx us," Owen said.

Someone behind Aderyn cleared his throat. A thrill of fear shot through her, and she spun around, her hand on her sword. A man stood there, not apparently armed. He was middle-aged, with thinning hair and a bald spot at the back of his head, and he wore a coat trimmed with squirrel fur. Instinctively, she Assessed him, though she guessed he was non-classed.

Name: Tevon

Traits: loyal, intelligent, difficult to offend, patient

"What do you want?" she demanded, still with her hand on her sword but not drawing it. Her voice shook. He'd sneaked up on them —if he'd been an armed adventurer, someone might have died.

Her words made the others turn around. Owen immediately drew Aderyn to one side so he stood in front of her. "Who are you?"

Tevon gazed at him fearlessly. "Fated One," he said, inclining his head. "My master would like to speak to you."

"Your master? And who is that?" Owen's tension covered the same fear Aderyn had had, the realization that if this had been an armed adventurer, some of them might be injured or dead now. Aderyn had never been so grateful that **[Read Body Language]** wasn't visible to everyone.

Tevon gestured at the armband he wore, which was a spotless white and looked like it had been ironed. "Why, Liander of the White, of course," he said. "You are new to our city, but surely you know of the factions?"

"The factions, yes. We don't concern ourselves with city politics. Why does Liander want to speak to me?"

Tevon bowed slightly. "My master confides in me only what I must know to carry out his instructions. He informed me he has a proposition for you that will be mutually beneficial."

"Does he." Owen took a few steps forward that put him face to face with Tevon, or almost; Tevon was an inch taller than Owen, but Owen's confident stance made him the dominant one. "So he's given up on assassination?"

"Assassination?" Tevon's brow furrowed, and he frowned. "My master would not stoop to assassination. I assure you he wishes only to talk."

"Wait there." Owen turned on his heel and walked in the direction they'd been going. Aderyn and the others followed until Weston nodded, indicating that they were out of Tevon's earshot. Owen put his back to the servant and said, "This Liander has to be the one who hired those thugs. What are the odds *two* factions have an interest in the Fated One?"

"It's possible," Isold said. "It might be a citywide concern. Tarani is Obsidian's most famous daughter, and even though we are the only ones who know the secret of her monument, I can imagine there are many Fated Ones who come here, for inspiration if nothing else."

"But even if that's true, we have to assume this is the man behind the thugs," Weston said, "because if he is, this meeting he wants is a trap, and the consequences of us walking into it blindly are much worse than if he really is just innocently interested in Owen."

"So we refuse," Aderyn said. "We get in and out quickly, we stay out of the White district, we watch for more thugs..." Her voice trailed off as she saw Owen shaking his head.

"Only two possibilities," he said. "Liander is our man, or he's not. And either way, we have to meet with him."

"Owen—"

"Aderyn, I know it's a risk. But if he isn't behind the attack, he could be an ally against the one who is. And if he *is* behind the attack, we need to know why he wants Fated Ones dead so we can defend ourselves. This won't take long, and we have to learn more about the memorial anyway before we tackle it."

He returned to where Tevon stood, patient as a stone. Tevon didn't look as if he'd been trying to eavesdrop, merely turned his attention on Owen as he approached. "We'll go," Owen said. "With the understanding that if we so much as suspect we're being surrounded, your life is forfeit."

"That won't be necessary," Tevon said, without a hint of fear. "While it would be my honor to die in my master's service, he never wastes resources. I assure you, you are in no danger."

"We'll see. Lead the way, Tevon."

Aderyn joined Owen right behind Tevon as the others formed up around him, with Livia and Isold in the center and Weston trailing behind. Aderyn dearly wished she could discuss Tevon's behavior with her friends. He didn't act like someone whose life was in danger, even though there was no way he could defend himself against the least of their attacks. Aderyn had never seen a non-classed person with such self-possession and calm.

She thought back over what **[Improved Assess 2]** had showed her. In the past, anyone non-classed had just showed up as a name and occasionally a profession. She couldn't remember the last non-classed person she'd Assessed—no, Phedera yesterday had displayed the same Traits information. This could be useful if she could figure out how to apply the knowledge. So, Tevon was loyal, intelligent, difficult to offend, and patient. All of that added up to someone who was more than just a servant. A spokesman, or a diplomat?

"Tevon," she said, "what can you tell us about your master Liander?"

Tevon didn't turn around. "He is powerful and influential in Obsidian. He commands the loyalty of hundreds and the respect of thousands. Whatever proposition he has for you, I suggest you take it. My master did not reach his position of dominance by allowing others to disrespect him."

"It's not disrespect to choose a different path," Owen said. "His proposition may be sound and still not be a good idea for us."

"Nevertheless, consider carefully, and then take his offer. That is the only warning you will receive."

"He can't be all powerful, or am I wrong and the Black faction doesn't hold the premier position in Obsidian?" Owen retorted.

Tevon jerked, and his step hesitated for a moment. Then he continued walking as if he hadn't been interrupted. "My master's interest in you is not relevant to his relationship with the other factions. You're new to the city, and I suggest you not meddle in affairs you can't possibly understand." As if in emphasis, the clock tower began to ring the twelve deep tones of midday.

"Liander's the one who dragged us into this," Weston said. "He's made those affairs our business."

Tevon waited for the clock to finish striking before replying. "If that is what you believe, I have misled you. I apologize. This business is between my master and the Fated One alone. You need not concern yourself with other matters." He quickened his pace until he was just short of running.

Aderyn reflected as she stretched to keep up with him that talking at this speed would be difficult. She wasn't sure if Tevon had sped up because Owen and Weston had hit upon a topic he found uncomfortable, or if he'd seen the foolishness of continuing to threaten adventurers of any level, but either way, he clearly wanted to end the conversation. Aderyn hated political matters—she always felt out of her depth—but even she could see faction politics were more complicated than usual. She hoped she and her friends weren't about to be dragged into them.

CHAPTER SEVENTEEN

They headed west rapidly, walking fast enough to draw the attention of others along their path. Tevon didn't keep a straight line, and he didn't move like he expected others to get out of his way; he dodged those they overtook, and nodded courteously to those headed toward them. It felt a little like being a cork bobbing around a boiling pot, though a cork under someone's control.

With most of her attention on Tevon, Aderyn didn't notice the white-banded lampposts until they entered a more upscale area. As in Red district, mansions occupied plots of land that separated them from each other. Unlike Red district, those plots left enough space between mansions that more mansions would fit easily between them. Wrought-iron fences topped with wickedly sharp spikes divided the streets from the gardens and grassy lawns surrounding the mansions, their bars spaced barely far enough apart for someone to stick their arm through the gap. As if Aderyn wanted to do something that stupid. She heard the barking of dogs coming from somewhere nearby. It wouldn't surprise her at all to discover the owners didn't want to count on bars and spikes stopping an intruder. Sticking an arm through might result in getting it ripped off.

Tevon slowed his steps when they reached a corner where one house dominated the street. A hill rose within that fence, lifting the mansion well above street level, but the height wasn't the only thing intimidating about it; bars covered all the windows at ground level, and a stone wall inside the fence encircled some of the property near the mansion. Aderyn guessed a garden, though it was hard to imagine anything as delicate as a flower growing in this sunless place.

About twenty paces from the corner, a closed iron gate and two armed guards indicated where people might enter, though it was hard to imagine why anyone would want to, given how forbidding the place was. Of course, *they* were going in, so maybe that meant something, like that only the truly brave entered. Or, in this case, the truly foolish. Aderyn reminded herself that Owen's point about needing to confront Liander was a good one that didn't make them fools. She stayed alert regardless.

As their little procession approached, Aderyn Assessed the guards.

Name: Clion
Class: Stalwart
Level: 7

NAME: RODRY
   ∞ **Tenalie**
   Class: Staffsworn
   Level: 6

She noted in passing that Rodry was married, so that must be as fundamental as class to an adventurer or traits to the non-classed. Her relief that the guards were too low a level to be a danger to her team vanished as she considered why someone as powerful as Liander would hire less than the best. Maybe he wasn't as powerful as they believed. Or maybe—well, it wasn't as if the average non-classed person could give a level six or seven fighter much of a challenge, so maybe Liander didn't need anyone stronger than these two on gate duty.

She tried not to let this unnerve her, but it was hard not to speculate further, like imagining an army of high-level fighters and spell-slingers waiting for them. That was stupid, because if Liander had an army, he'd have sent his most capable adventurer minions to attack their team. Unless—Aderyn made herself stop worrying. Soon enough, they'd know.

The gate guards Clion and Rodry opened the gate for Tevon without being prompted, and Tevon sailed through without acknowledging them. "This way," he said, though there was really only one way to go: a path paved in small white bricks and edged with stones painted a brilliant white.

Aderyn paid more attention to her surroundings now. There weren't any trees or bushes by the fence, nothing that would provide cover for an intruder, but about twenty feet in, the path was shaded by linden trees whose leaves grew thickly along their sturdy branches. Aderyn looked up as they passed beneath the first one and got an unlucky drop of rainwater in her eye. She blinked it away and surveyed the rest of the trees, which made a ring surrounding the mansion that would block its lower stories from casual view. The fragrance of the lindens filled the cool air.

Tevon didn't look around, merely led them directly to the mansion's front door. It, too, opened before he reached it, something Aderyn found more impressive than the gate because as far as she could tell, no windows overlooked the steps rising to the slab of stone where visitors, or petitioners, would stand and wait for admission. Again, Tevon continued to walk as if he expected this. "Please follow me."

Owen's rigid back told Aderyn he'd been about to insist that Tevon go first, and the fact that he didn't relax indicated that he now wasn't sure if Tevon going first was the best idea. Still, he squared his shoulders and entered the mansion. Aderyn kept close behind him.

Their boots echoed in the vast entrance, with its marble floor and ceilings rising two stories tall. Stairs broad enough for five people occupied the center of the room, but Aderyn didn't feel they were inviting—more like they were a mouth open wide to engulf anyone who dared set foot on them. The marble was pale pink with white streaks, and for half a second Aderyn was reluctant to step with her muddy boots on the shining surface. Then she remembered they might be in the house of their enemy and stopped caring.

"My master will see you in the great hall," Tevon said. "It is on the third floor. Don't worry about leaving footprints, someone will clean the mess."

"We weren't," Owen said. "The third floor?"

Tevon bowed. "I am pleased to guide you."

"I hope so," Owen replied. "We're still not sure this isn't a trap."

"It's not, but I'm sure my assurances mean nothing. I'm not insulted. I imagine adventurers must live cautious lives." Tevon began ascending the stairs.

The stairs let out on a long hallway easily thirty feet wide. Doors lined both sides, some of them open so Aderyn could see inside. Couches and chairs, small tables, cabinets—it was all more ornate and over-furnished than anything she was familiar with. She couldn't imagine how anyone could need that many small round tables.

She glimpsed a harp taller than herself in one room and rows of bookcases in another. The library was easily five times the size of her parents', but the books were so uniform in height and color Aderyn suspected it was just for show. Could *all* of this be for show? If so, how sad to have enough money to pay for it all and not buy the things that would make you happy.

Another staircase, this one half the size of the first, waited at the end of the hallway. It rose to a landing and then rose again to another hallway, this one short and with only three doors. Tevon walked to the one directly opposite the stair, an enormous double door with a curved top and heavy iron hinges and latch, and Aderyn waited for it to open automatically like the others. Instead, Tevon opened the door, which swung inward as easily as if it weighed nothing, and bowed to Owen, gesturing with his free hand to indicate he should enter.

Aderyn was close enough behind Owen that she nearly tripped over his heels when he stopped just inside the door. She quickly stepped to the left, and then saw what had brought Owen to a halt. The entire back wall of this room, which Aderyn guessed took up most of the third floor, was a series of stained glass windows depicting animals bowing before a male figure dressed in white. In full light, the display would be blinding. As it was, the colors gleamed dully, but were still impressive enough to command anyone's attention.

"Oh, the windows," a man said. "I'm so accustomed to them I forgot how they appear to newcomers. Gaudy, I know, but it's extraordinary workmanship, don't you think?"

Owen took a few more steps forward, making room for the others to enter and arrange themselves around him. "It's a little obvious," he said. "Worshipping at your feet—not subtle at all."

The man seated in the throne-like chair stood and turned as if to examine the windows again. "Oh, that's not me," Liander said. "An ancestor, someone who wasted the family fortune building this pile. He had delusions of his own competence, after besting the Gray faction and bringing White to preeminence in Obsidian, and ultimately it cost him his life, when his brother—"

He turned back around. "Sorry, I'm sure you don't care about that. Why don't you have a seat? No, wait, there aren't enough chairs —Tevon?"

"Of course, sir," Tevon said, bowing.

Aderyn dragged her attention away from the windows and surveyed the room. In addition to the throne-chair, four other wooden chairs, smaller but equally ornate, had been arranged in a line facing the throne, like a handful of petitioners that hadn't quite lost their dignity in the face of the lord. Armed men wearing white jerkins under chain mail, fourteen of them, stood like armored statues all around the room's perimeter. None of them met her eyes when she Level Assessed them. A mix of Swordsworn, Staffsworn, Deadeyes, and two Stalwarts, none of them higher than level eight. That suggested that Liander really didn't have anyone high level in his employ, which made sense if he'd had to hire mercenaries to try to take her team out.

She also noticed that there were more chairs against the walls, all of them identical to the four facing the throne, and that Tevon had picked one up and brought it to join the line. Liander watched as intently as if Tevon were handling explosives rather than an overdecorated chair. He wore his chestnut hair short, nearly as short as Owen's had been when he first arrived in their world, and his face was fleshy but not fat. He fit exactly Aderyn's idea of a middle-aged government official, all except for his eyes, which were deep-set and black so the pupils were invisible. Aderyn didn't like his eyes. They reminded her of pictures she'd seen of sharks, emotionless and uninterested in anything but savaging their prey.

Liander smiled. "Thank you, Tevon. *Now*, if you'll all take seats? I won't offer you refreshments, as I'm sure you're cautious enough not to accept food or drink from someone who might be an enemy." He returned to his throne and sat in it with a sigh of contentment, though to Aderyn it looked extremely uncomfortable, with no padding and a heavily-carved back and armrests.

"I appreciate your willingness to meet with me," Liander said, addressing Owen, who'd seated himself at the far left of the line instead of the center. "How are you liking Obsidian? I know, you've only been here a day, so perhaps you haven't formed an opinion yet."

"We aren't impressed with our welcome," Owen said. He didn't sound hostile or friendly, just indifferent, as if they were discussing the weather. "As I'm sure you've guessed."

Liander crossed one ankle over his knee, leaning back as if the carvings didn't dig into his spine. "I admit it, I sent men to kill you. I hope that won't make a potential accord impossible."

"Shouldn't it?"

"Of course not. What's a little test between—well, we're not friends, but perhaps we can become colleagues or even allies?"

"You think you're entitled to test us?" Now Owen sounded angry. "Two men died in pursuit of your 'test.' I don't put up with that in my allies."

"We won't quibble over whether or not I have the right to assess those who come into my city," Liander said, tapping his fingers on the chair's armrest in a quick one-two-three-four motion. "The fact is, you passed. You and your friends are quite powerful, though I'm told you're only level ten. Given that, I believe you and I can enter a mutually beneficial arrangement."

Aderyn blinked. "You were told?" she blurted out, and blushed when Owen's forearm tensed in a warning that he needed to do the talking. To cover her embarrassment, she quickly Assessed Liander.

Name: Liander

Traits: ruthless, intelligent, devoted, cruel

"Oh, I'm no adventurer or even a retired adventurer," Liander said, waving a hand languidly. "I couldn't afford to sacrifice my position here by heading off into the Forsaken Lands. I rejected the Call. That shocks you, does it, young lady?"

Aderyn kept her mouth shut this time. That Liander could command these resources, that he could control even these lower-level adventurers, meant he was no one to be underestimated, even non-classed as he was.

"It doesn't matter," Owen said. "I came because I want to know why you want me dead. Not for a bargain."

"I don't want you dead," Liander protested.

"Those thugs said otherwise."

"All right, I should say—I don't want you dead *now*. If they'd killed you, I would have known you were just another poser. But you survived, and survived completely unscathed—that's remarkable! That tells me you're more than an ordinary adventurer. And, as I said, I have a proposition for you."

Owen shifted his weight and rested his ankle on his knee, mirroring Liander's casual pose. "I admit I'm curious. What is it?"

The door behind them slammed open. Everyone but Owen turned to see who'd made the noise. A young woman stood in the doorway, silhouetted against the opening like she'd posed intentionally to be dramatic. She wore a shirt and trousers similar in cut to Aderyn's, but the shirt was dark pink silk and the trousers were so finely made Aderyn couldn't make out the stitching. Boots that gleamed with polish and a leather vest dyed black to match her trousers completed her ensemble. Chestnut curls bounced all around her heart-shaped face.

"*Papa*," she exclaimed. "There's a horse at the market I need to own, Papa, he has the sweetest face and I asked and they said he would cost only five hundred and fifty gold, I can have him, can't I, Papa?"

"In a moment, sweetness," Liander said. His formerly businesslike tone turned sugary, like a pool of melted caramel. "Papa is talking to these people. This is my daughter, Jessemia. Jessemia, these are Weston, Livia, Isold, Aderyn, and Owen."

That Liander knew their names sent a chill through Aderyn. She glanced at Owen, who alone hadn't stopped watching Liander. "You let your daughter interrupt your business negotiations?" Owen said.

"Not—" Liander said, but Jessemia overrode him.

"I'm not just his daughter," she said, tilting her head so her chin lifted. "I'm the Fated One."

CHAPTER EIGHTEEN

In the stunned silence that followed, Aderyn Assessed the young woman—a Full Assessment, because anyone claiming to be the Fated One was worth a little extra time.

Name: Jessemia

Class: Pathseer

Level: 6

<u>Skills</u>: **Assess (2), Bluff (3), Climb (1), Conversation (3), Intimidate (4), Sense Truth (1), Spot (4), Survival (1), Swim (1)**

<u>Class Skills</u>: **Improved Weapon Proficiency (4), Basic Armor Proficiency (4), Improved Sneak Attack (3), Tracking (5), Knowledge: Magical Beasts (3), Detect Traps (2), Spot (5), Awareness (4), Dodge (3), Acrobatics (3), Stealth (2), Dirty Fighting (4), To the Heart (0), Hide (1)**

She'd barely finished reading when Owen said, "The Fated One. In that case, you don't have any need of me, do you?" He stood, pushing back his chair so it scraped across the floor. The sound echoed in the vast room.

"Please, sit," Liander said. It was not a request despite his wording. All around the room, the watching fighters stirred from their statue poses, bringing weapons to the ready. Aderyn was terrifyingly aware of the Deadeye to their left whose arrow was pointed at Owen's chest.

Owen slowly resumed his seat, his eyes never leaving Liander's. "I get it," he said. "You know there are hundreds of would-be Fated Ones throughout the world. You want to clear the way for your daughter, so you kill off any who show up here. A pointless, dramatic gesture, but I'm sure to you it seems like a great idea."

"Then how do you explain your presence here, unharmed?" Liander said.

Owen shrugged. "I have no idea. I don't try to fathom the minds of sociopaths—of anyone who finds life that disposable," he amended. "Go ahead. I'm sure you're eager to explain your plan."

"Don't be rude," Jessemia said. She strode across the room and hugged her father, pressing her cheek against his. "You're just a fake Fated One. You're lucky Papa doesn't have you killed right now, isn't that right, Papa?"

"Of course, sweetness, but let Papa speak." Liander gave her a quick hug and straightened. "Jessemia is the Fated One, Owen. I'm certain of it. Her destiny has been evident since she was a child. All those other imposters' deaths prove it."

Owen crossed his arms over his chest. If he knew an arrow was aimed at his heart, **[Read Body Language]** didn't show it. "And what does my survival prove? Since I doubt you've suddenly given up your delusion based on one failed assassination."

Liander's lips tightened briefly. "It's you who labors under the delusion that you are the Fated One. But your strength in defending yourself tells me you're not like the others. In fact, it proves your identity as the Fated One's chosen companion."

"Excuse me?" Owen sat up straight. "The what?"

"It's in the prophecies, that the Fated One will be surrounded by those whose talents turn toward protecting and sustaining her. Obviously anyone who can defeat opponents several levels higher is a true champion of the Fated One."

Owen glanced at Isold. Isold looked as stunned as Aderyn felt. "It's true, there are prophecies that suggest that," Isold began. "It's why we—"

"Papa, do you mean these are my new companions?" Jessemia let out a little shriek of happiness and clapped her hands. "How delightful!"

"That is *not*," Owen began. The Deadeye pulled back on his bowstring just enough to draw attention to the arrow. Owen made a visible effort to control himself and said, "So what you're saying is that I only think I'm the Fated One because the system has been steering me to Obsidian all this time, with the intent of making me and my friends your daughter's team?"

"You're insightful. I'm sure I never said any of that, but it's true enough."

"How did she gain any levels at all?" Weston asked. "Level one adventurers living outside the safe zone have to travel there, protected by an escort or caravan, to adventure in a place where they won't instantly die. Obsidian isn't on the border of what's too dangerous for anyone, but it's far too dangerous for a beginner."

"Jessemia has been under the protection of many teams as she advanced," Liander said. He took Jessemia's hand and squeezed it gently. "She partners with those at the edge of what the system will allow, and as they encounter challenges, she is able to gain experience at an accelerated rate."

"That's *cheating*," Weston exclaimed.

"Hardly cheating. The system won't allow cheating, as I'm sure you know. Merely taking advantage of a loophole."

"Then that explains—" Aderyn shut her mouth before revealing what **[Improved Assess 2]** showed her of Jessemia's skill rankings. All of them except **[Tracking]** and **[Dirty Fighting]** were much too low for a level six Pathseer. If Jessemia ever struck out on her own, she'd be at a serious disadvantage—though, looking at her doting father, Aderyn doubted that would ever happen.

"You're saying you want us to babysit your daughter as she levels," Owen said flatly.

"Babysit?" Liander shrugged off this nonsense word. "You're going to team with her for a while. Just until she reaches level eleven or twelve. Then you're free to go if you still want to. Here, I'll make it official."

A system message appeared in front of Aderyn's face.

A new quest is available: [Help the Fated One]
Join the Fated One as she pursues her magnificent destiny!
Accept? Y / N

"You're a questgiver?" Owen asked.

"Certainly. Now, accept it, and you can be on your way."

"I see," Owen said. "You still haven't addressed the obvious question. I am the Fated One. I haven't denied that claim. What do you intend to do about that?"

"Nothing," Liander said. "You can believe anything you like. Jessemia's destiny grows ever clearer as she advances. I would think you would be grateful to be part of history being made."

"You make a good argument," Isold said. His voice hummed with subtle harmonics. "But I don't think you've considered all the possibilities. Adventuring at these levels is dangerous, and having the protection of higher-level companions may not be enough. Surely it would be better to send Jessemia to the safe zone, where she can level naturally."

Jessemia stomped her foot, sending more echoes through the chamber. "That's not fair! I'm the Fated One, and I shouldn't have to slog like ordinary people! You're mean to suggest it. You must want me to fail. Papa, why are you letting that man insult me?"

Liander, who'd looked as though Isold's **[Persuasion]** was working on him, shook his head like someone rising out of a deep pool. "He didn't mean insult, sweetness, and you know I won't let anyone treat you poorly. He's not wrong that adventuring with them will be dangerous."

"I'm not afraid! I'm an excellent fighter. You, there." Jessemia pointed at Owen. "I want to fight you."

Owen blinked. "You what?"

"Get up and fight me. I'll prove I'm capable of adventuring with you." Jessemia drew the narrow-bladed sword that hung at her hip and brandished it awkwardly.

"I'm not going to fight you, and we're not going to team with you," Owen said, rising from his chair. "This meeting is over." He jabbed at the air just where N would be. Aderyn swiftly dismissed the system message about Liander's quest.

"You're making a mistake," Liander said. "This is destiny."

Aderyn realized that Jessemia had accidentally positioned herself between Owen and the twitchy-fingered Deadeye. She rose and said, "If Jessemia is the Fated One, sir, you shouldn't have to do anything to protect her destiny. It will just happen."

Liander fixed his gaze on Aderyn for the first time. "So naïve," he said. "If you refuse my very reasonable request, you won't leave this room alive."

Owen's hand rested on his sword hilt, but he didn't draw the weapon. "That's up to you," he told Liander. "We're leaving."

Liander signaled. The three archers brought their bows to the ready. The other fighters drew their weapons. And Owen, quick as a cat, snatched the <**Twinsword**> from its sheath and thrust its tip against the hollow of Jessemia's throat.

Jessemia squeaked. Her sword fell to clatter on the marble with a terrible ringing echo.

"Stand down!" Liander shouted, leaping from his chair. He took a step toward Owen, then froze when Owen pressed harder so the tip of the sword dimpled the young woman's throat.

"That's better," Owen said. "Weston, take charge of her. We're leaving, Liander. Jessemia is coming with us as far as the gate."

"I'll see you killed personally if you so much as scratch her skin," Liander snarled.

"She's the Fated One. Don't you have any faith in her destiny?" Owen withdrew his blade as Weston took Jessemia's upper arm in his grip. Weston's other hand held a long-bladed knife he pressed into the young woman's side.

"Don't you *dare*," Jessemia said. "Let me go this instant! Papa, don't let them do this!"

"It's all right, sweetness, don't worry, Papa will kill them all." Liander followed at a safe distance as Owen led the way out of the room. "You should have killed *me*," he said. "You'll never be able to stop watching your backs so long as I live."

"Owen?" Aderyn frowned at Liander, then at Tevon, who'd come up on her other side but was also keeping his distance.

Owen shook his head. "We don't murder indiscriminately, unlike some people. But I suggest you leave us alone, Liander. You have no idea what else we're capable of."

Aderyn drew her sword and gestured at Tevon. "Stay back."

"You should have obeyed," Tevon said. "You're doomed." He said it calmly, but with a certainty that chilled Aderyn.

She was the last one through the door and shut it firmly in Liander's face. Then she threw herself to one side as Livia cast *iron spikes*. A hail of iron slammed into the door, nailing it shut. Immediately, people started banging on the door and calling out words muffled by the thick oak.

"Let's move," Owen said.

Jessemia struggled and fought despite Weston's knife until, exasperated by her attempts to use **[Dirty Fighting]**, Weston sheathed the blade and picked their hostage up to sling her over his shoulder, pinioning her legs. Jessemia began screaming. "Help! Somebody help! I'm being ravished! Stop this man!"

"Oh, shut up," Livia said, smacking Jessemia across the top of her head. "You're not being ravished."

"I know what you have in mind for me!"

"A muzzle," Weston muttered.

"Ignore her," Owen said. "We'll drop her at the gate and then haul ass out of this district."

Servants appeared at several doors as they pelted down the second-floor hallway. All of them looked shocked, but none of them tried to interfere. That gave Aderyn a good idea of how popular Jessemia wasn't among the staff. Jessemia kept thrashing until Livia hit her a little harder, stunning her but not knocking her unconscious. By the look on Livia's face, she'd hoped to knock her out.

When they emerged from the mansion, the clouds had blown westward, toward the ocean, and although more clouds loomed on the eastern horizon, the sun shone brightly. The companions ran down the hill, not slowing when the guards Clion and Rodry shouted at them to stop. Livia's boot sent *thunderstomp* racing ahead of them to knock the guards down. Weston paused to lay Jessemia on the ground, not roughly, and then they were off again, heading east.

CHAPTER NINETEEN

They didn't stop running until they were solidly in Gray district, on an anonymous street with very little traffic other than themselves. Aderyn leaned against a filthy building and sucked in air, her chest heaving painfully. "Should we have killed them?" she gasped.

"No good solution," Owen said. "Killing the leader of White faction would disrupt them enough to prevent them coming after us, but it would get Blue faction involved in a war, and Blue's leaders would want our heads. Leaving Liander alive maintains the status quo, but it means putting him in a position to strike at us again." He slid down the side of a building to sit on a crate that wasn't quite as broken as its neighbor. "I hope that was the right decision."

"You said it. We don't murder indiscriminately," Isold said. "Although in this case it would have been discriminating murder, but we all agree on the principle."

"All right, but now everything's become ten times harder," Livia said. "We have to avoid half the faction areas in this stupid city, we still know nothing about the memorial, and now White faction is after our heads."

"Try to be less optimistic, dearest," Weston said.

"You joke, but that *was* the optimistic version. I didn't mention how we have no allies, no one we can trust, and we still have to watch out for adventurers who have nothing to do with this mess but would still like to kill us for the experience."

Silence fell. Finally, Weston said, "So it will be hard. But is it too hard? Because Gamboling Coil is still outside, and I'm starting to think I'd rather take my chances with the sanguisuge."

Livia sighed. "I'm sorry."

"I'd rather we faced facts," Owen said. "Don't be sorry. But, now that we've established what's against us, we should evaluate our strengths. For one thing, I'm guessing there currently aren't many adventurers a lot higher level than us in Obsidian, if only because Liander would have hired them instead of the ones we killed. So that threat of others wanting to kill us for the experience is real, since even level twelve could be a threat, but it's not as serious a threat as Liander poses."

"And by that same reasoning," Aderyn said, "Liander isn't going to send any more teams to assassinate us. Which means that's not the threat we have to watch out for."

"At the risk of sounding pessimistic again," Livia said, "that only means we don't know what to watch out for, and we'll have to be extra vigilant. But we already knew that."

"In my opinion, we should pursue the information hidden in the memorial more diligently than we originally planned," Isold said. "It's the only thing keeping us here. Once we have Tarani's record, we can leave, regardless of anything Liander does."

"I agree," Owen said. "So let's go to the memorial and see what we can learn."

As if the sky knew their mood, the clouds rolled in as the companions crossed Gray district. They'd left the cobblestones behind and once more trudged through damp earth that just missed being mud thanks to the weak sunlight that at the moment had found a gap in the clouds. Aderyn breathed in deeply and wished she hadn't. Her previous day's theory about how bad Obsidian might smell when it wasn't raining came back to her, along with the nose-clenching smell of horse shit and urine. She breathed shallowly through her mouth until the stench faded into the background again.

Isold's pace slowed. "It's that one," he said. "My informant said it would be obvious. I understand why now."

He didn't point, but he didn't need to; there was only one building on the street that could be Tarani's memorial. For one thing, although it was one of the two-story buildings that elsewhere shared common walls with their neighbors, this one stood alone, with no other buildings closer than thirty feet away in any direction. For another, it was painted in shades of gray, its sides pale enough to be called dingy white, the cladding along its corners pewter, the hinged shutters thrown open beside its windows the color of the distant sea under clouds, and the slates of the roof charcoal. Five steps painted to match the shutters led up to the front door, which was stormcloud gray with pewter-colored trim.

The friends stopped on the corner some sixty feet from the house. "Well," Livia said. "I guess we know where her loyalties lay."

"I doubt she painted her house those colors," Owen said. "That does look like someone wanted to make Tarani's birth or allegiance clear, though."

"I'm intimidated," Aderyn said.

"You're not serious," Weston said. "It's just a house."

"I'm only mostly joking. Look at that place. Nobody's approaching it. It looks more like a shrine to a lost hero than anything anyone could enter."

"I agree with Aderyn," Isold said. "We will have to be cautious."

Aderyn glanced covertly at him. He hadn't sounded like he blamed her for nearly having gotten him killed. Guilt struck her, this time guilt that she hadn't properly apologized and made things right.

It wasn't the right time now, but with the monument right there, looming over them like doom personified, she couldn't help feeling she needed to make more of an effort to find the right time.

"Right," Owen said. "Then let's cautiously approach."

They stopped across the street under an overhang that didn't do much to shelter them. "I guess I'll take a look," Weston said. "Nobody's paying attention to anything beyond their feet and the pavement."

"Wait." Aderyn put a hand on his arm. "Let me see if [Improved Assess 2] tells us anything."

"It's not a dungeon," Livia said.

"Sure, but it doesn't hurt to look. It told me about the vines' weaknesses, right?" Aderyn focused on the memorial.

Name: Tarani's Memorial

Type: Questgiver

Available quests: [Defend Obsidian], [Divide and Conquer], [Fated One's Destiny: Discover the Path]

"That's so strange," Aderyn exclaimed. "I've never seen anything like it. It's got quests attached to it."

"I thought quests were only available from people or from the system," Owen said.

"So did I. Let me see if I can learn more." Aderyn selected the first quest, **[Defend Obsidian]**, and a message appeared.

Obsidian's position far from civilization leaves it open to attacks by monsters. This quest rewards those who successfully defend the city from such attacks over a period of seven days. This quest is repeatable. Reward: an additional 50% of the total XP gained from defeating enemies during this seven-day period.
Accept? Y / N

Aderyn selected N. "The first one doesn't apply to us, unless we want to hang around here killing monsters for a week." She moved on to **[Divide and Conquer]**.

> **Change the balance of power in Obsidian by bringing a new faction to preeminence. Reward: the XP reward varies commensurately with the power differential between the faction's beginning position and its final one.**
> **Accept? Y / N**

Aderyn shuddered and chose N again. "The second one is to disrupt the government by bringing a different faction into power."

"That sounds dangerous," Isold said. "And definitely not what we are interested in."

"I didn't think we cared about any but the final one, but I thought I should check. The last one is about the Fated One." Aderyn Assessed the last quest.

> **The adventurer Tarani left a record of her attempt to achieve the [Fated One's Destiny] quest chain. Retrieve the documents from her memorial to proceed.**
> **WARNING: This quest is only available to those who have accepted [Fated One's Destiny]. Accepting [Fated One's Destiny: Discover the Path] without having the previous quests in the quest chain will invalidate the quest. Repeated attempts to do so will result in XP penalties.**
> **Accept? Y / N**

Aderyn read the message aloud. "That worries me. I mean, the memorial's right there. How hard can it be? Which means there's something we don't know about."

"I'm more worried about how anyone who isn't a Warmaster is supposed to even be aware of the quest," Owen said. "I tried Assessing the memorial and got nothing."

"[Assess] improves over time for every class," Isold said. "I imagine at level fifteen or sixteen, we would be able to see it."

"Which means this quest is intended for high-level adventurers, not us," Livia said.

"We'll take it anyway," Owen declared. "We've come this far and done things no one believed possible at our level. I'm not saying we should be cocky, but we can at least try."

Aderyn selected Y and then, when prompted, set it as the primary quest. The quest shrank down to a golden dot just below and to the right of the first golden dot that indicated the [Fated One's Destiny] quest.

"Did [Improved Assess 2] show anything else? Any weaknesses?" Owen asked.

Aderyn shook her head. "I think we may have to take the direct approach."

"I'll see if there are any traps on the door," Weston said. "Maybe this will be simple, after all."

"Didn't I tell you not to say things like that?" Livia said.

Weston grinned at her. "You did, but I'm willing to risk a little optimism." He pulled his hood higher so it shielded his face and strode away, not toward the memorial, but down the street to the left and around a corner. Aderyn snugged her coat closer around her body and waited.

In less than a minute, Weston reappeared. He walked rapidly, just like everyone else on their way to shelter, and he kept his head bowed low so he looked as inattentive as the other pedestrians. Then, when he came even with the memorial, he veered and just as rapidly bounded up the five steps to the door. His body shielded whatever he was doing from anyone on the street.

Aderyn held her breath as two men wearing oiled rain capes and carrying swords approached from the other direction. They were having a conversation, gesturing broadly as if making points to each other, and they looked more alert than anyone else Aderyn had seen.

But they only glanced once at Weston's broad back before continuing on. Then Aderyn noticed their bright orange armbands and relaxed. Adventurers from Orange faction. They might not know the significance of Tarani's memorial, either what it meant historically or its secret contents, and they obviously didn't realize there was anything strange about someone standing on its doorstep in the rain. As the unseen clock tolled four, the adventurers paused, looking around for the source of the noise, and then continued on their way.

As the echoes of the peal faded, Weston glanced around, managing to make the motion look casual. When the Orange adventurers had passed by, he beckoned to the others. Aderyn hesitated. Nobody seemed to be watching, but she still had a feeling like they were doing something wrong in approaching the memorial, something they could get in trouble for. But Owen was already heading across the street, and Aderyn hurried to catch up. Maybe they'd find trouble, but at least they could find it together.

Weston was staring at the door, his brow furrowed. "It's painted on," he said.

"What do you mean, painted on?" Owen said. He touched the gray upright of the door frame.

"I mean just that. It's one of those illusions, not a magical illusion, but a trick of the eye. I've seen it done before, but never for something practical like a door. It was always art." Weston continued to glare at the painted illusion as if that would transmute it to a real door he could batter down.

"So... what does that mean?" Aderyn asked. "Is there a secret way in? Like, does the fake door conceal a real door?"

"No. Not only is the door fake, I can't find any evidence that this is anything but an ordinary wall."

"Let's circle around," Owen said. "Unless Isold's information is wrong—"

"Unlikely," Isold said. "And I say that not out of arrogance, but because my information about the memorial comes from multiple sources, all of which are in agreement. If they're all wrong, we have a much bigger problem, namely that Tarani's memorial isn't what we hoped."

"Right. So we know they turned Tarani's house into the memorial. They didn't tear it down and build a house-shaped box of solid wood. Which means there has to be a way in."

Livia hissed. "I can use *clairvoyance* to see what's inside. I can't believe that didn't occur to me before."

They all shuffled around on the steps to give Livia access to the wall. Aderyn, standing at the foot of the steps, turned her back casually on the rest of them and leaned against the rail, watching the street. As before, everyone passing had hoods up against the increasing wind that blew occasional spatters of rain against Aderyn's cheeks. She pretended nonchalance, though her heart was hammering. Livia was taking forever, they were all standing out in the open, and all it would take would be the wrong person seeing them.

Someone came around the corner where they'd stood moments before, dressed like everyone else in rain cape and warm trousers. Aderyn's gaze slid over him and then jerked back. The man had stopped and was looking in their direction. One hand rested on a club threaded through his belt, shifting the cape aside enough that Aderyn could see the chain mail shirt he wore beneath it. Warning bells rang through her head, and she Level Assessed him quickly.

Name: Birch

Class: Stalwart

Level: 10

"Someone's coming," she said. The Stalwart's pause had been only long enough for someone to Assess five people, and now he was crossing the street, not quite running, but moving with intent. "He's definitely after us. We need to run."

CHAPTER TWENTY

Owen followed the line of Aderyn's gaze. "Well, crap," he said. "It's too late to run. Guess we have to brazen this out."

"Maybe he's just curious," Weston said. "Livia, do you see anything?"

"It's dark inside, but it's the darkness of an unlit, windowless room, not the kind of dark where it's a solid object." Livia stepped back from the wall and turned around, leaning casually against the fake door.

The Stalwart, Birch, slowed his pace as he approached. He wasn't built the way Aderyn expected a Stalwart to look; he was heavyset and muscular, but shorter than Owen, and his hands were slimmer than the rest of him, with long fingers and short nails bitten nearly to the quick. He immediately focused on Livia. "Stand up straight, and show some respect for the memorial."

"Sorry," Livia said, immediately straightening. "I wasn't thinking."

"What are the lot of you doing? Don't you know approaching

Tarani's memorial is forbidden to anyone not of the Gray faction?"
Birch didn't sound angry or hostile, but his hand remained on the
club and he spoke like someone in authority.

"We didn't, sorry," Owen said. "It wasn't in the lecture."

"That's no excuse. You should have the decency to familiarize
yourselves with our customs."

"Well, now we know, and we'll be going."

Owen took a few steps, stopping when Birch didn't move out of
his way. "That's not good enough," the Stalwart said. "You'll have to
come with me."

"We apologized. There's nothing more to say," Owen said.

"There's a two hundred gold fine for interfering with the memorial. I'm guessing that wasn't in the lecture, either." Birch smirked.
"Right this way."

"You plan on making us go?" Weston said in his deepest, most
intimidating voice.

The short Stalwart looked Weston up and down and didn't seem
impressed. "You won't fight me if you know what's good for you," he
said. "Otherwise all of Gray faction will be on the lookout for you,
and you'll have more to worry about than a fine."

Isold stepped past Weston and held up a hand. "Now, there's no
need to argue," he said, his voice low and throbbing. "We meant no
disrespect, and of course we don't want to be in violation of law or
custom."

"See? He's sensible. Listen to your friend," Birch sneered.

"But this really was a misunderstanding," Isold went on, the
harmonics of [Persuasion] making his voice more beautiful than
ever. "We were carried away by our excitement at being so close to
such an important piece of history. You understand, of course. I can
see you've felt that way before."

Birch's sneer faded. "That's true. The memorial is unique."

"So I don't think we need to pay a fine, given that it was an honest mistake we won't repeat," Isold went on. A pulsing thrum joined the low, persuasive sound. "In fact, you should go back to your home, secure in the knowledge that you've taught five new people the importance of Tarani's legacy."

Aderyn held her breath. [Suggestion] was powerful, but the higher level the person it was used on, the greater the chance the victim would just ignore it—or, worse, shrug it off and attack Isold for trying to manipulate him.

Birch stared at Isold with a look of dawning realization. "I did, didn't I?" he said. He clapped Isold companionably on the shoulder. "Make sure you let everyone you meet know how important the memorial is. Wouldn't want anyone disrespecting it." He smiled broadly and strode off down the street.

Aderyn let out her breath in a great whoosh of air. "That was brilliant," she said, for once not remembering that she'd nearly gotten Isold killed with her timidity.

"Let's go. Quickly. He'll eventually realize what he's done," Isold said.

"I thought anyone you used [Suggestion] on didn't suspect it if it was successful," Owen said as they hurried down the street in the opposite direction to what Birch had taken.

"[Suggestion], yes," Isold said, "but [Persuasion] only lasts so long before the victim sees the discrepancy between what they intended and what [Persuasion] convinced them to do. I'm sure we have an hour, though." Isold frowned. "Unless he meets someone who knows he behaved unusually and brings it to his attention. In which case—"

"Let's run," Owen suggested.

The cloud cover grew denser as they retraced their steps to Blue district. The air felt heavy, waterlogged and too-warm in the way of some storms. Aderyn's coat weighed on her, still damp from the earlier rainfall, its thick padding no longer welcome. She reminded herself that she would be grateful for it once the rains fell again and trudged on behind Owen.

By the time they made their way the long way around through Red district, the clock had tolled once more and the clouds had darkened as the invisible sun sank lower in the sky. "Livia, what time is it?" Owen asked. "How long after five?"

Livia checked her pocket watch. "5:47. We're going to miss our gracious hostess's mealtime."

"I'm not sure I care," Owen said, "but let's hurry anyway. If we're late, we'll find somewhere else to eat."

They picked up the pace, not quite running, until they came around the corner onto the dead end street where the hostel lay. Owen came to a stop. "What's going on there?"

A group of armed men, all wearing blue shirts beneath hardened leather jerkins, stood at ease in front of the Blue Tern's front door. One of them noticed the friends and jerked to attention. They were too far away for Aderyn to hear words, but she saw the man's lips move, and gradually every one of the eight armed men stopped milling about and focused their attention on her and her friends.

"We should run," Isold said. "That can't be good."

"Where would we run to?" Owen pointed out. "If they're not after us, we have nothing to worry about, and if they are for some reason intent on rousting us, running will only postpone whatever they have in mind." He strode forward.

Aderyn held back to Assess the men. Most of them were low-level Swordsworn and Staffsworn, no higher than level five, though one was a Swifthands and two were non-classed. That struck her as odd, but Owen had nearly reached the group and she ran to join him.

"You're the level ten adventurers who entered Obsidian yesterday just before noon?" the Staffsworn at the front of the pack asked.

"We are," Owen said.

The Staffsworn squared his shoulders. "You will come with us to answer the charges against you."

"And what charges are those?" Owen asked. Though he sounded unconcerned about the possible threat the Blue faction fighters posed, his back was tense and his hand drifted to his sword hilt.

The Staffsworn noticed the motion. "Attacking us will constitute proof of guilt. Throw down your weapons."

"I just want to know what we're accused of," Owen replied. "Surely that's not a secret?"

"You know what you did." The Staffsworn's grip on his weapon tightened. "No more talk. You're coming with us. Come quietly, and our master will take that into account."

Owen didn't budge. "We've been in Obsidian barely a day and a half. We haven't committed any crimes, unless Obsidian has laws we're not aware of. Tell us the charges against us, and I swear we won't fight you."

"You're a nervy bastard," the Staffsworn sneered. "All right. You five are accused of murder."

"What?" Weston exclaimed. "Murder? Of who?"

"Still playing dumb, huh?" The Staffsworn pointed his staff at Weston. "You know you killed Rupart, the Gray faction's second in command. You've tangled our master up in a faction war."

"When was this?" Owen asked.

"I said no more questions." The Staffsworn stepped closer to Owen and pressed the steel-shod tip of his staff beneath Owen's chin. "Surrender your weapons and come with me. If you persist in pretending innocence, you can ask your questions when you're in custody."

Owen stared him down. Aderyn held her breath. Five against eight... but the eight were lower level, and the friends could take them easily. She watched Owen, waiting for his move.

Owen's hand went to his sword belt. "Okay. We'll come quietly."

"*Owen!*" Aderyn exclaimed.

"We haven't killed anyone in the factions, Aderyn, and we're not going to start with men who are doing their sworn duty."

Owen wrapped his sword belt around his <**Twinsword**> and handed it over. "And if we don't go with them, we can't untangle this mess."

It didn't take [**Read Body Language**] to see the Staffsworn relax out of his tense stance. "Very wise," he said. "You shouldn't mess with us. We're all experienced fighters."

"Of course you are," Owen said. "Come on, everyone, let's get this over with."

Aderyn gave her sword to one of the non-classed guards and glared at him when he leered at her. Next to her, Livia gave the Staffsworn leader her belt knife. "That's the only weapon I have," she said.

"You're an Earthbreaker. You should submit to being gagged so you can't cast spells," the Staffsworn said.

Weston growled and took a step toward the man, who cringed.

Livia put a hand on Weston's arm. "If I was going to cast spells to get us out of this, you'd already be dead," she told the Staffsworn. "And if you lay a hand on me, we're going to see whether I can entomb you faster than this one can tear your arm off and beat you to death with it."

"Livia, you're not helping," Owen said, his hand pressed to his mouth to conceal a smile.

"They've got orders to bring us in instead of killing us outright, Owen, which they could do without repercussions because we're of the same faction." Livia stared down the Staffsworn, who now looked a little green around the lips. "Something else is going on here. And I'm guessing these eight know their deaths could be the outcome if they piss us off enough."

"Yes, but threatening someone with a choice between a living burial or dismemberment..."

Livia smiled, a nasty expression that boded ill for the Staffsworn. "He knows neither of those things will happen, because he's not going to attempt to subdue me. Am I right?"

The Staffsworn nodded, his expression mingled fear and fury.

"Move along, the lot of you," he said. He prodded Owen in the back with the tip of his staff.

Owen turned, slowly, and fixed the Staffsworn with a look that had burning steel behind it. "You forget we don't know this city or where Blue faction's headquarters is. And... don't do that again unless you feel like eating that staff."

Aderyn snorted with laughter and made it sound like a cough. The Staffsworn withdrew his weapon abruptly. "Form up, and move out," he commanded, and strode away at the head of their little procession, the five friends surrounded by Blue guards. Aderyn realized they each had their own minder, with the two remaining guards bringing up the rear carrying the team's weapons. She wasn't enough of a fighter to do anything with this information, but she Assessed the non-classed fighter guarding her anyway and got a list of traits: stubborn, practical, cunning, willful. She tucked those away mentally for possible future use.

Aderyn had never wished so badly to be able to share thoughts with Owen. None of this made sense to her. Tactics on a battlefield, that she understood, but political maneuverings always left her feeling like she was missing key parts of a fiendishly difficult puzzle. It hadn't occurred to her, for example, that there was something strange about the Blue faction leader capturing them rather than having them all killed for embroiling him in a war. In fact, maybe offering up the heads of the ones who'd started the conflict was the fastest way to end it. So sending guards to bring them in instead of killing them made no sense.

What she *did* know was that they'd been set up, which meant Liander had struck at them. It was too big a coincidence otherwise. They hadn't been in Obsidian long enough to make more than one enemy.

Liander's plan was simple. He had this Rupart of the Gray faction killed and made it look like Aderyn and her friends as members of Blue faction had done it. Then Gray faction turned on

Blue faction in general and Aderyn's team in specific, and Blue faction got angry at these random adventurers who'd tangled them up in a war. Liander didn't have to kill the friends himself. He could get others to implement his revenge instead. And they'd all be dead regardless of which of the three wielded the knife. Aderyn could almost admire Liander's twisted plan. Almost.

CHAPTER TWENTY-ONE

Aderyn watched their route carefully, memorizing it although she didn't know why they'd need to find their way back to the Blue Tern in a hurry. More likely they'd be running for the gate if it came to fleeing for their lives. Aside from the blue-banded lampposts, the streets looked exactly as they did everywhere else in Obsidian. This struck her as absurd. Drop someone down anywhere in Obsidian and they would only be able to tell their location from the colored bands, not from unique architectural differences or smells or the number of people on the street.

Though there did seem to be more people than usual out and about, probably because it was dinnertime. Aderyn's stomach grumbled at the delicious smells wafting from every third doorway. Taverns, inns, or private homes, all of them advertised their cooking skills. It made the Blue Tern's humble offerings seem even less appetizing.

The Staffsworn led the way through narrow streets that grew wider as they approached what Aderyn assumed was the center of Blue district. Like Red and White districts, the houses here were taller and broader, with grassy lawns or hedges or rows of small trees dividing the properties. But there were differences, Aderyn noticed as she scanned the buildings and the streets looking for an escape route if that became necessary. None of them were as large as the mansions in White district, for one, and Liander's giant monstrosity of a house would have swallowed two of Blue district's largest buildings with room for stables and outbuildings for dessert. They were also plainer, without the elaborate carved eaves or fluted pillars of Red district or the marble facing most of White district boasted.

She looked up at the eaves of one of the mansions. An abandoned bird's nest perched at the corner where two rain gutters met. That couldn't be a smart place for a bird to build a nest, not with how rainy Obsidian was. It might be the reason the nest was abandoned. Just then, it seemed like an omen: their team was square at the intersection between Gray and Blue factions, with a deluge pouring toward them from both directions. Too bad fleeing wasn't an option.

Owen walked in front of her, looking fearless and unconcerned. She hoped he had a plan that would get them all out safely. At the moment, Aderyn felt as pessimistic as Livia: Liander was powerful, and whatever evidence he'd manufactured would be compelling. And Blue faction didn't care anything about them to defend them against Gray faction, who would want them dead. Maybe the Staffsworn and his gang were more important than Aderyn thought, if their presence would keep the Gray partisans off her team's backs. Aderyn considered this and then discarded the notion as improbable.

Eventually, the Staffsworn left the street for a path leading up to the front door of a mansion no different from the others. But he didn't walk to the front door. Instead, he followed a branch of the path around to the back of the house, down a short flight of stairs that put the top of his head even with the ground, to a narrower door of plain wood. He rapped on the door with the steel-shod tip of his staff, three quick knocks, and waited.

After a few seconds, a series of locks ground open, and the door swung inward a few inches. "Inside," a gravelly-voiced woman said.

The Staffsworn pushed the door open fully and stood aside for the others to enter. Aderyn's escort nudged her, not hard enough to be a shove, and she decided not to fight him.

She followed Owen into a darkened space lit only by indirect light coming from two other rooms on either side of the hall. The woman who met them had heavy eyebrows that made her look angry and resentful, or maybe she actually was angry and resentful and Aderyn had picked up on that. She wore a blue kerchief wrapped around her thick black hair and a white apron stained with the remains of a thousand dinners.

"Where's Kemper?" the Staffsworn asked.

"Taking a leak," the woman said. "You caught him with his trousers down." She smiled, not a nice expression. "Is that the bastards? You're to take them to the reception hall at once."

Aderyn Assessed the woman out of curiosity.

Name: Ferenna

Traits: suspicious, loyal, skilled, sly

Ferenna didn't hold herself like someone who felt inferior for not having a class. She certainly didn't look as if the Staffsworn intimidated her at all. The Staffsworn, for his part, looked like he was keeping out of her reach, though she was unarmed and couldn't have given him a fight if she was. He nodded curtly and walked on down the hall.

Stairs at the far end, barely wide enough for a single person to climb comfortably, led up out of the bowels of the mansion to a hall only a little wider than the stairs. Aderyn had seen very few large houses in her life, but comparing it to what she'd seen of Liander's mansion, she suspected these were servants' quarters. They smelled of polish and cleanser and very faintly of soot.

The Staffsworn was already out of sight around a corner. When Aderyn's minder prodded her in that direction, she discovered yet another door, a plain rectangle of wood that needed a good whitewashing. It stood open, letting in cooler air currents that weren't strong enough to be a breeze but still were palpably different from the close, smelly air of the servants' corridor.

Aderyn followed Owen through the door and stopped, astonished. The rest of the mansion couldn't compare to Liander's hulk of a house, but this room was half again as big as Liander's stained glass chamber and another twenty feet taller. It was completely empty save for the five of them and the Blue guards and echoed with the sounds of boots on the wooden floor. Aderyn found the floor fascinating, with how thousands of short planks of varying shades of wood were arranged to make geometric patterns, wheels connecting to wheels in a dizzying array. The room was chilly by comparison to the hall, and despite her heavy coat, Aderyn shivered.

She looked back as the door closed almost without a sound. From this side, it blended perfectly with the pale green walls, barely visible as a rectangular outline. Another, more obvious door looked like it took its job of guarding this chamber very seriously; it was of red oak, banded with iron, and had two iron rings below the latch for someone to pull the door open. The Staffsworn was doing this now. "Wait here, and don't touch anything," he commanded.

"There's nothing to touch," Owen pointed out.

"Though I want to rub my face against the walls now you've said something," Weston added.

The Staffsworn scowled and slammed the door shut behind him, or tried to; the door moved like a big man after a heavy meal, and he only succeeded in sending up a chill breeze and making himself look ridiculous. Leaving the door half open, he walked away, his footsteps gradually fading with distance.

Owen immediately turned on the two guards carrying the friends' weapons. "I don't suppose we get those back now?"

The guards stepped back. One of them swallowed nervously, making the prominent knot in his throat bob up and down.

"No talking," Owen's minder said.

"Oh, come on," Owen said. "The guy with the staff up his ass is gone. Who's going to know? Besides, just standing here silently is boring. What's your name?"

Owen's minder, a Swordsworn, said nothing.

"I mean, I Assessed you, and I know your name, but it's polite to let someone introduce himself, right? I'll go first. I'm Owen."

Aderyn watched this exchange, mystified. Owen couldn't think being nice to the guards would get them out of this, could he?

Owen's minder shifted. His eyes moved as he searched for help among his comrades and found nothing. "Tarlis," he finally said.

"Tarlis, hi. I don't suppose you can tell us more about what happened? Our supposed crime?"

"Shut up," the Swifthands said. "You think Lord Seburtan will be gentle with us if we give things away to criminals?"

"Lord Seburtan is the Blue faction leader?" Owen asked. "And we're supposed to have killed Rupart of the Gray faction, embroiling this lord in a factional fight. Maybe a war."

"Don't pretend this is all new to you," the Swifthands snarled. "Think you can come into our city, pretend to take on faction loyalties, and use that protection to kill someone?"

"I see." Owen didn't protest that none of that was true. Aderyn opened her mouth to do it for him, and he shot her a glance that said clearly *Don't argue, stay quiet*. If Owen had a plan, it wasn't something he could reveal with their enemies there, not even with **[Read Body Language]**. Aderyn controlled her impatience.

"Who's the leader of Gray faction?" Owen asked.

"Stop talking," said the Swifthands. "You're trying to trick us."

"Trick you how?" Owen asked. "I'm just asking questions."

"Asking questions is not your prerogative," someone said from the doorway. "You're lucky I didn't have you all killed. Speaking of prerogative."

The man in the doorway wore a heavy fur robe whose apparent warmth Aderyn was envious of, over which hung a gold medallion engraved with something she was too far away to see. Short dark hair thinning on the top lay tousled across his scalp as if he'd just risen, and his fur robe, on second glance, didn't look as if it had been made for him, the hem dragging on the floor and the long sleeves nearly engulfing his hands.

"Lord Seburtan," Owen said. "Why *didn't* you try to have us killed?"

Seburtan's lips quirked up at the corners. "Try?"

"I guarantee we wouldn't go easy on anyone you sent," Owen said. "Let me guess. You don't have anyone available, either among your permanent employees or on retainer, who is high enough level to be a threat to us. That means you had to find another way of neutralizing us."

The smile deepened. "You're a little too clever for your own good, young man," Seburtan said, and snapped his fingers.

Two more nearly-invisible doors sprang open, and armed men and women poured through. Aderyn automatically Assessed them. No one higher than level six, but there were acres of them, more than thirty, possibly more than forty. Aderyn gave up counting and realized she'd reflexively stepped closer to Owen.

"You're right, my retainers are lower level," Seburtan said when the flow had stopped and the room was more than half full of people. "But there are many of them, and you wouldn't escape unscathed, if you escaped at all. Have I made my point?"

"You have, my lord," Owen said, still not sounding afraid. "And now that we've established how much power you have, tell me why you didn't use it."

Seburtan advanced into the room, gesturing with one elegant hand so the fighters moved out of his path. Aderyn Level Assessed him quickly, hoping not to miss too much of the conversation in her distraction.

Name: Seburtan

∞ Vessa

Class: Spiritsmith (retired)

Level: 9

"...think I won't still exercise that option?" Seburtan was saying when Aderyn dragged her attention back to the chamber and the lord.

"Because you've gone to a lot of trouble to avoid it, and I would still like to know why," Owen said.

Seburtan paced forward, appearing to glide across the wonderful wooden floor thanks to the dragging hem of his coat. He stopped just outside lunging range if Owen decided to attack with his bare hands. "I want to know," he said, his voice slow and contemplative, "why Liander of the White set you up to take the blame for Rupart's murder. Given that you're Liander's allies."

Chapter Twenty-Two

"We are not!" Aderyn protested.

Owen raised a hand that to everyone else meant he was asking for silence. To Aderyn, it carried the further message *Save your outrage for if these people attack.* "What makes you think we're his allies?"

"I watch every adventurer who comes to Obsidian and takes my faction's aegis." Seburtan still spoke slowly, as if he was thinking about each word individually and the impact it would make. "My agent observed you leaving Liander's estate and hurrying to Gray district, clearly intent on an errand for your master."

"Your agent didn't see what happened inside Liander's house, or they wouldn't have drawn those conclusions."

"Why would newcomers to the city attend on Liander unless they meant to hire out to him?" Seburtan now sounded as if this was the most reasonable thing in the world. Aderyn clenched down hard on her back teeth to keep from bursting out with another denial.

"Liander wanted something from us. We refused. And then we got as far away from him as we could." Owen sounded as reasonable as Seburtan. "And if your agent was watching us, you know we didn't kill Rupart."

"As it happens, that's true." Seburtan's eyes narrowed. "I can only conclude that you were paid well to be the sacrifices for Liander's plot to embroil Blue and Gray factions in a war he would benefit from. He knew you strangers to the city couldn't reach Rupart, so he had his own man secretly do it and lay evidence it was you."

Weston shifted his weight. Seburtan's gaze immediately focused on him. "Don't make me remind you of the consequences of attacking me, big man."

"I wouldn't attack you," Weston said. "But you're out of your mind. How is this plot you've concocted the only reasonable possibility?"

"You're new to Obsidian, and you're fools, given that you were willing to accept Liander's offer," Seburtan said. "No one in power sleeps quietly here. We are all looking for ways to best one another—and watching carefully for signs that some other faction leader intends to move in on our position. Hiring visiting adventurers as assassins or stooges is common."

He took another step closer to Owen. "But you didn't kill Rupart," he said, again with that air of distracted contemplation. "I was informed that adventurers matching your description had done so, and if I hadn't had my own people watching you, I would have believed it."

"Then you ought to realize we aren't Liander's pawns," Owen said.

"I only realize that Liander might be playing a deep game," Seburtan replied.

Owen said nothing. He crossed his arms over his chest, tightening his shoulder muscles. Aderyn, from behind him, saw the clear message *Someone's going to die here.*

Seburtan raised both eyebrows. "Well? Not going to deny it?"

"You've made up your mind. There's no point." Owen said. "Now, are you going to give us back our weapons so this can be a somewhat fair fight, or are you going to order your minions to kill unarmed prisoners?"

"Bold words." Seburtan regarded Owen for a moment longer. "I admire that. And, in truth, I've been in power for seven years and even I can't figure out how the events in question might be Liander's plot. In fact, it's far more reasonable that it's *you* Liander is angry with and wants eliminated."

Owen's shoulders relaxed. "That's right."

"He made you an offer, and you refused. No. Mere refusal is part of the game, and no faction lord would hold it against you. Either you refused to do something he had his heart set on, something he couldn't accomplish without the five of you personally, or you refused in a way that humiliated him so he's now after retribution."

"Would you believe, both?" Owen said.

Seburtan's eyebrows rose nearly to his hairline. "Really," he said, once more in that contemplative way. "Then you're stupider than I gave you credit for. Or just ignorant. No one pisses off an Obsidian faction lord if they want to live to see the next morning."

"We weren't going to agree to his plan," Owen said. "The humiliation was a side effect of getting out of his house alive."

"I see." Seburtan gestured, and every armed man in the room relaxed his stance. "Come with me. I'd like to hear the story, and there's no point keeping you uncomfortable."

Owen didn't move. "I'd like our weapons returned, then. Since you're so concerned about our comfort."

Seburtan gave him another narrow-eyed stare. "When you leave," he said. "I assume you're not actually stupid. Neither am I. Nobody but my own trusted men go armed in my presence. You understand."

Aderyn couldn't help glancing at Livia, who looked perfectly at ease. Seburtan hadn't shown any interest in her, though if he'd Assessed them, he knew she was a spellslinger. Whatever Seburtan had in mind, he wasn't actually concerned about being attacked.

"Fine. Lead the way," Owen said.

He made as if to follow Seburtan, but drew up short when two men armed with swords inserted themselves between him and their lord. "I'm also not so stupid as to leave potential enemies immediately at my back," Seburtan said without turning around. "Don't think that just because I believe your version of events I consider you allies yet."

"Understood," Owen said, the word sounding tight and pained as if Owen was reaching the limits of his patience. Aderyn had already passed the limits of hers, but she could control herself until Owen indicated it was time to attack.

She followed Owen, ignoring the guards who paced them, out of the chamber and into a hall wider than the first, half-paneled in some aromatic wood she didn't recognize. Strips of wood carved with roses decorated the walls at waist height, and above that border murals of sun-drenched hills dotted with trees rose. The detail was almost perfectly real, like the door to Tarani's memorial, and that made Aderyn uncomfortable, as if she was seeing into a world not quite like her own. She glanced away from a pair of deer drinking at a forest pool, unsettling in their near-perfection. It wasn't hard to imagine them stepping out of the mural to stand before her, beautiful and subtly wrong.

Just down the hall, a couple of women wearing the same blue shirts as the guards stood like sentinel statues flanking another double door the same size as the first. As Seburtan approached, each woman opened her half of the door, walking awkwardly into the room beyond as they tried not to turn their backs on Seburtan. It looked more like respect than fear, especially when Seburtan passed through the doorway and the women bowed.

Aderyn expected another austere, mostly empty room. Instead, it was a library, with a fire burning in the grate that kept the chill at bay. One window let in dreary gray light through small glass panes set in an iron grid; the other walls were lined with bookcases, none of them very full. Even so, Aderyn judged Seburtan's library contained at least three times as many books as did her parents'.

Seburtan seated himself behind a desk positioned to catch the light from the window and waved a hand at the room in general. "Sit anywhere," he said. "Lieutenant, you're free to go. Make sure my, ah, guests' weapons are stored somewhere safe for when they leave, and post two guards outside this room."

The lieutenant, a burly man who looked like he might be able to give Weston a real workout, hesitated, his gaze falling on Owen.

"Lieutenant, did I stutter? Or are you perhaps having hearing difficulties?" Seburtan smiled as if it was a joke, but Aderyn could see his eyes, and there was no humor in them.

"No, my lord. I apologize, my lord." The lieutenant bowed and retreated, pulling both halves of the door closed behind him. Aderyn didn't hear the latch engage and, when she looked, saw a hair-fine crack indicating the door was ajar.

Seburtan either didn't notice or didn't care. Possibly he wanted the door open enough that the guards would come if he shouted. He leaned back in his chair and rested his hands, the fingers interlaced, on the desk. "So. You refused Liander and made that refusal personal. I'm interested in knowing the details."

"To what end?" Owen asked. "Shouldn't we worry that *you* intend to use us the way Liander did?"

"I have my own ways of dealing with this mess. I don't need to hire you lot." Seburtan flexed his fingers once and then stilled them. "But knowing what really happened will help me. Call it an exchange for me not having had you killed out of hand."

Owen slowly lowered himself into a highbacked chair upholstered in highly textured brown leather. "I assume you know that Liander's daughter Jessemia believes she's the Fated One."

Seburtan rolled his eyes. "I know Liander has been abusing the system to accelerate her leveling. Crippling her as an adventurer, of course, but he's no adventurer and I doubt anyone in his employ has enough of a death wish to tell him that."

Weston cleared his throat. Seburtan's gaze snapped to him. "You did? No wonder he's angry. Liander doesn't accept criticism."

"That wasn't it," Owen said. "He wanted us to take Jessemia into our team and participate in his scheme. We turned him down."

"As I said, that shouldn't have been enough for him to turn on you. What haven't you mentioned?"

Owen hesitated. "I'm the Fated One. *A* Fated One, if you want to be picky. Liander sent assassins after me because he eliminates anyone who challenges Jessemia for the title."

"I see." Seburtan looked Owen up and down. "I can't say your destiny is obvious on the outside, but there's nothing stopping someone from declaring he's the Fated One and trading on that identity. But to Liander, whether or not it's true is irrelevant. Any other claimant poses a threat to Jessemia's title, and must be eliminated. I'm guessing when he couldn't strongarm you, he attacked. How did you escape?"

"We took Jessemia hostage."

Seburtan choked, then covered his mouth as he coughed. Gradually, the coughs turned into laughter. "Oh, you poor young man," he said when he got himself under control. "You should leave Obsidian now and hope you can get far, far away before Liander finds you."

"We're not leaving yet. We have business here," Owen said.

"What business is so important you'd risk your life for it?"

Owen stared him down. "Private business. And that's not information you've earned."

"Fair enough, fair enough." Seburtan waved his words away. "Well. That certainly clears things up. Though in another sense, your information does nothing to help me stop this disaster. I can't exactly go to Eleora of Gray faction and ask her to take my word that my people didn't kill her lover, proof or no."

"What are the consequences of a faction war?" Owen asked. "I mean, say we really had killed Rupart. What would that mean?"

"If you'd done it without my approval, I'd send Eleora your heads in a large sack," Seburtan said. "Along with a smaller, heavier sack of gold coins as reparations. If I'd hired you to do it, well, that's different. We use adventurers to carry out our plans sometimes. They're better armed and better skilled than our retainers, except for Black faction. Depending on my choice of target, that would send my enemy a certain message. A warning, perhaps, or the elimination of someone my enemy relies on."

"Does that mean Eleora—"

"That's Lady Eleora to you."

"Fine. Does that mean Lady Eleora assumes something about your intentions from who you supposedly killed? Or is she waiting on a message from you?"

"I—" Seburtan paused. "That's something I hadn't considered. Since I didn't order Rupart killed, I didn't follow his death up with an ultimatum or warning. I've been preoccupied with figuring out what Liander intends. My assumption was that he wanted to stir up trouble between Blue and Gray to give White a better position to attack one or both of us."

"So what will Lady Eleora do next?" Owen leaned forward like he wanted his peripheral vision to be clear and unimpeded by the sides of his chair.

"One moment," Seburtan said. "I need to send word to Eleora. She won't believe me if I say we've both been manipulated, so I'll tell her... I'll tell her rogue adventurers acting without my permission killed Rupart and I'm searching for them to turn them over to her."

"You said you believed us!" Aderyn exclaimed.

"Calm down, young woman. This is a stalling tactic." Seburtan drew paper out of a desk drawer and wrote a few lines with a quill pen in blue ink. Blue ink, Blue faction—if there was a connection, then Aderyn thought it was, as Owen liked to say, cheesy. Seburtan waved the paper in the air to dry the ink and then left the room, closing the door firmly behind him.

CHAPTER TWENTY-THREE

"Well, what in thunder do we do now?" Livia exclaimed. She sounded as if she'd been holding in an outburst for half an hour. "He doesn't owe us anything. Maybe he won't tie us up and send us to this Eleora's door, but at some point he's going to realize cutting us loose to fend for ourselves is the best option for him. And then we'll have all of Gray faction and half of Blue coming after our heads."

"I know," Owen said. "We have to figure out how we can prove we didn't kill Rupart. Better if we can prove Liander was behind it. Damn, I wish I knew more about these stupid factions. If we knew where Blue and Gray and White all stand compared to each other, that would be something."

"I'd say we should set Liander up the way he did us, but we don't have the resources for that," Weston said.

"But how can we prove anything?" Aderyn said. "We'd need a witness to say what happened in Liander's mansion, and nobody who was there is disloyal to their master to the point of testifying on our behalf."

"Even if we had that kind of witness, all that proves is that we didn't take Liander's offer," Livia said. "Whatever evidence shows us killing Rupart doesn't disappear, and we're back to this Eleora woman being out for our blood."

"We need a witness that puts us elsewhere when Rupart was killed, then," Aderyn said. "Seburtan's man can prove it, but with Blue faction apparently responsible, Eleora won't believe him. So we're screwed either way."

She watched Owen, who sat with both hands gripping his chair's armrests and his head bowed so his blond hair, finally long enough to look normal, fell forward to obscure his face. "You have an idea," she said. "Owen, what do we do?"

"It depends on when Rupart was murdered." Owen raised his head and stared blindly at the window. "We met with Liander at around one o'clock. It was nearly six when we arrived at the Blue Tern to find Seburtan's men waiting for us. Subtract an hour on either side for putting the plot in motion and for Seburtan to learn about it from Eleora so he could send those men. So, call it a three-hour window during which Rupart was killed. Liander must have had something like this in mind for a while, if he was able to arrange an assassination so quickly."

"That's horrifying," Aderyn said. "But I'm not sure how it helps us."

"It means that if we can prove we were somewhere else during that three-hour window, we have an alibi. That's easier than trying to prove our every action over the course of a day." Owen sighed. "It's not much, I know."

"It's more direction than we had before," Weston said.

The door opened. "You're still here," Seburtan said, sounding surprised. "I thought you'd use my absence as an excuse to flee."

"Where can we flee to? We still have a task." Owen rose to face Seburtan. "Do you know when Rupart was killed? Exactly?"

"Not to the minute," Seburtan said. "I received Eleora's challenge at four-thirty p.m., so I assume no more than an hour before that. Is it important?"

"What were we doing at four-thirty this afternoon?" Owen asked the others.

"We were at the memorial," Aderyn said without thinking. She shot a glance at Seburtan to see if he felt this was an admission of guilt the way that Gray Stalwart, Birch, had.

"So you were in Gray district," Seburtan said. "That's not good for your alibi."

"But it is," Weston exclaimed. "Some Gray official, or guard, or something accosted us at the memorial right around four. He could prove we weren't in a position to kill Rupart, and El—Lady Eleora would accept the witness of one of her own."

"We'd have to find him, though," Livia said.

"Which means going into Gray district," Seburtan said. "You might as well deliver yourselves up for judgment immediately."

"You let us worry about that," Owen said. "If you're willing to write one more message, we'll deliver that and take our chances."

"A message like 'here are the criminals, do with them what you please'? Are you out of your mind?" Seburtan sounded genuinely concerned.

"We just need something that will get us through to Lady Eleora. I assume she'd want to see us killed in person rather than letting some flunky do it."

Seburtan shrugged. He seated himself and wrote another message in blue ink, showing its contents to Owen for approval. Owen nodded and took the piece of paper, tucking it away beneath his armor.

"Your weapons are at the front door," Seburtan said. "And I hope your deaths aren't too painful. I admire your nerve." He ran a finger down the length of the quill pen. "You know what? Come back here if Eleora doesn't kill you. I want to hear that story, too."

"What makes you think we'll survive?" Owen asked.

"Oh, I don't. Sorry. But you said you were the Fated One, and you laid a hand on Jessemia and managed not to get it cut off, so I'm thinking maybe you're not as doomed as I believe." Seburtan waved a hand languidly in the air. "Good luck."

None of their weapons had been damaged, and none were missing. They gathered outside Seburtan's front door, buckling things on in silence. Aderyn examined the street. It was thronged with people who had the look of men and women on their way to their dinners. Many of them gazed with interest at the five friends, but no one stopped to ask questions.

"We'll take off the armbands before we enter Gray district," Owen said. "We don't want to be obviously the Blue faction adventurers Eleora is after. Then we'll go back to the memorial and ask around, see if Birch is a fixture in that neighborhood. If not, then we'll expand our search until we find him. That's where my plan ends. I don't know how to compel him to speak on our behalf."

"Pardon me, but there's something I think you've all overlooked," Isold said. "Birch will by now realize that I used [Persuasion] on him. I doubt he'll be happy about that."

"That shouldn't change what he'll say, though. If anything, he might be more eager to reveal our interest in the memorial, if that might get us into trouble."

"I mean," Isold said, "that from Eleora's perspective, an unknown, possibly enemy Herald used his skills against one of her men to avoid the penalties of breaking one of Gray faction's laws. She might see that as an act of aggression. Meaning that we could find ourselves cleared of charges of murder only to be accused of magical manipulation instead—something of which we *are* guilty."

"But," Weston said, then fell silent.

In the silence, Isold added, "Maybe we should cut our losses and leave. Tarani's records are simply a shortcut to knowledge we can discover on our own, through research and questing. They aren't worth our lives."

Owen shook his head. "No," he said, "no, that's not right. Tarani's records aren't a shortcut, they represent us bypassing at least a year's worth of adventuring, during which we'll have ample opportunity to risk our lives, multiple times. Yes, this is a challenge, but I can't believe it's more dangerous than the alternative. But that means it can't be me calling the shots. We all have to agree. I say we take our chances with Gray faction. What do you all think?"

"I don't want to give up after coming all this way," Weston said.

"That's the sunk-cost fallacy, Weston," Owen said.

"Is it? Well, whatever you call it, we've endured plenty, and I'm willing to risk enduring more." Weston put an arm around Livia's shoulders. "And Livia agrees with me."

"Since when do you get to speak for me, you musclebound oaf?"

"Since you agreed I was the sensible one in this relationship."

"I would never do that. You have about as much common sense as a dandelion." Livia sighed. "But, as it happens, the musclebound oaf is right. I hate this city and its stupid factions and their stupider disagreements. Liander's an ass for dragging us into his politics, and there's no thundering way I'll let him or anyone else scare me into leaving."

"I don't like the idea of Liander getting away with murdering someone just to start a fight," Aderyn said. "Seburtan said it was Eleora's sweetheart, and just think how awful she must feel right now. But I think maybe this needs to be up to Isold. He's the one who would for sure be in trouble if Eleora takes offense at him using his skills against her man. Isold?"

"You know I won't force the rest of you to follow my whim," Isold said with a crooked smile. "But I do think this is a dangerous gamble."

"Then you want us to leave," Aderyn said, quashing her disappointment.

"Owen has a point that we wouldn't be leaving danger for safety," Isold said. "For all we know, the path to rediscovering Tarani's quests is far more dangerous than anything we face in Obsidian. I don't like our odds, but I don't think this cause is hopeless. So... I'm in."

"Okay," Owen said. "That's settled. Let's go."

"And hope we're not killed outright," Livia said.

They walked rapidly through Blue district as the sun dropped lower in the sky and the ever-present clouds gathered like they meant to chase it below the horizon. The temperature had dropped as well, making Aderyn once more grateful for her coat. Thunder occasionally rumbled, and the air smelled of rain as usual. Others on the streets made way for the friends, though Aderyn couldn't tell, thanks to how fast they were moving, whether it was fear or politeness that motivated them.

"We're going the wrong way," Weston said after a few minutes.

"No, we're going the *direct* way," Owen corrected him. "Through Orange district."

"That's not safe," Aderyn said, then blushed. "Like any of this is safe. But I thought we risked being attacked as outsiders if we entered a district that's at war."

"We do, but we're in danger of that everywhere, and the route through Orange is much shorter than going around through Red. It's a chance we'll have to take."

"I hope you're prepared for that chance to fail, because I think we're being followed," Weston said. "Don't anyone turn around."

Aderyn's heartrate sped up. "Are you sure? Who is it?"

"At least four on our trail. We're going too fast for me to Assess them. But they've been behind us for a full minute, acting like they've no interest in anything but dinner." Weston didn't look back. "Take the next right and stop at the first sign, whatever it is."

Owen nodded. He passed an orange-banded lamppost and turned right around a sharp corner that put them out of sight of anyone who might be following. The first sign, fifteen feet away, was a tailor's shop, closed for the night. The wooden plaque with a painted spool of thread rocked gently in the rising wind with a faint creak of iron chains.

Weston put his hands on Aderyn's shoulders and turned her to face the way they'd come. "We won't get more than a few seconds to Assess them if we want to go on pretending we don't know they're after us, so make the most of it."

Aderyn nodded. She wiped her sweaty palms on her coat. Behind her, the others struck up a loud conversation about how the tailor closed early, and they'd have to come back in the morning.

A handful of adventurers—armed and armored as they were, they couldn't be anything else—came around the corner and slowed their pace. There were five of them, three men, two women, but Aderyn didn't see anything else as **[Improved Assess 2]** filled her vision. She scanned the information without reading more than levels and classes. Names didn't matter.

"Let's just go get dinner, all right?" she exclaimed loudly. "It's not like this was a tailoring emergency." She strode down the street, away from the enemy adventurers, and waited for her friends to catch up before saying, "Level fifteen Swordsworn, level fourteen Spiritsmith, Staffsworn, and Flamecrafter, and level thirteen Lone Wolf. Please tell me we're outpacing them."

"They're hanging back," Weston said. "I think our boldness confused them."

"They might be the sort who want their prey aware of being hunted," Owen said. "You know, the thrill of knowing someone's afraid of you. But that won't keep them from attacking for long."

"Weston, do they act like they know this area?" Livia asked.

"Definitely. We'll need to stick to the main route or risk being trapped."

"No, we want a dead-end street, one they won't enter in a hurry for fear of having their ambush turned on them," Livia said. She was scanning the streets that crossed theirs, her eyes narrowed as if she could Assess them for their potential as escape routes.

"Turn left, then take the second right," Isold said, his eyes shifting as he examined the map the system showed him. "I'm guessing you want us *not* to lose them."

"Why not?" Aderyn asked.

"So I can *transport* us away and leave them scratching their heads and searching in all the wrong places," Livia said with a grin.

"They're still following," Weston said, "but they look like they're getting impatient."

"Almost there," Livia said.

Aderyn stopped trying to see over her shoulder without being obvious about it and focused on Owen, just ahead of her. The street Isold had indicated was less busy than the others, with a lot of shops closed for the night. None of them had windows at ground level, and only a few of the windows above were lit. Aderyn noticed in passing another tailor's shop, a general store, a seamstress's establishment—was it just her, or did Obsidian have a lot of shops relating to mending or sewing clothing?

She followed the others around the corner of the second right. Livia had stopped about ten feet in and beckoned to them all to huddle together. "For once it won't matter if I make noise," she said, and rattled off a long string of syllables that sounded like boulders rolling downhill. With a crack like thunder, something grabbed Aderyn and yanked her sideways so she stumbled and had to grab Owen's shoulder to stay upright.

Transport dropped them in a street Aderyn didn't recognize, but Isold was already striding off like he knew the way. She hurried to catch up, ignoring the stares from the people who'd seen them arrive. With luck, those enemy adventurers would be confused enough not to track them as far as this street. Violent factions, hostile adventurers, greedy merchants, bad weather... so far nothing about Obsidian impressed her.

CHAPTER TWENTY-FOUR

Rain began falling, a light pattering of drops, just a few minutes before Aderyn saw the first gray-banded lamppost. A Flamecrafter wearing a charcoal-gray cloak, the hood pulled up against the drizzle, stood beneath it, muttering a sharp pair of syllables that made the air smell suddenly of fire and smoke. The lamp kindled into light, blazing brightly for a second before trimming itself to a steady glow.

Owen approached the Flamecrafter before the man could move on to the next lamp. "Hi there. We're looking for a Gray faction member named Birch. A Stalwart we met near Tarani's memorial this afternoon. Any idea where we can find him?"

The Flamecrafter pushed back his hood and peered nearsightedly at Owen. "You *want* to talk to Birch?"

"Is that bad?"

"For you, probably. Birch doesn't like outsiders, which I'm sure you know if you met him before." The Flamecrafter squinted at the blue armband Owen hadn't yet removed. "You've got some nerve coming here after what some of your faction did today. My advice is for you to go home, stay out of Gray district, maybe buy a different affiliation. It's open season on Blue faction here."

"You're being awfully generous," Owen said. "Why aren't you attacking us?"

The Flamecrafter shrugged. "I don't work directly for Lady Eleora, and five against one isn't the kind of odds that are healthy for someone in my position. And it's not like I knew Lord Rupart for his death to matter to me. All I know is the Lady is rabid about getting her hands on Lord Seburtan's thugs and sending them back to him in pieces."

"Makes sense. So, you don't know where we can find Birch?"

"Still on that, huh?" The Flamecrafter shrugged again, making the hood slide farther back. "Look, you feel like dying young, go ahead. He lives on Ranwyn Street. But don't tell him I gave you directions, because I don't want him pissed off at me for disrupting his evening."

"We don't know your name to tell him," Owen said.

"That's right," the Flamecrafter said, and pulled his hood over his face and walked away.

"Ranwyn Street," Isold said, once more consulting his system map of Obsidian. "It's five streets north of the memorial."

Owen watched the Flamecrafter move off down the street, lighting lamps as he went. "Time to lose the blue armbands."

Newly anonymous, they followed Isold through the darkening streets. No one paid them any attention, at least as far as Aderyn could tell, and they reached the memorial street without being accosted. Aderyn eyed the memorial as they walked past. The differences between its shades of gray were less stark in the twilight. Now that she knew what to look for, it was obvious the door was painted on. She hoped they'd have a chance to find out what lay inside.

She walked into Isold, who'd come to a stop ahead of her. "Isold, what—"

"That's right," said an unfamiliar voice. "Stop there. What's your excuse for breaking curfew?"

A couple of men wielding clubs as Birch had blocked their path. Their rain capes didn't obscure the chain mail they wore over gray shirts. Aderyn Assessed them.

Name: Halsey

Class: Staffsworn

Level: 10

Name: Gaven

Class: Lone Wolf

Level: 11

<u>**Skill Alert**</u>**: Hand and Foot (6), Intimidate (5)**

"We didn't know there was a curfew, but I'm sure that doesn't matter," Owen said.

"That's right. You're smart for an adventurer," Gaven the Lone Wolf said, in a voice that sounded like he gargled with gravel. "You want to tell us your destination?"

"Why, are you going to give us an escort?"

Gaven smiled nastily. "Something like that."

"We don't want any trouble," Owen said.

"Should have thought of that before you tried to pass as nobodies," the Staffsworn, Halsey, said. "You've got some nerve walking around like you didn't slaughter Rupart like a dog."

"You can't prove—"

"Save it," Gaven said. "We all have your descriptions. Half of Gray faction is out hunting you right now. Guess we're the lucky ones." He hefted his club, then to Aderyn's surprise tossed it aside and took up a fighting stance she'd seen her friend Dashan, a Swifthands, use in combat. "Go ahead and draw your weapons. It won't make a difference in the end."

"We outnumber you," Owen said. "And we don't want to fight."

"Owen," Weston said in a low voice, "we're surrounded."

Aderyn whipped around. Five more men dressed as Halsey and

Gaven were had come up quietly behind them. She Assessed the lot: all of them Swordsworn, all of them level ten or eleven. Two of them had their swords drawn. "Oh, that's honorable," she said, cursing the tremor in her voice. "Keep us distracted while your friends cut us down from behind. Very noble."

"No reason to deal honorably with the dishonorable," Halsey said. "Go on. Draw."

Livia opened her mouth to cast a spell, and Owen grabbed her arm. "We have a message for Lady Eleora. Something she'll want us to deliver personally. Or am I wrong, and she wouldn't prefer to see us killed in front of her?"

Gaven lowered his club. "It's a trick."

"The message is written, and it's not a secret. Here." Owen fished the somewhat crumpled paper out of his brigandine and extended it to the two men.

Gaven carried it to beneath the nearest lamppost and squinted at its contents. When he returned, he handed it back to Owen. "Stand down," he told the others. "We're taking them to Lady Eleora."

Aderyn didn't look away from the Swordsworn at their rear until all their weapons were sheathed. They didn't look as angry as Aderyn thought they should, not as if Rupart's death were personal. She wished she could think of a way to make use of that. As the guards collected their weapons, she avoided looking at their faces. If she looked at all uncertain, she didn't want to give them that extra weapon, too.

The fighters tied Owen, Aderyn, and Weston's hands in front of them. Weston growled when they bound Livia's hands behind her and gagged her, but he did nothing. Livia didn't fight. Neither did Isold when it was his turn to be subdued. This was far more serious a situation than being apprehended by Seburtan's much less powerful men.

Gaven got up in Owen's face. "Walk where we tell you, and don't put a foot out of line. You can still be killed while trying to escape."

"We won't try to escape."

"Nobody else has to know that." Gaven prodded Owen's chest with one bony finger. "And you give us trouble, well, accidents have been known to happen. Maybe we killed you before we saw that little paper. You get what I'm saying?"

"Clearly," Owen said.

"Let's go!" Halsey shouted, and Aderyn jerked into motion, walking too close to Owen for a few paces before leveling out her gait.

She didn't notice their surroundings as they walked through Gray district. She was keenly aware of the men with swords following them. Seven against five... she had confidence her team would win—well, if they were untied, for sure—but fighting these guards would only make it worse for her team when it came to convincing Eleora they weren't the enemy. That the guards had no such problem hadn't escaped her.

The rain was falling harder now, soaking the shoulders of her coat, and she ducked further into her hood and wished she had a waterproof rain cape like their captors. She'd liked rain a million years ago when she was in a position to sit inside with a good book and watch it pelt the windows. Now if she never saw another rainstorm again, she could die happy.

She wished she hadn't just thought about dying.

The creak of rusting iron startled her out of her reverie. She realized they'd come to an iron fence set in a stone foundation, with a wide, wrought iron gate that now creaked open to admit them. Ahead, almost invisible in the darkness, rose a mansion, in size somewhere between Liander's obscene pile and Seburtan's more modest home. Few lanterns lit its façade, but Aderyn had the impression of rain-slicked stone that was probably light gray when it was dry and many, many glass windows.

Their guards hurried them up the walk and through the front door into a well-lit space that smelled of damp wood and varnish.

The chamber was nearly a perfect cube, with doors and unlit halls opening off it like tunnels into an earthen mound. Wood paneling covered every surface, including the ceiling, a reddish-brown that should have made the room feel warm. Instead it was cold, colder even than the rain-soaked outdoors. Aderyn tried to avoid dripping on the floor, which was a masterpiece of parquet work similar to the one in Seburtan's house, but only succeeded in splashing Isold as she shifted her feet.

"Wait here," Gaven said. He hurried off down one of the halls without lighting a lamp and immediately disappeared into the darkness. Aderyn hugged her arms close to her chest to keep from shivering. She didn't know why there weren't stairs when the house was at least three stories tall. Granted, it wasn't like she'd seen a whole lot of mansions in her life, but all of them had had stairs in their entrance chambers to provide access to the upper floors. To distract herself, she considered reasons why someone might want those stairs concealed. To prevent an enemy from accessing the private areas of the house directly? To control what kind of welcome the owner showed guests?

Footsteps sounded, far too many for one person, and soon Gaven reappeared at the head of a knot of people. [Improved Assess 2] revealed that most of the five newcomers were non-classed. The one exception was a woman who strode as if she meant to conquer the ground she walked on. She wore her dark brown hair loose around her face, which was pinched and angry-looking. She bore no weapon, and alone among all the group wore no gray; her trousers were brown leather, and her shirt was black.

The group stopped a few steps into the chamber, all except the woman, who continued striding toward the friends without slowing her pace. Before she could reach Owen, Aderyn pushed past him and exclaimed, "But—you're a Warmaster!"

The woman stopped and switched her keen focus from Owen to Aderyn. "Who do you think you are?"

"I'm a Warmaster, too," Aderyn said. "I've never met another one of us, definitely not another one who's such a high level—you're level nine, which is amazing—how did you do it?" She knew she was babbling. She knew from Assessing her that this was Eleora, their enemy. But none of that mattered now that she'd met another Warmaster.

Eleora stared at her like she was an insect who'd just proclaimed they were sisters. "Get out of my way," she said. "You. You think you can get away with killing one of my people and then just walk in here like nothing happened?" She pointed a shaking finger at Owen.

"I have a message from Lord Seburtan," Owen said, "and an explanation."

"I'm not interested in explanations," Eleora replied. "Give me the message."

Owen once more dug the now very battered piece of paper out of his armor, awkwardly thanks to his bound wrists, and extended it to Eleora. She snatched it out of his hand, tearing it slightly, and unfolded it. Her eyes moved rapidly as she scanned its contents. Then she crushed it into a ball and tossed it over her shoulder, where one of the non-classed people in her entourage fumbled to pick it up. "Irrelevant," she said. "Take them outside. I don't want their blood staining this floor."

"You know what Lord Seburtan swears to," Owen said, ignoring the Swordsworn who moved to grab his arms. "We aren't the ones responsible."

"He thinks he can start a war and then pretend innocence?" Eleora roared. She grabbed Owen's chin and forced him to look at her. "My men will hold you down and cut out your heart, you bastard, like you cut out mine."

Aderyn hadn't taken her eyes off Eleora the whole time this exchange had passed. She noticed more details: how red-rimmed her eyes were, how not just her finger but her whole body was trembling, how her clothes hung on her haphazardly, like she hadn't cared what she put on or how well it fit. And a sudden dread certainty struck her to the heart.

"Oh," she breathed. "Oh, no. Rupart wasn't just your sweetheart. He was your *partner*."

Eleora's gaze returned to Aderyn. "What?"

Tears prickled Aderyn's eyes. "I am so sorry, Lady Eleora. No wonder you're furious. You've lost everything that made you who you are."

Eleora took a step back. "Who are you?"

"You know," Aderyn said. She stepped away from the Gray guard menacing her. "Assess me. See why I'm the only person in this room who can even come close to understanding your loss."

Eleora's eyes narrowed, then took on the glazed look of someone reading the Codex. Her tight frown relaxed slightly. "A Warmaster," she said. "And you killed him anyway. You knew exactly what that would do to me and you killed him anyway."

"No, we didn't," Aderyn said. "I swear on my own partner's life I would never do that. That wouldn't be just war, it would be salt the earth destruction. If it were me, anyway."

Eleora stared at her in silence for a moment. Then she snapped her fingers. "Watch them," she ordered Gaven. "You, come with me." She crooked a finger at Aderyn.

"No!" Owen shouted. Two guards grabbed him, holding him back as he lunged for Aderyn.

"It's all right, sweetheart," Aderyn said. "I promise."

Eleora said, "That was stupid. Telling me who your partner is so I'll know to kill him slowly while you watch."

"I did it on purpose," Aderyn said calmly. "So you'll know I'm sincere when I tell you we had nothing to do with Rupart's death."

"Aderyn!" Owen shouted.

"Don't worry about me," Aderyn said, though her calm façade was a lie. Sweat had broken out all over her body, and her hands trembled enough she didn't think she could hold a sword if she'd had access to one.

Eleora walked back the way she'd come at a slower pace than before. Aderyn cast one glance at her friends, her gaze lingering longest on Owen, before hurrying after her.

The dark hall was lit only by the light spilling into it from the entrance chamber at one end, and by a single lamp at the foot of a narrow staircase at the other. But Eleora didn't ascend the stairs. Two doors faced each other at the far end of the hall, and Eleora slammed the right-hand door open like she meant to tear it off its hinges. Aderyn followed quickly, though the violence of Eleora's entrance made her heart skip in terror. It didn't help that Aderyn didn't have any other options; she was still conscious of being alone with someone who hated her and had the power to kill not just Aderyn, but everyone she cared about.

The room was a study, but not a very welcoming one. It was small, cramped, and smelled of mildew. The one bookcase held a handful of volumes bound in fraying black leather and a lot of miscellaneous objects. Aderyn had the impression of trinkets collected over a lifetime of adventuring. The desk wasn't much more than a block of wood on four spindly legs that shouldn't be able to support it, and the three chairs didn't match each other or the desk.

Eleora flung herself into one of the chairs that wasn't behind the desk and waved at another. "Sit. You get five minutes to convince me not to kill all of you."

CHAPTER TWENTY-FIVE

Aderyn sat, wishing her mind hadn't just gone blank. She wasn't great at convincing people of things, not like Isold or Owen. All she could think to do was tell the truth. "Liander of the White had your partner killed. I don't know if he knew that's what Rupart was, or if he intended to strike at you so personally. I'm guessing not, because he's not an adventurer and nobody but a Warmaster or her partner knows what that relationship means."

"Nice story, but you have no proof. Though I admire your balls of solid steel at daring to implicate someone as powerful as Liander." Eleora lounged in her chair, but Aderyn could see the tension in her hands and didn't need **[Read Body Language]** to know the pose was a lie.

"Liander tried to get us to team up with his brat of a daughter, to help her level quickly," she said. "We turned him down. This is his way of getting revenge."

"You must be new to the city," Eleora said. "Liander wouldn't start a war to get rid of adventurers who rejected him."

"What about starting a war to get rid of adventurers who humiliated him by taking his daughter hostage?" Aderyn shot back.

Eleora choked on a laugh. Her smile transformed her whole face. "You didn't."

"It was the only way to get out of his house alive."

"I see." The smile disappeared. "Still, you have no proof. And Seburtan, blast his hide, is clever and devious enough to concoct a plan this convoluted."

"We do have proof. One of your men, a Stalwart named Birch, stopped us from approaching Tarani's memorial at about the time Rupart was killed. At just after four o'clock this afternoon. He'll remember." Aderyn tried not to think about what else Birch might remember.

Eleora gazed at Aderyn in considering silence while Aderyn squirmed inwardly. "So you're putting the burden of proof on me," she finally said.

"Not on purpose. We were looking for Birch when your men caught us. We hoped he'd be willing to speak on our behalf."

"You don't know Birch. He's not the altruistic type." Eleora tapped her finger against her lips. "How sure are you that Birch will give you an alibi?"

"I'm one hundred percent sure his witness will prove our innocence," Aderyn said. "But I'm not at all certain he'll be willing to share it."

Eleora once more fell silent. Aderyn said, "I don't blame you for wanting vengeance. I would want the same if it were my partner. But I'd want even more to make sure the right person suffered. That's not us."

"You're a starry-eyed idealist," Eleora said. "You wouldn't last two seconds in Obsidian politics. Don't you have any sense of self-preservation?"

"My friends all say I don't always think before I act. I only know I hate injustice." Again, tears rose to Aderyn's eyes. She wasn't sure if she was weeping for Eleora's loss or for fear of what would happen to her if Owen were killed.

"How did you know?" she asked impulsively. "About how the Warmaster class works. I've never even heard of another Warmaster who didn't think it was a useless class."

Eleora smiled again. "Rupart and I grew up together, and we got our Calls within days of each other. Rupart refused to abandon me to head out with another team that didn't want a Warmaster along. It didn't take many battles with vermin to discover how our skills enhanced each other's. He was—" She covered her trembling lips with one hand. "He was such a good swordsman. I still don't know how he was defeated, unless your partner is as overpowered a swordsman as Rupart was."

"I don't want to incriminate us further, so I won't answer that."

That drew a chuckle from the Gray faction leader. "So you're not a total starry-eyed idealist. Fine. But if Birch refutes your story... I'll make sure your deaths are quick. One Warmaster to another."

Aderyn nodded. The lump in her throat prevented her from speaking.

They returned to the entrance chamber, where it didn't look like anyone had moved. Eleora addressed Gaven. "Send someone to bring Birch here. Make it quick."

Gaven didn't react like he thought this order was bizarre. He spoke to Halsey, who left the house. Cold rain blew in as he opened the door, with a wind that made the chilly room positively icy.

Aderyn started to return to Owen's side, but Eleora brought her to a halt with a hand on her shoulder. "You wait with me," she said. "If I'm not satisfied, you'll watch your friends be killed before I take your life."

Aderyn nodded. Her eyes were on Owen, who looked ready to erupt. She assessed the room, not with a skill but with her Warmaster's eyes, looking for tactical weaknesses. The two men holding Owen weren't paying attention to him, and their swords dangled at their sides within Owen's reach. With [**Two-Weapon Fighting**], he could cut his way through the guards—but they were all still bound, and cutting themselves free would take time those guards weren't likely to give them. Even so, they had a chance of escaping, but not without taking damage or even losing one of them.

Her gaze returned to Owen. He had stopped straining against the guards' hold, but as their eyes met, he flicked a glance at the sword of the guard on his left and then back to Aderyn, a clear indication that he'd seen her tactical assessment and was waiting for her signal. Aderyn shook her head, the tiniest motion, telling him *wait and see*.

Owen's eyebrows twitched in the silent query *Did you convince her?*

Aderyn shrugged. That ought to convey her uncertainty even without [**Read Body Language**]. Owen's lips tightened in frustration.

The door opened, admitting two very wet men with their hoods pulled well over their faces. The guards nearest the door stepped back as both men shook rain off their coats in putting their hoods back, revealing that they were Halsey and Birch. Halsey looked like this had been just another task, but Birch's frown creased his forehead and made a V in the middle of his eyebrows, as if he was close to taking out his anger on anyone who deserved it.

His gaze shifted from Eleora to Aderyn's friends, grouped exactly like prisoners at the center of the room. Aderyn knew the instant he remembered who they were, because he lunged at Isold with a hand outstretched. One of the guards stepped between them, Aderyn thought reflexively because the guard couldn't possibly care if Isold was hurt.

"You caught them!" Birch shouted. "You foul, disgusting—Lady Eleora, that one used magic on me and I demand his execution!"

Eleora turned to Aderyn, puzzled. "What's this about magic?"

"Ah," Aderyn said, "well, it's true Birch found us approaching Tarani's memorial. We didn't mean any harm, and we didn't know it was forbidden for anyone not of Gray faction to try to get inside. Birch was so angry, and Isold—he's a Herald—he calmed him down with **[Persuasion]**." In her excitement and terror she'd temporarily forgotten the drawback to having Birch as an alibi.

"He convinced me not to fulfil my sworn duty!" Birch raged. "She makes it sound so innocent, when what happened was that bastard used magic on me so they wouldn't be held responsible for breaking the law!"

Eleora closed her eyes and tilted her head back, clearly searching for patience. "You misled me," she told Aderyn. "Though it's not like I can kill you twice."

"Is death the punishment for trying to enter Tarani's memorial?" Aderyn asked.

"No, but using magic to avoid punishment might be."

Aderyn let out a deep breath. "It's true I didn't mention that part," she said. "I wasn't trying to mislead you. I just hoped we could resolve one accusation before dealing with another."

"It's not an accusation," Birch shouted, "it's fact! Lady Eleora, you should—"

"Don't tell me what to do, Birch," Eleora said calmly. "What time did this happen?"

"Why, it—" Birch looked confused. "What—you mean, their vicious attack on me?"

Eleora glared at him.

Birch swallowed. "I apologize, my lady. It was just after the clock tolled four this afternoon."

"And you're sure it was these five adventurers?"

"I'd swear to it on my life! I'm never going to forget *that one's* face." Birch again pointed at Isold. "He might have made me do anything, any act of perversion."

Isold rolled his eyes and scowled as best he could through the gag.

"Enough," Eleora said. "I accept that these are not the ones who killed Rupart. Cut them free. Gaven, Halsey, Liander of the White has been accused of that foul deed. Find the truth and report to me immediately."

As Gaven and Halsey left, Gaven passing into the dark hall, Halsey heading back out into the storm, Eleora turned to Aderyn, who was massaging her wrists now that the ropes were gone. "And now we have another serious charge," she said. "You were willing to risk death to avoid paying a twenty-gold fine?"

"No—*twenty* gold?" Aderyn's gaze shifted to Birch, who wouldn't meet her eyes. "He said it was two hundred."

"She's lying," Birch said. "I told them twenty gold."

"You did not," Aderyn said hotly. "You wanted us to come with you to someplace where for all we knew we'd be beaten when we couldn't afford your fine. I don't see why we should be ashamed of not wanting to put ourselves in harm's way. Or acting to defend ourselves."

"Stop trying to distract her ladyship," Birch said. "It's my word against yours, and you're just a bunch of wandering adventurers who don't care anything about Obsidian's traditions or respect for Tarani."

Aderyn's eyes met Owen's, asking a question. Owen nodded. Aderyn cleared her throat. "Owen is the Fated One," she declared. "We respect Tarani's heritage because it's his heritage. I'm sorry we didn't pick Gray faction when we entered, because that would have solved this whole problem, but I'm not going to apologize for wanting to see what Tarani left behind."

Eleora gripped Aderyn's arm painfully tight. "The Fated One?"

"I'm sure you know what quest is attached to the memorial," Aderyn said. She no longer knew where she was going with this or if it might still get her and her friends killed, but she was floating on adrenalin and rage at how stupid Obsidian was. "Maybe you'll call us stupid like Birch did for not knowing the rules, but unlike Birch, I hope you'll accept that we acted in good faith as well as ignorance."

Eleora's eyes narrowed. "Prove you're eligible for the **[Fated One's Destiny]** quest chain."

Aderyn's heart sank. "How? You'd have to be able to read Owen's Codex."

"All the faction heads have power to act as magistrates," Eleora said, "which includes the ability to read someone's Codex." She released Aderyn's arm and strode to face Owen, taking his chin in her hand, but gently this time. Owen didn't resist.

Eleora stilled, even her constant trembling subsiding. The room fell so quiet the rain pattering the roof and door sounded like hail. Aderyn watched Eleora rather than Owen. The Gray faction leader's expression was neutral, but occasionally Aderyn saw her frown, or smile, and once or twice her lips pursed thoughtfully.

After a time Aderyn felt was much longer than Eleora needed to confirm what quests Owen had accepted, the woman stepped back and released Owen. "Twenty gold fine, for approaching Tarani's memorial without proper authorization."

"But—" Aderyn protested.

"That's the law, Warmaster," Eleora said. "It won't be a problem again now you have authorization, right? You." She pointed at Birch. "I've had complaints about your overenthusiastic performance of your duties before. Do I want to investigate how much you took in 'fines' that you didn't report?"

Birch took a step back. "I—"

"Consider this a warning. It's the only one I'll give. Now, get out of my sight."

Birch ran out the front door without putting up his hood against the rain.

Eleora sighed. "You bought into Blue faction when you arrived, right?"

"It was all we could afford at the time," Owen said.

"I suggest you change your allegiance so we don't have any more confusion over Tarani's memorial." Eleora snapped her fingers, and a non-classed woman of her entourage left the room. "And don't try swapping armbands so you can move freely in both districts. I won't protect you from those consequences."

"We won't," Owen said. "And, for what it's worth, I'm really sorry your partner was murdered. That's a foul thing even if Liander didn't realize how serious it is."

"You're not defending him, are you? After what he tried to pull?" Eleora's eyebrows raised in astonishment.

"No, just saying I know how I would feel if Aderyn were gone. Liander doesn't deserve any sympathy, and I hope you take him down hard." Owen put his arm around Aderyn's shoulders and pulled her close.

"Once I have more information, Seburtan and I will talk. Liander can't be allowed to get away with manipulating us into a war." Eleora's smile was wicked. "It's past time he learned he's not all-powerful."

The woman returned with a fistful of gray cloth that turned out to be armbands. She handed them to Owen. "How much?" Owen asked.

"No charge. Call it repayment for making sure I went after the right target. Though it's still twenty gold for the fine."

Aderyn, blushing, dug in the <**Purse of Great Capacity**> and handed four smallish gold coins to the servant woman. "Sorry."

"Rules are rules," Eleora said, so blandly the sarcasm was evident. "And I'm going to have you escorted to lodgings in Gray district. I may have need of you later, and I wouldn't put it past Liander to have more than one scheme going directed at hurting the five of you."

"We won't get involved in your retribution," Owen said. "I'm sorry, but we really did want to avoid faction entanglements of any kind."

"I'm surprised you don't want a piece of Liander for your own revenge, but that's up to you. No, it's not that I was thinking of—

but we'll talk when this is resolved." Eleora turned as Gaven came back into the room. "Gaven, take your squad and escort these fellows to Raintree Inn. It shouldn't be beyond your means," she told Owen.

To Aderyn, she said, "I've never met another of us who was successful, either. I wish you luck, both of you."

Her lips trembled, and her eyes shone with tears. Impulsively, Aderyn hugged her. "I don't know the answer," she whispered. "It's not like you can replace him, even if you found another partner. I hope someday it's easier."

Eleora didn't return the embrace, but when Aderyn let her go, she was smiling. "Starry-eyed idealist," Eleora said. "I hope that too. It just won't be today. Now, get out of here, and I hope you don't die."

CHAPTER TWENTY-SIX

The Raintree Inn turned out to be only a few streets away. It was a modest two-story building whose stables were bigger than the inn, but despite the obvious care the owner had for horses, the inn itself was warm and dry and welcoming. On learning the rates, Isold negotiated for three rooms, and the friends left their wet coats in those rooms and met again in the taproom. They sat at a table near the fireplace where most of a tree burned and basked in the heat without speaking.

Aderyn was leaning against Owen with her eyes closed when Isold said, "That was luckier than we deserve. I wish I hadn't used my skills on that greedy little Stalwart."

"There's no point revisiting the past," Owen said. "We're free, we have the right affiliation, and Liander is going to get crushed. I say the small matter of having used mind control on someone isn't worth fretting about."

"And you're always careful with your skills," Livia said. "It's not like you depend on them in every interaction. You didn't use [Suggestion] to get us a better rate on those rooms, right? So I wouldn't worry about it."

Aderyn said nothing. She was still uncomfortable around Isold, fearing he was still angry with her for not striking that attacker when he was helpless, and on top of that, she had lingering fears about Isold using his skills on one of them. Why she worried about that when she never feared Weston would steal from her or Livia *thunder punch* her, she didn't know, but however irrational, she still feared.

She opened her eyes as the smell of roast chicken reached her nostrils. It was late, and she was hungry, but her appetite was gone, killed by the excitement and terror of the evening. She choked down half of what Owen served her and stirred the rest around on her plate so it would look like she'd eaten more. The last thing she wanted was for her well-meaning friends to pry into what was wrong with her, given that she didn't know the answer herself.

But when the meal was over, and they all returned to their rooms, Owen shut the door and said, "What's bothering you?"

"Who says something's bothering me?" Aderyn regretted those words the instant they left her lips. They sounded so petulant.

"I do. You barely ate anything, and you were so quiet I kept expecting to find you'd fallen asleep. You want to talk?" Owen guided her to sit on the bed and dragged the room's one chair over to sit opposite her.

Aderyn shrugged. "I can't stop thinking about Lady Eleora. She lost her love, her partner—that's so awful it hurts me to imagine it."

"You mean, hurts you to imagine it happening to you," Owen said.

She shrugged again. "I suppose that sounds selfish."

"Not selfish. Natural to put yourself in her place." Owen took Aderyn's hands and rubbed his thumbs gently over her knuckles. "Is it something you fear? Because I guarantee I won't go without a fight."

"Neither did Rupart. Lady Eleora said—" To her horror, tears welled in her eyes, and her throat began to close up. "I didn't fear it before, but now I hate myself because my first grief wouldn't be for my sweetheart, it would be for myself. For going back to being a useless Warmaster with no partner. That's what hurts."

Owen nodded slowly. "Come here," he said, and drew her into his arms while she cried. "It's been a terrible, exhausting day, and I don't think, in all the battles we've fought, all the challenges we've faced, we've ever been closer to death as a team. It's natural that your emotions are high."

"Is it? When I was about to be shredded by that spinning blades trap, what were *you* thinking?" Aderyn didn't know what had prompted her to fling that at him, but the part of her that knew his words came from a place of love was shouted down by the bitter, heartsick part that said he was being condescending.

Owen stiffened. "I don't think this should be a competition over who feels what more deeply."

"It doesn't have to be a competition for me to feel like a heartless, selfish bitch. Even before I knew I loved you, all my worries for you were really about what would happen to me when you went back to your world. Doesn't that bother you?"

Owen released her and sat silent for a moment. Aderyn swiped an arm roughly across her eyes. Finally, Owen said, "Why would it bother me that you fear losing yourself more than you fear losing me?"

Aderyn blinked. "I didn't say that."

"But that's what this is about. Aderyn, if I got killed tomorrow, would you find the first person you could convince to take a chance on you and make him or her your partner?"

"Of course not! Owen, I will never find anyone to replace you."

"That's not true. Now that you know what you're capable of, it shouldn't be hard for you to find another partner."

His words opened a hole in her heart, an aching emptiness that made her feel like crying again. "But they won't be you," she managed to say through shaking lips.

Owen smiled. "And you don't see what that means? Aderyn, I

know your feelings for me are tangled up with your feelings about your partner. It doesn't mean you love me less just because you have some fears about the future. In fact, I think it's because you love me that the thought of losing your partner hurts so much. Any other person you partnered with, you'd always be comparing." He wiped away tears from her cheek. "And, not to be arrogant or anything, but those comparisons would always come up short."

Aderyn hiccupped a laugh. "They would. Oh, Owen. I wish I could make you promise not to die, but we're in the wrong line of work for that."

"Like I said, I can promise I won't make it easy on anyone who kills me. And they'd have to deal with you as well." Owen put his arms around her again, and this time Aderyn returned his embrace. He smelled of dinner and sweat, not unexpected, and she found the scent reassuring.

Owen kissed the top of her head. "I'm exhausted. Come to bed, and let's see about sleeping off some of this turmoil."

Aderyn nodded. Sex felt like too much work at the moment, but cuddling with her sweetheart, that she could manage.

They snuggled together, but despite her tiredness, sleep eluded Aderyn. Long after Owen's breathing had deepened into slumber, she lay awake, staring at the rectangle of blue that was the window. The waning moon had set hours before, and the sky was a grand sweep of stars that dimmed to a paler blue where a lamp burned near the window. It wasn't close enough for Aderyn to see the light, just the glow it shed over the street, but it made the sky look like a painting done by some apprentice just learning color theory.

Finally, she eased away from Owen and dressed, then went downstairs to the taproom. She didn't know exactly what time it was, though thanks to the tolling bell of the clock she was aware it was after eleven, but the taproom was still busy with drinkers all focused on Isold, drumming and singing near the fireplace. Isold's eyes met hers, but he didn't acknowledge her, which made her feel empty again. Without the rest of the team around, maybe he didn't feel he had to pretend he wasn't angry with her.

She found a seat at the edge of the crowd and listened to the music. Isold's magnificent voice changed depending on what he was singing, melodic for a love song, bold and powerful for a martial anthem, tinged with humor for a country song. It was hard to understand how Isold hadn't known from childhood what class awaited him, but he'd wanted something different and convinced himself that was enough for the system.

She still didn't know how the system made decisions. True, Isold's musical gift made him a natural for a Herald, but Weston was by his own admission built like a brick shithouse, and by that logic the system ought to have made him a Stalwart. All sorts of people trained through their childhoods in hopes of influencing the system, but half of them ended up disappointed. Aderyn's own father had studied magic in his youth, and he'd become a Swordsworn.

And then there was herself. If it was true the system considered natural talents and so forth—it probably wasn't true, but just for the sake of argument—then what about her screamed "Warmaster"? She'd never been exceptional at strategy games as a child and young adult; she'd never led a team to victory in any of the childhood games they'd played in Far Haven. She'd liked learning about monsters, but not to the extent of memorizing monster qualities and statistics and attacks. She had no innate qualities that had been there before she accepted the Call.

The crowd roared with laughter and applause as Isold came to the end of his mildly ribald song and bowed. He rose, gathering up his small drum, and pushed through the crowd to Aderyn's side. "Can't sleep?"

"No. I'm restless. I thought you'd have gone to bed already. You've had as long a day as any of us."

"I'm restless, too. Wait a moment." He left his drum on the table and crossed the room to the bar, where he had a word with the bartender. A minute later, he returned with two foaming mugs. "Here. Call it a sleeping draught."

Aderyn sipped the ale, then took a longer drink. "It's good."

Isold drank down half his mug and set it aside. "The house brew. Slightly more alcoholic than the usual offering, but I judged we both need a relaxer."

His banal words, his neutral tone of voice, sent guilt spiking through Aderyn again. Before she could stop herself, she said, "I'm sorry, Isold."

Isold's gaze fixed on her. "Sorry? For what?"

"For not killing that assassin when you had him subdued. He would have killed you—I shouldn't have hesitated—"

"Aderyn, stop." Isold put a hand on hers. "Has that been bothering you all this time?"

Aderyn nodded. She ducked her head and examined the grain in the wooden tankard, how a dribble of ale had found a path over the lip to follow the deep lines in the wood. "I was weak, I know. I guess I couldn't bring myself to kill a helpless man. It's so different from monsters, except if the monsters are human, is it really all that different? And it was like a waste of your skill."

"I thought you were behaving strangely around me." Isold removed his hand. "And you believed I blamed you for not acting quickly."

"Didn't you?"

"Honestly, Aderyn, I haven't thought about those men until this minute. I'll admit at the time I was frustrated that you didn't act immediately, but then he went for you with his knife and that pushed everything else out of my head." Isold wrapped his long fingers around his tankard, but didn't drink. "It *is* different, killing humans, and even more different killing helpless humans. I shouldn't have expected you to be able to strike readily. But I swear I never held it against you."

Aderyn let out a long, deep breath of relief. "I meant to say something earlier, but it's been a busy day."

"Don't worry about it." Isold laughed. "I thought maybe this had something to do with how my skills frighten you sometimes."

Aderyn froze. "I... I didn't think you knew about that."

"I like to think I have some skill at reading people. It goes with being able to charm others, maybe—the ability to see their reactions, their emotions, and work on those to help or harm. You get tense sometimes when I use my skills on humans. Are you afraid of me?"

"No!" At Isold's look, she blushed. "Really, no. Not of you in your right mind."

Isold blinked. "What does that mean?"

Aderyn hesitated, then forged ahead. "You're not the only Herald in the world, and those other Heralds aren't necessarily friendly. If one of them, someone higher level, used those skills against you, they could convince you that we were enemies. And you never hesitate to use [Charm] or [Persuasion] or [Suggestion] on enemies. That scares me. I don't know why."

"How odd," Isold said. "I have that exact fear."

"You do?"

Isold nodded. "I feel I already constantly watch myself as I interact with people, always considering the consequences if I use my skills on them. I never want to become like that Herald we defeated in Asylum, feeling entitled to control and manipulate others, or go even farther and gain the evil class Beguiler. There's no way I would ever use my skills to do that to my friends. But you're right. It's not just other Heralds—there are monsters that can sway humans, control their minds. If one of them managed to control our team, well, we're all powerful and getting more so by the day, but you know as well as I that my skills aren't easy to resist."

"I guess I'm afraid of those monsters or Heralds doing that to me, too. I don't know why being manipulated is so frightening to me, but it is. And then I think how you would feel if you were forced to turn on us—I mean, when you recovered—and that just makes it worse. Because I think I would fear you then."

Isold winced. "I couldn't blame you. It wouldn't matter that I hadn't done it of my own free will."

"But it should! You're my friend. I just—" Aderyn took another drink of ale. "It's irrational. I hate being irrational."

"For someone who depends on her instincts rather than rational analysis, that's amusing," Isold said. "But I understand what you mean." He clasped her hand again briefly. "Promise me this. If it ever happens, I want you to knock me out before I can act. Or at least do your best to. That ought to resolve both our fears."

The idea did ease Aderyn's heart. "You're right. I promise."

Isold drained his tankard and set it down with a hollow thump. "You know, I feel better? I didn't realize what a burden I was carrying until now. Thank you."

"Thank *you*, Isold." With a smile, she added, "Where do you plan to sleep tonight?"

"Sadly, I'm too tired to take advantage of any of the suggestive, inviting looks I received tonight," Isold said with an exaggerated sigh. "But once this business with the memorial is through, who knows?"

Aderyn finished her drink and set the tankard beside Isold's. "I think I can sleep now."

"Then—good night, Aderyn, and I'll see you in the morning."

She let herself into her room with barely a squeak of hinges and a click of the latch, but she'd forgotten how light a sleeper Owen could be. She heard a rustle of bed linens, and then Owen said, "Aderyn? Did you go somewhere?"

"Just to get a drink." She found she didn't want to share the conversation she'd had with Isold. That Isold had shared her fears felt like a private thing she couldn't tell even her partner. "Sorry I woke you."

"I'm not." He took her in his arms as she settled back into bed. "I feel the need to kiss you, something I can't do if I'm asleep."

"You wouldn't feel that need if you were asleep, either," Aderyn teased.

Owen slid his hand down her back. "Touching you is also something I wanted to do." His lips found hers in the darkness, kissing her breathless. "And, well—"

"I thought you were exhausted—oh! Do that again."

Owen chuckled and kissed his way down her neck to her collarbone. "You know," he murmured against her skin, "I have it on the highest authority that this is immoral behavior."

"Really?" Aderyn said. "Then you should—ah, yes!—you should probably stop."

"Is that what you really want?" His fingers brushed the soft skin at the base of her spine.

She kissed him, her lips lingering on his, and it was his turn to gasp. "What I want," she said in a low, provocative voice, "is to make love with you until we can't remember what 'immoral' means."

"That might take a while," Owen said. "I have a good memory."

"Good thing we've got all night," Aderyn replied.

CHAPTER TWENTY-SEVEN

They left the Raintree Inn later the next day than Aderyn had wanted, but even Weston had slept heavily and risen late, and really, it no longer mattered if they hurried or not. For once, the skies were clear, and the sun shone brightly, warming the air and drying the streets. Aderyn chose to take it as a good sign.

When they reached the memorial, they stood in front of it for a few minutes as Livia examined it with *clairvoyance*. Now that Aderyn knew what to look for, the door and the windows nearest it were obviously false, though the illusion was a good one. She tilted her head back to look at the second story windows. Those were too far away for a clear view, but she thought they were painted on, too.

"No windows," Livia said, as if she'd heard Aderyn's thoughts. "No doors. No entrance points at all. And yet I know there's empty space there."

"So, you could cast *transport* to get us inside," Owen said.

"I can try. If someone is serious about keeping people out, there might be a forbiddance or block or something over the house the way there was at Gamboling Coil." Livia glared at the painted door. "It depends on how clever the quest wants us to be. But if entering requires a different approach, we won't find that out by standing around. Everybody huddle up."

"Are we worried about being noticed?" Aderyn asked. "Because people are staring." The streets were busier than they had been the previous day, and many of those passing did stare at the little group on the steps of the memorial, though no one stopped or looked interested in accosting them.

"Let them stare," Owen said. He put his arms around Aderyn's shoulders and Isold's. With all of them joined, Livia chanted the long syllables of *transport*. The familiar jerk that felt like it meant to loosen her joints tugged at Aderyn, and then she was surrounded by darkness. Immediately Livia summoned her *orb of light* and tossed it into the air.

They stood in a cramped, low-ceilinged room, furnished only with a couple of chairs and a round-topped table between them. Their arrival had disturbed a thick layer of dust on the floor, and Aderyn and Isold both sneezed. The upper corners of the room, brightly illuminated by the orb, were festooned with cobwebs that drifted in the same breeze that had stirred up the dust. No paintings hung on the walls, and the floor was bare of rugs.

"That's strange," Weston said. "The door is real on this side."

Owen tried the handle, then pulled the door open. Boards blocked the exit. "So, they did build a box to surround the place," he said. "Weird."

Aderyn twitched back the curtains covering one window and sneezed again at the puff of dust she raised. Beyond the glass panes was nothing but flat wood. "I don't understand this at all."

"These rooms lead right into each other," Livia said. "There's a kitchen back here, and what looks like an office or library or something through here." She'd summoned more lights and tossed them into the other two rooms. "And stairs through the last door."

"Let's spread out, then," Owen said. "Isold, do we know what we're looking for? What form her record will be in, I mean?"

"Aside from 'written,' no." Isold was already peering with interest at the library's shelves. "My guess is either a bound journal or loose pages in a portfolio."

"Then that's what we'll look for first," Owen said. "If we can't find it in those forms, we'll try something else." He clasped Aderyn's hand briefly. "I'll see what's upstairs."

"I'll join you," Livia said. "I'll look for any hidden compartments with *clairvoyance*."

"And I'll check for secret places down here," Weston said.

Isold had already entered the library and was pulling volumes off the shelves. "I guess I'll help in here," Aderyn said, and started taking books down from the bookcase opposite Isold.

She and Isold worked in silence, with the only sounds being those of leather rubbing against leather and the thump of discarded books being replaced on the shelves. Aderyn didn't like the idea of dropping them on the floor or even moving them to the table in the middle of the room, so she pulled each one out, wiped the dust off the top, and put it back in its place once she'd flipped through it and determined it wasn't Tarani's writings.

After only a few minutes, her urge to sneeze had disappeared, though the dust hadn't. Her sleeves were gray from elbow to wrist, and her skin felt itchy and dry. She finished one shelf and moved down to the next.

"It's too bad we don't have time to read these," Isold said. "Some of the titles are intriguing."

"I haven't stopped to read the titles, other than to know anything with a title probably isn't what we want." Aderyn wiped dust from a tattered book whose binding was loose and opened it with care. Its pages were spotted and yellow with age, and the title printed across the first page, *Mathematical Conjectures*, did not sound at all enticing.

"That's not a good assumption. We don't know what Tarani did with her record. It's true, it's likely to be simply a diary, but she might have rewritten her record in a different form in anticipation of it going to her successor." Isold sneezed. "Excuse me. What worries me is the possibility that we won't be able to read it, or that we'll overlook it because the text isn't legible. People's handwriting has changed over the centuries, and Tarani lived a long time ago."

"That hadn't occurred to me." Aderyn reached out to one of the books she'd already looked at, but then she remembered she'd been able to read everything she'd found so far. "Does that mean what we're looking for won't be printed? Because that was the other thing I've been assuming."

"Printing it would make no sense, not for just one book. And Tarani struck me as secretive when we heard her witness back in the Repository. She wouldn't trust her record to anyone who'd have to read it in the process of preparing it for printing. No, you're right, what we're looking for is handwritten. Oh, I've always wanted to read this!"

"You could take it with you," Aderyn suggested. "Or... no, I'm sure Lady Eleora would view that as a breach of etiquette, if not actual law." Aderyn finished the second shelf and moved to the third. "Though it's sad, having all these books with no one to read them."

"I agree. Something tells me this wasn't anything Tarani wanted."

A system message interrupted Isold before he could continue.

Congratulations! You have completed the quest [Fated One's Destiny: Discover the Path] You have been awarded [7500 XP]

Footsteps sounded on the stairs, and Owen entered the room, followed by Livia. "You can stop," he said, waving a small, fat book bound in red leather and a scruffier, more worn brown leather volume at them. "This is it. Or them. There were two."

"I choose not to see Aderyn's and my efforts as a waste of time," Isold said with a grin.

"We had no way to know where it would be," Owen said, "so you're right. But they were between the mattresses of one of the beds upstairs. And I figured we might as well read them in the library."

"It's a good thing we did search, because I found a passage between the walls," Weston said as he entered. "Evidence of a space, anyway. The rooms' sizes don't add up. I was about to look for a way in when I heard you come downstairs."

"Let's look at that first," Owen said. "The journals aren't going anywhere."

They returned to the sitting room, where Weston rapped on a section of the wall it shared with the kitchen. The empty sound of the thud clearly indicated that part of the wall was hollow. Weston began searching the floorboards and wall as Livia cast *clairvoyance*. "It's too dark to see anything," she said.

"Give me a minute—oh, there it is. That's clever." Weston poked a fingertip into a hole where the head of the nail was sunk below the surface of the floor, and a panel that had looked like wood grain popped away from the wall an inch. Weston swung it open further as Owen moved the chair blocking it, and they all peered inside.

The disguised cubby was six inches deep and filled the space in the wall from floor to ceiling. Inside, adventuring gear hung on pegs or sat piled on the floor. There was a coil of glistening white braided rope, a set of goggles with green lenses, a belt with two pouches dangling from it, an empty knapsack huddled on the floor, and a fist-sized cube of bronze atop the knapsack.

Livia whistled. "Those are all magical!"

Isold had already picked up the rope. "This is a **<Ensnaring Rope>**. You whip the end at your target, and when the rope makes contact, it entangles the victim, restraining him completely. It's not as good a restraint as Livia's *immobilize* spell, because depending on how they're ensnared, the victim still has limited mobility, but it is effective."

"Not bad," Owen said. "The goggles?"

"<**Cat's Eye Goggles**>. They grant the wearer the ability to see clearly in darkness. And the belt is a <**Forager's Belt**>. Each of those pouches is like Aderyn's <**Purse of Great Capacity**> in that it holds much more than its apparent size. The difference is that these pouches are always full of fresh food, however much you take out." Isold frowned. "I'm afraid its power might be at the limit of my [Identify] ability, because there are a number of details I can't recall, such as what kind of food it produces. I also think 'always full of food' has a daily limit, like perhaps only ten apples a day, but it will produce ten apples a day every day until the end of time."

Weston was already reaching into the first pouch. "Grapes," he said with satisfaction, and popped one green globe into his mouth. "Seedless grapes. I've never heard of such a thing before."

"Seedless grapes are popular in my world," Owen said. "It's taken me some getting used to here, spitting out seeds. How do they taste?"

"Incredible," Weston said, helping himself to a few more and then passing the bunch around. "And this other pouch has dried meat, only it's not dried hard, it's still flexible." He tore off a mouthful of meat. "This is amazing. It's actually juicy, but not in a squishy, disgusting way. And it tastes like real beef. Here, try." He handed a piece to Owen.

Owen's eyes widened as he chewed. "This is like the best beef jerky in the world," he mumbled with his mouth full. "It's what rations want to be when they die and go to heaven."

"I'll assume that's a good thing," Isold said. "This knapsack is something we've talked about the possibility of before, but it would be far outside our resources to buy if we ever found one in a shop. It is the larger version of the purse, called a <**Knapsack of Plenty**>. And that really is all I know about it. Some of these items are very high level."

"What about the cube?" Aderyn asked.

"Such a high level I don't recognize it at all," Isold said. "Normally when I find something [Identify] doesn't recognize, I feel a sense of straining for knowledge I once had that I've forgotten, like the name of a childhood friend twenty years later. In this case, it might as well not be magical for all I know anything about it, which tells me it is quite powerful."

"We'll take it anyway," Owen said.

"Should we?" Aderyn asked. "I mean, we aren't going to take the books in the library. I guess if these were hidden this well, nobody knows about it to protest if we take them."

"That, and I think Tarani's legacy extends to these items," Owen said. "She knew there was a chance she wouldn't come back from that third quest, and she left information for anyone following her. That means us. And it's not a stretch to believe she left this stuff for us, too."

"I think these items were put here by whatever teammates survived the encounter that killed Tarani," Weston said. "If they'd turned the items over to Tarani's family, or to the city, the stuff would be long gone. It's too valuable to lock away. So I bet those teammates were doing what Tarani wanted, and this stuff is meant to help the Fated One who comes after."

"I don't see the point in us leaving them here," Livia said, "whatever Tarani might have wanted. Think of what we can use that knapsack for."

"Aderyn, I think you should carry the knapsack," Owen said. "You're already managing the team's funds."

"I was going to suggest it." She took her own knapsack off and transferred its contents to the <**Knapsack of Plenty**>. There was no sense not using it immediately, and putting it into her ordinary knapsack would look ridiculous. Also, she'd tried putting the <**Purse of Great Capacity**> into her knapsack and it had fought being confined like a small animal in a trap, and she guessed anything that was bigger on the inside would react like that.

"Weston, the goggles are obviously yours," Owen said, "and Isold, why don't you take the belt?"

"I was about to say I should take the rope, because I'm used to the strategy behind *immobilize*," Livia said, "but it makes sense for more than one of us to have that attack."

"So, I'll take the rope," Owen said. "And I don't know that it matters who has the cube, since we don't know what it does, but Livia hasn't gotten anything yet."

"I'm the only one of you lot who won't mess around with it, trying to figure out how to make it work and getting us all sucked into a vortex or something." Livia turned the cube in her fingers. Each side was imprinted with a varying number of V's, placed the way pips on a die would be, one through five, with the sixth side bearing a single, larger V with a circle around it.

"Close the panel up," Owen told Weston. "I want to take a look at these journals."

Chapter Twenty-Eight

They returned to the library, where Livia made more *orbs of light* until the room was brightly and warmly lit. Owen opened the red leather book and held it where they could all see it, though for Livia and Isold it was upside down. "Tarani had good penmanship," Owen commented.

"You won't know this, Owen, but her handwriting is simple, like that of someone who has only just learned to write and hasn't yet developed sloppy habits," Isold said. He didn't sound like upside-down writing was a hardship to read. "Either she wasn't much of a scholar, or she *was* a scholar and knew how handwriting changes across the years. And thought far enough ahead to guess it might take a while for someone else to find her record."

"I'm grateful for whichever of those things it was," Owen said. "And it looks like this is a fair copy from some other writing. There's no dates like there would be with journal entries, and no scribbles or strikeouts."

"That was Isold's guess," Aderyn said.

She let out a squeak of protest as Owen turned the page before she was done reading the first. "I think we shouldn't all try to read it at once," she said.

Owen nodded and handed the book to Isold. "You're the one who knows something about Tarani. This might have greater meaning to you."

"Not much, but it's a fair point." Isold began turning pages, more rapidly than Aderyn would have been comfortable with. "I'll skim this now and see what kind of direction it gives us, and read it more thoroughly later."

Aderyn controlled her impatience, casting her gaze about the room as an attempt at distracting herself. Three bookcases, another window shrouded in curtains, the table they all stood at. No chairs, not even plain wooden ones. Sitting and reading comfortably was impossible. She began counting books on the shelves: seventeen, fifteen, twelve—

"This is it," Isold said, startling Aderyn. "The first pages are an introduction, who Tarani was, her Call, how she knew she was the Fated One. It's fascinating stuff, but then she gets straight to the point: 'I know my destiny, but I'm not so arrogant as to believe being the Fated One makes me invincible. And the system is a bastard, controlling our lives—'"

"Daring words," Weston said.

"She does not have good things to say about the system, which surprises me," Isold said. "At any rate, she writes, 'If I fall, there will be others. Most of them will be false, only interested in the fame and unaware that they have to actually do something to earn this destiny. But some will be like me, and unless I'm really unlucky, anyone reading these words is either one of those or her teammate.'"

"This is so exciting!" Aderyn exclaimed.

Isold nodded. "'What follows is the details of the quests I undertook as part of the Fated One's Destiny quest chain. To access the first, travel to the rock outcropping that overlooks the sea, north of Obsidian. There's a brass statue of a dolphin in its shelter, and it has the quest attached to it. From there, completing one quest will automatically offer you the following quest, and then it's just a matter of finishing them off. As if it's so easy.'"

Owen was nodding slowly. "That's convenient, not having to travel the world in search of the quests. Though we might still have to do that."

"There's more," Isold said. "'I'm sure the system wants the Fated One to go into this blind, but I don't give a damn about the system's desires. So I'm writing down every secret I discovered, every trick I learned, and of course how I ultimately completed each quest. I want my successor to have every advantage. There are four quests in the quest chain, or at least that's as many as I have proof for. I don't know anything about the fourth, but as I write this, I'm about to head out to complete the third. I'll write as much as I can about that in my other journal, and copy it here when I'm finished.' She was nothing if not confident."

"So the other journal is that brown book?" Aderyn asked.

Owen opened it. "The handwriting is much harder to read, and there are dates. I think. I still don't know much about timekeeping in this world." He handed it to Aderyn, who flipped a few pages.

"It's hard for me to read, too, and the dates aren't exactly the way we write them today, and also there's no year," she said. "But there's a lot of choppy sentences the way someone might write notes to herself. 'Reached point of Mt S today,' that sort of thing."

"So it's reasonable to assume this is the other journal she meant." Isold extended a hand to Aderyn, who gave him the brown book. "Between these two, we'll have everything we need to complete the first two quests in the chain, and a good start on the third."

"It's still early," Owen said. "Let's get out of here and get moving. I want to find this statue and accept the first quest, even if we don't leave for it right away."

"I don't think I could bear to wait," Aderyn said. "And really, what would we be waiting for?"

"Exactly." Owen waited for Isold to stow the journals in his knapsack, then directed everyone to form up around Livia. "Too bad *transport* can't take us there directly," he joked.

"Give me a couple of levels, and who knows?" Livia replied.

"I HAVE A BAD FEELING ABOUT THIS," WESTON SAID AS they walked east through Gray district.

"About the quest? Why?" Owen asked.

Weston shook his head. "Not about the quest. About leaving the city. You want to bet that lieutenant makes us surrender our armbands? Because I can see her being the type to want to charge adventurers for faction affiliations every time."

Owen stopped. "I wouldn't take that bet. And we don't know if we'll need to get back into Obsidian after this."

"We have enough money to pay again," Aderyn said, "but I don't want to."

"Fine. Let's go back to Blue district first. We'll change armbands —I know what Eleora said, but this will only be for a short time. Then, if it turns out Weston is right, we'll give back the blue armbands and keep the gray ones concealed." Owen started walking again, more quickly this time. "And hope nobody who matters knows what we did."

Having switched armbands, they proceeded to the gate. Lieutenant Araceli wasn't there. Instead, a burly, unshaven man who teetered on the brink between muscular and fat accosted them as they approached. "Armbands," he said, snapping his fingers.

"We're coming back soon," Owen said. "Can't we keep them?"

"Rules," the man said, not sounding like he cared about them or about rules. "Come on. Hand them over. You can buy another affiliation when you come back."

"But we'll only be gone a day."

"Not my problem."

Aderyn thought Owen was protesting too much, but maybe it would look strange if they complied without a fight. It was a lot of money they were talking about. She handed over her blue armband with pretended reluctance.

They left Obsidian and, instead of following the road, circled the great wall, heading north and west. The pine trees grew close to the wall, but not right up against it; there was a strip of bare ground some fifty feet wide between the wall and the tree line. The friends stayed in that empty space rather than make their way beneath the low-growing pines. With the sun shining, it was a pleasant walk. The air smelled fresh and sharp and resinous, birds sang sweetly in the trees, and Aderyn relaxed. They were headed into danger, or would be once they accepted this quest, but for now, everything was peaceful and still.

The bare strip widened as they rounded the curve of the wall until it became a broad plain. A rushing sound like wind over long grass filled Aderyn's ears, growing louder until it couldn't possibly be what it sounded like. Her confusion cleared up when Owen said, "We're nearing the ocean."

"I've never seen it," Livia said.

"None of us have," Isold said.

"I have. My family vacationed at the coast a couple of times, in California. I tried surfing and sucked at it. But boogie boarding was fun." Owen's step quickened. "Let's see what it looks like from up here."

After a few minutes, they left the plain behind for rocky ground covered with a thin layer of pebbly soil. Aderyn couldn't imagine anything growing there, but tiny plants pushed through cracks in the stone, their little leaves defiant, and she avoided stepping on them as a courtesy to their persistence. The stone sloped upwards now, not much, but enough to feel a strain in her calves. Ahead, the edge of the rock made a sharp line against the sky, as if it came to an abrupt halt.

In a minute or two, she discovered this was true: the rocky slope ended abruptly at a cliff's edge, a sheer drop at least a hundred feet to the shore below. The sea lay spread before them, a glistening, constantly moving expanse of bluish-gray touched here and there with white. "Those are waves," she said. "I read about them in one of Mother's books. I didn't think they were so small."

"That's just distance," Owen said. "When you're down among them, they're enormous, bigger than the biggest Stalwart. And they're strong enough to drag someone down beneath them."

"They're so beautiful." Aderyn watched a wave hump and curl its way toward the shore, where it turned into white foam without reaching solid ground. There were ships anchored there, big ones that rode the waves some distance from land, small ones dragged onto the beach where little wavelets lapped at their sides. People hurried from sheds built back along the cliff's base to the small boats, loading them with boxes and bags. Other people toiled up the path that ran back and forth across the cliff face to Obsidian, high above, or loaded packages into wooden boxes dragged straight up the cliff-side by chains.

"So is this," Livia said.

Aderyn turned from her contemplation of the ocean. Livia stood where the cliffside rose in a sharp jag, looming over where they stood as if something had cut a chunk out of its side to make a shallow niche. Stones arranged in too orderly a way to be called a pile made a sloping pillar, its base twice as wide as its top.

Atop the pillar, a brass rod was jammed between the stones, supporting a brass statue of a leaping dolphin. It was only partly shielded from the elements in its niche, but it looked new, not at all corroded or pitted by exposure. Aderyn, astonished, stared at it until Owen said, "What does **[Improved Assess 2]** say, Aderyn?"

"Oh! Wait a moment." Aderyn focused her skill on it and read aloud.

Name: Dolphin Rampant

Type: Questgiver
Available quest: [Fated One's Destiny: The Great Old One]

"Great Old One?" Owen said. "If it wants us to take down Cthulhu, I'm noping out."

"I don't know what that is," Aderyn said.

"It must just be coincidence, calling it a Great Old One, whatever that is," Owen said, mostly to himself. "But Winter's Peril liked Earth culture..." He shook his head as if clearing it. "Never mind. We need this to move forward, so we have to accept it."

"Let me see what else I can learn before we do," Aderyn said.

The dread Sarnok walks the woods north of Obsidian. Defeat this monster to receive the next quest in the quest chain. Recommended minimum adventurer level for this quest is 14. WARNING: This quest is only available to those who have accepted [Fated One's Destiny]. Accepting [Fated One's Destiny: The Great Old One] without having the previous quests in the quest chain will invalidate the quest. Repeated attempts to do so will result in XP penalties.
Accept? Y / N

"What is a Sarnok?" Weston asked. "I've never heard of it."

"Neither have I, which worries me," Isold said. "My **[Knowledge: Monsters]** skill is quite advanced, but we are still only level ten, and my skill does have limits. The level fourteen recommendation tells us what we suspected, that these quests were intended for adventurers at a higher level than we. Given all that, while I'm sure Tarani's record will tell us all about the Sarnok, including its weaknesses, that may not be enough to let us defeat it."

"So what do we do?" Aderyn asked. "I don't want to give up without trying, but it sounds like we need to work on leveling up before going after this Sarnok, or the other quests in the chain."

She looked at Owen, who was gazing at the dolphin statue as if he were the one who could Assess it. "Maybe we should put this off," he said, again as if to himself. "Am I being impatient?"

"If you are, it's nothing the rest of us don't feel," Aderyn said. "We went through so much to get Tarani's record, it feels like betraying her not to take advantage of her knowledge immediately. To me, anyway."

"I say we take the quest," Livia said. "It's not like there's a time limit or date of expiration on it. Take the quest, read Tarani's notes about it, and then if we decide the Sarnok is too much, we go get a few more levels and come back later."

"I agree," Weston said. "This isn't any different from anything else we've done. We took on Winter's Peril and survived because we're cautious as well as daring."

"Can someone really be both at once?" Isold asked in amusement.

"Of course, because we are." Weston's smile fell away. "Seriously, if it had turned out that the first quest starts in, I don't know, in Finion's Gate or somewhere equally far away, we'd take this quest just so we don't have to come back for it after leveling up elsewhere. Let's learn what Tarani says about it, and then make a decision. But accept the quest first."

Owen nodded. "You make sense, all of you. All right. Go ahead and accept it, and then we can sit and eat lunch while Isold reads us the information on the Sarnok."

"Lunch," Weston said with satisfaction. "Supplemented by grapes and—what did you call it, Owen? Beef jerky?"

"The beef jerky of the gods," Owen said.

Aderyn watched the quest title shrink to a glowing golden dot in the periphery of her vision. "What are gods?"

"Complicated," Owen said, "and as far as I can tell, nothing your world has any concept of, unless the system... no. Let's just say it's a way of saying something is exceptionally good, and leave it at that."

CHAPTER TWENTY-NINE

They walked back to the field and sat together beneath some pines, eating and listening to Isold read aloud. Based on her own words, Aderyn thought Tarani might have been difficult to get along with. She had very strong opinions, didn't like being contradicted, ruled her team instead of them all working together, and never backed down from a fight. Those were good traits for a Fated One who knew what her destiny should be, but bad ones for a person who wanted to be liked. Maybe that hadn't been something Tarani cared about. She certainly never made mention of friends, or a sweetheart, just the teammates who supported her.

"What class was Tarani?" she asked, interrupting Isold.

"She was a Lone Wolf," Isold said.

"That fits," Aderyn said. "I was just thinking how she sounds like someone who wishes she didn't have to depend on others for anything, let alone to complete the Fated One's quests."

"And matches what we heard from her in the Repository," Owen said. "Sorry, Isold. Please go on."

"Tarani lists all three of the quests in the chain that she was aware of," Isold said. "The first is, of course, **[The Great Old One]**. The second is called [Free the Penitent]. The third, the one that killed her, is called [The Maze of Doom]."

"That sounds bad," Livia said.

"That sounds exciting," Weston said at the same time. They pretended to glare at each other.

"This next section is about the Sarnok," Isold said, "and rather than describe their encounters as they happened, Tarani wrote down its information the way it appears to [Assess]. I'll pass it around."

Aderyn waited for the book to come to Owen and then read over his shoulder.

Name: Sarnok
Type: Monstrosity
Power level: 16
Attack: Claw x 2, Bite, Tail slap
Vulnerable to: ?
Resistant to: bladed weapons, arrows, bolts, mind-affecting magic
Immune to: bludgeoning damage, unarmed attacks
Special abilities: Fire breath, regeneration, tough hide

"I wonder why there's no more information," she mused.

"This is plenty," Owen said.

"No, I mean, when I Assess a monster, the system tells me all this, plus some words about the monster's tactics. I guess that's a Warmaster thing."

"Or it's on the next page," Owen said. He turned the page, and stilled so completely Aderyn couldn't even hear him breathe.

"Owen, are you all right?" she asked.

"Holy shit," Owen said. "It's Godzilla."

"It's what?" Isold asked.

Owen held up the book so everyone could see the drawing that filled the next page. It was of a lizard-like creature in a forest, its open mouth displaying rows of jagged teeth. It stood erect on powerful hind legs and wielded a pine tree, by its dangling roots apparently just pulled from the ground, in its much smaller forearms. A long, muscular tail balanced it at the rear against its thick neck and sloping forehead. The artist had drawn other pine trees around the monster for scale. Its head overtopped the trees by several dozen feet.

"What's Godzilla? Isn't this the Sarnok?" Aderyn asked.

"Yes, but it looks exactly like a monster from my world. An imaginary, made-up monster," Owen clarified. "And it has heat beam breath, and its hide is nearly indestructible... it might as well be Godzilla."

"You look like someone hit you, Owen," Isold said.

"It's stupid, because Godzilla isn't real, and the Sarnok is," Owen said, "but the second I saw that picture, I had a flashback to cities burning and a big-ass lizard stomping all over them. Nothing we could defeat. Never mind. I'm letting my imagination run away with me." He handed the book back to Isold.

"Tarani gives extensive space to describing the Sarnok's habitat and—excuse me, Owen—stomping grounds," Isold continued. "As well as directions to find it. She writes also that it took all six of her team members to deliver enough damage to kill it, thanks to its regenerative powers. There's no mention of what level they all were."

No one spoke. Aderyn was thinking about a monster capable of smashing Obsidian to rubble and setting fire to the remains. "Maybe the picture exaggerates its size," she finally said.

"That's comforting, but I doubt Tarani included anything in her record that wasn't as accurate as she could make it," Owen said. "It's looking more and more like avoiding the Sarnok for now is the way to go."

"Yes, and I don't think there's even any point to searching for it so we can Assess it," Weston said. "Too great a risk of being spotted."

"Not to be critical, but where does this leave us?" Livia said. "Gamboling Coil again?"

"We'd still need to have a direction to give it," Owen said. "I think we should spend one more night in Obsidian, working out where we want to start our leveling journey, then tackle Gamboling Coil in the morning."

"I like this plan," Weston declared. "And as for where to level, I think we should head for Finion's Gate. That area might be a little high level for us, but not by much, and the experience rewards will be rich. We've got to be close to level eleven now after everything we've done."

"Really? Because it's only been a few days since we reached level ten," Livia said. "I've always heard leveling slows down once you reach the halfway point. I bet we've got a long way to go still."

"I like my answer better."

Owen heaved himself to his feet and gave Aderyn a hand up. "Argue while we walk."

They returned the way they'd come, with Weston and Livia bickering amiably and Isold singing, not a magical song, but a popular love ballad that Aderyn had always liked. She was so caught up in the familiar tune she didn't at first realize it was discordant. "What's that sound?" she asked.

"You mean, something other than music and verbal foreplay?" Owen said. "I don't hear anything unusual."

"It sounds like someone singing along to Isold's music, but out of tune." Aderyn stopped and turned her head, trying to pinpoint the location of the other song.

Isold stopped singing and tilted his head. "I hear it," he said. "But it's not out of tune. Not anymore." He took a step in the direction of the forest.

"It's beautiful," Livia said.

"Am I the only one who thinks this is dangerous?" Owen said. "Beautiful songs enticing us to follow—that can't be anything but a trap."

"It's just as likely to be something wonderful," Isold said. "A Virtuous Songstress, or a Peace Bird. Those are harmless, beautiful creatures. We should investigate. Peace Birds give boons if you can entice them to your side." He took off running for the trees.

"Isold!" Owen shouted. "Crap. We have to catch him." He sprinted after the Herald. Aderyn and the others followed.

[Keep Pace] brought Aderyn level with Owen after a few seconds, but Isold was the fastest of them, and however hard they ran, he was always just out of reach. The pines closed in around them, their branches low enough that even Aderyn, who wasn't tall, had to duck to avoid them. The song was louder now, still beautiful, and Aderyn realized Isold was right that it wasn't discordant, it just hadn't been in the same key as his song. "What if he's right?" she wheezed. "Maybe it's nothing dangerous."

"There could be a hundred things in this forest that *are* dangerous even if this one isn't," Owen gasped. "And he's not a fool. Whatever's making that song, it's captivated him."

"Can't possibly be something harmless," Weston panted. He slowed. "I'll stay with Livia and watch your backs. Try to stop him, and we'll catch up."

Owen nodded, and Aderyn felt the tug on her calves that said he was running faster.

Isold's shape was still visible ahead, though partly concealed by the trees. He didn't seem to be having any trouble with the branches. Ahead, the pines were thinning out, and the sunlight was brighter. A clearing.

When Aderyn and Owen reached the clearing, they found Isold standing in the middle of it, gazing upward. The song was so loud as to be deafening, and it no longer sounded harmless. A brisk wind from the west, scented faintly with sea water, rustled the tall grasses and tossed the limbs of the pine trees, sending up more of their sharp, resinous scent.

Owen grabbed Isold's arm. "We have to go back. Now."

"They're coming," Isold said. "I can hear them. Just wait, Owen. This will be a sight to remember."

"I'll bet," Owen said. "Don't make me drag you out of here."

The wind shifted to blow from the north instead of the west, bringing a different smell with it. Aderyn wrinkled her nose. "That's awful. What is that?"

"Nothing good," Owen said. He grabbed Isold and lifted him off the ground.

Isold broke free and staggered backward, intent now on Owen. "You're making a mistake."

"I don't want to have to knock you out," Owen said. The wind gusted, bringing more of the terrible scent. It smelled of decay and rotting flesh and bitter old smoke.

Isold opened his mouth and began to sing, a wordless tune that throbbed with the subtle harmonics of [Persuasion]. Terror struck Aderyn to the heart, and she leaped forward, wrenching her sword from its sheath. Owen shouted something her panicked brain couldn't understand. In the next moment, she whacked Isold across the left temple with the pommel of her sword.

Isold's eyes rolled up in his head, and he collapsed. Aderyn dropped her sword and fell to her knees beside her friend, feeling for a pulse. Isold was still breathing, though he looked far too pale.

She heard Owen shout again. This time, he sounded terrified. Then the stench of a thousand rotting corpses enveloped her, and she gagged, her eyes watering. The song disappeared, replaced by the sound of enormous wings beating the air. Aderyn looked up and screamed. A flying creature with the upper body and head of a naked woman merged with the bottom half of a bird of prey dove at her. The monster's wingspan was twice as wide as Aderyn was tall, and its feathers were gray and filthy, some of them broken off so they were only stubs. She flung herself flat across Isold as the creature's talons snatched at her, tearing at the <Knapsack of Plenty> but missing her flesh.

Then Owen was beside her, helping her stand. "We have to

defend Isold until Weston and Livia get here," he shouted over the tremendous wind. "What is it?"

Aderyn, her eyes still watering from the stink, focused on the monster.

Name: Giant Harpy

Type: Monstrosity

Power level: 12

Attack: Talons, wing strike

Special ability: Captivating song

Giant harpies, like their smaller cousins, lure prey to their death with their music, a form of compulsion that makes those who fall victim to it run unerringly to the monster. The scent of a giant harpy is so foul it can cause those not captivated by its song to become violently ill and thus helpless to fight off its attack, but if you're close enough to it to see this warning, you already know that. Giant harpies hunt in pairs and only eat live prey.

"There's another one of them somewhere!" she told Owen. "Try not to breathe in the stink." As she spoke, she watched the blue lines of **[Discern Weakness]** slide across the monster's body, finally focusing sharply on the female torso and abdomen in fat points of blue light. "And it's vulnerable where it's naked!"

The giant harpy had gained altitude and was now hovering, its great wings flapping, as if deciding which of the tasty humans to eat first. Then it dove, moving faster than Aderyn expected. Owen waited for it, sword raised, and thrust for its belly as it descended. It rolled in midair, and his blade scored a glancing hit down its side that made it shriek with rage.

Aderyn took advantage of its distraction to position herself on the opposite side from Owen, carefully avoiding Isold, who was making little movements like he was waking up. She swung at the giant harpy's tailfeathers, shearing off a few of them. The giant harpy again took to the sky, but it wobbled as it flew.

"What did I—" Isold murmured.

"Stay down!" Owen shouted.

"It's coming for you again, Owen!" Aderyn said.

Owen swung as the giant harpy dove. The monster struck him a resounding blow with the edge of its wing, making him cry out in pain and drop his sword. Aderyn leaped over Isold and deflected the giant harpy's talons with her sword, then sliced at its belly. The creature backwinged with a great rush of air that nearly knocked Aderyn over.

The sound of chanting, just audible over the wind, startled Aderyn into nearly dropping her guard. A stone sphere three feet across slammed into the giant harpy's chest, knocking it backward to impact against a pine tree. Aderyn raced toward the creature to finish it, but a system message appeared before she was most of the way there.

Congratulations! You have defeated [Giant Harpy]. You have earned [8500 XP]

She stopped running, observing that not only was the giant harpy's chest caved in, a broken branch had impaled it through the back of the neck. Definitely dead. Aderyn lowered her sword, breathing heavily. She felt along the bottom of the **<Knapsack of Plenty>** and was astonished to discover it intact despite the giant harpy's raking talons.

With a sigh of relief, she turned and ran back toward her friends. Weston and Livia stood near Isold, who had the **<Healing Stone>** out and was running it over Owen's arm. "Be careful!" she shouted. "There's another—"

The stench of giant harpy was the only warning she had before a second creature dropped out of the sky on top of her. She heard Owen shout her name once, and then talons gripped her around the waist, cutting sharply into her stomach and back, and the ground fell away as the giant harpy carried her off.

Chapter Thirty

Panicked, she twisted and flung her arms around the creature's ankles, visions of being dropped from a great height filling her head. She felt her knapsack shift, then slide off one shoulder. Instinctively, she tried to stop it falling with one hand, the hand still holding her sword. The sword overbalanced in the harsh wind of the giant harpy's flight, twisting in Aderyn's sweaty grip. In the next moment, it was gone.

Aderyn grabbed hold of the ankles again, and the **[Knapsack of Plenty]** stopped sliding. She tried not to breathe the monster's funk through her nose. Its ankles' rough, abrasive surfaces tore at the bare skin of her hands, but gripped her clothes as she clung to the legs' dubious safety. The talons still dug sharply into her stomach and lower back, painfully but not so deep as to cause serious damage. That frightened Aderyn further. If the giant harpy hadn't torn her to bits in its first strike, it might have anything in mind.

She ignored the pain as best she could and made herself look down. Heights frightened her—she was always conscious of the ground that lay at the bottom—but now was not the time for fear, not when she needed to stay alert. The view from above was amazing, she had to admit: miles upon miles of pine forest, a shining blue lake or two, and the distant slopes of the Pinnalore Mountains, growing nearer by the second. Then she realized what that meant, and struggled to get free for one terrified moment before remembering that getting free meant being free to fall to her death.

She held on tightly and told herself not to despair. Yes, she was far from her companions, and yes, that distance kept increasing, and *yes*, she had no sword, but that didn't make her defenseless. She wasn't going to give up.

They had nearly reached the foothills, and the giant harpy swooped low to glide along the rocky ground before lifting to the top of a small cliff, little more than an outcropping of rock in a bigger formation. Aderyn guessed the giant harpy was about to land and let go of the creature's legs just before the talons released her. Her fall became a controlled tumble, and she ended in a defensive crouch, whipping out her belt knife. It was barely five inches long, but it was a weapon.

The giant harpy took a few running steps to slow herself to a stop. She turned around to face Aderyn. Aderyn shouted, "Come on! I won't make this easy on you!"

The creature didn't respond. Aderyn took a closer look at her human half. The giant harpy's female body looked roughly molded, with no discernable musculature, no nipples on its pendulous breasts, no navel. Its hair was as gray as its feathers and lank with grease and dirt. Its mouth hung slackly open as if the monster was asleep and dreaming, but its eyes, with their vertical slit pupils like a cat's, were keenly alert and fixed on Aderyn.

The wind blew across the rock outcropping, keening like a mourner, but Aderyn realized she was hearing other sounds, too, rough grunts and whistles like air through a blocked nostril. She backed away, not daring to take her eyes off the monster even to find out what made the sounds, until her foot slid just enough to warn her that she was at the edge of the outcropping.

The giant harpy's gaze fixed on the knife as if considering how much of a threat it was. Then it smiled, a loose, open-mouthed smile that revealed sharply pointed teeth stained dark with old blood. It sidled toward the back wall of the outcropping. The grunting and whistling became louder and more urgent.

Aderyn followed the monster with her gaze, taking a few steps away from the edge, and realized there was something else on the bare outcropping, an irregular pile of branches ranging in size from twig to sapling. Charcoal-gray feathers intertwined with the messy pile. With a growing sense of horror, she perceived this was the source of the sounds.

Something moved in the pile, something dark gray that clambered to the top of the pile and stared at Aderyn. It was a miniature harpy—miniature, not childlike; though it was the size of a five-year-old human child, its body was a smaller version of its mother's, down to the nipple-less breasts. Its wings were fluffy, with no long flight feathers, but still filthy. It stared at Aderyn with the same intent hunger the first giant harpy had had, the one Livia had killed with *stone sphere*. Aderyn swallowed and took a step back before remembering the drop.

More heads of lank gray hair were popping up, three, four, five. The giant harpy croaked, the sound of something that had died long ago and was expressing the last air from its lungs. The young harpies scrambled over the edge of the nest and lunged at Aderyn.

She'd already Assessed them when they first appeared.

Name: Giant Harpy, Immature

Type: Monstrosity

Power Level: 2

Attack: Talons

The immature offspring of a giant harpy lacks the ability to perform a *captivating song* and is considerably weaker than a full-grown adult. It is also not strong enough to break bones with its wing attack. However, its sharp talons are not to be

ignored. **Immature giant harpies are trained by their mothers to rend and devour live prey. That's not you, is it?**

Aderyn held still and let [**Discern Weakness**] do its job. About half a dozen weak spots appeared, blue dots of light at abdomen, chest, neck, and the base of both wings. With her sword, she could have killed any of them easily. With only a knife, that would be harder. With only a knife against *five* of the little monsters...

She sheathed her knife and, rather than wait for them to overwhelm her, dove at the one leading the pack and slammed into it. Her attack took the creature off its taloned feet as she rolled with it, hugging it to her chest and tumbling past the rest of the harpies almost to the nest. She clenched her back teeth together to keep from retching at the stink so close to her face. The creature lay still beneath her, stunned. Aderyn sprang to her feet, bringing the harpy with her, and ran for the cliff's edge. As she ran, she shifted her grip until she was holding the monster under one arm around its midsection.

The creature began to struggle just as Aderyn reached the edge, but it was too late—Aderyn shifted her grip and flung the harpy over the edge. The sound of its whistling grunts faded as it fell out of sight. A second later, Aderyn saw the system message:

**Congratulations! You have defeated [Giant Harpy, Immature].
You have earned [150 XP]**

The giant harpy screamed and clawed the rock with its talons, but it didn't attack. Aderyn had no time to wonder why, because the remaining harpies had regrouped and were coming for her. Aderyn drew her knife. She wouldn't be able to repeat that maneuver.

She fell into a defensive crouch and sidled along the edge until she could put her back to the sheltering cliff. The harpies followed slowly, their cat-eyes gleaming with malice and hunger. Aderyn made herself look at them with a Warmaster's eye. They weren't working as a team, however much it might look otherwise; they got in each other's way, shoving and ducking to get the best shot at her. Aderyn had the impression that none of them wanted to attack first. Obviously they couldn't fly, and although [Improved Assess 2] had said their wings were no threat to her, the harpies themselves protested when one sibling smacked another with the edge of a filthy wing.

The scuffling press of bodies shoved one of the harpies out ahead of the others. As if that was a signal, they all rushed Aderyn, grunting and wheezing like asthmatic pigs with razor-sharp talons. Aderyn dodged the first, drove her knife into the belly of the second, then shoved that one off her blade into the first and almost dodged the talons of the third. That blow raked her stomach, slicing through her coat but not reaching skin. She'd never been so grateful for the padding.

To her surprise, the one she'd gutted was down, being torn at by its sibling, and for the moment Aderyn faced only two opponents. She aimed a blow at the chest of one, who dodged enough that the hit was a scratch rather than fatal, then slashed at the legs of the other, hoping to disable at least one of them. The two darted back, and the one she'd scratched let out a keening wail that tugged at Aderyn's heart like the memory of grief. She shook her head clear and pressed the attack.

She dodged as another swipe of the vicious talons struck harder, sending a streak of pain through her shoulder instead of her throat. Blood seeped into the shredded padding of her coat, but Aderyn ignored it. To strike her higher than her waist with their talons, the monsters had to leap into the air because they were shorter than she, leaving themselves defenseless as they returned to earth. Aderyn thrust again with her knife, and this time, the one she'd scratched cried out as Aderyn's blade found its heart.

**Congratulations! You have defeated [Giant Harpy, Immature].
You have earned [150 XP]**

She blinked away the system message. The one who'd torn up its sibling's body turned on the new corpse, tearing at its flesh. Only one opponent remained, but this was the cleverest one, the one who'd wounded her and hadn't taken any damage in return. It paced outside the reach of her knife, eyeing her with a malevolent gaze. Aderyn's legs shook, and blood loss dizzied her, but her hand on the knife was steady, and she was not going to be taken down by the likes of this creature.

The rush came when she wasn't expecting it, the harpy running at her and throwing itself against her legs in an attempt to knock her down. Aderyn tottered and stepped backward from the impact. Her foot slid, revealing that she'd once again come close to the edge. Instinctively, she plunged the knife into the vulnerable spot at the base of the harpy's right wing. The creature screamed and pulled free, staggering back, and as it curled its wing around itself, Aderyn struck again, this time at the base of its spine. Spasms wracked its body, and Aderyn snatched her knife free and shoved the harpy over the edge.

She saw the system notice distantly thanks to fog clouding her vision, the silver letters dim and tarnished. She leaned heavily against the sheltering wall, not sure her legs would support her if she tried to stand. The last harpy had finished its meal and was approaching her, slowly but confidently, its mouth stained with its siblings' blood. Aderyn thrust the knife before her. "Stay away," she said, but her voice shook, and that terrible mouth smiled more broadly.

It was still a good fifteen feet away, and Aderyn searched her surroundings for something that would save her. Why couldn't **[Improved Assess 2]** work on terrain? Maybe that happened with **[Improved Assess 3]**. But if she couldn't find a way out of this situation, she'd never learn the answer.

The cliff wall behind her was too sheer to climb—worse than that, it curved inward, and Aderyn wasn't a spider to cling to inverted walls. There was nothing in the nest that was a better weapon than her knife. The slope—Aderyn risked a glance at the cliff. It wasn't as sheer as the wall. In fact, it sloped more than she'd realized. And she was no more than thirty feet off the ground.

With her free hand, she detangled the **<Knapsack of Plenty>** from her body. It remained as flat as if it were empty. She brandished the knife at the harpy, making it pause just long enough to give her a few more seconds. Then she threw down the knapsack, dropped to sit on it, and kicked herself over the edge.

CHAPTER THIRTY-ONE

There was more of a slope than she'd realized, but it still wasn't much of one. She leaned as far back as she could without her head hitting the loose scree of the slope and crossed her legs in front of her, hoping to slow her descent. In the first seconds, she heard the horrible cry of the giant harpy and was terrified that she'd left her escape too late. But nothing clawed her, nothing grabbed her, and she slid faster and faster down the slope.

It wasn't a smooth glide, but a bouncing, jolting descent that rattled her teeth and turned the wounds in her shoulder and around her stomach into lancing streaks of pain. After only a few seconds, she was sure she'd made a mistake. True, she'd rather die free than at the talons of monsters, but odds were she wouldn't die instantly, she'd shatter her bones at the foot of this cliff and die slowly.

Then she felt herself slowing, and gravity stopped trying to pull her over headfirst. Leaning back became easier. In the next moment, she shot off the stone and bounced and rolled across the ground until she came to a tumbling halt. Breathing heavily, she stared up into the pine trees that miraculously she hadn't fallen against headfirst. Slivers of blue sky were visible between the branches, but no giant harpy descended to finish her off.

Aderyn tried to rise. She had to get away, as far as she could, in case the giant harpy wanted vengeance for what Aderyn had done to her children. Her body refused to move. She ached everywhere.

She drifted in semiconsciousness for a while in which time had no meaning, listening to the birds call to one another and dreading the sound of the giant harpy's cry or the less terrifying but still awful grunting, whistling noise of its offspring.

As darkness began to fall, Aderyn came to herself. She propped herself on her elbows and looked around. Immediately, she guessed why the giant harpy hadn't come after her: she had tumbled between the trees of a thick grove of pines, which grew close enough together the giant monster couldn't fit. She felt as if she'd struck several of the trees on her tumble down the mountainside. She'd gladly take that over being disemboweled by monstrous talons.

In addition to her wounds and the aches from tumbling down a cliff, she was hungry. She pushed herself to her feet and was grateful to discover she hadn't broken any bones, though she would be nothing but bruises for a while. Her shoulder had stopped bleeding thanks to the remaining padding of her coat, as had the wounds the giant harpy had made in carrying her off. She'd need to clean and bind them properly eventually, but that would have to wait until she found water.

She trudged back along the path of torn-up undergrowth she'd made and found the <Knapsack of Plenty>, which was completely unscathed. The cliff's slope became shallow for the last ten feet, a gentle rubble-covered curve that had probably saved her life. She was too tired to feel properly grateful.

Slowly, feeling a million years old, she rummaged through the <Knapsack of Plenty> to see what she had. There wasn't much. Spare clothes, her mess kit, a package of dried meat, not the nice kind from the <Forager's Belt> but standard rations. Everything she'd attached to the outside of the knapsack, including her waterskin, was gone, scattered by her headlong descent. Her <**Purse of Great Capacity**> was still attached to her belt, with all its contents intact. Aderyn fingered the <**Wayfinder**> and sighed. This could have turned out so much worse.

Dried meat in hand, she walked southeast, not because she knew where she was going but because she wanted to put some distance between herself and the giant harpy. Soon it would be too dark to see, and she would have to find a spot to hole up for the night, but in the morning she would use the <**Wayfinder**> to find Owen and her friends. She refused to dwell on how far the giant harpy had carried her from Obsidian. She would find them eventually, or they would find her—Isold's system map was detailed, and they might return to Obsidian to find someone to scry her location—and there was no sense falling into despair.

As soon as she could only barely see the outlines of the trees, Aderyn searched for shelter. There wouldn't be much of it in the open forest, but this was summer, and she didn't need much. What she did need was water, both to drink and to wash her wounds. She hadn't come across a stream yet, and this worried her, but there was nothing she could do about it tonight.

She found a hollow between the roots of a giant pine, and once she'd determined no one was already using it and that it didn't smell of an animal who might come back and be upset at having been evicted, she curled up with her head on her knapsack and settled in to sleep.

She didn't know what woke her, because when she came alert, the forest was silent, with nothing but the high droning of insects filling her ears. But she was convinced she'd heard something. She sat up, searching the darkness. Pale moonlight came from somewhere, not bright enough to be directly overhead, and almost none of it reached the ground from between the pine branches, but she could see the outlines of tree trunks and her fingers in front of her face.

Distantly, the ground shook.

Aderyn heard the noise at the edge of her hearing, the sound of someone striking hard ground with a stone mallet. Her heart leaped, imagining it was Livia searching for her—but that made no sense, because no spell Livia could cast that sounded like that would be used to locate a missing person. And surely her friends couldn't be close enough for Aderyn to hear if they were in a fight.

The sound came again, and this time the shaking was more noticeable. Aderyn rose and turned her head, trying to identify the origin of the sound. The third time, she realized it was coming from the west.

The fourth time, she identified the sound as giant footsteps.

Aderyn snatched up the knapsack and prepared to run. Immediately, she knew it was a terrible idea. She could barely see to run anywhere, and she didn't know what the creature was or if it meant to attack her. It was big—

Finally, the fog of sleep lifted fully from her mind. There was only one big creature in these woods, at least from what Tarani had written. And it was definitely capable of shaking the earth when it walked.

Aderyn shrugged into the knapsack and tightened its straps. Then she set out into the darkness to find the Sarnok.

It was the only plan that made sense, Aderyn told herself as the footsteps drew nearer and the earth shook ponderously with every one. If she fled from the creature as it approached, it might crush her without even knowing before she could get out of the way. In the darkness, small as she was by comparison, she could locate it, see where it was going, and run the other direction. Yes. This made sense.

She reached for the <**Wayfinder**>, but touching its smooth surface brought her to her senses. At night, surrounded by trees, there was no way she could move quickly and pay attention to its guidance. Besides, she could hear the Sarnok clearly, ahead of her to the west. Its thunderous footsteps shook the ground more powerfully with every step, making the branches quiver and the needles send up a hissing noise as they brushed against each other. The Sarnok's pounding steps didn't do more than send shudders through Aderyn. For now.

As they neared each other, the smell of the Sarnok filled the air, overriding the scent of the pines and the hard-packed earth. It wasn't as awful as the giant harpies' stench, that odorous mixture of rot and death; instead, it smelled musty, like the inside of a cave filled with mushrooms. Musty, and unpleasantly sweet with a hint of decay. Aderyn slowed her steps. The Sarnok's steps now shook the earth hard enough that she had trouble keeping her balance.

In the distance, the crack and splinter of a tree snapping echoed through the woods, immediately followed by the thump of the Sarnok's foot. Berating herself for a fool, Aderyn turned in that direction. She no longer felt that seeing the monster would keep her safe, but she felt compelled to continue, as if the night and the Sarnok had cast a spell over her.

Someone called her name, a long, drawn-out distant cry that echoed the way the breaking tree had.

Terror shot through her, the fear that there was some creature in this midnight woods who knew her name and meant to use it against her. She spun about, searching for this new enemy. The sound came again. This time, she knew it for a human voice, and in the next second realized it was Owen.

She bit back a cry of relief that might have drawn the Sarnok's attention and ran toward the sound, not caring anymore about the monster at her back. After only a few steps, she knew it was a mistake. She couldn't run blindly into the darkness and expect to find Owen and her friends, especially since it was unlikely they'd stay in one place and wait for her. Swiftly, she pulled out the <Wayfinder> box and spilled the spiked orb into her shaking hands. In only a few seconds, its directional spike glowed deep cherry red. Maybe it was a stupid impulse, but she had to take the risk.

She couldn't run and watch the <**Wayfinder**> *and* avoid the trees, so even though her heart urged her to hurry, she kept a steady, normal pace. The ground still shook as powerfully as before, but the steps came at longer intervals, as if the Sarnok had slowed its pace when she did.

Owen shouted her name again. Aderyn drew in a breath to scream a response, and the loudest sound she had ever heard shattered the night. The cry was deep, but resonated with higher notes so it sounded like a cross between a roar and a shriek. The Sarnok's scream touched some primal fear deep within Aderyn, rooting her to the ground like some small animal who hopes the hawk won't see it if it stands perfectly still.

Then the footsteps grew more rapid. The Sarnok was coming her way.

Aderyn ran. She strained to see into the distance enough that she could risk glances at the <**Wayfinder**> to keep her on her path to Owen. Occasionally she caromed off a tree trunk, sending pain flashing through her many bruises, but after a while she found a rhythm that let her move at more than a jog and less than a full-out sprint. Behind her, the Sarnok roared again. The ground shook so hard she stumbled once or twice, but she never lost her footing completely and she never dropped her precious magic item.

Owen shouted her name again. "Shut up!" she screamed, but she was out of breath from running and didn't think the sound went farther than a few feet. The Sarnok had to be nearly on top of her, homing in on the sound of Owen's voice. She blinked away tears. Being blinded by stupid, pointless weeping was the last thing she needed.

Something big hit the ground only twenty feet to her right. She choked back a scream and flung herself behind the shelter of a tree on her left, panting and terrified. In the darkness, the Sarnok wasn't more than a shadowy shape, legs three times the size of the biggest tree trunk, feet like clawed round platters that could feed a hundred people, a tail that swept the ground behind it and made more trees snap and break like twigs. She had the impression of spikes at the end of the tail before it moved past her, not rapidly, but with a terrible inexorable stride that would never need to stop and rest. Not like her. She was almost certainly going to die.

CHAPTER THIRTY-TWO

Aderyn clung to the tree for a moment, her mind numb. Then she shook herself out of her stupor and ran again. Her teammates weren't stupid. They would hear the Sarnok coming and stay out of its way. She just had to find them before they ran and made her journey that much longer.

Owen had stopped shouting, which reassured her. How they had reached this place so rapidly, she had no idea. It was at least a four-day trek through the wilderness. But what mattered was that they were almost reunited, and they would survive this night and get far away from the Sarnok until they were strong enough to defeat it. Having seen the monster, Aderyn wanted that time to be long from now.

At the speed the <**Wayfinder**> constrained her to, she was slower than the Sarnok. Running, she could outpace it. But outpacing it was pointless if she didn't know where to go. Her heart screamed at her to hurry, that her friends were in danger, but she made herself maintain a jogging pace, her eyes flicking now and then to the red spike to keep her oriented.

When it unexpectedly dimmed, her initial fear that something had happened to Owen was shouted down by her knowledge that this meant he and the others were on the move. The Sarnok, and Aderyn, were moving southwest; Owen had started heading east. Hope rose within Aderyn, and she changed direction, following the <Wayfinder> and her heart's desire.

The Sarnok's roar split the night, still far too close, but not close enough to terrify Aderyn with the thought that it might have found her. Again, Owen's direction changed, from east to southeast. Away from her.

Aderyn's earlier hope died. She was going to spend all night chasing him, exhausting herself, and it wasn't as if the Sarnok would go away with the daylight. She shoved the <Wayfinder> into her purse and slowed to a walk, too exhausted to run, putting one foot in front of the other as inexorably as the Sarnok. At least she could put some distance between herself and the monster as she prepared to trek back to Obsidian... through miles of dangerous wilderness... armed with nothing but a knife... She stopped herself thinking about all her many disadvantages. That wouldn't get her to safety.

The rustling of the undergrowth snapped her out of her dream-like reverie. She drew her knife, brandishing it and hoping she looked fierce. Forgetting about the Sarnok, she shouted, "Back off, or you'll get a taste of this!"

"*Aderyn!*"

Several human figures burst out of the dimness, and Aderyn lowered her knife as Owen grabbed her. She cried out as his hand closed on her wounded shoulder, and he released her, looking horrified. "You're wounded. I'm so sorry. Isold—"

"We are almost out of charges of the <Healing Stone>," Isold said. "I choose to be thankful it is only 'almost.' Get the coat off her."

Aderyn held still, too exhausted to help as Owen and Livia removed her tattered coat and Owen cut the ruined shirt away from her wounded shoulder. Blood began flowing again, sluggishly, but Isold pressed the <Healing Stone> against the wound, ignoring the blood. Green light glowed deep beneath her skin, making her bones visible as shadows within her flesh. The stone itself felt almost hot, as if Isold had plucked it from the edge of a campfire, but rather than cooling, it grew warmer, its heat spreading out to fill not only her shoulder, but her arm and the top of her chest. The heat felt so nice Aderyn didn't notice she no longer hurt until Isold removed the stone and said, "Do you have other injuries?"

Aderyn nodded and raised the hem of her shirt, revealing the puncture wounds. Isold took out the **<Wand of Minor Healing>**, then paused. "Was that—"

Weston held up a hand. "Quiet." He moved silently through the underbrush, his head held high, until he had almost disappeared into the darkness to the west. Then he ran back to the others. "Later," he said. "It's coming. We have to move."

"Where do we—" Livia said.

"Northeast," Weston said. He swept Livia up over his shoulder. "And we have to move fast. It's figured out we can track it by its roar."

Aderyn heard it then—the distant *thump, thump, thump* of the Sarnok's approach. She froze. As terrifying as the roar had been, the steady thumping was much worse.

She let Owen pull her along, grateful for his hand and his reassuring presence. The spike of fear that had jolted through her had given her fresh energy, but after only a few minutes she was flagging again, and Owen's grip was all that kept her moving.

"Stop," Owen said. "Aderyn can't go on much longer. And we can't run all night."

"We have to keep moving," Weston said, setting Livia down. "It's got our scent. All we can do is get far enough ahead that it either loses interest or forgets about us."

"We don't know if that will happen," Isold said. "Or how long it will take."

"If we don't at least try, it won't matter. And I don't want to die, least of all at the jaws of that monster. Did you see its jaws?" Weston looked weary. They all did.

"You're both right," Owen said. "And you're both wrong. We have another option. We need to take the Sarnok down."

"You're out of your mind," Weston said. "It took Tarani's six-person team at a much higher level than we are to do a massive amount of damage before killing it. Not only are there only five of us, Livia's at a disadvantage because it's immune to bludgeoning damage, and it won't respond completely to Isold's mind control. And Aderyn is near collapse. How are we supposed to take it down under those circumstances?"

"Then we don't attack directly," Owen said. "We'll have to set a trap. Turn its strengths against it."

"A trap," Weston said, less vehemently. "What kind of trap?"

"I was hoping you could tell me," Owen said, clapping the giant Moonlighter on the shoulder. "It'll be dawn in a couple of hours. We have to figure out how to maneuver it into a vulnerable position and trap it, preferably before full light."

"But we'll have an advantage after sunrise," Aderyn said.

"So will it. If it could see in the dark, it would have caught us before now." Owen put an arm around her shoulders and hugged her. "Can you go a little farther? We move faster than it, so every step takes us closer to safety. Or the semblance of safety, anyway."

Aderyn nodded.

"Think about the problem as we go," Owen told Weston. "It has weaknesses, we just have to use them against it."

"Weaknesses," Weston mused. "What weaknesses? The Assessment didn't mention any."

"There was a question mark next to 'vulnerable to,'" Livia reminded him. "To me, that means it has weaknesses Tarani's team didn't know about or weren't sure about."

"No bludgeoning damage," Weston said, "but... hmm. Maybe

manipulate the terrain. We really need—" He glanced at Aderyn and shut up.

Aderyn knew what he hadn't said. "We need a Warmaster's **[Improved Assess 2]**. If I can get close to it—"

"You need to rest," Owen said. "You're about to collapse. In fact, we need to find a defensible place, just in case the Sarnok catches up faster than we think." He put his arm beneath Aderyn's shoulders to support her as she stumbled.

"We've almost reached the foothills," Weston said. "I'll go ahead and scout. Keep moving northeast." He sped up and soon disappeared into the darkness.

"What if he can't find us again?" Aderyn said. Her voice sounded weak even to her.

"He's a Moonlighter. He can find us anywhere." Owen stopped her and crouched to lift her into his arms, cradling her like a baby. "Just rest. It will be fine. We've bought ourselves some time. Hey, for all we know we've already outrun it!"

Aderyn smiled without meaning it, but he hadn't been serious either. She rested her head against his shoulder as he walked on and after a moment drifted into semiconsciousness again. She woke when Owen set her down on something soft and springy that prickled. Nearby, a fast-moving stream burbled. The smell of fresh water mingled with the strong scent of pine reached her, and she suddenly realized how thirsty she was.

She pushed herself into a sitting position. The springy surface was a pile of pine branches, much more comfortable than the bare ground. Weston had found a cave, or at least a shallow cleft in the rocks, with a stream of water flowing from somewhere above and pouring over the lip of the overhanging rock into a shallow pool some three feet away. Owen and Livia knelt there, filling waterskins. She didn't see Isold or Weston.

Owen turned and noticed that she was awake. He came to her side and offered her the waterskin, still dripping. "Isold says you're dehydrated, so drink as much as you can," he said. "I can't tell you how relieved I was to see you wielding that knife at me. You were still on the heads-up display, but your health bar kept dropping. We saw the system notices that you'd killed harpies, and then nothing."

The water tasted bitter, like stone and earth, and it was the best water she'd ever drunk. She gulped until her belly felt full, then handed the waterskin back. "How did you get here so fast? I was sure we'd all be walking for days."

"Once Weston kept me from racing into the wilderness after you, we ran back to the city." Owen drank, not as thirstily as she had, and set the waterskin aside. "We didn't want Livia to exhaust herself with a million little *transport* hops—"

"I swear I'm getting a better transportation spell the minute it's available," Livia said. "I'm not made for running."

"We got to Obsidian, argued for far too long—"

"It was less than five minutes," Isold said, coming around the curve in the rock. "I want to finish healing you, Aderyn."

"Keep talking," Aderyn said. "You had to argue?" She peeled what remained of her ruined shirt off the puncture wounds and tossed it aside. Isold lifted the edge of her shift and held the tip of the **<Wand of Minor Healing>** a few inches from one of the wounds.

"We managed to find the one guard in all of Obsidian who actually cares what happens to adventurers without a faction allegiance." Owen grimaced. "We couldn't exactly whip out the gray armbands, and we couldn't buy even the cheapest faction affiliation without some guard or other reporting it to whoever pays for his information. Finally, we convinced Mr. Helpful that we were willing to take our chances, and we headed straight for Lady Eleora's mansion."

Green light bubbled and frothed from the tip of the wand, tickling the sensitive skin of Aderyn's belly. Between the healing and the water, she already felt much better. "I can't believe she was willing to help."

"She wasn't there. Seems she was at Seburtan's mansion, plotting revenge on Liander. I almost feel sorry for the guy. Eleora is not someone to piss off. Anyway, her second in command, or rather third in command, that Halsey fellow, he let us in and told us all that. I begged him to help us find a spellslinger who could cast *world door* and wouldn't charge us thousands of gold. It hadn't escaped us that you had all our money except the pocket change we each had for emergencies. It was enough to pay the entrance fee, but not much more."

"I joke about how indispensable I am because I've got all the coin, but I didn't think it might actually become an issue." Aderyn clasped Owen's hand. "But you found someone."

"A level sixteen Earthbreaker who calls himself Virros the Rock," Owen said. "He's built like a rock, too, round like a boulder, with fists you could imagine cracking stone. Gray faction, even, so we didn't have to worry about being accosted. We threw ourselves on his mercy, and he agreed to take payment when we return."

"Daring of him, considering he couldn't know if we would ever return," Weston said, dropping to his knees beside Aderyn. "But I think he's a romantic. He was much taken with Owen's wild-eyed story about the loss of his sweetheart, swept away by a monster."

Aderyn's hand closed more tightly on Owen's. Owen put his other arm around her and hugged her close. "I was more than a little upset," he said.

"I understand." She leaned into him, feeling even better than before.

"Virros couldn't get us directly to you, because he doesn't have *scry* and *world door* doesn't home in on people automatically. But he dropped us about three miles south of that end of the Pinnalore Mountains, and I shouted in the hope you'd hear and know to use the <**Wayfinder**> to reach us. But then we heard the Sarnok coming and had to run."

"I don't understand how you found me at all. I thought you were running away from me, southeast, but it turns out I just didn't know which way on that heading you were moving. I should have noticed the <**Wayfinder**> warming—I guess I was more lightheaded than I realized. What other magic did you have?"

"The magic of desperation and luck," Owen said. "We didn't know how far the monster would chase us, and we were afraid of bringing it back to Obsidian with us. So we ran east for a while and then turned northwest, hoping to draw it back to its lair, or wherever it lives. I was thinking maybe if it was comfortable, it wouldn't feel like chasing us. It was a complete surprise to stumble across you." He hugged her again. "I guess we were due some good luck."

At that moment, Aderyn felt the ground tremble.

The others felt it too. Everyone fell silent, waiting for the Sarnok's next footstep, and the next. "It's advancing," Livia said. "The steps get closer together, and the tremors are stronger."

"That's all right," Weston said. "I have a plan."

CHAPTER THIRTY-THREE

With the <Cat's Eye Goggles> firmly in place, the world looked, not bright as day, but clearly outlined in shades of gray. Aderyn examined their shelter, if you could call it that. The crevice was too shallow, even with the over-hanging rock, to protect against any but a northern wind, and it stood at the top of a shallow rise that didn't elevate it enough to give it a clear view of oncoming enemies. It was also backed into a bare stone cliff that at the moment looked more like a trap than a shelter.

Another crack and the pattering of stone shards on the ground drew her attention to where Livia clung to the cliffside, creating holes in the rock with *stone ladder*. Aderyn saw clearly that the series of climbing holds didn't rise in a straight line, but veered around bumps that would have been difficult to get over, all the way to a sort of ledge about twenty feet off the ground. Livia clambered back down. "See if that helps," she told Aderyn. She cast a glance over her shoulder at the trees. "It hasn't sped up yet. Either it's lost us, or it thinks it has us trapped."

"I hope Tarani's picture was right, and it's taller than the trees,"

Aderyn said, and scrambled up the *stone ladder*, her recovered sword bouncing at her hip.

Livia had judged the distances between holes well, and despite having to move sideways occasionally, Aderyn reached the ledge easily. She pressed her back to the wall and surveyed the tree tops. Her heart lurched at the sight of the Sarnok, no more than a hundred yards away. She'd thought it was terrifying when it was nothing but a shadowy shape, as if her imagination made it more horrible than it was. Now she knew her imagination had fallen short. The Sarnok towered head and shoulders above the tree tops, its jaw hanging open like it meant to taste the air for their scent. Teeth like daggers as long as her arm gleamed dully in the light of the waning moon. Its thick, muscular neck bulged as its head turned, casting about for its prey.

Aderyn swallowed her fears and Assessed it.

Name: Sarnok

Type: Monstrosity

Power level: 16

Attack: Claw x 2, bite, tail slap

Vulnerable to: radiant damage, *daylight, sunburst*

Resistant to: bladed weapons, arrows, bolts, mind-affecting magic

Immune to: bludgeoning damage, unarmed attacks

Special abilities: Fire breath, regeneration, tough hide, tracking

The Sarnok hunts the westernmost end of the Pinnalore Mountains, north of Obsidian. Despite its size, it is sustained by magic rather than food, which frees it to pursue its prey according to its whim, small or large. It tracks both by scent and by eye, and if you're unlucky enough to come within range, it is likely to pursue you forever. Bright light hurts it, but practically nothing else does. Are you discouraged yet? Because you really should be.

Aderyn ignored the last two sentences and watched the blue lines of light play over the creature's body. She cursed. The trees blocked her view of the creature's lower body, and if it had weaknesses there, they would stay a mystery. Above, she saw only what she'd expected: two blue dots where its eyes were, taunting her with their inaccessibility.

As if aware of her scrutiny, the Sarnok stopped moving. It lifted its head higher, as if scenting the wind, and roared. The wind carried the sound of its roar away, but even the edge of the sound terrified Aderyn. Before the sound faded completely, the monster started moving again, faster and faster until it was running straight for her.

Aderyn bit back a scream and clambered back down, skinning her palms in her rapid descent. "We have to go. It's on the move. Is Weston back yet?"

"No. How close is it?" Owen asked. He had his pack on and held the <**Knapsack of Plenty**> in one hand.

"Less than a hundred yards." The ground shook with the monster's approach. Aderyn slung the knapsack over her shoulders and fumbled the <**Wayfinder**> out of her pouch. "Go!"

She ran arm in arm with Owen, eastward along the cliff base where the trees didn't grow, and in gasping breaths summed up what she'd learned from her Assessment. Behind her, Isold and Livia's breathing said Isold was lagging behind on purpose to keep Livia with them. The <**Wayfinder**> glowed brightly, so Weston must be close. Aderyn stumbled, was kept upright by Owen's grip, and kept running. She hoped she was right about being able to outrun the Sarnok in a race. That assumed it was a race with an end, though, and after what Aderyn had Assessed, she didn't believe that was true anymore.

She was intent enough on her path that Weston's appearance in front of them startled her into dropping the <**Wayfinder**>. She scrambled to pick it up as the others gathered around. "I've found a spot, but we have to hurry," Weston said.

"Aderyn learned it's vulnerable to bright light," Livia said. "But *daylight* is a close-range spell. It will take perfect timing."

Isold and Owen threw out their arms to steady themselves against the growing tremors. Livia stood as if rooted, even when Weston put a hand on her shoulder for balance. "Go, go!" Owen urged.

They ran south and east, into the forest. There hadn't been time to give the goggles back, and Aderyn saw everything clearly outlined, all the trees seeming covered in pale ash, the roots outlined starkly so there was no chance she might stumble. Too bad she would have to return them to Weston, but he'd make better use of them in general than she could.

They stumbled into a smallish clearing, no more than twenty feet on its longest side. Weston said, "Is there any point in hiding, Aderyn?"

"It tracks by sight and smell. The point of the trees is to keep it from using its tail slap attack freely, not to hide us. But we might be able to confuse it if it thinks we don't know how it found us. Nothing in [Improved Assess 2] said it's intelligent. So we should pretend to hide."

"That works." Weston surveyed the clearing. "Aderyn, where should we stand?"

Aderyn followed his gaze. "Owen and Livia, on opposite sides *here* and *there*. Isold, all the way at the far end where you can catch its eye. Resistant to mind-affecting magic isn't the same as immune. Weston, you back up Owen, and I'll put myself in a flanking position. Now, hide us."

The shaking of the ground had become constant. Wherever the Sarnok was, it was close and moving faster. Aderyn crouched in the spot Weston picked. On a whim, she removed the goggles and tucked them inside the knapsack. She didn't know what would happen if she saw Livia's *daylight* spell through them, but it couldn't be good.

The tremors stopped.

Her heart pounding as if the Sarnok were trampling it, Aderyn peeked out in time to see the Sarnok's enormous head thrust through the trees into the clearing. In the next moment, Livia shouted a string of nonsense syllables, and light burst over the clearing, bright as the brightest summer day.

The Sarnok screamed in pain and jerked back. Somewhere nearby, a dozen trees splintered and crashed to the ground as its tail swiped through the forest. Owen darted out of hiding and waved and shouted at the monster, brandishing a coil of white rope with one long trailing end.

The Sarnok blinked, its head weaving as if trying to focus on Owen. Then it stumped toward him, moving faster than before. Owen snapped the end of the **<Ensnaring Rope>** at its legs.

The **<Ensnaring Rope>** whipped out of Owen's grasp and lashed itself around the monster's ankles. The Sarnok stumbled, teetering, and Aderyn balanced on the balls of her feet, ready to lunge when it fell.

The Sarnok roared again, a sound more furious than before. It got its balance and strained at the thing that dared restrain it. The rope stretched and then snapped, its pieces flying in all directions. The monster screamed in defiance and took another ponderous step, clearly intending to crush Owen.

When its foot landed, the ground disappeared from beneath it.

This time, the monster fell.

It hit the ground with a convulsive thump that rippled the ground and knocked Aderyn over. She scrambled to her feet and ran. Everyone else was ahead of her, Livia and Isold approaching the head, Weston racing toward it from the north just behind Owen.

The Sarnok lifted its head, and a beam of light and heat so intense it dried Aderyn's eyes and nose from thirty feet away burst from its maw and struck Livia and Isold.

Aderyn screamed. She ran, sword bared, for the fallen monster only to stop short in amazement. A curved wall of earth, its surface glassy from being hit by intense heat, stood where Livia and Isold had been. In another moment, the two backed away from the protective shield and fled.

Owen threw himself atop the monster's shoulder, but before he could reach the vulnerable eyes, the Sarnok pushed itself to its knees and roared again, forcing Owen to cling to the monster's rough hide or be thrown free. Owen drew back his sword for a blow to the neck.

"*Watch out!*" Aderyn screamed. Owen ducked as the Sarnok swiped at him with its vicious claws, three on each hand. The Sarnok got to its knees, and Owen jumped and tumbled away. With another cry, a beam of burning light scythed across the tops of the trees to the north, sending Owen and Weston running as fire spread through the branches. Blood dripped down the Sarnok's neck where it had clawed itself trying to reach Owen.

The friends gathered around Aderyn. "We have maybe ten seconds before it comes after us again," Owen said. "Aderyn?"

Aderyn frantically reviewed what **[Improved Assess 2]** had told her. "If Isold could **[Fascinate]** it, we could stab it through the eye. That's the only weak spot it's got."

"I tried. It didn't respond at all," Isold said. "Maybe a deeper pit? Something to bring it down to our level?"

"*Hungry pit* is too small for the Sarnok to fit inside," Livia said.

Something nagged at Aderyn's memory. "We need it subdued for only a few seconds, long enough—oh, *I know!*" She grabbed Isold's arm. "Do you still have that euphorium we got to drug the bees?"

"It's not going to sit still for us to spray it," Isold said.

"It won't have to. What's the most magical item we've got? That weird cube, right? Let me have that, Livia, and Isold, pour the euphorium over it." She snatched the cube from Livia and held it out to Isold. Isold dumped what was left of the sticky liquid over the cube and Aderyn's fingers. She hoped the drug couldn't be absorbed through the skin. The liquid coated the cube's surface and pooled in the grooves of the largest V.

The roar of the Sarnok shattered the forest air. "Run, *run!*" Aderyn yelled, and threw the cube at the Sarnok before taking her own advice. They all pelted for the trees at the eastern end of the clearing and ducked into their dubious shelter. Aderyn turned, terrified that she was wrong in her understanding of what **[Improved Assess 2]** had told her.

But the Sarnok hadn't chased them. It stood in the middle of the clearing, awkwardly holding the cube in both its three-fingered hands. Slowly, it raised the cube to its face and sniffed it. Its fleshy black tongue curled around the cube and drew it into its mouth. The Sarnok didn't move, didn't roar. Then, like a great tree hewn down at the roots, it toppled, falling to lie on its side with a tremendous thump that shook the earth like *thunderstomp.*

Owen and Weston were already sprinting for it. Aderyn ran after them, counting seconds even though she had no idea how long euphorium would affect a monster the Sarnok's size. Owen reached it first, clambering up its chest and shoulder to balance atop its head. Weston was barely seconds behind. Owen reversed his grip on the <Twinsword> and struck the monster's eye with a two-handed thrust that drove the blade nearly to the hilt. The Sarnok's spasm nearly tossed Owen off, but as he steadied himself, Weston struck at the other eye from below, and with another deep shudder, the Sarnok fell still.

Aderyn stumbled to a halt a few steps away, not quite believing the monster wasn't playing a trick on them. At any moment now, it would toss Owen into the air and swallow him.

**Congratulations! You have defeated [the Sarnok].
You have earned [25,000 XP]**

**Congratulations! You have completed the quest [Fated One's Destiny: The Great Old One].
You have been awarded [10,000 XP]**

Welcome to Level Eleven

Aderyn sagged in relief. Owen slid down from the Sarnok's head and embraced her. "How did you know that would work?" he asked.

"The Assessment said the Sarnok lives on magic, not food," Aderyn explained. "I thought it might mean that it likes to consume magic. And it's not like we know what that cube does, so I figured it was no real loss if it devoured it."

"That was brilliant," Weston said. He was holding his hand, gory from monster ichor, out to Livia to wash clean. "And level eleven, too. Let's get out of here before it respawns, and not fight any more great old one monsters for a while, all right?"

"We have a problem," Isold said.

Aderyn realized the Codex hadn't cleared, and another message had taken the place of the level up notice. "'A new quest is available,'" she read aloud. "How is that a problem? Didn't Tarani say the quest chain is automatic after this?"

"That's not all Tarani said," Isold said darkly. "Read the whole thing."

Aderyn focused on the Codex.

A new quest is available: [The Fated One's Destiny: Fire and Ash]
Accept? Y / N

"This seems pretty straightforward," Owen said. "Is there something Tarani wrote about it that we should know?"

"Tarani didn't write anything about it," Isold said. "That's not the second quest."

Chapter Thirty-Four

I t came to Aderyn all at once. "That's right. Tarani's second quest was called **[Free the Penitent]**. What happened? Did we do something wrong?"

"This **[Fire and Ash]** is clearly marked as a Fated One's Destiny quest. We can't have done something wrong." Owen squinted at the air, scowling as if that would make the Codex change.

"Done something..." Isold dug through his knapsack and brought out the red-bound journal. "Done something... give me a second." He flipped pages rapidly and then stopped, stabbing a finger at the page. "Tarani said it took all six of her team dealing damage to kill the Sarnok. Four powerful fighter classes, a Flamecrafter, and a Windwarden. As she put it, 'we stabbed it until it was pulp and even its regeneration couldn't save it.' We didn't do that."

"We *couldn't* do that even if we wanted to," Livia pointed out.

"Yes, but we still defeated it. Two different approaches, both successful." Isold clapped the book shut on his finger. "I think the quest chain isn't static. I think it changes according to how each Fated One and their team succeeds."

"Is that possible?" Owen said. "Wouldn't that put us back where we started, not knowing which way to go?"

Isold was shaking his head. "No, I think Tarani got some things right. There probably are four quests in the chain, and we both had the Great Old One quest to start. And the next quest did appear automatically. But she couldn't have known the second quest is dependent on how you complete the first. She used brute force. We used cunning."

"That sounds like the system testing the Fated One again," Weston said. "Presenting quests that will prove different abilities."

"It makes sense," Aderyn said to Owen, who still looked torn. "It's an extension of the system giving us secret quests and throwing overpowered monsters at us. Suppose the system wants the real Fated One to be able to handle any challenge?"

"I get it," Owen said. "But I liked the idea of knowing what comes next. If Tarani's journal doesn't give us an edge, we're back to fumbling in the dark."

"I don't think it's that bad," Aderyn protested. "More like... seeing only a few paces at a time. Let's see if we can get more information about this one." She brought up the Codex again and focused on the new quest.

A new quest is available: [The Fated One's Destiny: Fire and Ash]

A threat from the Lonely Tor puts the surrounding communities in danger. Find and eliminate the threat to proceed. Recommended minimum adventurer level for this quest is 16.

WARNING: This quest is only available to those who have accepted [Fated One's Destiny]. Accepting [The Fated One's Destiny: Fire and Ash] without having the previous quests in

the quest chain will invalidate the quest. Repeated attempts to do so will result in XP penalties.

Accept? Y / N

Aderyn let out a deep breath. "Well, that was less informative than I hoped."

Owen was squinting at his Codex. "The Lonely Tor is a long way off, and in the opposite direction from Finion's Gate. There isn't anything about a time limit, is there?"

"I don't see one," Weston said. "But it's possible if we leave without accepting the quest, we'll have to defeat the Sarnok again to get the system to offer it to us. We should take it, and set it aside for now."

"Sounds like a plan." Owen flicked a finger at the air, then stiffened. "What's this?"

Aderyn selected Y. A new message appeared.

WARNING: Your average team level is 11, making you ineligible to complete the quest at this time. [The Fated One's Destiny: Fire and Ash] will remain inert until average team level reaches 14.

"Well, it looks like our decision was made for us," Livia said. "I'm glad the first quest didn't have that restriction. We'd still have had to defeat the Sarnok and we wouldn't have gotten anything out of it."

"We'd have gotten twenty-five thousand experience," Weston pointed out.

Livia shrugged. "There's that."

"It's still a good outcome," Aderyn said. "We have the quest, and we aren't going to accidentally fall into it at much too low a level. We got lucky with the Sarnok, but we can't count on that happening twice."

Owen nodded. "Let's get out of here. It's stupid, because the Sarnok probably won't respawn for a while, but I feel superstitious about hanging around this corpse while we find out what changes level eleven made—what the *hell* are you doing, Isold?"

Isold shoved the Sarnok's wet, muscular black tongue to one side of its slack mouth. "That cube saved our lives, and it's extremely magical. We shouldn't leave it here if—ah, found it." He raised the gleaming bronze cube to where they could all see it. "But I could use a wash."

A gush of clean water poured over his shoulder, arm, and outstretched hand. "Thank you, Livia," Isold said, shivering.

"Do you know anything more about it now?" Owen asked.

Isold examined the cube. "I feel I should, but the knowledge escapes me, so I'm getting closer. I know it makes things, and that's all." He handed it to Livia, who turned it over a few times before putting it in her knapsack.

"Then let's walk until daylight and see where that puts us," Owen said.

Aderyn walked beside her sweetheart and marveled at the beauty of the woods just before dawn. The birds were already awake and singing like they meant to serenade the friends, or perform some stirring anthem in praise of their exploits. They'd killed the Sarnok! That was cause for amazement, or celebration, or something.

"What a marvelous day," she sang. "Marvelous, marvelous. See, even the birds agree!"

"Aderyn, are you all right?" Owen asked.

She ran her hand up his arm to his shoulder and caressed the side of his neck. "I'm wonderful, and so are you. You look like a noble hero out of a story, so handsome, so strong—I can't wait to get you alone so I can kiss—"

"Um, Aderyn, you need to stop there," Owen said, blushing.

"I think she absorbed a touch of the euphorium," Isold said.

"No, I didn't drink one teeny tiny droplet, not one," Aderyn trilled.

"That's not good," Owen said. "How long before it wears off?"

"I have no idea. We can hope we aren't attacked by anything serious until after she recovers." Isold's eyes gleamed with amusement. "But she is quite funny at the moment."

"I told you we should have tried it," Weston said. "She looks blissed out."

"If we had, we'd all be dead now because we couldn't have used it on the Sarnok," Livia said.

"Good point," Weston said.

Aderyn couldn't take it anymore. She skipped ahead, singing with the birds, ignoring her friends' shouts. They ought to dance, too, stuffy old boring sticks as they all were. Then Owen's hand on her shoulder brought her to a halt. "How about you sing for us? Don't run ahead or we won't be able to hear your, um, your beautiful song."

She twined her fingers with his. "Only if you sing too, handsome."

Owen reddened again. "I don't sing."

"Everyone sings! Listen to the birds, they'll teach you." Aderyn warbled a bird song and listened as the jays in the trees sang it back to her. Owen, his face crimson, joined her, and after a moment they were all singing, with Isold's tenor rising above the rest. Aderyn's heart swelled with happiness. This was the best day ever.

Half an hour later, she let her song die away and said, "What did I just do?"

"Something we can all be grateful we weren't in civilization for," Isold said, grinning.

Aderyn released Owen and covered her face with her hands. "I've never been so embarrassed."

Owen took her in his arms and kissed her. "If that's the only fallout from killing the Sarnok, we're all grateful. Besides, it was fun.

But only because we were in the forest. And now that you're in your right mind again, and the sun has risen, let's stop for food and decide what to do next."

Aderyn let Owen find them a comfortable seat in the hollow of a dead pine and leaned against him. "Did I really offer myself to you as your willing slave?"

"You did, and as I'm a gentleman I turned you down." Owen smiled and kissed her again. "Don't worry, Aderyn. Your idea saved our lives. And I think we all needed a laugh."

"Still." She shrugged. "I want to see what level eleven looks like."

She brought up the Codex and whispered, "Advancement."

Name: Aderyn

Class: Warmaster

Level: 11

Skills: Bluff (7), Climb (3), Conversation (7), Intimidate (4), Sense Truth (11), Survival (4), Swim (1), Knowledge: Monsters (10), Knowledge: Demons (1)

Class Skills: Improved Assess 2 (18), Awareness (11), Knowledge: Geography (9), Spot (11), Discern Weakness (16), Dodge (10), Improvised Distraction (9), Outflank (11), Draw Fire (5), Keep Pace (12), Amplify Voice (9), See It Coming (7), Basic Weapon Proficiency (Swords) (5), Read Body Language (3), Basic Map Access (2), Compel (0)

"I wonder what [Compel] is," she murmured. "Suppose I can make monsters do what I want? That would be useful."

"I have [Overrun] as a new skill," Owen said. "It looks like it's related to [Charge]. And I'm reminded that I haven't done anything about [Two-Weapon Fighting]. I'm going to need a second sword. Or something. My skill applies to all bladed weapons, right?"

Aderyn nodded. Owen sounded like he was speaking from very far away. She yawned. "Any bladed weapon, yes."

"So maybe I don't want to limit myself. I wonder what kinds of swords there are in this world? So far, they've all been familiar ones. I mean, it's not like you have…"

She drifted off to sleep with his voice in her ears, comforting her.

When she woke, the sun was nearly directly overhead, as far as she could tell through the branches. She was lying with the **<Knapsack of Plenty>** pillowing her head, with Owen snoring nearby. When she sat up, Weston shifted his position from where he'd been sitting with his back against a tree, keeping watch. "Feel better?" he asked.

"Much. Have you slept?"

"Not yet. I'm not very—" A jaw-cracking yawn interrupted his words. "Maybe I am sleepy." He rested one hand gently on Livia's blonde head, lightly enough not to wake her from her sleep. "Do you mind watching?"

"Not at all." Aderyn rose and stretched as Weston lay down next to Livia. She strolled around their… it wasn't so much a campsite as the place where they'd all collapsed in degrees of exhaustion. That she wasn't still tired surprised Aderyn. The healing she'd received must have revitalized her as well.

The cool air beneath the pines invigorated her further and roused her appetite. She thought better of waking Isold, who wore the **<Forager's Belt>** but had one hand draped across it protectively, and dug through her knapsack for that packet of dried meat. It was better than nothing.

Owen stirred and blinked up at her as she closed the flap. "What time is it?"

"I don't know. About noon, I guess. Want some meat?"

"That stuff in the **<Forager's Belt>** has spoiled me for rations," Owen said with a grimace, but he accepted a hunk of dried meat and gnawed on it without complaint.

They ate in silence, reminding Aderyn that one of the things she loved about her relationship with Owen was that they could sit together, not needing to talk, and let that bring them closer together. She idly brought up her Codex and read her Advancement again.

[Compel]. She wished there was some way to learn more about skills that wasn't trial and error. Well, maybe there was. It wasn't as if she'd be penalized for failure.

She focused on [Compel] and Assessed it with a long blink.

[Compel]: Force one enemy to target an ally of your choice.

Aderyn gasped. Owen sat up and looked around. "Is something wrong?"

"I just discovered a new element to [Improved Assess 2]. And now I wonder how long I've had this ability. I might have been able to do it several levels ago!"

"What is it?"

"If I Assess a skill, I learn more about what it's for and how to use it." She Assessed Owen and focused on his class skills list. "[Overrun]—do you know what that does?"

"I assume it's a refined version of [Charge]. But I'm not sure."

She Assessed the skill and squeaked in excitement. "My skill works on you! [Overrun] means a charge in which you knock your opponent down and move into position behind him. It's like doing damage before getting in a position for [Outflank]. This is so exciting!"

"See if it works on someone who isn't your partner," Owen suggested.

A quick Assessment of the sleeping Weston revealed that it didn't. This didn't ruin Aderyn's mood. "I couldn't see others' skills for a while after I was able to see yours," she said, "and this probably means I haven't had the skill for very long. Which is reassuring. I hate the idea of having a skill for levels and levels without knowing it. It feels so wasteful."

"What's wasteful?" Livia asked, sitting up and running her fingers through her short hair.

"Nothing. I'm surprised you're awake."

"Something was digging into my side." Livia patted the ground all around her and the surface of her knapsack. She brought out the mystery cube. "I must have rolled onto it."

"I wonder what it does," Aderyn said.

"We should get it identified," Owen said. "There must be Heralds in Obsidian. Or is there an identify spell?"

"Not that I know of," Livia said. "There's a *heritage* spell that reveals the history and provenance of an item, and that sometimes identifies magical qualities, but this is high enough level that spell might not be effective." She turned the cube around and stilled. "Huh."

"Did you figure it out?" Aderyn asked.

Livia shook her head. "Not really. It's just that I don't think these are letters. The sides curve out too much. If you look closely, there are fainter lines coming off them, and if you turn it upside down, well, they look like tents." She crossed to where Owen and Aderyn sat and offered them the cube.

Aderyn squinted. There were faint lines, and they did look like guy ropes supporting the upside-down V of a tent front. "Do you think it's an alarm for a campsite? Something that protects a tent?"

"I have to believe whatever it does, there are six versions," Owen said. He moved to press the big circled V or tent, and Livia whisked the cube out of his hand.

"Sorry," she said, "but we shouldn't randomly press magic items. Not in this confined space. I have an idea, though." She walked away through the trees, slowly, scanning the ground as if searching for something.

"Don't go too far away," Owen said.

Livia waved an acknowledgement. She came to a stop in a place where the trees were maybe a little more widely spaced, held the cube at arm's length, and with her other hand pressed her thumb against one of the cube's sides.

Nothing happened for about three seconds. Then the faintest sound of a trumpet playing a fanfare filled the air, and Livia was suddenly at the center of a whirlwind. Aderyn shouted and lunged for her, but pulled up short when Livia said, "It's all right! I'm not hurt."

The whirlwind expanded, filling the tiny clearing with what looked like small humanoid figures moving fast enough to be barely more than a blur. Then they were gone, and Aderyn gaped in wonder. The clearing now held a tent barely able to fit the space, with a roof high enough to walk under, and a neat little ring of stones contained a small fire that crackled merrily.

"Wow," Livia said. "That's more than I expected. I thought maybe it would summon a length of canvas and some rope to tie between two trees. This looks more like something a noble would take on a picnic. I guess if the cube is as magical as Isold says, that's reasonable." She pressed the side of the cube again. The whirlwind returned, and after three seconds and another, different fanfare, the clearing was once again empty. Not even a trace of ash from the fire remained.

Livia walked back to join them. "That was the side with one tent," she said. "I'm guessing it will produce up to five tents, and this sixth side, I'm afraid to test in among all these trees, in case it's enough tents for a regiment."

"More than enough for us, though," Owen said.

"And it didn't suck us into a vortex," Aderyn said with a grin.

"More dumb luck," Livia said with an answering grin. "Seems we haven't yet used up our share."

CHAPTER THIRTY-FIVE

They reached the road leading to Obsidian at noon four days later, coming onto it just a few hundred feet from the great gate. The forbidding black walls and the ridiculous black-painted doors were a welcome sight after days of trudging through the wilderness and seeing nothing but endless trees. Aderyn stopped in the middle of the road to Assess the city, just in case level eleven improved her findings, but she didn't see any differences.

"Aderyn, come on. I want a real meal," Owen said. "Not that I haven't been grateful for the **\<Forager's Belt\>**. I can't believe none of us are good at hunting."

"I'm great at hunting," Livia said. "I hit my target every time. It's not my fault *stone sphere* pulverizes small animals."

"I can't believe you were willing to do that," Weston said. "You with all your proud talk about bunnies being too cute to kill."

"I didn't kill a single bunny," Livia said, pretending haughtiness. "Only someone with a heart of stone would expect me to eat rabbits."

"Maybe, but those deer were also cute."

Livia shuddered. "Deer are terrifying. Unnatural. Those big eyes, and the way they're always slightly smiling—you know they're plotting something, and the cuteness is just to throw you off guard."

"Fortunately, Gamboling Coil's instantaneous travel means we don't have to be good hunters," Owen said, looking queasy as if he was remembering the results of Livia's attempts at killing prey for the cookpot.

"We ought to check to see if Gamboling Coil is still there," Weston said, sobering.

"Why wouldn't it be? Who would know about it to defeat it?" Aderyn gazed with longing at the city. A hot meal, a bed with a mattress...

"That's why we shouldn't take it for granted that we'll have access to it. We need to prepare for the possibility that would most disrupt our plans. Just in case." Weston set off down the road, away from blessed civilization. Aderyn couldn't believe she'd just thought of Obsidian as civilized.

Aderyn didn't remember exactly where Gamboling Coil had settled, but Weston strode confidently along the road for a few miles and then took a sharp turn into the trees. The rest of them followed him up a hill into a clear space. Which was completely empty.

"Well, crap," Weston said. "I'm never paranoid, and this is why. I hate being right about the worst-case scenario."

"It's not paranoia if you're right. Then it's realism," Livia said.

"It might not be the right..." Aderyn's voice trailed off as Owen walked into the clearing and kicked a deep gouge in the turf that looked exactly like a giant foot had torn it up. More of them disturbed the ground all around the clearing, the marks of Gamboling Coil's froggy feet digging in and leaping high into the air.

"Well, crap," Owen said. "I totally forgot. Steering the dungeon somewhere resets its pattern, remember? Which means if no one else came along, it moved five days after we arrived. Which was two days ago."

"There's still that fellow, that Earthbreaker," Aderyn said. "The one who cast *world door* to get you close to me. He could transport us to Finion's Gate."

"Well, about that," Owen said. "We had to promise him a lot of money payable when we returned. More than we have, possibly. I'm sure we won't have enough for five more castings of the spell."

"So, we'll walk," Livia said.

They all stared at her. "Walk?" Weston said.

"It's a very long way to Finion's Gate," Isold reminded her.

"Sure, but we have to level up to access the next quest, right? I bet we'll level at least once between here and there, just by killing monsters. So it's tedious. It's not like we have another choice."

"Livia, since when are you the optimist?" Weston exclaimed.

"I'm a realist, dearest. And realistically, this is the option we have." Livia glanced at the sky. "Let's return to Obsidian, settle our business, resupply, and head out in the morning."

"I agree," Aderyn said. "And honestly, this isn't so bad. Except for the small matter of feeding ourselves on something other than grapes and beef jerky."

Owen put his arm around her. "We'll figure that out, too."

When they approached the city gate, Lieutenant Araceli was there, her spectacles glinting in the sunlight, so rare for Obsidian. "You again," she said. "You look like shit. Been sleeping rough?"

"It's ten gold entrance fee, right?" Aderyn said. "We won't be needing armbands."

Araceli raised both thin eyebrows. "Daring as well as scruffy," she said. "You want to get yourselves killed—"

"Actually, we have a standing invitation from Lady Eleora of Gray faction," Owen said. "You can tell your master that. Hope you get paid in advance, because he won't last long."

"I have no master," Araceli said with a sneer. "And Liander of the White isn't in a position to hear anything from me or any other informant."

"Is he dead?" Aderyn exclaimed.

"No, but I'm sure he wishes otherwise. The faction power structure has been rearranged, and White has lost its position to Blue and Gray. Did you all have something to do with that?"

"You want information, you'll have to pay for it. That's how things work in Obsidian, right?" Owen returned her sneer and brushed past her to enter the city. Aderyn handed over the entrance fee and hurried after him.

"Well, damn," Owen muttered. "White lost power."

"I hope you don't mean to suggest we should be sad about that," Isold said.

"No, but if we'd taken that quest about the factions, we might have gotten experience for helping Blue and Gray."

"What we need now is money, not experience," Weston said. "We need eighteen hundred Obsidian gold. How much do we have?"

Aderyn blanched. "Not eighteen hundred, that's for sure. Maybe we'll be stuck here for a while, earning money to pay that Earth-breaker off."

"We're not going to worry about that now," Owen said. "We're going to see Eleora and find out what's been going on. I'm not saying I feel like we owe her anything, certainly not help with her political game, but I'll admit I want to see Liander taken down a peg or two."

They stopped out of sight of the gate and Araceli to put on the gray armbands, then strolled through the city toward Gray district. Obsidian was a different city in the sunlight, with most of its citizens thronging the streets. Shouts from street vendors mingled with the laughter and cries of men and women buying everything from produce to live pigs. The happy clamor made it impossible for Aderyn to be downhearted despite her eighteen hundred good reasons for depression.

Eleora's mansion, like the streets of Obsidian, looked much different in daylight without the rain battering its stone walls. Though it rose three stories tall, with crenellated walls and towers flanking the entrance, it felt more homey than intimidating, and

Aderyn didn't know why. Maybe it was all the windows. There were dozens of them, all sheets of thin, perfect glass like Aderyn had never seen before, and with the mansion facing east they would be blindingly bright in the morning. Aderyn had seen houses similar in size and construction to this one, and none of them had had windows, just narrow slits you could shoot a bow or crossbow through. This one looked like it was only pretending to be tough.

The grounds were much smaller than Liander's and were laid out plainly, with no large trees, just shrubberies lining the outer wall and rosebushes beneath the windows of the ground floor. Petals littered the ground around the rosebushes from where the flowers had taken a beating during last week's storm, suggesting that the rains hadn't been heavy while the friends were gone.

They walked up the path to the front door, and Owen pulled a bell rope dangling next to the door. Someone had knotted an orb of malachite at the end of the rope, and Owen examined it after ringing the bell. "How valuable is this stone?"

"Not very," Livia said. "Even if you cut it and faceted it, set it in jewelry, it still wouldn't sell for much. It's pretty, though. Maybe someone liked the look."

The door swung open, revealing Halsey. "You again. You found your teammate. Go you."

"Don't be so enthusiastic," Owen said. "We'd like to speak to Lady Eleora, if she's available."

Halsey opened the door wider and gestured for them to enter. "Wait here," he said, and disappeared down one of the many unlit halls, not the one that led to Eleora's study.

The entrance chamber cube was as cold as before, but now that they weren't captives in danger of death, it didn't bother Aderyn so much. For lack of anything better to do, she examined the parquet floor. Thousands of pieces of wood the size and breadth of two of her fingers made up a geometric pattern of light and dark that Aderyn couldn't help trying to trace with her eye, searching for an end or a beginning. Was it the work and design of one person, or had many hands put it together? Or maybe some artist had drawn the concept and a dozen workers had brought it to life. She liked imagining who that artist might have been.

Footsteps sounded in the hall. The person who emerged wasn't Halsey, but a woman wearing a drab apron spattered with dried paint over an ordinary shirt and trousers. Since Aderyn had been looking at the floor, she noticed the woman's shoes first. They were of soft fabric stitched to leather soles that were the source of the sound, with flowers in many colors embroidered all over the fabric. Why the contrast between her shoes and her clothes, Aderyn didn't know, but it intrigued her.

"Eleora will see you upstairs," the woman said. She sounded not at all servile, and again the contrast made Aderyn curious. Surely this woman couldn't be an ordinary servant, especially if she referred to Eleora so informally.

They followed the woman back down the hall and up the staircase at its end, which led to a long gallery with windows on one side and portraits on the other. Everyone in the paintings was extraordinarily beautiful or handsome, unrealistically so, Aderyn thought. She envisioned generations of Eleora's family instructing artists to make them look better than they actually did, with successive portraits getting less and less representative of reality.

The door at the end of the gallery stood open, and the smell of fresh paint wafted from the room beyond. The woman entered without saying anything more, and after a brief hesitation, Owen and the others followed her.

Half the smoothly plastered wall of this round chamber was a drab brown the color of poorly-bleached leather. The rest of it, the half that smelled of fresh paint, was an extraordinary raspberry pink. Couches and tables had been pushed to the center of the room and draped with sheets of fabric, and the floor beneath the newly-painted sections was covered with heavy canvas rumpled here and there where people had rucked it up by walking across it.

Eleora stood with her back to them, dressed as the other woman was, with her hair bound up loosely out of her face. "I redecorate when I need to relax," she said without turning around. "Painting soothes me. Do you like it?"

"I didn't know paint could be that color," Aderyn said.

"There's a Windwarden in Orange district who has a passion for inventing new paint colors. I pay her a retainer to put my requests first. Haven't been able to convince her to move here." Eleora laid her brush across the top of a large bucket filled with raspberry paint and wiped her hands on her apron. "Halsey told me what you came here for while I was gone. You were successful."

"Yes, and we appreciate the—" Owen began.

"Don't thank me for doing what anyone in the city could have done. Virros the Rock is famous. All I did for you—or more accurately, all Halsey did for you—is give you a shortcut." Eleora looked Owen up and down. "And now you're back here. What can I do for you this time?"

Owen ignored her sarcastic tone. "We hoped you'd tell us how things stand with Liander of the White. We want to know how careful we should be."

Eleora turned to the other woman. "Miretta?"

"Liander has until midnight tonight to accede to our demands," Miretta said. Her voice was low and sweet and nothing like Eleora's. "My informants tell me he's stalling so he can hide most of his valuables and pretend he doesn't have enough to pay you and Seburtan, then offer you a pittance and hope you'll take it on the grounds that a little is better than nothing." She smiled, and in that expression she looked so much like Eleora Aderyn knew they were related.

"My sister," Eleora said as if confirming Aderyn's guess. "And supervisor of my informant network. Seburtan and I offered Liander a deal: pay us off, and he can stay in Obsidian at a lower rank. In practice, that means he'll be able to move against us someday, but that's a hazard of politics in Obsidian. If he chooses not to pay, we'll destroy him and take his property anyway."

"It's your city. I assume that's reasonable," Owen said.

"More than reasonable." Eleora smiled wickedly. "Of course, there's a stinger attached. Once we've destroyed him—"

"I thought he was going to pay," Aderyn said, horrified.

Eleora snorted. "Liander loves his wealth, as is evidenced by what Miretta just said. Anyway, we won't kill him, if that's what you're worried about. That's against the laws of Obsidian. Also, dead men can't suffer humiliation, and I intend him to suffer greatly for what he did to me." Her lips trembled, and she pressed them together to still them. "Once he's destroyed, we're going to make him send his daughter somewhere far away."

"That seems cruel," Isold said, but he didn't sound judgmental, only thoughtful.

"Crueler to her what he's been doing," Eleora said. "Jessemia is a bubble-head and more arrogant than all the rulers of Obsidian put together, but she's been spoiled all her life and that's not her fault. Maybe she won't learn humility fast enough, and maybe she'll end up dead, but she'll have the same chance all of us did."

"And it will break Liander's heart, losing the person he loves most," Isold said. "I imagine you find that very satisfying."

"Deeply," Eleora said. Her wicked smile broadened.

"It's a good solution," Owen said.

"I appreciate your approval," Eleora said, again with a sarcastic edge to her voice. "Which is fortunate, because I have a job for you."

Owen's eyes widened. "No," he said. "Absolutely not."

"You haven't even heard my offer."

"I don't have to. It's obvious," Owen said. "You want us to escort Jessemia to the safe zone."

CHAPTER THIRTY-SIX

Aderyn gasped. "We can't do that!"

"Of course you can," Eleora said. "When you're finished here, you're leaving. I'll pay you to take her with you. Nothing could be easier. You don't even have to team with her if you don't want to."

"That obnoxious, prissy, stuck-up mouth on legs?" Weston said. "We'd end up leaving her for the monsters to devour."

"You're too nice for that," Eleora said. "No, you'll take her. Get her as far as Guerdon Deep. That's not too high a level, and if she has to, she can take a caravan south to the safe zone."

"You can't force us to do this," Livia said.

"I can't. But I can make your lives miserable for as long as you remain here. I can ensure you get no jobs. You'll never pay back Virros—hah, you didn't think I knew about that, did you? Virros is my loyal man, and he doesn't conceal things from me." Eleora's eyes were cold and hard. "So you have a choice. Do as I tell you, and you'll leave here tomorrow. Reject my offer, and you'll call Obsidian your home for a good long time. Which will it be?"

Aderyn watched Owen anxiously. The set of his shoulders practically shouted his desire to attack Eleora, who was unarmed and a good deal shorter than he was. "Owen—"

"How much?" Owen said, the words grinding past his gritted teeth. "And it had better be a lot."

"Five thousand gold," Eleora said promptly. "Enough to pay Virros, equip yourselves, and have a little left over to buy your partner something nice." She smiled, this time pleasantly. "I'll even cover your bill at the Raintree Inn to show my appreciation."

"It's the least you can do," Aderyn said, overriding whatever Owen was about to say that [Read Body Language] told her would be something obscene about Eleora's mother.

"If you want to think of it like that, sure." Eleora waved a hand in the direction of the door. "Go, get yourselves cleaned up. You look like you've been dragged across a hundred miles of bad terrain. I'll send word to the inn when I'm ready for you to pick up Jessemia— and I'll pay you at the same time. Don't worry, Virros isn't in a hurry to get his money back. I told him not to be."

Owen stormed out of the room before she finished speaking, nearly mowing down Miretta in his haste. Aderyn felt the tug of [Keep Pace] in her calves as she ran after him. "Owen—"

"Not a word until we're on the street," Owen said quietly, with none of the anger she'd expected.

Once they left Eleora's mansion, Owen kept walking rapidly until they were deep in Gray district and the mansion was well out of sight. Then he stopped and threw his head back to stare at the blue, cloudless sky. "It's fine," he said when Aderyn said his name. "Five thousand gold ought to be enough to clear our debt and pay for six castings of *world door* at Virros's rates. We'll take the brat to Guerdon Deep and be off again. I realize it means losing out on the experience an overland trip would give us, but I think that's balanced by how we'd kill Jessemia if we took her the long way."

"And she's probably not worth much experience," Livia said.

"Just so we get rid of her as fast as possible," Weston said. "She irritates me. And don't think I was kidding about the muzzle."

Aderyn said nothing. Jessemia irritated her, too, with her casual assumptions that she was better than everyone else and her complete lack of self-awareness or understanding of just how crippled an adventurer her father had made her. But she couldn't help feeling sorry for the woman regardless. No real friends, no one who respected her—Aderyn wouldn't trade places with Jessemia if she was the richest woman in the world.

"Much as I hate to admit it, Eleora was right about one thing. We're a mess." Owen glanced around as if getting his bearings and headed off down the street. "Let's go talk to Virros."

"Eleora said not to worry about him," Isold said.

"Not to pay our debt. I want to confirm that he can send us to Guerdon Deep or, failing that, the safe zone. Don't forget that Wind-warden back in Elkenforest knew *world door*, but not how to open it on Obsidian. We shouldn't count on a solution without confirming it's possible. And I want to lock in Virros's price for sending us." Owen let out a huff of breath. "After discovering that Gamboling Coil is gone, I'm inclined to a little paranoia."

"Livia assures me it's called realism," Weston said.

THE HOUSES ON THE BORDER BETWEEN ORANGE AND GRAY district faced off across a single long street, wider and straighter than any Aderyn had seen before in Obsidian. They were also identical, two rows of two-story houses, all with slate shingles, all faced with plaster cracking from the constant onslaught of rain and salty sea air. The plaster was painted a white that had faded to pale gray years before. To Aderyn's eyes, it looked like poverty.

"It's not what you're thinking," Owen said in a low voice, though the many men and women thronging the street ignored them, too busy with their own pursuits to bother with scruffy adventurers.

"How do you know what I'm thinking?"

"I can read your body language, remember?" Owen jogged up three steps and knocked on one of the identical doors. "You'll see."

The door didn't open immediately. Owen pounded hard with his fist and waited. Weston said, "He might be asleep."

"It's almost one," Aderyn said.

"Yes, but he sleeps odd hours, or so he told us when we apologized for rousting him in the middle of the night." Weston nodded politely at a pair of women passing who sped up, giggling, at his notice. Livia elbowed him in mock reproof.

The door swung open. Aderyn gasped and turned away, blushing. The man who stood there wore nothing but a pair of thin cotton undershorts through which Aderyn refused to admit she'd seen anything. "Hey, it's you," Virros the Rock said. "And this must be your sweetheart. Glad to see you found her. Something wrong, miss?"

Aderyn shook her head violently.

"Well, come on in. Sorry for the delay, but I was asleep. Days like this one make me tired. You remember the way." Virros turned and stumped away down a short hall. Aderyn made sure Owen was solidly between her and the Earthbreaker in all his amazing near-nudity. What she could glimpse past Owen's shoulder told her her friends' description of Virros had been totally accurate. The man was nearly as short as Livia, and round with muscle rather than fat. From behind, it looked like his head sat directly on his shoulders, which were broad and sturdy; his arms bulged so much they stood out slightly from his body, giving him the look of a wrestler permanently ready for a match; and his thighs were easily as big around as Aderyn's waist.

Low couches with fat cushions filled the room Virros led them to, all of them upholstered in heavy silks stiff with embroidery. Virros waved a thick-fingered hand indicating they should sit and exited the room through another door. When he returned, he was wearing a dressing gown that strained across his shoulders and stomach. It was covered with pockets, some of which were in fabrics that didn't match the rest of the gown, and a stylized dog's head was embroidered over the left breast pocket.

"I've set water on for coffee. I need it on a day like this," Virros said, seating himself next to Livia.

"What's different about today?" Aderyn said, pretending her embarrassed reaction hadn't happened.

"Oh, I'm allergic to sunlight," Virros said casually. "Makes me break out in hives. That's why I live in Obsidian, and even with its fantastic weather I sleep the day away." He punched Livia lightly on the arm. "It's not really an Earthbreaker trait, but sometimes it feels like it, eh?"

"I know I'd sleep until noon if they let me," Livia said with a grin.

"Anyway, I didn't expect to see you again for a while. Though I didn't doubt you'd return. I have a good sense for people's trustworthiness." Virros tapped the side of his fleshy nose. "You in a rush to get things settled?"

"We don't have the money to pay you yet," Owen said. "We will tomorrow, don't worry."

"Like I said, I trust you." Virros unselfconsciously scratched his crotch. "But I am wondering why you're here, if not to square our account."

"This is more about seeing what our options are. We're about to leave Obsidian, and we were hoping to shorten our journey back to the safe zone."

Virros whistled. "That's a long way off. I can see why you might not want to travel cross-country. Where, specifically?"

"Any of the safe zone towns. Guerdon Deep, if those aren't an option. We know *world door* has limitations, and you might not know all of those places." Owen casually rested his hand on Aderyn's knee, and she clasped it.

"Well, I hate to disappoint you, but I'm afraid I don't know any destinations that far east." Virros did look discouraged, as if he'd denied himself a treat as well as having to turn them down. "As an adventurer, I located a lot of places where quests are available, and I specialize in sending adventuring teams to those. But none of them are farther than maybe five hundred miles from Obsidian, and the journey you're talking about is almost three times that. I'm really sorry."

"But you could cast it if someone could *scry* one of those towns," Livia said. "I took *scry* as one of my fifth-level spells, and Asylum is my home town. Even with my inexperience at the spell, I'm sure I can get a good enough look at Asylum for *world door* to work."

Virros brightened. "What a great idea!" He chuckled and patted his stomach. "I keep meaning to replace one of my fifth-levels with *scry*, but that takes something like two weeks of rigorous fasting, and I love food."

"Man after my own heart," Weston rumbled.

"We'll need six castings of *world door*," Owen said. "I hope that's not impossible."

"Not at all." Virros sniffed. "Coffee's ready. Let me bring it out, and we can talk price."

When he was gone, Isold said, "That was almost too easy."

"Don't you go pessimistic on us," Weston said. "Why should it not be easy? It's a matter of having the right spells, which we do, and even if it takes all the money Eleora pays us, we'll be free of that mouthy wench Jessemia in no time and in a position to get back to our quest."

"With everything we've been through in the last week, I'm suspicious now when things go our way," Isold said with a rueful smile. "More paranoia, though possibly not the realistic kind."

Virros returned with a tray laden with coffee pot and thick ceramic mugs that made Livia's eyes gleam in anticipation. She helped pass mugs around as Virros poured. Aderyn stirred cream into hers and sipped the scalding liquid cautiously. It smelled divine and tasted better.

"So, how about this?" Virros went on when he had his own mug. "You pay me the seven thousand gold tomorrow, and we'll see if we can make this trip work. Does that sound good?"

Owen choked. "How much?"

Virros looked concerned. "Did you swallow the wrong way? Hot coffee can burn if you do that."

"No, I'm fine. *How* much will it cost?"

"Seven thousand. I'm giving you a discount because I like you. Plus the eighteen hundred from before. That's not a problem, is it?" Virros's concerned look deepened.

"I thought you charged four hundred and fifty gold per casting of *world door*," Aderyn said. She'd done the math on the way back.

"The farther the distance, the greater the power expenditure," Virros explained. "That translates to me having to charge more for those long-distance hops."

"But the Bonemender in Elkenforest only wanted five hundred each to send us all the way here!"

Virros's expression stiffened. "I hope you don't suggest that I'm cheating you just because some spellslinger in some other city doesn't understand economics."

"No, of course not. I'm sorry. It's not what I expected, that's all." Aderyn drank more coffee to cover her confusion. That was not quite twelve hundred gold per person!

"I wish I could offer you more of a bargain, because I really do like you all." Virros stirred another thin stream of cream into his already milky cup. "But I have to make a living."

"We understand. And it's not your fault we can't afford that much. You've been very generous." Owen drained his mug. "We shouldn't keep you up. Can we return tomorrow evening?"

"That's very understanding of you. I'll see you then." Virros yawned. "But not before five in the evening, if you don't mind."

CHAPTER THIRTY-SEVEN

On the sidewalk outside Virros's house, Owen said, "Damn."

"Then we're stuck walking all the way to Guerdon Deep," Isold said. "I wish I hadn't jinxed us by suggesting things were too easy."

"Not having enough money was not what I expected our problem to be," Owen said. "Having to wrangle that selfish idiot through a *world door* was the extent of what worried me. And now we're stuck with her for six to eight weeks, during which time we'll be fighting monsters we'll have to protect her from, and she'll be an impediment the whole way."

"An impediment and a burden," Livia said. "Weston, we could use some optimism right now."

"I have no optimism where she's concerned," Weston said. "She's going to demand special treatment and refuse to do her share of the work, and she'll yammer on about how cruel we are while she does that. I swear we'd better level at least once or I'm going to feel very ill-used."

"Maybe she'll change once she knows she can't manipulate us the way she does her papa," Aderyn said.

"That's better. We need that kind of optimism," Owen said.

"I was kidding. The only thing that will change her is a *poly-morph* spell. You don't know that one, do you, Livia? It was in a story I read once."

"Sadly, I do not." Livia sighed. "We have to make the best of things. It only makes a situation harder if you dwell on all the negatives."

"My grandma always used to say 'Spit in one hand and wish in the other, and see which fills up faster,'" Owen said. "Meaning when you want something, you have to make it happen rather than dwell on wishing for things to change. We're stuck with Jessemia, so we need to deal with that."

"Your grandma had some disgusting habits," Weston said, making a face.

"She was a hoot. She grew up on a farm and then left to become a journalist traveling the world—someone who goes places and writes about what they're like," Owen clarified. "I think she liked to put on the down-home airs so people didn't expect her to be educated and sharp."

Mention of his grandma got Aderyn thinking about Marrius. She wasn't sure she wanted to go home yet, but the idea of seeing her parents reunited with him had appeal. "It's just to Guerdon Deep," she said. "But maybe we could go farther than that. So long as we're grinding experience to level."

"Do you really call it that?" Owen said. "That's what we say in roleplaying games in my world. It's amazing how much of this world seeped into mine."

"I wish we had that glowing line thing you talked about when we first met," Aderyn said. "The one that shows the path to your next quest. How useful that would be."

"I'm intrigued," Isold said, "but let's talk on the way back to the inn. I could really use a wash and a real meal."

"They have baths. I checked," Aderyn said.

Owen let out a low groan. "A bath, and real food. This day is looking up."

THE NEXT MORNING, ELEORA SENT A MESSAGE: *LIANDER'S house at three p.m. Come ready to travel.* She also sent the full five thousand gold. Owen's lips thinned in anger when he saw it, conveying to Aderyn the clear message that he knew Eleora was taunting them. She knew they wouldn't cut and run. Aderyn almost wished they weren't honorable.

The teammates spent the time before lunch buying supplies for their long trip, basic necessities and enough food for a week. They'd have to figure out hunting in that time. Livia's assurances that she had new ideas for creative spell use in killing prey unnerved Aderyn.

She and Owen went out to buy him a second weapon and discovered, after buying supplies and reserving money for Virros, they couldn't afford a magic sword. They ended up getting a long, thin dagger with a slim guard and a minor enchantment of increased damage. The knife merchant called it a <**Deadly Blade**>, something Aderyn thought was overselling its virtues. Owen called it a +1 pigsticker.

They met back at the inn at noon and sat together in the taproom, waiting for the serving boy to bring them whatever was on offer that day. Owen displayed his dagger and compared it to Weston's new throwing knives, which were shorter and weighted differently. "We're running through the gold fast," Owen said, "but it's not as if there's anything to spend money on in the wilderness."

"I'm afraid most of it went to recharging the <**Healing Stone**>," Isold said. "I successfully charmed the Bonemender who did it—my natural charm, not a skill," he said to Aderyn. "And I also sold the <**Wand of Minor Healing**> and used that money toward getting a <**Wand of Healing**>, which is more powerful and has more charges."

"That's the best use of our money I can think of," Owen said. "Livia, did you pay Virros?"

"He wasn't happy about being woken before noon, but then, who is?"

"I am," Weston said promptly.

"You're known to be insane, dearest. Anyway, with us leaving at three, we couldn't wait on his requested time. And I thought I'd see if he knew *heritage*. My guess was that he'd feel mildly guilty at disappointing us and might cast that spell on the cube for free. And he did."

"That was a clever idea," Aderyn said. "Did the spell reveal anything useful?"

"The cube is extremely powerful," Weston said. "We knew that, but according to *heritage* it's more than we expected. It's called <**Soldier's Friend**> and there are only five of them in existence, so it's famous enough that *heritage* had plenty of information on it. Aside from building the magic campsite, it sets an *alarm* spell that goes off if anything hostile crosses the perimeter. The fire burns without fuel until the campsite is disassembled. And the campsite will last for up to seventy-two hours or until commanded to break camp, whichever comes first."

"Oh, and that big tent in the circle?" Livia added with a gleeful grin. "Turns out that produces enough tents for an army. Specifically, one thousand tents. Good thing I didn't let you press that button, huh, Owen?"

"I'm very grateful," Owen said.

After lunch, everyone retired to their rooms to finish packing for the journey. Aderyn laced shut the <**Knapsack of Plenty**>, which looked completely empty and weighed almost nothing. "I feel almost guilty about not carrying a real load."

"You carry the cookware and almost all the food, and no one cares whether it's not a fair burden," Owen pointed out. "It's not like anyone wants the others to suffer under huge weights."

"I guess not." She turned around and embraced Owen, resting her head on his shoulder. "I think I want a nap."

"If you're interested, this is our last time having a real bed for the next two months." Owen ran his hand down her back.

Aderyn laughed. "I'm sleepy. Maybe later."

"Of course." He kissed her and lifted the knapsack off the bed. "I'll join you. I have a feeling I'm going to need all the rest I can get before this afternoon."

They lay together, not speaking, fingers intertwined. For no reason, Aderyn found herself remembering their first days together, not as sweethearts, but all the way back to the road from Far Haven, when they barely knew each other and Owen had been withdrawn and uncertain and Aderyn had sometimes been impatient. "I'm sorry I wasn't nicer to you when we were first partners," she murmured.

"I never felt that. You were always patient with me, or at least acted patient. If you felt otherwise, you hid it well."

"I was surprised when you turned out to be a good leader, after how diffident you were at first." Aderyn squeezed his hand lightly. "Surprised in a good way."

Owen laughed. "I was so disoriented those first few days. I had no experience that would prepare me for this world, killing monsters with a sword and eating strange foods. Walking all day. And—you'll laugh—I was intimidated by you."

"Owen!"

"See, I told you it was funny. You were so confident, and you knew the answers to all my questions, and it never seemed to bother you that I'm from another world. And you're beautiful. I thought I was self-assured around women, but you are so different from the women I know."

Aderyn blushed. "You keep saying that. No one's ever thought I was all that beautiful before. Pretty, maybe."

Owen scooted closer. "Then those people are idiots." He kissed her, slowly, running a hand across her shoulder and down her arm. "Because you're the most beautiful woman I've ever seen."

She shivered and kissed him fiercely in return. "You're terrible."

"I am? What kind of—"

Her kiss silenced him. "Terrible," she said, "because I really did want to sleep, and I have totally changed my mind now."

"That was not my intent, Aderyn." Owen drew her into his arms. "But when a beautiful woman tells a man she wants him, the smart man doesn't turn her down."

"You're the smartest man I know," Aderyn said.

WHEN THEY APPROACHED LIANDER'S GREAT MANSION ON its hill at quarter to three that afternoon, no guards stood at the gate, and the gate itself was ajar. Owen pushed it all the way open, and they trudged up the white-brick path to the front door. Here, the door was shut, and unlike when they'd come this way with Tevon, it didn't open at their approach.

Weston checked the latch. "Not locked," he said, and opened the door. "This is eerie. It feels abandoned."

"It might be, if Eleora and Seburtan stripped Liander of most of his support." Owen followed Weston inside. "Now I'm wondering just how far Liander fell."

"Do you think they let him keep this house?" Livia said. "If they took all his money, he might not be able to maintain it. Certainly not to be able to pay servants."

"Honestly, I don't care so long as it leaves him unable to strike at us. If he hadn't been so high-handed, he'd still have all his power, so anything that happens to him is ultimately his own fault." Owen pointed at the stairs. "I'm guessing we go to his audience chamber. One last look at those awful stained glass windows."

They retraced their steps from their first visit. This time, all the doors lining the second-floor hall stood open. The rooms were all empty, the art removed, the harp gone. If not for the thick carpet they walked on, Aderyn was sure their footsteps would have echoed. She knew better than to pity Liander, but the empty rooms saddened her. If Liander did lose this mansion, she hoped whoever owned it next would fill it with things they cared about rather than showing off their wealth in that tasteless, vulgar way.

Though today wasn't as bright and clear as the day before, the weak sunlight was still bright enough to show the stained glass windows at their finest. The white robe of the male figure on the center window glowed, translucent and bluish like skimmed milk. It seemed to Aderyn like a taunt aimed at White faction's degraded leader.

If Liander felt that way, though, he didn't show it. He stood beneath that panel, facing Seburtan and Eleora, his shoulders squared like someone ready to take a punch. All the chairs, including Liander's throne, had been removed, and the warriors that had surrounded the friends last time were gone.

Liander, with his back half-turned on the stained glass, saw them first. He shoved past Seburtan and advanced on Owen. "You did this," he raged. "I offered you a place in history and you turned on me. I will see you destroyed."

"Big words from the man who's already lost almost everything," Owen said, not reacting to Liander's violent approach. "You did this to yourself, Liander, and you know it."

"That's *Lord* Liander to you, you whelp."

"I really think it isn't." Owen turned his back on Liander and approached Seburtan and Eleora. "We're here. Now what?"

"We're just waiting on your new team member," Eleora said.

"We're not teaming up with her. That's outside the scope of our agreement."

"That was more figurative than literal. I told you you wouldn't have to if you didn't choose to." Eleora scanned the group, and her eye fell on Aderyn. "Warmaster. Are you satisfied with my revenge?"

"It's not my business to judge you," Aderyn said. "But I think you were more generous than you might have been. And I told you how I'd feel if it were me."

"Well said." Eleora's lips quirked in a wry smile. "Remember, they can't suffer if they're dead."

"I hope I never need that advice," Aderyn said, concealing her unease at the turn the conversation had taken. If she were in Eleora's position, she'd want revenge, but she wasn't at all sure she'd be able to take her revenge in cold blood as Eleora had.

"So do I," Eleora said.

CHAPTER THIRTY-EIGHT

A piercing shriek from the hallway brought everyone to attention. The shriek was followed by loud, hysterical sobbing that gradually got louder. Tevon appeared in the doorway, bringing Jessemia with him. Today, Jessemia's silk shirt was a deep sapphire blue, and her leather vest was bleached so pale it was almost white. Her splendid appearance was marred by how disheveled she looked, like she'd rolled down the stairs or been in a fight. Her chestnut curls had once been caught up at the back of her head, but now they were tangled and coming down on one side. Her eyes were red with crying, her cheeks blotchy, and when she saw Owen and the others, she let out another shriek that turned into a sobbing wail.

Liander hurried to her side and put his arms around her. "There, there, sweetness, you shouldn't cry. They'll think you're weak."

"I am *not* weak," Jessemia exclaimed through her tears. "I'm the Fated One. They can't do this to me!"

"I know, dear one, I know." Liander patted her head like she was a favored puppy. "This will all be over eventually. They'll suffer when your destiny is made clear."

Jessemia glared at Owen over her father's shoulder. "See? You're going to pay for taking me away from Papa. I hope you die horribly."

"Let's hope not, because if I do, you'll go next," Owen said, sounding as calm as if Jessemia wasn't clearly willing his death to happen right now in this room. "Say goodbye. We want to get on the road and put some distance between ourselves and this city tonight."

"*Now?*" Jessemia cried. "I'm not ready!"

Owen turned to Eleora. "You said we should come prepared to travel. Are we going to waste time for this... Jessemia to pack her things?"

"Gaven and Halsey packed for her," Eleora said. She snapped her fingers, and Gaven, who'd been standing unobtrusively near the stained glass windows, hefted a knapsack with a bedroll tied atop it and dumped it at Jessemia's feet. The woman stared at it in confusion.

"Isn't someone going to carry this?" she asked, prodding it with the toe of her shiny leather boot that showed no signs of wear.

"Yes. You are." Owen set his own knapsack on the floor and glared at Eleora. "Do you have any other commands, my lady?"

"Oh, you're in a rare temper, aren't you," Eleora said. "I figured you would be. How about we sweeten the deal?"

A system message flashed before Aderyn's eyes.

**A new quest is available: [Escort the Spoiled Darling]
Take Jessemia of the White safely to Guerdon Deep without
succumbing to your desire to leave her to be devoured by
wolves. Reward: [10,000 XP] and the satisfaction of dumping
her on her ass.
Accept? Y / N**

Aderyn snorted with laughter. Owen glanced quickly at her, then back at Eleora, but Aderyn had seen him smile, the barest curve of his lips. "You're a questgiver, too?" he said.

"Anyone with magisterial authority can issue quests. Where are you from that you don't know that?" Eleora shrugged. "It doesn't matter. See her all the way there, and you'll gain a substantial experience reward."

"Fine," Owen said. Aderyn touched the Y, then N when the system message asked to set it as their primary quest. It might be the one that was currently active, but she never wanted to forget their actual purpose in adventuring.

Jessemia had stopped crying and was staring at Owen in increasing horror. "You're not serious," she breathed. "Papa, don't let them do this! I promise I'll behave, I'll live like a commoner, I'll give up all but three of my favorite horses—just don't let them take me away!"

Liander hugged her again. "Sweetness, it's out of my—"

Jessemia wrenched away from him. "You could if you wanted to. You're Liander of the White! You're more powerful than these awful people."

"Is the muzzle still an option?" Weston asked of no one.

Jessemia let out a shriek of rage and leapt at him. Gaven restrained her easily. "I hate you all!" she shouted. "You, and you, and especially *you!*" She pointed at Seburtan, and Eleora, and finally Owen, with a shaking finger.

"Stop it!" Liander roared. Jessemia, her mouth open to deliver more verbal abuse, froze. Liander's face was pale, and tears streaked his cheeks, but his voice was firm. "You're making a fool of yourself, Jessemia. I'm sorry, but I can't protect you anymore. This is out of my hands. Now, be a good girl, and someday I'll see you again, when you come into your destiny." He kissed her forehead and stepped back.

Jessemia still shook with rage. Eleora regarded her dispassionately for a few seconds before saying, "Who knows? You might even thank us someday."

"I'll never be grateful to you for anything, you bitch," Jessemia snarled.

Eleora smiled as if Jessemia had just given her a tremendous gift. "I'm sure it will disappoint you to know your ire won't keep me up at night. Owen. You're free to leave."

Owen nodded. "I won't thank you either."

"I wouldn't expect it. Consider us even."

The set of Owen's shoulders told Aderyn he was suppressing half a dozen scathing retorts. He walked over to Jessemia. "Let's go. Pick up your things."

"I refuse," Jessemia said, ostentatiously not looking at him. "Pick them up yourself."

Owen shoved the knapsack a few inches with his foot. "No one's going to carry it for you."

"Then I'm not going."

"Jessemia," her father began.

"You're going, and you know it," Owen said, in that same calm voice, "because if you stay, someone's going to put a knife in your back—out of revenge against your father, out of hatred of your entitled behavior, maybe even out of a desire to become the Fated One. You appear to be the only person in this room who doesn't realize that."

Jessemia gaped at him. "You're trying to scare me."

"If the plain truth scares you, then sure. So, you've got two options. Stay here and be killed, or come with us and maybe live to become a real adventurer. Now. *Pick up your bag.*"

Those last four words thrummed with power as if Isold had spoken them. Jessemia's eyes widened. She bent, picked up her knapsack, and awkwardly put it on. Owen made no move to help her. When she had it mostly settled, he said, "Let's go," and walked away without looking back.

Aderyn hurried after him so they could walk side by side down the stairs. "*I* didn't realize that," she whispered.

"I was exaggerating to get that idiot to fall in line. But it's true. Liander's coddled and protected her from the consequences of her behavior her whole life. Now that he doesn't command more than Tevon and maybe a couple of faithful retainers, she's a target for anyone who ever suffered at Liander's hands." Owen blew out his breath. "I'll deny saying this later, but maybe I'm not so pissed off about being manipulated by Eleora. No, that's wrong, I am extremely pissed off about that. But I feel a shred of sympathy for Jessemia."

"I won't tell," Aderyn said.

With Jessemia bringing up the rear, the five friends left Liander's mansion—not Liander's anymore, Aderyn reminded herself—and walked through the city to the gate. The realization that she wouldn't miss Obsidian at all startled Aderyn. All the cities they'd visited before were memorable and even beloved in some way, like the stony houses of Guerdon Deep that concealed beautiful, lush interiors or the gardens of Ashenfell. Even Elkenforest, a city she hadn't cared for or thought beautiful, was where Owen had told her he loved her. When she contemplated returning to any of them, it was with pleasure.

But Obsidian had none of those good memories and plenty of bad ones. They'd been threatened, captured, almost killed, and black-mailed. And Aderyn couldn't stop remembering her impression of the city, how the streets of each district were interchangeable and yet everyone behaved as if the districts altered the people living in them. No, she had no desire to return to Obsidian ever again.

Lieutenant Araceli met them on the inner side of the gate. "Armbands," she said. "And don't think I was fooled by your little game. I'll let it go—"

Owen slapped his armband into her hand and drew his sword. "All right. Let's do this."

"What?" Araceli said.

"You're a bully, and I hate bullies," Owen said. "I'm calling you out. You and me, personally, no faction involvement, just your sword and mine."

Araceli stepped back. "I could order my men to take you down."

"You could. And then everyone will remember that you were too afraid to duel a Swordsworn five levels lower than you. Aderyn? What do you think of my chances?"

Aderyn Skill Assessed the lieutenant and was relieved at what she saw. Owen was good with a sword, but against someone that much higher? "Oh, no," she said, pretending horror. "The lieutenant hasn't been practicing. I wonder how much experience she's worth?"

"You're bluffing. You can't possibly know that," Araceli said. "I'm level sixteen. There's no way a level eleven Swordsworn can give me a fair fight."

"A level eleven Swordsworn partnered with a Warmaster," Owen corrected her. "You're right. It won't be anywhere close to a fair fight."

They'd gathered an audience of guards and citizens who all seemed intrigued by what was going on. Aderyn glanced over the guards, checking to see if anyone might be willing to shoot Owen to defend Araceli. To her surprise, though there were a few men with crossbows and one Deadeye holding a short recurve bow, none of them aimed their weapons at Owen. The Deadeye in particular looked like she found the fight amusing.

Araceli looked like she'd come to the same conclusion about her support Aderyn had. Slowly, she drew the sword hanging at her side and then without warning lunged at Owen. Owen sidestepped the attack as easily as if he'd been warned, which, since Aderyn's observations were being sent to him via the <Twinsword>, was true. He slapped Araceli's backside with the flat of his blade as she stumbled past, sending up a roar of laughter from the crowd.

Araceli turned and took up a more solid stance. "You think you're clever," she said.

"Not clever. Better than you, certainly." Their blades clashed as they tested one another, first tentatively, then with growing sureness. Aderyn hadn't recently been in a position to watch Owen fight, thanks to being preoccupied with not dying at the talons of a giant harpy. He'd definitely improved, and he was just as definitely toying with Araceli, offering his sword for her to swat at, pretending to give ground only to force her back a step or two.

The crowd shifted as Araceli backed toward it. Araceli snarled and went on the attack, driving Owen backward as he'd done her. Owen parried several increasingly wild swings, following each with a thrust Araceli had to dodge to avoid. Still neither of them had landed a blow, Araceli because she couldn't, Owen because he chose not to.

In a flash, Owen struck. Araceli's sword hit the ground at her feet. The next moment saw the tip of Owen's blade press against the hollow of Araceli's throat. Araceli froze, holding her hands away from her sides in a gesture of defeat.

"I concede," she said hoarsely.

"No, you lose," Owen said. He was only barely out of breath.

Congratulations! You have defeated [Araceli the Pathseer]
You have earned [19,000 XP]

"Go on, then," Araceli wheezed. "Finish the job. You know you want to."

"Maybe you would, in my position. But I'm no murderer." Owen lowered his sword, and Araceli breathed out in relief. "Remember this the next time you feel like persecuting someone lower level than you. That person might not be as compassionate."

He strode toward the door, which was still closed. A couple of watching guards hurried to open it. Aderyn walked beside him, not daring to speak, until they'd left the city behind and were a good two hundred feet down the road. Then she said, "That was risky. Suppose I was wrong about her sword skills?"

"I have faith in you. Plus, you were watching, so the

<Twinsword> kept telling me where she was going to strike next. The only danger I was in was of looking like a prat taking advantage of a weaker opponent."

"You didn't look like that," Weston said. "You also didn't look like a level eleven Swordsworn. I wish we were in a position for me to bet on your fighting."

"You don't like gambling," Livia said.

"I don't like risk when the reward is so uncertain. This would be a sure thing."

"Is that what you do? Fight stupid guards and then not finish them?" Jessemia asked scornfully. Aderyn had forgotten she was with them.

"I didn't think you cared what we did," Owen said.

Jessemia shrugged. "If you're going to be my protectors, I want to know you're the best."

Owen stopped, making them all come to a halt, even Jessemia. He squeezed his eyes shut as if searching for patience. Then he turned on their unwilling guest. "Time to set things straight," he said. "We're not your protectors. We were not hired by your father to babysit you. We are taking you to Guerdon Deep as a quest, which means you are nothing more to us than a juicy little bundle of experience."

Jessemia squeaked. "How dare—"

"I'm not finished," Owen said. "If you're going to travel with us, there are some conditions we'll insist on. You will carry your own knapsack. You will help with chores when we camp. You will stay out of the way when we encounter monsters. If one of us tells you to do something, you do it. If *I* tell you to do something, you do it faster. And if you whine or complain even once, I'll add something heavy to your knapsack, and I will go on doing that until you shut up. Have I missed anything?" he asked his friends.

"That covers it," Weston said. "Since I forgot to buy a muzzle."

"Thank you." Owen turned back to Jessemia. "If you have any

questions, ask them now, because I was serious about getting as far from Obsidian today as we can."

Jessemia glared at him. "I wouldn't give you the satisfaction. And I still hope you die horribly."

"It's a long trip. You might get your wish." Owen started down the road again, with Aderyn beside him. The others fell into their usual formation, Weston at the rear, Isold and Livia near the center. Jessemia straggled along behind.

"Should we worry about her running back to her papa?" Aderyn whispered after seeing where Jessemia walked.

"If she does, I'll consider the contract void. Eleora blackmailed us into taking her, but she can't control what Jessemia does. You have the cookware in there, right?"

Aderyn patted the apparently empty <**Knapsack of Plenty**>. "All of it. Why?"

"Just double-checking in case Jessemia starts whining sooner than I expect." Owen grinned. "Is it bad that I hope she whines?"

"She does sort of make you want to slap her," Aderyn agreed.

"Isold, how far is it to Guerdon Deep?" Owen called out.

"One moment." Isold stopped, and they all, even Jessemia, gathered around him while he consulted his system map. "My estimation is between twelve hundred and thirteen hundred miles. If we walk at top speed, with no deviation or obstacles, that will take us six weeks. It will likely be—" He glanced at Jessemia— "closer to eight."

"Plenty of time to kill monsters and level up," Weston said.

"And for me to practice hunting," Livia added. "I promise I've got a plan that doesn't use *stone sphere*."

"Okay." Owen cast an eye on the sun, already beginning its descent. "Let's see how far we can get before sunset."

"That's more than four hours from now! You expect me to walk for four hours?" Jessemia exclaimed.

"We take breaks, don't worry," Aderyn said.

"That's ridiculous! I can't walk that long!"

Owen sighed and unlaced the flap of the <**Knapsack of Plenty**>. He pulled out a mid-sized iron pot, the one Livia usually boiled water for coffee in. Strolling casually, he walked around to behind Jessemia and wedged the pot into her knapsack. Jessemia sagged briefly at the weight. "What—"

Owen held up a finger. "We have two more. They're each bigger than that one. Want to find out first hand how much they weigh?"

Her face crimson with fury, Jessemia said nothing.

Owen returned to his position beside Aderyn. "That felt way too good," he whispered.

"I'm surprised she shut up so readily."

"Oh, she's plotting my grisly death. Yelling at me would interfere with that." He gripped her hand briefly. "You up for a new adventure?"

"You sound like you're resigned to it now. What changed?"

He shrugged. "We're on the road now. That always changes my perspective. Well? What do you say?"

Aderyn smiled and shook her head. "I say it's going to be a long eight weeks."

APPENDIX: CHARACTER SHEETS

NOTE: These character sheets represent the status of the companions at the end of the book, which means it reveals everything the companions learn about their skills throughout the story. If you haven't finished the book, don't read this unless you don't mind spoilers!

Name: Aderyn
    Class: Warmaster
    Level: 11
    <u>Skills</u>: Bluff (7), Climb (3), Conversation (7), Intimidate (4), Sense Truth (11), Survival (4), Swim (1), Knowledge: Monsters (10), Knowledge: Demons (1)
    <u>Class Skills:</u> Improved Assess 2 (18), Awareness (11), Knowledge: Geography (9), Spot (11), *Discern Weakness* (16), Dodge (10), Improvised Distraction (9), *Outflank* (11), Draw Fire (5), *Keep Pace* (12), Amplify Voice (9), See It Coming (7), Basic Weapons Proficiency (Swords) (5), *Read Body Language* (3), Basic Map Access (2), Compel (0)
    *italics are paired skills with partner

Name: Jacob Owen Lindberg

   Class: Swordsworn

   Level: 11

   Skills: Assess (8), Awareness (10), Climb (5), Conversation (7), Sense Truth (10), Spot (8), Survival (3), Swim (10), Knowledge: Demons (1)

   Class Skills: Advanced Weapons Proficiency (18), Improved Armor Proficiency (11), Knowledge: Monsters (9), *Exploit Weakness* (16), Dodge (12), Parry (10), Improved Bluff (10), *Outflank* (11), Trip (3), *Keep Pace* (12), Disarm (3), Intimidate (6), Charge (3), Two-Weapon Fighting (0), *Read Body Language* (3), Basic Map Access (3), Overrun (0)

   *italics are paired skills with Warmaster

Name: Weston

   Class: Moonlighter

   Level: 11

   Skills: Assess (9), Climb (5), Conversation (7), Intimidate (5), Sense Truth (11), Survival (5), Swim (2), Knowledge: Social (9), Knowledge: Demons (1)

   Class Skills: Pick Locks (7), Improved Sneak Attack (12), Advanced Weapons Proficiency (10), Improved Armor Proficiency (9), Improved Detect Traps (11), Disable Traps (9), Spot (15), Awareness (12), Dodge (11), Stealth (12), Improved Bluff (11), Dirty Fighting (6), To the Heart (10), Hide (6), Basic Thrown Weapons Proficiency (3), Disguise (1), Hide in Plain Sight (3), Evasion (4), Basic Map Access (3), Escape Artist (2)

Name: Isold

   Class: Herald

   Level: 11

   Skills: Assess (10), Awareness (11), Climb (4), Conversation

(11), Intimidate (2), Sense Truth (10), Spot (9), Survival (3), Swim (1), Knowledge: Demons (2)

Class Skills: Perform (singing) (14); Knowledge: Magic (9); Knowledge: Monsters (11); Knowledge: History (7); Knowledge: Social (7); Knowledge: World Lore (10); Identify Magic Items (11); Charm (13); Distraction (9); Map Access (10); Inspire Courage (7); Fascination (5); Persuasion (6); Perform (drum) (7); Suggestion (4); Resist Magic (2); Shout (2); Hypnotize (0); Find Object (0)

Name: Livia

Class: Earthbreaker

Level: 11

Skills: Assess (6), Awareness (8), Bluff (3), Climb (1), Conversation (6), Intimidate (10), Sense Truth (8), Spot (7), Survival (2), Swim (1), Knowledge: Demons (1)

Elemental Powers: Earth, stone

Class Skills: Knowledge: Magic, Elemental Blast (earth spray, shower of small stones, rain of large stones) (11), Earth to Mud/Mud to Earth (4), Mage Armor (shifting stone slabs) (5), Excavate (2), Summon Elemental Hammer (0), Basic Map Access (2)

Spell List

0-level spells: Daze; Drench; Light; Telekinesis, minor; Mending; Freezing Ray, minor; Root, Spark

1st Level spells

Air Bubble; Break; Force Shield; Grease; Heat Metal (slow); Loose Bonds; Mudball; Sunder Weapon; Thunder Punch

2nd Level spells

Create Pit; Dust Cloud; Earth's Endurance; Thunderstomp; Mirror Image; Mud Minion; Improved Mending; Protection from Fire, Mass (big earth dome); Skip

3rd Level spells

Iron Spike Attack; Thunderstomp, Greater (directed); Clairvoyance; Dispel Magic; Immobilize; Telekinesis, Greater; Daylight

4th Level spells

Stone Ladder; Stone Sphere; Transport, Minor; Invisibility (self); Earth Glide; Stone Fist

5th Level spells

Hungry Pit; Dismissal of Demons; Scry; Lighten Object

About the Author

In addition to the Warmaster series, Melissa McShane is the author of many fantasy novels, including the novels of Tremontane, the first of which is *Servant of the Crown;* The Extraordinaries series, beginning with *Burning Bright;* and *The Book of Secrets,* first book in The Last Oracle series.

While her home remains in the mountains out West, she currently lives in Kerala, India, with her husband and two rambunctious Persian kittens. She wrote reviews and critical essays for many years before turning to fiction, which is much more fun than anyone ought to be allowed to have.

You can visit her at her website
www.melissamcshanewrites.com
for more information on other books and upcoming releases.

To subscribe to her newsletter, which is published monthly, visit **www.melissamcshanewrites.com/contact-me-2/join-my-mailing-list**

ALSO BY MELISSA MCSHANE

WARMASTER

Warmaster 1: Dungeon Spiteful

Warmaster 2: Winter's Peril

Warmaster 3: Gamboling Coil

Warmaster 4: Sorrowvale (forthcoming August 2024)

THE BOOKS OF THE DARK GODDESS

Silver and Shadow

Missing by Moonlight

Shades of the Past

Path of the Paladin

Bright Moon Deception (forthcoming 2024)

THE LAST ORACLE

The Book of Secrets

The Book of Peril

The Book of Mayhem

The Book of Lies

The Book of Betrayal

The Book of Havoc

The Book of Harmony

The Book of War

The Book of Destiny

THE LIVING ORACLE

Hidden Realm

Hidden Enemy

Hidden Pursuit (forthcoming)

THE EXTRAORDINARIES

Burning Bright

Wondering Sight

Abounding Might

Whispering Twilight

Liberating Fight

Beguiling Birthright

Soaring Flight

Discerning Insight

THE NOVELS OF TREMONTANE

Pretender to the Crown

Guardian of the Crown

Champion of the Crown

Ally of the Crown

Stranger to the Crown

Scholar of the Crown

Servant of the Crown

Exile of the Crown

Rider of the Crown

Agent of the Crown

Voyager of the Crown

Tales of the Crown

COMPANY OF STRANGERS

Company of Strangers

Stone of Inheritance

Mortal Rites

Shifting Loyalties

Sands of Memory

Call of Wizardry

THE DRAGONS OF MOTHER STONE

Spark the Fire

Faith in Flames

Ember in Shadow

Skies Will Burn

THE CONVERGENCE TRILOGY

The Summoned Mage

The Wandering Mage

The Unconquered Mage

THE BOOKS OF DALANINE

The Smoke-Scented Girl

The God-Touched Man

Emissary

Warts and All: The Deluxe Expanded Edition

The View from Castle Always

Winter Across Worlds: A Holiday Collection

Made in the USA
Middletown, DE
08 November 2024

64147611R00192